Sweet Southern TROUBLE

MICHELE SUMMERS

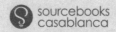

sourcebooks
casablanca

Sourcebooks and the colophon are registered trademarks of Sourcebooks, Inc.

Published by Sourcebooks Casablanca, an imprint of Sourcebooks, Inc.
P.O. Box 4410, Naperville, Illinois 60567-4410
(630) 961-3900
Fax: (630) 961-2168
www.sourcebooks.com

Printed and bound in Canada.
MBP 10 9 8 7 6 5 4 3 2 1

To my sweet sister, Carol Lynn, the best cheerleader ever! You believed in my writing and this story way before I did. This one's for you, girlfriend!

Chapter 1

MARABELLE DIDN'T SUCK AT EVERYTHING. SHE MADE a mouthwatering orange pound cake with chocolate ganache. She made the Wicked Witch come to life when she read aloud to her students. And she had a mean slice backhand that gave her opponents trouble on the tennis court. But when it came to biting her tongue and taking direction, she sucked.

"Marabelle, are you listening?"

Marabelle blinked several times to keep from dozing off as Mrs. Crow droned on and on at the tedious gala meeting. She forced her tired eyes to focus on the blue-and-gold-bound agenda in front of her. Marabelle's cell phone beeped, indicating a text.

"*Marabelle!*"

Marabelle straightened her posture, grappling to turn off her phone.

"Mrs. Evans is suggesting that you help with the auction as well as the coordination of the golf and tennis tournaments." Mrs. Crow enunciated as if Marabelle had comprehension problems.

Oh brother. Another project to add to her ever-growing list.

Marabelle shifted her attention to the bleached-blond Mrs. Evans, head of the gala committee, and then to the other members seated around the conference room table, all staring back as if a third eye had grown on her forehead.

"Why me?"

But Marabelle Fairchild already knew the answer to her question. Brandon Aldridge. A five-year-old in her kindergarten class. Well, not him exactly, but rather his uncle, Nick Frasier, the famous NFL quarterback-turned-head-coach of the North Carolina Cherokees. Besides his impressive football career, Nick Frasier held the distinguished title of most eligible bachelor in the Raleigh-Durham area *and* the most smokin' hot and sexy. And Trinity Academy for Boys and Girls wanted this particular available hunk helping out with their fund-raiser. To be specific, the women across the polished mahogany conference table with undisguised lust in their eyes wanted him in ways that Marabelle did not care to contemplate.

"Marabelle, honey, you need to use your connections and…assets to convince Coach Frasier to participate." Carol Evans stumbled over the word *assets* as she clasped her yellow-diamond-encrusted fingers together.

Assets, my left toe. Compared to these perfectly coiffed women, who looked as if they had stepped out of the pages of *Vogue* on steroids, Marabelle felt like the poster child for unwanted orphans. Her wardrobe didn't help. She wore a navy-blue cardigan over a white button-down blouse, and could've passed for one of her kindergartners rather than a thirty-year-old with a master's degree in elementary education.

"We need to raise a considerable amount of money if we want to improve any of the playing facilities and add a permanent teaching position to the staff." Carol Evans spoke with a Yankeefied Southern twang that grated on Marabelle's true-blue Southern ears. It was a well-known fact that Carol Evans hailed from Trenton, New Jersey. But she'd married a native North Carolinian and had taken to her new identity faster than you could say "Nothing could be finer than to be in Carolina."

At the mention of the teaching position, Marabelle's attention ratcheted up. She'd been barely eking by on a teacher's assistant salary for the last three years, and she wanted nothing more than to be hired as a certified, permanent teacher.

Mrs. Crow said, "The board will seriously consider allocating monies we raise from the gala toward creating another teaching position if—"

"*If* I do what…exactly?" Marabelle leaned forward in her chair and waited. She hated the age-old twisted plot of high society women out to one-up each other in the name of charity. She recognized the competitive gleam in their eyes and the tension around their mouths. Her mother had worn that exact "game on" expression more times than Marabelle cared to remember. But she knew how the game was played, and she was ready to deal.

"Clearly, you don't understand what's at stake here," Mrs. Burrows, a native Tar Heel, interjected as she played with a strand of perfect South Sea pearls around her neck. She and Mrs. Evans gave each other "we're doomed" looks with the rise of their perfectly waxed eyebrows.

Marabelle definitely knew what was at stake…a significant increase in salary so she could continue to pay her mortgage without her mother bailing her out. A stand she took very seriously three years ago when she said no to her inheritance from her mother in order to gain her independence. Marabelle put on her best schoolteacher face and said, "I know exactly what's at stake. You want to raise huge funds, and you want Brandon Aldridge's famous uncle to participate by calling in a bunch of favors from all his celebrity friends and pro athletes, who will donate sports memorabilia and money." This wasn't Marabelle's first rodeo.

"Well, yes, that's precisely what we want," Mrs. Evans said, sounding a bit startled at Marabelle's acumen. "Marabelle, honey, what we're all trying to say is that you don't exactly have the best track record. You remember last year's carnival?" Carol Evans sounded sympathetic, while looking anything but.

Reaching for her water bottle, Marabelle took a huge gulp before addressing the committee. She needed to make a good impression. These women may have thought she had nothing in common with them, but they were dead wrong. Marabelle had lived in their world for years and had learned from the master. "Once again, I'm sorry about the mishaps at the carnival last year. But in my defense, the *minute* I noticed the clown was drunk, I had him escorted off the grounds. And the carny apologized for setting the Tilt-a-Whirl at warp speed." She omitted the part where he'd proceeded to proposition her.

"*Three* of our first graders were thrown into the holly bushes." Beak-Face Crow scowled. "Thanks to Mrs. Evans's husband, our school attorney"—she fluttered her hand in Carol's direction—"we avoided a costly lawsuit."

Marabelle had been thrust into taking over the volunteer job at the last minute, from a faculty member who'd suffered a broken foot. For the past three years, she'd been forced to "volunteer" a lot. Even though she hadn't booked the carnival company, her reputation had been on shaky ground ever since.

"So the committee, faculty, and I thought we would offer you another chance to…you know…shine, so to speak, *if* you acquire Coach Frasier's sponsorship…" Mrs. Crow's voice trailed off.

So, *that* was the catch. They planned to hold a teaching position hostage until she had hooked Coach Frasier for their cause. Brilliant! But her parents, Edna and Ed Fairchild, hadn't raised an idiot. Sarcastically, she blurted, "Why don't we raise some real money and have all the eligible bachelors auction themselves off to the highest bidder?"

The school conference room grew so quiet Marabelle could hear the sweep of the second hand on the oversized black-and-white clock hanging above the closed door. Mr. Turner, the only male member of the committee, stopped swiveling in his high-back leather chair. All eyes fixed on her. Marabelle twisted her hands in her lap to keep from clapping them over her mouth. She'd just catapulted herself from the frying pan into the fryer.

Beak-Face Crow cleared her throat, appearing very interested in the papers she was shuffling between her bony fingers, while the Blondie Twins, Mrs. Evans and Mrs. Burrows, grinned like the Grinch contemplating diabolical ways to steal Christmas.

Mrs. Cartwright, the eldest member of the committee, continued to work on her needlepoint and, without looking up from her stitches, spoke in her gravelly voice. "You've just come up with the only idea that might work. A live auction with the best-looking bachelors we can find."

Marabelle pitched forward, grasping the edge of the table until her knuckles turned white. "I was being facetious," she said through cold lips. "Nobody is going to agree to auction himself off to a room of drooling, miserable housewives with too much money. It's degrading."

"It's da bomb!" Carol Evans shouted in all her New Jersey glory. "A live bachelor auction! The perfect addition to this year's gala. I can see it now." Her eyes took on a dreamy quality while her hand floated in front of her face as if reading a marquee.

"It will be a huge success. The mothers at St. Michael's are going to be *pea green* with envy," Mrs. Burrows added.

The image of besting her good friends, who gave of their time and money at St. Michael's, probably danced in Carol Evans's over-bleached head. Raleigh's high society had stringent requirements: children needed to attend either Trinity Academy or St. Michael's. The schools shared a long, bitter rivalry, and just mentioning them in the same sentence was risky.

"I'm bidding on Coach Frasier. His abs make a great six-pack," Mrs. Cartwright cackled as she snipped the end of a black thread.

Beak-Face Crow, the Blondie Twins, and even Mr. Turner talked at once as their excitement escalated over the racy new element to be added to this fine Christian event.

Marabelle watched in horror. The tornado was heading her way, and there was no stopping it.

～～～

Nick Frasier strolled into room B12, where his nephew attended kindergarten. He glanced around the empty classroom and then at his Rolex Submariner. Three minutes past four. The room appeared to have been swept clean of debris from a day of active kids. The small chairs pushed under the laminate desks looked like obedient little soldiers, and a hint of Lysol hung in the air as if the desktops had been wiped down. But no signs of life.

Until he heard grunting.

Nick's eyebrows rose as he caught sight of an attractive, heart-shaped ass poking out from under a wall of cabinets below the windows across the room. He spied hot-pink panties peeking from the bottom of a pleated skirt.

He double-checked his location.

This *was* where his nephew went to kindergarten. Hand-painted pictures tacked up willy-nilly, toys lining one wall, Play-Doh, paint smells. Yep.

So what kind of place were they running around here, where young women showed their butts off to anyone who happened to walk by? Nick cleared his throat just as Miss Cute Ass yelled "Gotcha!" and bumped her head scooting her way out from under the furniture.

"Shhhugar. That hurt."

A petite person struggled to stand, with a very large ball of caramel fur cradled in her arms. He remained unnoticed as she marched to the guinea pig cage on a nearby table and placed the furball on its wheel. She turned while brushing hair off her front, glanced up, and stopped short.

"Whoa, you're huge."

Miss Cute Ass gawked, but whether from fascination

or fear, he couldn't tell. He figured she'd seen him on TV, of course, when the camera would pan the sidelines of a Cherokees game. He always wore a billed Cherokees cap like the one he had on today, but with a headset attached, and he usually paced up and down the sidelines, barking orders or reviewing plays on a beat-up clipboard. But against the other players, the Carolina blue skies, and evergreen pine trees, he imagined it could be hard to determine true size.

He smiled as she started babbling.

"I'm so sorry. I didn't mean to imply… It's just that you look much smaller on TV." She motioned with her hand. "Would you like some hand sanitizer?" She squirted some onto her palm from a huge, commercial-size pump that sat on the edge of the teacher's desk. "You can never be too sanitary around here."

Nick couldn't agree more, but declined as she rubbed the clear goop over her palms and around the backs of her hands as if she were scrubbing up for surgery.

"Well, now we can shake hands without spreading germs." She thrust her small hand forward. "Hey, I'm Marabelle Fairchild, Brandon's teacher's assistant. Mrs. Harris is on maternity leave."

Brandon's *teacher*? She had to be kidding.

Nick masked his surprise as he engulfed her much-smaller hand in his, shaking it firmly but gently. "Nick Frasier, Brandon's uncle. I believe you wanted to meet with me about something?"

———

"Uh…Ms. Fairchild?" Coach Frasier gently shook her palm again. Marabelle stared at the end of her arm where her hand used to be, swallowed up within his warm grasp.

"Oh." Marabelle snatched her hand back as if she'd gotten too close to a burning flame. Her face blazed. God's nightgown, she needed to get herself back in the game.

Coach Frasier towered over her. He had to be about six four. *A fine specimen indeed.* Chiseled from his jaw down to his toes, the perfect proportions created by his broad shoulders and trim waist. Naturally sun-streaked, sandy-blond hair curled out from under his red cap. And golden-brown skin only highlighted his piercing blue eyes. The gods had kissed this guy but good. *No wonder all the women in this town want a piece of him.* Marabelle remembered the painful meeting the day before and what she had to do, and her stomach muscles tightened into a cramped ball.

"Take a seat, Coach Frasier, any seat," she said, dreading her next course of action. Coach Frasier arched a brow at the room full of miniature furniture.

"How 'bout I just prop myself up against your desk?"

Coach Frasier had a deceptively soft but husky voice. Marabelle had the strangest sensation of melting butter on top of a steaming bowl of homemade grits. Lord, this man was dangerous with a capital *D*!

Marabelle gave Coach Dangerous a covert glance from beneath her lashes as he rested one hip on the top of her desk. It wasn't so much what he wore as *how* he wore it. He made ordinary clothes look extraordinary. His off-white Nike fleece pullover with the Cherokees tomahawk logo hugged his mile-wide shoulders, and his well-worn jeans, snugly fit to showcase his muscled thighs, dropped comfortably over expensive brown ostrich-skin boots. *Why do all football players have to play cowboy?*

A large hand waved in front of her face. "Ms. Fairchild?"

"Sorry. I was having a moment." Marabelle erased the fantasy of playing cowgirl to his sexy Clint Eastwood and marched around her desk. "Um, just let me get my folder." She rustled through a stack of papers, hoping to get her mind back on track and out of the gutter.

"Is Brandon in some kind of trouble? Is he doing well in school?"

Marabelle's head popped up, the shuffled papers forgotten. "Oh no. Brandon is completely out of control and in danger of becoming much worse, but that's not why I called you here."

Coach Frasier's head jerked back. "Excuse me? Do you really teach here?" he asked.

Wishing she could shove her words back down her throat, Marabelle gulped. Probably not the best time to bring up Brandon's awful behavior.

"Uh, yes, and I'm sorry if my comment offended you. But don't you think it would be better if you knew the truth? About your nephew, that is."

Was this some kind of joke? Stumped, Nick openly studied the woman before him, not caring if she noticed.

No, make that half woman, half urchin with curly brown hair wrestled on top of her head in some claw-like device. She couldn't be more than five feet, if that. Nick's gaze tracked from her head to her feet. The extra-large gray Trinity Raiders sweatshirt she wore swallowed her entire upper body and fell somewhere midthigh, and a black-and-white-plaid pleated skirt peeked out as if gasping for air.

The only thing with any shape was her legs, and they were nicely formed. Slender ankles and muscled calves showed that she exercised regularly. Small, narrow feet sported a pair of Nike tennis shoes. No glamour in that footwear. Nick's gaze traveled back up her bulky form and landed on a faint blue paint smudge on her right cheek, which somehow seemed fitting. After sizing her up, he couldn't help but mentally question the credibility of the school. She should be *taking* the class, not teaching it.

Marabelle twisted her hands and gnawed her bottom lip. "Coach Frasier, may I be perfectly frank?"

"Have you ever been anything else?"

She hesitated before answering. "Well, no, but I think it's an admirable trait."

Nick bit the inside of his cheek to keep from smiling. "Then certainly don't change on my behalf."

Blinking huge, chocolate-brown eyes, Marabelle looked more determined. Her face—sans the paint—was attractive. Faint freckles were scattered across her small, pert nose, but her mouth—by far the main attraction— had that bee-stung look that Hollywood stars coveted. For a moment, he wondered if her lips were as soft as they were full, if she tasted…

Where had those thoughts come from? *She's a kindergarten teacher, for chrissakes.* He punted those unwanted thoughts right out of the stadium, and got his head back in the game by focusing on her small hands, which seemed to talk even more than her sexy, full mouth.

Marabelle paced in front of the large white dry-erase board. "Trinity Academy has a very important fundraiser every spring that the whole community supports, and this year is going to be extra special, because they're raising money to improve the football field and add two more tennis courts. And—"

Nick had heard this pitch a million times. Same setup, different location. "And you want me to contribute to the fund? Right?"

She stopped pacing. "Well, it's more than just your money. Don't get me wrong, your money is *huge*." Nick chuckled at her lack of tact, but she ignored him, intent on lining up dry-erase markers in alternating colors.

"We need your help in contacting your celebrity friends and asking them to participate in the golf and tennis tournaments," she said, leaning the markers against the board. "And we want you to ask the single, eligible men you know to sell themselves in our bachelor auction," she finished all in one breath and turned, knocking all the markers to the floor.

"Um, what?" Nick shook his head as he bent to help her gather the scattered markers. This had to be a joke. "Are you secretly filming me for YouTube or something? Is this some sort of practical joke?" He'd had enough of being secretly filmed to last a lifetime, and if this fairy-tale character thought she could pull a fast one on him, she had no idea who she was up against. His gaze darted around the classroom, searching for a hidden camera. The room looked clean. Then he smirked. "Did my offensive coordinator set this up?"

Kneeling on the floor with puckered brows, Marabelle asked, "Who?"

Nick handed over three reds and two blues. "Coach Prichard. We've been arguing about the draft, but I didn't think he was *this* upset."

Right on cue, she turned stern schoolteacher. Standing, she released the handful of markers on the metal tray, her back as straight as if fused with a goalpost. "Coach Frasier, this is not some reality TV show, and I don't even know your offensive coordinator. But if he's upset, I suggest you make nice, and maybe you guys will start winning some ball games."

Splaying hands on his hips, he delivered one of his fiercest stares. "You tetched in the head or something? Are *you* telling *me* how to coach a professional football team?"

Marabelle didn't flinch. A room full of five-year-olds must be tougher than he thought. Curling her fingers around a ruler in the metal tray as if she might rap his knuckles, she said in the same firm, schoolteacher voice, "If there's dissension among your staff, it would be prudent to smooth things over. Arguing with your staff is bound to affect the players. It just goes to reason." *Tap, tap* went the ruler in her palm.

Nick swore under his breath. Many a rookie had backed down from his most intimidating stare. Its effect was legendary. But not on crazy Marabelle. "Ms. Fairchild, you don't know jack shit about coaching football." Nick rarely lost his temper off the field, but she'd managed to push all his buttons. He knew his young team had struggled last season. He certainly didn't need reminding from Little Miss Muffet. He had the team's owner, general manager, and the press for that. But Nick believed in his team. They had raw talent, and with good coaching and proper discipline, they'd only get better. Yet it still rankled when he was confronted with their less-than-stellar record.

He didn't need this hassle. "I'm out of here," he muttered, starting for the door.

"Coach Frasier, please wait!"

Nick whipped around to squash the crazy, ruler-toting fairy once and for all, when three high school boys barged through the classroom door, carrying large tennis bags over their shoulders.

"Hey, Coach, you comin' to practice today?"

"What?" The theme song from *The Twilight Zone* played in his head. Why would he be coming to practice here?

"Whoa! You're Nick Frasier," said the tallest of the boys as all three gazes landed on him.

Nick plastered on a smile, not wanting his scowl to be reported all over social media. "Hey, guys. What's up?" All three eagerly shook his hand, talking at once. "You boys play for the tennis team?" Nick asked in between introductions and hand pumping.

"Yeah. We're heading to practice and wondering if Coach is coming."

"Coach?" Still confused, he searched their faces.

"Surprise, surprise," Marabelle chimed softly next to him.

Chapter 2

"Listen, guys, start your warm-up without me," Marabelle said.

After several more minutes of slobbering over Coach Frasier and posing for selfies, the boys left for the courts. Marabelle pushed the heavy classroom door closed to the celebratory high fives, taking a moment to inhale much-needed air to calm her nerves. She turned, facing the man who stood between her and a successful auction…and her future.

"Um, could we start over?"

"You're a *coach*?"

Marabelle barely refrained from smacking her forehead with her open palm. She half chuckled, half smirked. "For the varsity tennis teams."

Surprise lit Coach Frasier's expression. "You actually play?"

"Since I was six." Time to steer the conversation back to her cause: approval from the board and a permanent teaching position. Marabelle clasped her hands together, and in a steady voice, said, "Let's see if we can focus here. I'll start by apologizing for fouling this whole thing up—"

"You don't look like a tennis player. You look like you can barely ride a tricycle."

Marabelle stepped closer, ignoring her quivering belly, determined to say her piece and get back to the reason for this meeting. "There's an entire world of sports beyond football out there. You should give some of them a try. Besides, what I lack in stature, I make up for in guts. Now, can we get back to the business at hand?"

Coach Frasier peered down at her, his gaze zeroing in on her mouth. Heat crept up her face under his intense scrutiny. She nervously slicked her bottom lip with her tongue and could've sworn he groaned.

"Okay, Ms. Fairchild, start from the beginning."

The tension in her shoulders eased as she exhaled. She explained how she was responsible for the tournaments and securing eligible men for the auction, barely managing to omit that her independence, pride, and sense of worth all were at stake. Marabelle had thrown away a fortune…literally. She couldn't afford to screw this up.

"So will you do it?" She squeezed her crossed fingers behind her back.

Coach Frasier relaxed his hip against her desk again. He crossed his powerful arms and tilted his head, his mesmerizing blue eyes making a slow glide from her forehead down to her tennis shoes. Marabelle nervously shifted her weight from one foot to the other. If she'd been the kind of woman who fussed over her appearance, she would've been insulted by his blatant perusal. But she wasn't here to win a beauty contest. She had a job to do.

His scrutiny felt like it lasted hours instead of mere seconds. Finally, his gaze landed back on her face. "No offense, Ms. Fairchild, but are you the best this school has to offer?"

"None taken. And yes, compared to the rest of the

staff, I actually look pretty good." She gave a nervous laugh. "Hard to believe, huh?"

Coach Frasier's gorgeous head fell back as he burst out laughing, flashing straight white teeth. He had one of those warm, masculine laughs.

Marabelle liked it—a lot.

Smiling, she pushed up the sleeves to her sweatshirt. "Okay, okay, so I'm not in the big league." Damn, her small stature always put her at a disadvantage.

"Honey, you aren't even in the Pee Wee league," he said between hoots. "Has the committee ever conversed with you? I'm no expert or anything, but you kinda lack the finesse for winning friends and influencing people." Coach Frasier grinned.

Marabelle shot a grin right back, mimicking his body language by folding her arms. "I have zero tact. That particular gene skipped me. But I'm a damn good teacher, and the students love me. Crazy as this sounds, I relate much better to children—"

"Now *that* I believe!"

"—and if I strike this deal with the sexiest, most famous guy Raleigh has ever seen, I will improve my status here at the school in a big way." Now there was the understatement of the century.

She bent to straighten a cup of crayons on one of the small desks when Coach Frasier entered her space. "You think I'm sexy?" he said in his smoky voice.

Marabelle straightened her shoulders. "Give me a break. Like I'm telling you something you haven't heard since coming out of the womb. You and I both know that every single woman and half the married ones would sing 'The Star-Spangled Banner' *naked* on the fifty-yard line at the Super Bowl just to go out with you."

"Now that sounds promising. Would you?"

Coach Frasier moved so close, the glittery blue of his eyes showed flecks of steel gray. An involuntary shiver ran up her spine. Marabelle knew what the feeling meant and didn't like it. At. All.

"Good God—no! You are not my type." She flapped her hands as if to brush him away, swaying back to regain her equilibrium.

"What do you mean I'm not your type?" Coach Frasier boxed her in with the door to her back. "Are you gay?"

Of course he would think that was the only logical reason not to want him. This close, the intoxicating smell of spice and lemon filled her nose. Marabelle's mouth watered. If he'd been a dish, she would've eaten him on the spot.

She chose to refocus on his face instead of his edible, broad chest, and almost whimpered at the unfairness of it all. Swallowing her frustrated sigh, she said, "Why is it that every time a woman says she's not interested in a man, she's automatically assumed to be a lesbian?"

"Because she usually is." Amusement lifted the corner of his mouth.

"Hardly. Because your inflated ego cannot fathom that a woman might not be interested in you."

Coach Frasier moved back, allowing Marabelle to draw air into her deprived lungs, but her breath clogged her throat as he pulled keys from his pocket.

He can't leave now. He jiggled the keys in his hand. "Ms. Fairchild, as stimulating as this conversation has been, you haven't said anything compelling to convince me to sell my friends and myself for the cause. I'm afraid I need to be going, unless there's something important you have to tell me about Brandon."

Marabelle's hard-earned independence flashed before her eyes. If she didn't get his cooperation, her mother's prediction of failing would come true.

Unthinkable.

———

"No, wait," Marabelle said.

Nick peered down at the small hand gripping his forearm. Marabelle released him as if embarrassed. Man, he'd been working too hard if that innocent touch caused heat to shoot from his arm straight to his groin.

Marabelle reached for a folder on top of her desk. "I know I'm not the best salesperson for the job, but if you would take this packet and read it over, I think you'll change your mind." Hope shimmered in her huge brown eyes, and Nick felt like crap for crushing it.

What the hell. He gave a quick nod and took the glossy marketing packet, slapping it several times against his thigh.

Then Marabelle smiled. Really smiled. It lit her entire face, and Nick felt dizzy. A megawatt smile capable of making him forget about her abrupt personality, hideous outfit, and the fact that she was probably gay.

Spellbound, he said against his better judgment, "Okay, Tinker Bell. I'll read your packet." Her smile turned high-beam like the sun breaking over the horizon. "I'm not making any promises," he quickly amended, still unable to avert his gaze.

"Got it. So, when can we meet to discuss the prospects?"

Nick hesitated and then glanced at the keys he'd palmed. "Uh…I'll call you." The oldest line in history, and it failed miserably. Marabelle's megawatt smile faded like a lightbulb growing dim. He needed to get the hell out of here before he made promises he didn't want to keep.

Nick extended his hand. "Tinker Bell, it's been interesting, to say the least."

"Coach Frasier, I'm afraid I can't let you go."

"What?" Nick's hand hung in midair.

Suddenly, he watched in shock as Marabelle threw her back against the classroom door, spread-eagle, barring his exit. "You're going to have to agree to another meeting before I allow you to leave."

Nick's jaw dropped. *Allow me to leave?* "Or what? You threatening me?"

Marabelle's chin shot up a notch as she remained plastered to the door. "Y-yes. You gotta go through me if you want out this door. Or…we could be civilized about this, and you can agree to another meeting."

Nick rubbed his hand over his face. "Did you forget to take your meds? Because I outweigh you by at least a hundred and ten pounds, and I don't want to hurt you."

Marabelle audibly gulped. "Yeah, but I'm tenacious, not to mention desperate."

"Tinker Bell, I'm warning you. *Move away from the door.*"

Her stubborn chin quivered, but she ignored his threat. "Promise to meet me next week."

Professional football players had more fear than this crazy fairy, or maybe they just had more sense, because

Marabelle Fairchild shook in her little Nike shoes, but she was sticking.

At some point, Nick had made up his mind to meet with her again, because she'd been the most interesting weirdo he'd ever encountered and she made him laugh. And lately, there'd been a shortage of laughter in his life. But *no way* could he let her think she could take him.

Nick cursed low. "You can't say I didn't warn you." Dumping his keys back in his pocket and tossing the gala folder on top of a small desk, he wrapped his hands around her waist, lifting her away from the door. Marabelle flung her arms around his neck and coiled her legs around his hips, clinging to him as if he were a life raft in a turbulent sea.

"*What the—?*" Nick's jolt matched the utter shock written on Marabelle's face.

"Promise me, and I'll let go!" she blurted.

Nick froze. This was no girl he held in his arms. Womanly curves teased his hands through her hideously bulky clothes. She was luscious and soft in all the right places. The urge to peel away the layers to see what lay beneath flexed his fingers. Flashes of hot-pink panties covering a heart-shaped ass replayed in his head.

Nick's entire body stiffened...including his cock. Marabelle's eyes flared even wider.

"*Marabelle.*" He tried disengaging her arms without hurting her, but she squeezed tighter.

"Please," she begged.

"Monday afternoon. My office. Same time," Nick gritted through his locked jaw. Anything to get her out of his arms before he did something really stupid.

Her stranglehold loosened, and slowly, she slid her legs down his rigid thighs.

The betrayal of his body pissed him off. He pushed away temptation a little more roughly than he intended. "Agreed?" The tic in his right jaw flared to life.

Unaware of his tenuous control, Marabelle nodded. "Thank you so much, Coach Frasier. Sorry about my strong-arm tactics, but I had to make you see reason. I *swear* you won't be sorry." Nick watched as her face morphed into an innocent cherub, making him instantly leery.

"I already am," he snapped. "Is it safe for me to leave now, or are you hiding a hand grenade in your desk drawer?"

"No. But I almost forgot." Marabelle lunged toward her desk and scooped up a manila folder sitting on top. "This is the progress report on your nephew. We can discuss it on Monday when we meet. Monday afternoon. Your office. Same time, right?" she confirmed, shoving the gala file inside.

With the folder in his hand, he reached for the door. "Until Monday, Ms. Fairchild." Then he touched the bill of his cap in a mock salute and walked out.

—⁓—

"What the hell just happened?" Nick mumbled to himself as he slid into his silver Porsche 911 Carrera. Dumbfounded, he sat in the parking lot at Trinity Academy, drumming his fingers on the leather steering wheel, staring out his windshield at the playing fields. That had to be the most bizarre encounter he'd ever had with a woman.

And being a famous quarterback and now a coach in the NFL, Nick had known a lot of women.

He could have his pick at any time, any day. But he had chosen not to go through women like a PEZ dispenser. These days, he chalked it up to being older and mellower. Retirement and coaching did that to a man. But he couldn't remember the last time he'd gotten hard in five seconds flat, especially over a woman who didn't appeal to him on so many levels. Nick shoved the key in the ignition and stopped. He generally preferred his women on the glossy side, but for some reason, Marabelle had gotten under his skin. A smart-ass—albeit cute—who tried to appear tough.

He tossed his ball cap onto the seat next to him and tunneled his fingers through his hair. The women who floated in and out of Nick Frasier's world always dressed to impress and were very single-minded with their agendas. They either wanted to land a professional athlete…or they wanted to destroy him.

Nick leaned back against the headrest and groaned. Anyone who really knew him knew he hadn't arranged to meet Jenna Williams while vacationing in St. Barts. Nick didn't do married women. Especially a woman married to his good friend and offensive coordinator.

It didn't matter that it had all been a ploy for attention, or that Jenna admitted her role in the debacle. The photos were damning, and the damage had been done. He'd stopped counting how many Internet media rags had run the pictures with fictitious headlines. Nick's business Twitter account had to be shut down. His team of assistants had jumped on damage control, trying to put an end to the speculation. But the photos had done their job. And now…Nick's future and job hung in the balance.

He squeezed his eyes shut. What a royal screw-up.

Marty Hackman, the tough-as-nails owner of the Cherokees, had read him the riot act, and it hadn't been pleasant. One more slip, and his ass was grass. Nick had worked too hard and come too far to let any conniving, gold-digging, attention-grabbing wannabe ruin his life.

Which brought him back to Marabelle Fairchild. He wasn't gonna be used for someone else's gain. Good cause or not. The fallout was not worth the risk.

As if his thoughts conjured her up, Nick caught sight of Marabelle crossing the back campus, heading straight for the tennis courts, pushing a wire basket of practice balls with several rackets tossed on top. She had traded the ugly schoolgirl skirt for an equally ugly pair of gray sweatpants to match the ugly sweatshirt she still wore.

When she reached the courts, some of the boys ambled over to speak with her. Nick could see the boys teasing Marabelle, making her laugh. All but two of them towered over her by at least a foot.

Then Marabelle surprised him by banging tennis balls at all the boys who weren't already practicing. They scattered like flies as she started the drills. Nick observed for the next fifteen minutes, impressed at how she reined them in. Tinker Bell got one thing right: she may be small, but she sure had guts.

Chapter 3

"Did anybody order pizza?" Nick asked at the sound of the doorbell.

Beau Quinton, the Cherokees' star quarterback, and Tyrone "Ty" Washington, tight end, were shooting pool in Nick's living-room-turned-game-room. Nick and Coach John Prichard lounged on the overstuffed chairs, drinking beer and arguing about plays flashing on the flat-screen TV centered over the stone fireplace.

"Nope. I'll see who it is," Beau offered since Nick's housekeeper didn't work Saturdays. Beau stepped back into the room a few minutes later, confused.

"Uh...Coach? There's a deranged Girl Scout or something selling cookies. Says she needs to see you."

"Maybe it's one of the neighbors' kids. I'll get rid—"

"Hey, Coach Frasier."

Nick's head jerked up. There on the threshold stood Marabelle Fairchild, holding a large wicker basket with what smelled like homemade baked goods. Nick frowned. She'd plagued his thoughts since their last meeting.

"How the hell did you get past the gates?" He glowered, hands planted on his hips. Nick lived in a gated community in North Raleigh, where large, new homes sat on several acres.

"I told the guard I'm your long-lost bastard child who wants to reconcile with the daddy I never knew." Marabelle batted her big, dark eyes. Beau laughed out loud, Tyrone dropped his cue stick, and Coach Prichard lowered his head, trying to hide his grin.

Nick blinked hard…twice. He didn't think Tinker Bell could look any worse than the other day, but he was wrong. Dead wrong. Her curls were caught on top of her head with some sort of tie-dyed rag. A Trinity Academy letterman jacket drooped from her small shoulders like a wet blanket, over a man-sized Atlanta Braves jersey. Both tops flopped over baggy jeans. Nothing, with the exception of a pair of clunky brown clogs resembling baked potatoes, fit her tiny frame. She looked like a child playing dress-up in her daddy's clothes.

"*Marabelle,*" he growled at her bright face.

"Okay, before your head explodes, I know the guard. He works security at the school part-time. I bribed him with some of my homemade cookies. Please, don't take it out on him. My cookies are hard to resist." Marabelle moved farther into the room, holding the basket out as an offering. "Would you gentlemen like some? I made plenty."

"They smell great," Beau said, reaching for a chocolate chip right off the top. "Aw, man. They're still warm." He shoved the whole cookie in his mouth.

"There's chocolate chip, oatmeal raisin, and coconut cupcakes to die for."

"Dang, girl. I want a cupcake." Ty reached into the basket with a shy smile.

"I'll try the oatmeal raisin," Coach Prichard added.

All three guys had their hands in Marabelle's basket of baked goods, and Nick started to see red. "Dammit!" He snatched the basket and shoved it at Coach Prichard. "You're coming with me." He gripped her upper arm and swung her around, dragging her from the room.

Marabelle called over her shoulder, "Y'all let me know how you like 'em. Ya hear?"

Nick hauled Marabelle through the spacious foyer and dining room, into a huge, industrial-size kitchen overlooking a wooded lot at the back of the house. Stopping at the large island, he yanked her in front of him, caging her in on both sides with his arms.

"Now, would you mind telling me why you are at *my* house on Saturday afternoon instead of my office on Monday afternoon?" he said between clenched teeth.

"Because when I called your office on Friday to confirm our appointment for Monday, your assistant told me you had no appointments that day. You were going to be out of the office on a road trip. You...you were planning to stand me up!"

Marabelle's brown eyes snapped with anger. Nick couldn't help but gape at her upturned, defiant face. No doubt about it...she had more nerve than sense. He blinked, noticing she wore makeup. Just a little mascara, elongating her already long eyelashes, and some pink lip gloss giving off a faint berry smell. The strangest urge to eat the berries right off her lush lips came over him. Shaking his head, he roughly pushed himself away and faced the windows to his wooded lot.

"What the hell am I going to do with you?" He gave a chest-heaving sigh, asking no one in particular. "You're gonna dog me until I agree to help out. Right?"

"Wow, you're not a dumb jock after all."

"Anybody ever tell you you're a real smart-ass?" Nick crossed his arms.

She nodded. "Practically every day."

Nick couldn't believe her gall. She showed up uninvited and then sassed him as if she had every right. On a deeper level, he probably respected her nerve, but right now, he needed to take charge. He'd admire her temerity later, when he could think straight.

"Listen up, Tink. All I'm agreeing to help with is the celebrity tournaments. I'm not making any commitment to the slave auction—"

"But—"

"No buts. Take it or leave it. We're going to do this my way or *not* at all. There's only one quarterback on this team, and I'm it." Nick leaned against the driftwood-inspired wood cabinets and crossed his legs at the ankles. "So, what's it gonna be?" Marabelle huffed, annoyed with his ultimatum, but he didn't give a shit. He could never be too careful these days.

She gripped the edge of the island top. "Fine. But won't you even consider—"

"Nope. I call all the plays. Don't you dare go announcing that I've committed to the auction, because I haven't." He moved to loom over her again, and she gave a wary step back. "Do we have a deal?"

"Deal." She nodded.

From the glint in her eyes and the way her mouth twitched to keep from smiling, he knew she was up to something. Nick kept his scowl in place, but on the inside he laughed out loud. He couldn't wait to see what Marabelle tried to pull next.

"Good. Now, I want to play pool and try your homemade cookies to see if you bake as well as you brag."

Back in the great room, he made the introductions.

"Marabelle, this is my offensive coordinator, John Prichard, and these two pretty boys playing lousy pool are Beau Quinton, quarterback, and Ty Washington, tight end for the Cherokees."

Beau and Ty both pumped her hand enthusiastically.

"Miss Mary-bell, your cookies are delicious. What else can you do?" Beau asked, winking in her direction.

Marabelle gave Beau one of her amazing smiles and slanted a furtive glance at Nick. "My baking is only surpassed by my cooking," she boasted. "And today's your lucky day, because Coach Frasier has asked me to cook in that professional kitchen of his." Nick snorted at her ability to sell horseshit.

Marabelle turned her back on him and continued to talk as if he didn't exist. "Bet you guys haven't had a great homemade meal in a while. So, what'll it be, boys?"

No one had ever called Nick Frasier dumb. Asshole, maybe, or cocky son of a bitch, but never dumb. He could read scheming Marabelle Fairchild like the jumbotron at the Cherokees games. The longer she snowed these guys, the easier it would be for her to sway them to support her cause. From the looks of things, Beau, Ty, *and* John were already entranced. Shit. Ruthless didn't begin to describe Tinker Bell. He'd have to watch her every move.

"Why don't you surprise us," Nick said with a challenge in his tone.

"Great. I'll be back before you have time to miss me." Marabelle removed her pup tent disguised as a varsity jacket, dumped it on the back of the leather chair he'd occupied earlier, and raced from the room.

Nick relaxed on a cushioned chaise on his brick patio, finishing the last of a cold beer. The weather in March could be tricky in Raleigh. One day the temperatures could hit seventy-five degrees and the next, there could be snow. But tonight was prime with crisp, cool air and rustling leaves, accompanied by the loud hum of crickets.

Nick smiled, remembering Marabelle in his kitchen, up to her elbows in flour, making homemade biscuits. Flour had covered her face and hair, and she still looked pretty darn cute. True to her word, Marabelle cooked a great meal along with the biscuits—chicken and wild mushroom casserole. The guys ate until they couldn't move, and Nick had a hard time getting them to leave.

Nick quietly chuckled as he recalled her comment to Ty about improving his footwork if he learned to play tennis. Ty appeared flabbergasted and then surprisingly agreed to a lesson. Marabelle also recommended children's books on tree sprites and wood nymphs for Coach Prichard to read to his four-year-old daughter, Hailey. Beau had poured on his usual charm and flirted outrageously, which Tinker Bell did nothing to discourage. Nick had no claim on her, but still felt a twinge of annoyance to see her all dreamy-eyed in front of his star player. Nick placed his empty beer bottle down on the brick pavers and folded his hands behind his head as he squinted up at the star-filled sky. His mouth tightened into a severe frown.

Beau was a marquee quarterback, and Nick was lucky to have him, but Q got more prime pussy in a month than most guys did in a lifetime. Beau didn't need to add Tinker Bell to his long list of conquests. Marabelle

Fairchild didn't fit into the same category with the ditzy, sex-crazed football groupies. She was smart, sassy, and a real ballbuster. Dangerous combination.

—∿∿—

Early Sunday morning, Marabelle went out for a jog in her neighborhood. Not because she loved the exercise, but because if she didn't, she'd never be able to eat the food she made. She settled into a comfortable stride as she allowed her thoughts to drift back to the night before. Even though Coach Frasier had shot down the live auction, she'd laid the groundwork to convince Beau Quinton and Ty Washington…one cookie at a time. The old adage, the way to a man's heart is through his stomach, was her modus operandi. Marabelle used cooking the way some women used their bodies. Her chocolate cream pie could make a man salivate better than any red-satin bustier. At least that was what she told herself. She knew all about her physical limitations, thanks to her mother's constant harping.

Edna Fairchild was a force to be reckoned with. She specialized in bridge playing, cocktail drinking, and party planning among Atlanta's high society. She also worked with a vengeance at molding Marabelle, like the perfect tomato aspic served at a Junior League luncheon. And her idea of perfection equaled extreme thinness and a St. John knit suit. Thank goodness Marabelle's older sister, Phoebe, a clone of their mother, relieved some of the pressure.

Edna had secured her position in the kingdom of her making with money she had inherited from her parents. Because she held all the cards, Edna kept everyone on a short leash, dangling their inheritance like chum over a shark tank, waiting for her daughters—and her husband—to bite. But if you displeased her or didn't live life according to the edicts of Edna, she threw the chum out or fed it to some other starving fish, like her charities or societies. Wherever she thought her legacy would hold the longest. Because for Edna, it was all about her mark. The mark she left on Atlanta's society at the expense of all else. Including her family.

Marabelle had dared to walk away from all of it. She'd not only said no to her mother's choice of potential husbands, but also to her portion of the inheritance. Marabelle did the unthinkable and then packed her bags and moved out. But Edna Fairchild would not accept defeat. She did everything in her power to lure Marabelle home and back under her control.

Marabelle caught herself as she almost stumbled on the uneven sidewalk. She swiped at the wetness around her eyes. It had been three years since she'd walked away, and she had no regrets. Except she missed her dad and sister every day. She didn't dare visit very often, because her mother always came up with reasons to make her stay. Edna was not malicious, but she'd always been needy and selfish. Deep down, Marabelle knew cutting ties with her mother and her lifestyle was for the best. And since she'd given up her safety net, she couldn't call for help when her car needed new tires, or when her health insurance went up, or when her roof sprang a leak and needed patching. Not that her parents wouldn't give her the money. Her dad would drop everything and bail her out at any time, but Marabelle wanted to prove to her mom, once and for all, that she could make it on her own without relying on them for financial support and...*without* a husband.

The air smelled of pine spiked with early morning damp moss. Thank goodness her ambush of Coach Frasier had seemed to go well. She rounded the corner toward her cute bungalow when her thoughts strayed to last night's dinner again. Coach Frasier had been a good sport, after he got over the shock of seeing her in his home. Marabelle had held her breath from the moment she'd barged through his front door until she'd opened his two stainless Sub-Zero refrigerators to find something to cook. All her years of competitive tennis had taught her a simple truth: close in for the kill when your opponent is down. Do not ease up on the pressure.

Marabelle started her cooldown from the top of her oak-shaded street. She waved to Lilah Dawkins—her next-door neighbor—sweeping her walk in a pink, printed housecoat under a heavy purple cardigan, giggling at Lilah's matching pink hair. Lilah sported a different hair color every other week. Marabelle would've stopped to chat, but her cell phone rang.

"Good morning!" Beau Quinton chirped on the other end of the line. "Hope I didn't wake you."

"Not at all. Just finished my run. What's up?" Marabelle said, catching her breath and wondering what had prompted this call as she pushed open her front door.

"What would you say to a tennis lesson with Ty and me? And maybe another home-cooked meal. We know you can cook, but can you back up all that big talk on the tennis court?" Marabelle could hear the smile in his voice. "We'll spring for the groceries, and if you're really good on the court, we'll double your going rate."

Shoving the phone between her chin and shoulder, she reached inside the refrigerator for a water bottle. Hot damn. Win-win. "You're on, big guy. Meet me at the school. Courts are around back by the playing fields."

"Three o'clock?"

Marabelle closed the refrigerator door with her hip. "Perfect. And you better bring your A game," Marabelle added with a laugh.

"Count on it."

———*ᴠᴠᴠ*———

Beau and Ty showed great promise on the tennis courts, which had everything to do with their exceptional athleticism and Marabelle's excellent instruction. From the groceries the guys provided, Marabelle made her famous chicken marsala with a side of pasta and homemade tomato sauce, along with salad and tangy lemon vinaigrette dressing. For dessert, Beau surprised her with her favorite ice cream: Cherry Garcia.

Beau and Ty entertained her all through dinner with funny stories about training, practices, and road trips. They described Coach Frasier as tough but fair, never asking them to do anything he couldn't or wouldn't do himself. Marabelle carefully mentioned the auction without committing Coach Frasier's participation one way or the other. With a clear conscience, she could still carry out her duties for the school without breaking her promise to Coach.

"We'd be happy to sacrifice our bodies for a worthy cause," Beau said with a chuckle. "Our record for pleasing the ladies is unsurpassed." He winked, and his brown eyes twinkled as he stretched out his long legs and folded his hands behind his head of thick, dark hair.

"In exchange for some home-cooked meals, we'll do just about anything." Ty gave a shy smile. With his warm brown eyes and buff physique, Marabelle could see he had no problems attracting the opposite sex.

"You're kidding, right? Why would you two stud-puppies want to hang around me, when you could have any woman out there?" Marabelle teased.

"None of those gals cook or whale on a tennis ball as hard as you," Beau said.

Marabelle chuckled. "Well, it's hard work being beautiful. Do you have any clue what it takes for those women to maintain themselves just so they can appeal to you gorgeous guys?"

"How do you do it then, Miss Marabelle?"

"Do what?"

"How do you stay beautiful *and* cook?" Ty asked, slaying her with the perfect aw-shucks expression.

"Ty honey, you must have me confused with some-one else." Marabelle lounged on her white slipcovered sofa dotted with lavender-and-green-striped pillows.

Ty smiled. "I think you're the prettiest thing ever. And I'm not the only one. Coach Frasier does, too."

"What?" Marabelle straightened, her relaxed pose forgotten. "Coach Frasier thinks I'm a hot mess and exer-cises great control, I might add, in not strangling me."

"From where I was sitting, Coach couldn't keep his eyes off you last night, and he didn't seem real happy with Q's flirting."

"Ty's right, Mary-bell." Beau spooned the last of the ice cream from his bowl. "Coach will probably run my butt off in minicamp next week. I've a good mind not to show up until he cools down."

Marabelle clutched a striped pillow to her chest. "You guys need to pee in a cup? Because Coach Frasier thinks I'm a child who doesn't know how to dress and drives a wind-up car."

"He does have a valid point on the dressing part." Beau slanted a dubious look her way, obviously not appreciating the comfort of her school sweats. "With a little sprucing up, you'd be damn near perfect."

Marabelle studied Beau and Ty's faces, waiting for the punch line. When none came, she said, "Okay, now I'm going to *pay* you! You guys are welcome to homemade meals anytime. You're the best thing that has happened to my ego since the year I won the Southern Regionals."

"That's a deal, Mary-bell." Beau rose, pulling Marabelle up by the hand. He planted a big kiss on her forehead, and Ty pecked her on the cheek.

Marabelle waved good-bye from her front porch and then rushed to the bathroom mirror. Nothing had changed. Freckles, cow eyes, unruly curls, and swollen lips. *Yep, those guys need their eyes checked.*

Chapter 4

THE NEXT AFTERNOON, MARABELLE RAPPED HER knuckles on the office door at Cherokee headquarters. The thick wood door intimidated her almost as much as the hulking guy lurking behind it. She'd been announced by Chantal, his blond, busty secretary, who sat behind an illuminated reception desk with the Carolina Cherokees logo etched in the center. The last time Marabelle had seen such a perfect, plastic-looking person, she'd been standing in the Barbie aisle at Toys "R" Us, buying carnival prizes for her students. Chantal, all lit up, confirmed what Marabelle already knew about Coach Frasier: he was a professional jock who liked his arm candy to stand out.

Marabelle furtively glanced down at her khaki golf skirt and Nike tennis shoes, grimacing at the yellow handprint—courtesy of Brandon Aldridge—on her navy cable-knit sweater. Too late for regrets, she plowed through the door.

"Oh man. This is wrong on so many levels." Nick shook his head as he stood from behind his massive mahogany desk and pointed at Marabelle's outfit. Instead of jeans and cowboy boots, he looked even more imposing wearing a gray cashmere sweater and tailored charcoal slacks with black Gucci loafers.

"What?" But she already knew.

"Tinker Bell, I wish TLC's *What Not to Wear* was

still on the air. I'd love for Stacy and Clinton to get a hold of you and your god-awful wardrobe."

Marabelle glanced at her sweater, buttoned up the front, and smiled at the fact that it could've housed a small family. "There's nothing wrong with my wardrobe, well, except for the handprint. It's…it's very functional," she lied.

Nick pointed a finger at Marabelle's hair wadded on top of her head. "Why'd you stab your hair? Trying to kill it?"

Marabelle touched the #2 pencils she'd shoved in her hair like chopsticks. "What are you, the fashion police? And how do you know anything about *What Not to Wear*? Is *Monday Night Football* aware of your habit of watching fashion shows?"

Suddenly Nick towered over her, and she couldn't figure out how he had moved so effortlessly. "When you've stayed in as many hotel rooms as I have, you watch a lot of things. I'm confident in my sexuality and sure know a damn bit more about fashion than you."

Marabelle gave an unladylike snort. "My kindergartners know more about fashion than I do. Even Clay knows more about it, and he's a terrible dresser. Obviously, it's not important to me."

Nick gave her a puzzled look. "Who's Clay?"

Marabelle waved her hand dismissively. "At one time, a boyfriend, but not really. Ex-boyfriend doesn't seem right. A friend. A friend who happens to be a boy."

"Friend with benefits?" Nick scowled down at her.

"No. Not anymore. We only slept together twice, and I sucked at it, so we decided not to go there again." Marabelle slapped a hand over her mouth. "Did I say that out loud?" she said, the words muffled behind her hand.

Nick stood frozen in place; his expression changed from scowling to one of complete astonishment. "You 'sucked at it'?" he said as if he had trouble forming the words.

"Crap," she grumbled. "Busted."

"How do you know *you* sucked? Maybe he sucked and you're a sexual dynamo."

Face heated, Marabelle brushed past Nick, plopping her navy-blue JanSport backpack on one of the tan leather guest chairs in front of his desk and pulling out several folders.

"Yeah, right. Anyway, it's no big deal. I'm aware of my limitations. Now—"

"Maybe you haven't slept with the right person."

Nick's husky voice now warmed the back of her neck. Maybe she *hadn't* slept with the right person. Maybe Nick was the right person with his big, warm hands and—*Oh, shut up!*

With a nervous laugh, she said, "Don't tell me you're volunteering for the job, because I have to tell ya, you're still not my type."

"You finally admitting you're gay?"

Marabelle's head jerked up. Nick was no longer behind her but on the other side of his desk, flashing his mind-numbing, lopsided grin. Rockin' roller coaster loop went her stomach. Okay. She needed to tread with great care. This highly competitive athlete wielded his sex appeal like a weapon to lure any and all unsuspecting women foolish enough to fall under his spell. And for some inexplicable reason, he'd set his sights on her.

"Nah. It's some allergic reaction to sex and relationships in general. I can't tell you how frustrated my mother is on this topic. She has support groups to help her cope. From what I hear, I've been written up in medical journals as a lost cause."

Nick could've melted Marabelle into a puddle of simple syrup right there on the plush red carpet with his sizzling gaze. Then he burst out laughing as he dropped into his leather desk chair.

"What am I going to do with you?" he said, still chuckling.

Marabelle smiled and rubbed her hands together. "For starters, you could give me the names of the celebrities I can contact for the tournaments."

He motioned toward the chairs. "Take a seat, Tinker Bell, and try not to mess anything up."

Nick had agreed to lend his name as the major sponsor to drum up excitement in the community for the event. He read off names and numbers—from a list supplied by Chantal—of all the celebrities he felt comfortable asking for favors. Marabelle spied Keith Morgan's name on the list, one of the world's top tennis players, and could hardly contain her excitement.

"You *have* to persuade Keith Morgan to come," she gushed. "Do you know him personally?"

"He trains in Miami. I knew him when I lived there."

Marabelle's gaze wandered to the large picture window behind Nick with a view of the practice field. "He's, like, my all-time favorite player. I'd die to be on the same court with him, like, I might not be able to hit the ball…"

"Jeez, Tinker Bell, *like*, you're getting all junior high on me over Morgan," he mimicked.

"For him, I will wear a tennis skirt."

Nick dropped the pen he'd been using to take notes. "Well, I'll be damned. I might pay him to come, just to see that."

Marabelle turned back to her notes. "He'd bring in major bucks for the live auction," she rattled off without thinking.

"I thought I told you I wasn't discussing the auction right now. Maybe never."

"But…but Beau and Ty already agreed to do it. They think it's a great idea."

"*Excuse me?*" Coach Frasier's voice got scary soft.

Marabelle wished she could insert her size-six Nike tennis shoe with foot attached into her mouth. "Before you chew me out, I can explain."

"This I've got to hear." *Tap, tap, tap* went his pen on his desk blotter. Nick's lips had thinned into a grim line, and some sort of tic appeared around the right side of his jaw.

Hidden in the folds of her skirt, Marabelle's hands twisted as she told him about yesterday's tennis lesson and dinner, and how she accidently let it slip about the auction, but they'd gladly volunteered without any persuasion on her part.

The tapping pen stopped. "You mean to tell me Beau and Ty had dinner with you again last night?"

The disbelief in his tone struck a nerve. "You're missing the point. They don't need to ask your permission to eat, do they?"

Nick rested his forearms on his desk. "You expect me to believe Q contacted you? Not the other way around?"

"As hard as it is for you to believe, Coach

High-n-Mighty, some people actually enjoy my company." Marabelle leaned forward, with her forearms on his desk, closing the space between them.

"I don't doubt that for a minute. What I do doubt is that you didn't plot this meeting somehow."

"I most certainly did not!" Marabelle resorted to her best schoolteacher voice. "Just ask Beau. I cannot believe you're being so bullheaded about this."

"Look, we had a deal, and you broke it by going behind my back and soliciting my players when I specifically told you not to." Nick stood as he spoke and planted his fists on the desk, doing a fine imitation of Hank from *King of the Hill*.

"You didn't *specifically* say not to contact your players. You said you didn't want anything to do with the auction." Marabelle rose from her chair.

His eyes narrowed. "Uh-huh. You knew what I meant. A deal's a deal. If you don't agree to stop your covert tactics right now, I'm withdrawing all my support *and* my money."

"Fine!" she shouted at his scowling face.

Marabelle and Nick were standing nose to nose over his desk when Chantal poked her head around the door.

"Coach Frasier? Is everything okay in here?"

"Yes. Thank you. That will be all for today." Coach Frasier's disapproving gaze remained on Marabelle.

Chantal gave Marabelle a suspicious look before closing the door.

"Tinker Bell, I'm going to hold you to that." Nick's face was so close Marabelle could feel his hot breath skim the side of her cheek.

Nick rounded his desk and jerked his thumb toward

her things. "Grab your bag and papers, and let's get out of here."

"But we haven't discussed your nephew. He's the reason for the yellow paw print on my sweater." Marabelle gathered her notes and legal pad, shoving them in her backpack.

"Good for him. Now you can burn it."

"You know I teach four- and five-year-olds. Not all of us can look as put together as Chantal." Nick guided Marabelle out of the office with his hand on the lower part of her back, warming her down to her toes.

He leaned close and whispered, "I think there's more to it than that."

Marabelle was too distracted to process his meaning, because her mind was busy devising ways to bottle and sell his delicious, spicy-lemony scent.

"Where are we going?" she asked when she realized they weren't heading for the parking lot.

"Training room, and then we're going to grab a bite to eat."

"We are?" Marabelle halted her steps. "You're presuming… What if I have a date or something?"

"Don't tell me you have another date with Beau, because you're gonna have to break it," he bit off in a clipped tone.

Marabelle sighed. "Stop worrying about your team. I don't have dates with anyone." No point in pretending she lived a party-girl lifestyle.

Nick led her toward a large state-of-the art training room. Shiny, stainless steel equipment sparkled in front of floor-to-ceiling windows. Several players with their trainers spied Coach Frasier and stopped their workouts to call him over. The smell of sweat hung heavy in the air, and the repetitive clinking of weights as the athletes pushed their straining muscles held Marabelle's undivided attention.

Near the entrance, Marabelle saw Beau Quinton off to the right. She drifted closer as he lifted a large set of free weights. He caught Marabelle staring at his bulging muscles and winked. Beau set the weights down with a thud and ambled over, wiping his face with a white towel draped around his neck.

Marabelle's mouth went dry. Her gaze followed a drop of sweat as it slid its way down Beau's chest and rippled over his six-pack. "Oh my," she breathed.

"Mary-bell, what're you doing here? Missed me already?"

"Q!"

Marabelle peeled her gaze off Beau's rock-hard abs in time to see a determined Coach Frasier storming their way.

"What's up, Coach?"

"You have dinner last night at Marabelle's?" Nick blocked Marabelle's view of Beau's glorious torso with his broad back and shoulders.

"Yeah, she cooked another awesome meal. Why?" Beau said from behind the white towel as he dried his face.

"She discuss her idea of a live auction with you?"

"Yeah, she might've mentioned it," he hedged, pulling the towel from around his neck.

Marabelle scooted around Coach Pain-in-the-Ass. "Hey. I'm right here."

Nick continued to ignore her. "Forget about it. Marabelle's having second thoughts, but she could use a signed football and jersey from you."

"Sure. Whatever Mary-bell wants." Beau grinned at her.

"Wait. I never—"

Nick snagged Marabelle's wrist, turning and pulling her behind him like an errant child, as he called over his shoulder, "One more thing, did you arrange for the dinner last night or did she?"

"I did. We're meeting again next Sunday. Why?" Beau replied.

"No reason. I'll be sure to be there."

Chapter 5

"I TOLD YOU I DIDN'T ARRANGE YESTERDAY'S MEETing." Out in the parking lot, Marabelle pulled on her hand to halt Nick's progress. She would've been more successful trying to stop a freight train.

Nick sighed. "Look, if Q hadn't called first, you would've found another way to get in front of him. I know how your devious mind works."

"Great minds do think alike."

He stopped next to his shiny silver Porsche and opened the passenger-side door for her. "Uh, why don't I follow in my car?"

"Because I don't trust you." Nick herded her in with his hand on her head and closed the car door.

Marabelle marveled at the cool interior as she ran her hand along the lacquered burl-wood dashboard. "Great car. Can I drive?"

"No. Sit back and don't touch anything."

Marabelle did just that as she relaxed in the firm black-leather bucket seat, more than thrilled to be riding in an awesome Porsche with an equally awesome sports celebrity. She didn't make a habit of flirting with danger, but when danger came as temptingly packaged as the coach, she gave herself a pass. She studied Nick from the corner of her eye as he drove. His nose was straight and Romanesque. His five-o'clock shadow, which covered a strong, square jaw, grew in a little darker than his sandy-blond hair, which, of course, had that perfect tousled look, more from tunneling his fingers through it than styling. She'd seen him do it during their meeting, whether from frustration or habit, she didn't know. He could be the perfect modern-day Prince Charming to her Cinderella scouring the locker room floors. Or not. He punched a contact on his cell while keeping one hand on the wheel. "Hey, Nat. Give me a call. We need to talk about Brandon. He's turning into a real monster, and I'm not okay with that." Nick disconnected the call.

"Who was that?" Marabelle straightened in her seat.

"My sister, Natalie. She's off licking her wounds in Paris or somewhere." He didn't disguise his disgust as he tossed the phone down.

"How long will she be gone? Because Brandon is becoming a real pain. I have a high tolerance, but he's even getting to me."

"I don't know. But I plan on finding out."

Nick turned into the parking lot of Franklin's Steak House, a popular place for the Who's Who in Raleigh, and managed to score a space right up front.

"Don't we need reservations to eat here?" Marabelle asked, peering through the windshield.

"Normally, but they always accommodate me." Coach Frasier jumped out and rounded the hood of the car to open her door. "Being rich and famous does have some perks." He flashed his lopsided, cocky grin.

Marabelle made no move to leave the car. Instead, she nervously glanced at the flickering gas-lantern sconces on either side of the black-and-white-striped canvas awning. "I can't go in there looking like this. With *you* of all people." She tried tamping down her panic, but her sweaty palms and constricted throat weren't helping.

Nick reached down and pulled her stiff form from the car. "Don't worry. You're fine. No one will be looking at you anyway. They'll all be looking at me." His white teeth flashed in his tanned face.

She tried to swallow. "That's just it. Aren't you embarrassed to be with me? I know I am." Marabelle hugged the side of the car, trying to work her way back inside.

"Tinker Bell, this is all the more reason to rethink your wardrobe. For occasions like this one." Nick began unbuttoning her sweater.

"That's why I stay away from occasions like this. What are you doing?" she shrieked as he started to remove her sweater.

"What I've been itching to do since you stepped foot in my office." He peeled away the bulky sweater. "To see what lay beneath," he said in a calm voice. His gaze flicked to her chest. She wore a snug blue polo shirt with the words *US Open* plastered across her chest in red. He whistled softly. "You've been hiding a real woman under all that bulk."

He had no idea what she was hiding and why. She'd waged this war for years, arguing there was more to life than presenting a false image of yourself. The reality: she'd started this line of attack to irritate her mother, and it had worked beautifully. And now that she'd made her point, it was time to give it up. But somewhere along the way, Marabelle had fallen into the trap of not caring, and it was costing her…a lot.

Marabelle tried to wrestle her sweater back, but Nick held it off easily behind his back with one hand.

"I can't go in there looking like this," she hissed for the second time.

"Why? Because you have great breasts?"

"Yes. No! Look, don't get too excited there, Coach," she stammered.

Just like that, her nipples stood at attention. Nick's gaze slid from her traitorous breasts to her hair. He plucked out the pencils and watched the tresses tumble down past her shoulders.

"Unbelievable," he murmured as he stared.

Marabelle rushed to wad her hair back up, but Nick covered her hands.

"Stop. Leave it down." His hand smoothed the curls hanging in disarray around her face, gently tucking one behind her ear, and brushed her cheek with his fingers. He sucked in a breath, his nostrils flared, and his eyes narrowed to slits.

"Tinker Bell, you've been hiding under a bushel, and I'm going to find out why," he said in a rough, husky voice. Exactly what she'd been afraid of. Marabelle had no experience with this type of foreplay. The type where sexual innuendos were lobbed like tennis balls and everyone knew their position on the court. She wished she were more skilled.

Abruptly, he reached into the backseat. "Here. Put this on." He held out his jean jacket. Thankful to have something else to do besides contemplate the fifty ways of gettin' down with Coach Dreamy, Marabelle turned and slipped her arms into his jacket. The worn, soft denim gave the sensation of being wrapped in his arms. More comfortable than her awful sweater, and it smelled way better too.

"Thanks. I don't think—"

"That's right. Don't think." He rolled up the sleeves, which fell past her hands. "Take your papers on my nephew, and we can discuss how to keep him out of jail." Nick shoved the folder at her and spun Marabelle in the direction of the entrance. "Now smile and play nice."

Like magic, the maître d' seated them immediately upon entering the already crowded restaurant and bar. Every few feet, someone stopped Nick to shake his hand and bask in the golden boy's glory. Some people shot Marabelle strange looks. Mostly women, but overall, Coach Fabulous garnered most of the attention. They finally worked their way to a cozy table near the windows, overlooking a lush courtyard with a stone fountain, affording them some privacy. The smell of grilled Angus beef made her mouth water, and the tension that had seized her stiff shoulders began to subside.

"That must get exhausting," she said after the waiter placed a crisp white linen napkin in her lap and left to bring their drinks. "All those people want a piece of you. Don't you ever get tired of it?"

Nick shot her a pointed look that spoke volumes. "Yeah, but I'm used to it. Maybe now you can understand my reservation about holding a live auction where a bunch of guys have to unwillingly be put on the block."

"Oh, but it wouldn't be anything like that." Marabelle hitched her chair closer. "It would be tastefully presented."

Nick scoffed, lowering the menu to glare at Marabelle. "You know as well as I do we're going to be viewed as sex objects, no matter how you present it."

Like that was such a hardship. "It's about time,"

Marabelle mumbled. "Women are viewed in the same manner every day. Look at the Miss America Pageant. Is the bathing suit portion really necessary? And what about all the sleazy topless bars?" She smacked her palm on the table for emphasis. "Don't even get me started on porn." Steam practically poured from her ears. "We're not asking you guys for a pole dance or to pose for *Playgirl*. Mrs. Cartwright, who's pushing ninety and is loaded, thinks you have great abs. You'll probably end up with her, big guy. If you stripped in front of her, she might expire on the spot."

The waiter had stopped midstride with their drinks on his tray, and conversation from the neighboring tables had ceased. Coach Frasier seemed to be struggling with allergies or something, because tears filled his eyes.

When would she ever learn? Everyone's gaze was glued on her as though she were green-glowing toxic waste. And to make matters worse, Nick gave up the fight and burst out laughing. So much for being inconspicuous.

"Aw, honey, come on now. Sit up, and let's call a time-out," Nick said between hoots of laughter as she slumped lower in her chair. "As much as I'd like to debate the battle of the sexes with you, why don't we order first?"

Marabelle fantasized falling down a manhole, never to be seen again. Damn. Something about this guy made outrageous things pop into her head and discharge from her mouth without warning. She needed the success of this auction. She needed to make her parents proud. And she needed to stop sounding like an idiot!

With a little encouragement from Nick, Marabelle recovered from her mortifying outburst and ate her perfectly cooked petite filet without further incident. Nick steered the conversation to more stable ground, asking questions about her teaching. She shared her thoughts on Brandon's behavior in school, her concern that he might be acting out because he felt abandoned by his parents. She stressed how Brandon needed his family, including Nick, because it wasn't healthy for him to be raised solely by his nanny. Nick nodded in agreement, never interrupting or pooh-poohing anything she suggested.

Toying with the stem of his wineglass, he said, "Your dedication to your students is admirable. They're lucky to have someone so enthusiastic and hardworking."

Marabelle glanced over her shoulder in confusion. *Is he speaking to me?* Nick gave a knowing nod as he tipped his glass in a silent toast.

Adoring fans managed to make their way to his side. Most of the interruptions came from women…young and old. Marabelle watched in astonishment at how deftly he deflected all the advances and not-so-subtle propositions without seeming to offend. It never occurred to any of the women he might be on a date, because one look at Marabelle set everyone straight on that account.

Over coffee and after-dinner drinks, Marabelle groaned when she spied Carol Evans and JoAnn Burrows, both decked out in the latest St. John knit suits, weaving through the crowded restaurant toward their table. Leaning forward, she whispered, "Don't look now, but you're about to meet the Blondie Twins." Nick quirked a brow, but before he could question her, he was accosted once again.

"Coach Frasier," Carol Evans purred as she neared

the table. "What a wonderful treat." Carol acknowledged Marabelle with a simple nod. Nick pushed away
from the table for the umpteenth time and stood.

"Ladies, I don't believe I've had the pleasure." His
oozing charm had the Blondie Twins at a loss for words.
A first, for sure. Watching them struggle to untangle their
tongues had Marabelle jumping in for the introductions.

"Mrs. Evans and Mrs. Burrows are the brilliant
minds behind the *live* auction," Marabelle added for
good measure.

"Please, call me Carol," she gushed, grasping both
of his hands.

"Call me JoAnn…all my friends do." JoAnn curled
her claws around his forearm. Both ladies drank him in
like a cool mint julep.

"Would you like to join us?" he graciously offered.

"We'd love to, but we're meeting friends for dinner."

Marabelle released a huge breath, not wanting them
to horn in on her connection. Nick was hers, dammit.
Her eyes widened at her ridiculous thought.

"Imagine our surprise seeing you with Ms. Fairchild,"
Carol said. "I'm so thrilled you're discussing business,
because I'm afraid we might've overwhelmed her with
the enormity of this task. She's going to need all the
support we can give her." Carol laughed as if everyone
agreed Marabelle was incapable of pulling off this job.

Nick's charming facade slipped, and his eyes turned
flinty. "Actually, ladies, we weren't discussing business at
all." He paused for effect, making sure he had everyone's
undivided attention. A frisson of alarm skittered over
Marabelle's skin. "We're on a date, and I was about to
ask Marabelle back to my place…before you interrupted."

Marabelle's jaw smacked the table at the same time the Blondie Twins' eyes bugged out, *boinging* as if attached to springs. Uncomfortable silence filled the air.

Instead of coming clean, Nick gave her a conspiratorial wink, causing her knees to tremble and her palms to sweat. "What the heck, we might as well come clean, right, honey?" Nick paused, drawing out the suspense until Marabelle came close to bursting into maniacal laughter. "Ladies…Marabelle and I are actually…engaged."

"NO!" All three women shrieked at the same time.

Shitdamnfire. Marabelle scrambled out of her seat with hands outstretched pleadingly. "Uh, Mrs. Evans, Mrs. Burrows, what Coach Frasier means—"

"From the moment I met Tinker Bell, I was hooked. It's hard to explain."

Ya think? Marabelle narrowed her eyes at his gorgeous soon-to-be-bashed-in head.

Nick disengaged himself from the cloying Blondie Twins and pulled Marabelle under his arm. "She's still not used to the idea. We're going to give it some time, but not too long. We're a little anxious, if you know what I mean." Nick actually waggled his eyebrows at the horrified women.

Giving her a warning squeeze, he pulled her in tighter. Head smashed against his chest, Marabelle inhaled his delicious scent before she inched away in time to see the Blondie Twins shooting switchblades at her with their eyes.

"Ms. Fairchild, obviously you've been up to more than securing bachelors for our auction and have over-stepped the boundaries of what is proper behavior for a Trinity Academy kindergarten teacher." JoAnn had designated herself the moral police. *What a load of crap.*

"Your role on this committee is very important, and we were assured you'd put your work above all else. Clearly, you've lost your focus," Carol said in cool tones.

It was obvious the Blondie Twins had considered Marabelle "safe," figuring none of the potential bachelors would be interested in her. She felt Nick stiffen by her side.

"Quite the contrary, ladies. Marabelle has been doing a stellar job. I've been against the auction, but with her sound arguments, she has managed to change my mind." No one could mistake the steel behind his words, working in direct contrast to his warm hand rubbing her side. "If you ladies will excuse us, Marabelle will have a full report at your next meeting."

"But, Coach Frasier, what…why…? You've never dated her type before," JoAnn wailed, on the verge of hysterics.

"Are you referring to Marabelle's wardrobe? Because I've got to tell you—"

"I'm a real dynamo in the sack," Marabelle blurted. Both women looked as though they'd been doused with a cooler of icy Gatorade, and Nick didn't hide his surprise either. It was official: she needed to be surgically fitted with a muzzle.

Carol Evans recovered first, her tone downright frosty. "Ms. Fairchild, we look forward to your report. Wednesday at four o'clock, *sharp*."

"Good evening, Coach Frasier." The Blondie Twins stormed off together with their heads inclined, undoubtedly recounting the devastating disaster they had just witnessed.

Chapter 6

"Tinker Bell, we need to talk."

Nick had hustled Marabelle from the restaurant and into his car before any more outbursts could come from her.

"Right. Thanks for the heads-up in there. What in the hell got into you? I hope I still have a job tomorrow," she said between gritted teeth.

"Everything was under control. You're the one who went off half-cocked. Do you have Tourette's? Because you seem to blurt things out—"

"*Me?* I'm not the one who said we're engaged. Have you lost your mind?"

Nick rubbed his hand over his neck. "I only wanted to help. Those ladies pissed me off, talking about you as if you didn't matter." Marabelle jerked her head sharply toward him. "You're working your ass off teaching those snot-nosed kids every day, and then they want you to change gears and convince a bunch of spoiled celebrities to donate to their cause. It didn't seem like they were giving you any support, that's all."

Nick wasn't lying. He didn't like their treatment of Marabelle. But something else had made him announce his engagement. Marty Hackman had given him another earful earlier about cleaning up his personal life and presenting a respectable, stable front to the press and the fans. He wanted Nick to settle down. No more pictures with women who looked like they knew Hef personally. Or didn't know a football from a soccer ball. Marty wanted respectability and credibility. And after spending time with likable but ballsy Marabelle, the perfect solution had suddenly popped into his head. Who better than a kindergarten teacher?

Surprise lit Marabelle's features. She'd probably never, in her wildest dreams, expected him to support her. Now to get her on board without blowing his cover. In a soft voice, she said, "Thank you. I don't know what came over me. It was a knee-jerk reaction." Her brow furrowed, and she twisted her hands in her lap. "We can undo this. I'll apologize on Wednesday. I'll tell them I mixed alcohol with cold medicine and didn't know what I was saying."

"No."

"What?"

Nick hated to see her visibly struggle not to appear miserable. The wind had been knocked from her sails, and he'd bet his Super Bowl ring it wasn't the first time. He didn't want his sassy, funny, frumpy fairy apologizing to anyone. Especially those overdressed, oversexed, jaded housewives.

"If anyone should apologize, it should be those rude women. They were out of line."

"But, Coach Frasier, you announced we're engaged. They're on their cell phones right this minute, spreading that bit of gossip all over Raleigh, Durham, *and* Chapel Hill. Not to mention social media." No sooner had the words left her mouth than Nick's phone starting pinging with new tweets. Yep. Poor Chantal. He might have to raise her salary for managing his exploding accounts.

Marabelle continued to babble. "…I'll tell them it was all a joke. Maybe if you send flowers or—"

"We're not changing our story." Nick covered her balled fists with his hand and squeezed. "If I say we're engaged, we're engaged. No one is going to challenge me on this."

"Huh? Of course they will. Look at me and look at you." Marabelle yanked her hand free, pointing her index finger back and forth. "No one is going to believe you're suddenly engaged to me. They'll suspect drugs or blackmail or something illegal. Please don't do this. I'm a big girl, and I can take care of myself."

The more he listened to her pathetic excuses, the more he liked his plan. She may be used to taking care of herself, but everyone could use a little help now and then. Besides, he enjoyed her company. She was funny and smart and different from anyone he'd ever been with.

Nick eased back in his seat. "Darlin', all I can say is being engaged to you is going to be one helluva ride."

Curls danced around her shoulders as she shook her head. "We can undo this before it gets out of hand. It's not too late."

He brushed a lock of hair behind her ear. "It's like this." His thumb followed a lazy trail from behind her ear and down her soft throat. "I could use a fiancée to keep unwanted women from coming on to me. You were a witness. Some women are relentless. I could use a little peace from all the activity." His fingers felt her pulse jump. "There's a new season to prepare for and the draft weighing on my mind. It's no secret the team is going through some major changes. We have to improve our record this year; too many jobs are at stake. I don't need the added pressure of juggling my personal life."

Marabelle swallowed hard. "So I'm going to be like a decoy?"

Nick laughed. "That's one way of putting it. More like a buffer. You get to keep the aggressive women at bay. I give you full rein to be a total badass."

Marabelle smiled, leaning away from his touch. "What's in it for me?"

Now we're talking. Nick had known Tinker Bell would find an angle to turn this to her advantage. "Hmmm, you play my fiancée for the next few months, and I'll go along with your slave auction."

Marabelle's eyes lit up like the Rockefeller Center Christmas tree. Nick held up his index finger. "There's one catch. I'm *not* one of the participants."

"*Wh—?*"

"You can have Q, Ty…whoever you can con into selling themselves on the block, but I'm off-limits. Besides, how can a happily engaged man put himself up there to be lusted after? It just wouldn't be fair to you, Tinker Bell—"

Marabelle gave an unladylike snort. "I'm telling you, no one is going to believe we're engaged."

"Let me worry about that. Do we have a deal?" Nick leaned toward Marabelle, crowding her space, forcing her to bump the back of her head against the passenger window.

"Let me get this straight. I pretend to be your fiancée, and you allow me access to all your single players and celebrity friends for the tournaments *and* auction. And as long as I discourage those pesky, gorgeous women from throwing themselves at you, you won't interfere. Does that sum it up?"

"You've covered the highlights."

"Okay, hand it over." She held her hand out, palm up.

"Hand what over?"

"The number that Pamela Anderson wannabe stuffed in your back pocket." Nick's eyebrows rose.

"She's not waiting for you to call her to discuss next year's draft picks. Now, hand it over." She wiggled her outstretched fingers.

Nick laughed as he lifted his left hip and reached into his back pocket. "You catch on real fast. I'm depending on you to keep me in line." He placed the slip of paper in her palm.

Marabelle unfolded it. "Tiffani with an *i*…seriously? Do they make these names up?"

Nick grinned, started the engine, and pulled out of the parking lot.

———

Marabelle mulled over the pros and cons of Coach Frasier's outrageous proposal as they drove in silence. Even in the land of make believe, she could feel this charade coming back to bite her. As they neared Cherokee headquarters, where she'd left her car, she asked, "Why the sudden change of heart? You were dead set against the auction."

"Because I'm the quarterback, and I call the plays. And there are times when you have to call an audible."

"Mmmm." Right. An audible. Whatever that was. "What happens when you decide you want one of those gorgeous groupies? Am I just supposed to be an under-standing fiancée and look the other way?" Marabelle crossed her arms and cocked her head.

Nick shot her a quick glance. "Aw, honey. How can I think of wanting another woman when I've got you?" he teased, and Marabelle sighed, knowing she'd have her work cut out for her.

In the near-empty parking lot, Nick cruised into the space behind Marabelle's blue Honda Civic, cutting the engine. "But, you know, it goes both ways."

"What do you mean?" Her bullshit meter was pinging.

He opened her door. "I'm the real jealous type and don't want you trifling with my affections with what's his name…you know, Romeo."

As soon as Marabelle's tennis shoes hit the asphalt, Nick pinned her in with his arms. The cold car to her back and his scorching heat to her front.

Marabelle smacked her hands flat against his hard chest. "Clay. Clay Spencer." The rapid beat of his heart against her palm matched her own, fluttering like a hum-mingbird's wings. The pole light nearby cast his face in shadows but highlighted his sun-kissed hair.

"And what should I tell him? Hmmm? Today, he's my friend, but tomorrow, he could be the one…maybe." So unlikely, but Marabelle needed to serve an ace down the T to keep Nick from winning this game. "Clay may not be patient and wait until this charade is over."

Nick chuckled, his straight white teeth flash-ing against his shadowed face. "Don't worry about Casanova. He's not the right guy for you." He slipped his arms around her back, cradling her against his body. Marabelle took full advantage and curled against her own personal heater to ward off the chilly March night. Pushing him away would've been the wise thing to do, but why deprive her body of such a good time?

"He's perfect for me," she murmured. "Unlike you and me. We don't fit at all." Their bodies belied that very statement. They fit together real good...*too good*. Nick settled Marabelle more closely to him.

"Darlin', you haven't even tried me on for size. I assure you, I know how to satisfy." He spoke in a lazy Southern drawl as he nuzzled her neck, causing Marabelle's eyes to flutter closed. She couldn't think of a better sensation than having Coach Hottie nibbling on her neck as she started to melt like butter in a hot skillet. *Oh boy, he's good.*

Marabelle wiggled away from his arms and mouth, holding up her hand like a stop sign. "Nick, this is not going to work out. You're every girl's fantasy. Believe me, I've noticed. It's just that you're not my fantasy," she managed to say with a straight face. *Liar!*

His loud burst of laughter cracked against the other-wise still night. Marabelle rushed on. "Please don't take it personally. I just don't have very good experience with this sort of thing, whereas you have enough experience to write a book. And really, mercy sex has never been my thing. Let's just agree not to go there." Marabelle moved backward, and Nick stalked her, eating up the ground with his long strides.

Overkill. She'd just thrown down the gauntlet, and now he was in battle mode. "Tinker Bell, honey"—he grabbed her hand, pulling her back into his addicting embrace—"let's get one thing straight. You and I both know that I could change your mind in less than two minutes. And from your own admission, your experience in the satisfaction department is nonexistent. I can change that, too." Nick's grin turned positively wicked. "So don't be convincing yourself we're not going to happen, because I promise you…we are."

Marabelle gulped. "Okay. Maybe there's the tiniest possibility…but not tonight." *Maybe never.*

His left hand curved around the back of her neck as he fed his fingers through her hair, causing all kinds of sparklers to ignite and singe her already heated skin. His steely blue eyes glittered as his other hand pressed into her lower back. Her breath caught. Girls like her didn't get this opportunity very often, right? A fairy tale come true.

His head dipped, their mouths merged, and all thoughts of inadequacies escaped her mind as he molded his firm lips over hers. He teased the seam of her mouth with his tongue, and when her lips parted, he plunged his tongue inside and rocked Marabelle's world.

He left her no choice but to lean into him and weave her arms around his neck, pressing against all that delicious hard muscle. His spicy, lemony scent drugged her into wanting more. His kiss drugged her into wanting him. She could get really used to this.

Erp!

Marabelle broke contact and blurted, "Just as I thought…nothing." Her fingers fluttered to her tender lips where he had left his indelible mark. "Look, I tried to tell you. I am no good at this. Let's just forget all about it."

Nick's talented mouth curved into a fiendish grin. "Keep it up, Tinker Bell, because I love a challenge, and I always win."

Marabelle wanted to stay and argue but knew when to cut her losses. She wasn't above cowering and retreating. She tossed over her shoulder as she walked away, "I'm leaving now and going to bed—*alone*—and when I wake up, this nightmare is going to be just that...but over." His crafty laugh did nothing to settle her jangled nerves.

"You'll be dreaming, all right. About me, and it won't be any nightmare."

Dang it. He was probably right. She picked up her pace and ducked her head to hide her embarrassment.

"Hey, Tink."

Marabelle hesitated at the open car door and glanced back, against her better judgment.

"Don't forget your security blanket." Nick threw her ugly blue sweater with the yellow paint and hit her in the head.

"Hey!" Marabelle shoved the sweater in the car, slammed the door, and drove off, still wearing his jean jacket.

Chapter 7

NICK PRESSED END ON HIS PHONE AND SMILED. HE'D called Mrs. Crow, the headmistress, to inform her the gala had his support because of his fiancée, Marabelle. He hated to be responsible if anything bad had happened with Marabelle's job. The stammering on the other end of the line didn't go unnoticed, but he stuck to his story.

Nick stared out the windows at the practice field. He'd arrived early for work, since sleep had eluded him. Half the night he'd spent thinking about crazy, funny, soft Marabelle and their perfect, hot kiss. And the other half trying to figure out what made her so appealing. The beautiful women of his past, with movie-star breasts, cover-model faces, and mile-high legs, skidded across his mind. More than he cared to count. But he couldn't come up with one who intrigued him the way Tinker Bell did.

And all that ugly crap she wore didn't disguise her real beauty. Her milk-chocolate eyes sparked to life when she spoke, and her long, curly brown hair felt like silk to his touch. Most women he knew worked out to sculpt their bodies to perfection, but Nick had reveled in Marabelle's curves. The perfect combination of toned versus softness…in all the right places. Nick liked a woman to *feel* like a woman, not rock-hard from hours with a trainer.

Marabelle's feisty personality had captivated him,

and he sure needed the distraction. Especially now. The latest debacle with Jenna Williams, and even before that his nightmare relationship with his old girlfriend, had taught him a heavy lesson. Lola had made Nick's life a living hell when he played ball in Miami. He bore the relationship scars to show for it. Cured for life, Nick didn't do serious relationships.

His high-profile job was a real pressure cooker, and he had a young, eager team to mold into champions. Last season, the offense had held strong, but the defense, plagued with injuries, had sputtered repeatedly. The Cherokees lacked execution and consistency. Not for long. Not if he could help it.

Swiveling his chair around to face his desk, he tapped the keyboard to his computer, pulling up his emails. Yep. Marabelle posing as his fake fiancée was perfect. No strings attached. No expectations. No drama. Marabelle showed zero interest in a relationship. Hell, she showed zero interest in him, and he was okay with that. Eventually, the press would die down, and he and Marabelle could go their separate ways. In the interim, he'd enjoy arguing and bantering with her. A little levity could go a long way. And if Tinker Bell was anything, she sure was funny.

Marabelle dropped her forehead, along with her cell phone, on top of her desk and sighed. She'd made dozens of calls and left dozens of messages for the celebrities on Nick's list. Her head throbbed from the drama of the fake engagement and, oh yeah...*that kiss*.

She'd played right into his big, warm, sexy, capable

hands like any starstruck groupie. How she'd walked away last night when she really wanted to stay and continue what he'd started, she had no clue. Face it...she wanted to jump his gorgeous, rock-hard body.

And it wasn't merely his incredible good looks—although they were mighty fine. He reeked of charm, good looks, and intelligence, but the greatest of all had to be his charm. His charm, coupled with his mouthwatering sexuality, put her at a huge disadvantage.

Marabelle's desk vibrated from her buzzing cell phone. She palmed it, hoping for a return call from a celebrity.

Nope. Even better. Her dad.

"Hey, Daddy! When are you coming home?" Edgar Fairchild worked for a large manufacturer, handling most of their marketing abroad.

"Funny you should ask. I've been summoned. Your mother's hosting another benefit at the country club and expects you and me to be there," he informed her.

Edgar and Edna Fairchild had not lived together since she had turned ten. At the time, Marabelle had easily blamed her mother for driving her dad away, but as she matured, she started to see things in a different light. Ed had a way with women, with his tall stature and handsome features. Marabelle favored him in looks, but not height, sharing his dark-brown hair and eyes. Even after marrying the prettiest girl in Atlanta, he'd still managed to keep a few on the side. To keep the peace, they'd lived apart for years. He and Edna had never divorced, because Edna wouldn't stand for it and Edgar couldn't afford it.

"Gah. Seriously?" Marabelle moaned. "Daddy, I can't go. I hate her parties. I hate me at her parties. Please don't make me do this."

"Marabelle, if it was up to me, I would never make you attend another one of your mother's outlandish benefits. But I'm warning you, she'll be calling, and you know how she gets. I suggest you buck up and make the most of it. Besides, misery loves company. If I have to, you have to."

Marabelle slumped back in her chair like a recalcitrant child and frowned into the phone. Another one of her mother's ploys to control her minions. If her dad had refused, then Marabelle would have flat out said no. But she couldn't let him suffer Edna on his own. "Okay, Dad. When is it?"

"In two weeks. How about I send you something wonderful to wear from Paris? Will you feel better?" Ed always treated Marabelle special…when he was around.

"No thanks, Daddy, I'm fine. I'll scrounge up something. How bad can it be?"

Ed chuckled. "Marabelle, it pains me to say this, but *real* bad."

"Tinker Bell, we need to talk." Nick caught up with Marabelle on the courts the next afternoon shortly after the gala committee meeting. She was in the middle of running drills for the team. She growled in his direction like a feral cat, but that didn't deter him. He opened the gate to court one and forged ahead.

"I have nothing to say to you." She continued to feed balls like a machine, with a death grip on her racket.

He watched the boys hitting behind the baseline. "Now, honey, is that any way to talk to your intended?"

"Get back on your court and keep drilling," she ordered the boys as some of them started to gawk and work their way over to him. She threw her racket in the basket of balls and grabbed his arm to pull him off the court.

Nick allowed himself to be turned and then stopped. "Where're we going, Thumbelina? Behind the bleachers to neck?"

"Fat chance. Away from the courts. Those guys have a fanboy crush on you, and I don't want them to hear us."

Nick strolled next to her toward the bleachers. "I think their crush is on you, not me."

Marabelle stopped, eyes snapping as she dug her small fists into her hips. "What's that supposed to mean?"

"It means…those teenage boys have the hots for their tennis coach."

Marabelle's eyebrows shot so far up they got lost under her tennis hat. "Are you insane?" She put up both hands. "*Don't* answer that. What kind of fiancé are you? You don't write; you don't call. I'm sitting on pins and needles here. This charade has gone on long enough," she whispered fiercely.

Nick bit back a grin. "Awww, it's only been two days. Have you been missing me?"

"Of course not. That's not what I meant." Nick started to chuckle. "I don't think I can keep up this lie. In case you didn't notice, those committee members want to lynch me," she said, eyes flashing. "They're very upset that the man of their dreams has taken himself off the market and gotten engaged to me."

Nick had shown up at the meeting unannounced, and walked in on complete pandemonium with a lot of hysteria thrown on top. He'd managed to settle everyone down. Pledging a shitload of money will do that. Marabelle should be kissing his ass for saving hers.

"And that's a problem because…" Nick shrugged.

"Because now the entire committee thinks I'm a slut. Hazel Cartwright asked how long I'd been 'boinking' you."

"Really? Well, maybe we should—"

"Look, can't we pretend we had a big falling-out and broke up? I'll tell everyone you dumped me for…for Jennifer Aniston. That's totally plausible."

Nick hated to burst Marabelle's bubble, but he needed her more than she needed him. Marty Hackman loved the idea of his "engagement" and told Nick not to *fuck it up*…his exact words. And Nick had no intention of disappointing the gruff, cigar-chewing owner of the Cherokees. If he asked Nick to join hands and sing Joni Mitchell songs, then he would do exactly that.

Nick placed his hand over his heart. "Tinker Bell, I'm wounded. Besides, Jennifer and I didn't get along all that well."

"You've actually dated Jennifer Aniston?" Marabelle drew back as her mouth formed a perfect *O*.

"We went out a few times. What's the real problem here? I think the committee bought our story. We had them eating out of our hands."

"Eating out of *your* hand. Look, it's time we go our separate ways." Marabelle ticked off on her fingers. "You do what you do best…date groupies. And I'll do what I do best…make my mother's life miserable. It works."

Nick gave an exaggerated sigh and rubbed the back of his neck. "Anybody ever tell you you have no sense of adventure? You need to get out more."

"I'm adventuresome. I'm all about adventure. Adventure is my middle name."

Nick shook his head. "Huh-uh. My mind is made up.

We're engaged, and you're just going to have to accept it. The sooner you do, the sooner we get to the good stuff." He waggled his eyebrows at her scowling face.

"How can someone so gorgeous be so wicked and depraved?" Marabelle wondered aloud. "Why don't you pick on someone your own size?"

"Honey, I'm not picking on you. I'm playing with you." Nick allowed his gaze to roam over the tennis sweats swallowing her petite body. "I can't wait to play doctor and get to the part where I undress you," he said in a husky voice, moving in close and invading her space.

"Oh my God…you're impossible."

"Sh-h-h, you're drawing a crowd." Nick pointed at nobody over her head.

Marabelle whipped around to see who was listening, and Nick took advantage by gathering her in his arms.

"Marabelle, honey, stop fighting. Trust me." He slipped his arm around her waist and lifted her up on her toes.

Then he kissed her silly. Or did she kiss him silly? Because the second his lips met hers, he forgot what they were arguing about. He'd never had to work this hard to get a girl on board. Frustrated didn't begin to describe his feelings. Maybe he was losing his touch. He lifted his head, and Marabelle's whacked expression matched his. Nah.

"See, that wasn't so bad, was it?" he murmured.

Marabelle lowered herself and licked her bottom lip as if tasting him there. "Mmm. Okay. We'll pretend. But only when others are around. And *no* sex." She narrowed her eyes to slits. "I'm no groupie. I worship only from afar. It's safer that way."

He pressed another hard kiss to her lips, wishing he could scoop her up in his arms and take her home. "Get back to work. I'll call you later."

"Yeah, right," she mumbled. Nick watched as she trotted back to the courts, wondering how he was going to survive the next few months.

Marabelle chopped fresh vegetables for her favorite chicken stir-fry as fast as any professional chef, thinking how her life would've made a good reality TV show, when it suddenly dawned on her. Coach Sneaky had never agreed to her "no sex" ultimatum. He was cocky and confident he had her under his thumb. *Thumbelina, my ass.*

Marabelle stopped chopping before almost cutting off her finger. *Dammit.* She needed her wits about her. She had no intention of being his pawn. She blew out a breath. Juggling Coach Naughty, the hyped-up committee, her teaching job, and now her mother's latest ploy to convince Marabelle to drink the Kool-Aid had her on edge. Marabelle craved reassurance, along with a good bottle of pinot noir. She smiled, ready to pour a glass and call Paula, her BFF, when her phone rang right on cue. Snatching it up, thinking it was Paula, her smile faded at the name on caller ID. She was surprised it had taken her this long.

"Hey, Mom."

"Hello, dear. Have I caught you at a bad time?"

Does the sun set in the west? Yes. "No, I'm making dinner."

"Are you cooking for a man? For that Carl fellow?"

Marabelle let out a tortured sigh. "No, Mother. I'm not cooking for *Clay*."

"I'm glad. He was not your type."

Because he didn't bring in seven figures and own a yacht named "Who's Your Daddy." Good thing her mother didn't know about Nick. Marabelle had no doubt he could be her type, and her mother would be whistling the "Wedding March" and tossing out bushels of birdseed.

Edna started in on her usual blah-blah lecture. "Are you still determined to make it as an elementary school teacher?" Edna made it sound as if Marabelle panhandled on the corner. "You know, if you were living in Atlanta, I could help put your life in order."

Marabelle's chest tightened. She also happened to be a pretty good tennis coach, but that skill never registered with her mother. She shoved the phone between her chin and shoulder and transferred the crisp stir-fry onto her dinner plate. She sat down to eat, knowing that anything she said to defend her choices would fall on deaf ears. Edna lived to criticize. And since Marabelle always came up short on whatever her mother deemed acceptable, she became Edna's project in need of rescuing.

"For a capital city, Raleigh is so, so lacking. Maybe if you secured a real teaching job at the university." According to Big Edna, no CEO or gazillionaire was looking for a simple kindergarten teacher. "Or maybe if you joined the Junior League. I understand Sally Kingston has reached out to you numerous times, and you have not responded. Your lack of interest is very embarrassing, dear. I don't know why you're insisting on this ridiculous course of action. If hurting me is your goal, you have succeeded admirably." Edna sniffed.

And then there was the guilt, mounting like garbage at the city landfill. Edna turned guilt trips into gold medal events.

And she was off. "You are my daughter, and you know I love you, but if you can't come home for me, then do it for your sister. She misses you terribly." Marabelle missed Phoebe too. But Phoebe was not wasting away because Marabelle didn't live in Atlanta. Her social calendar was brimming with activities, stamped with Edna's approval, of course. Marabelle sighed, sometimes wishing she was more like her sister, allowing Edna to orchestrate her life to her heart's content.

"…and you haven't dated a decent man since I set you up with that chiropractor…oh, what was his name? Such nice, strong hands—"

"Uh, Mom," Marabelle interrupted the tirade. "Is there a point to this call? Because we've been down this road before, and the scenery is boring."

"Marabelle, your manners are deplorable. Another bad habit you've picked up." Edna's voice dripped with disapproval. "I'm calling about the fabulous party I'm hosting at the country club to benefit the restoration of Magnolia House on Peachtree. I insist you be here for it. You know, they say Scarlett O'Hara stayed in that house when she was in Atlanta." Edna's voice lowered as she dropped that piece of juicy news. *Oh brother.*

"Mother, Scarlett O'Hara is a fictional character in a book. She never existed."

"Fiddle dee dee. What matters is for my whole family to be here to support me and make this party the talk of the town."

Marabelle speared a perfectly cooked piece of red pepper, thankful her dad had already warned her.

"Sure, Mother, I wouldn't dream of missing it." Only because she'd get to see her dad. Marabelle gritted her teeth. She pushed her plate away, having lost all enjoyment in her meal, while Edna rambled on about the benefit, clothes, shoes, bridge, marriage, and, oh yeah, procreating. She always managed to sneak that into the conversation. Marabelle seriously eyed the butcher knife as a means to end her own misery.

"You need to catch a man while you're young, darling." Her mother's favorite mantra.

"Oh, God, I would rather stick hot pokers in my eyes."

"I heard that! Now listen up, I've already sent you some suitable clothes. Don't dare come home with your…your atrocious wardrobe. How a daughter of mine can have such terrible taste in clothes is beyond me. Sometimes I wonder if you weren't switched at birth."

"Nice thought…even for you, Mother," Marabelle grumbled. And that comment only rubbed salt in the wound. The one where she questioned if her family knew she existed. If they ever cared about her as an individual, not simply an extension of her mother's legacy.

"Oh, darling, perk up. This party might be just the thing for you. There's a handsome man, the son of Mavis and George Stone. You remember the Stones, dear—"

"Oh! I almost forgot," Marabelle interrupted, inspired.

"What is it?"

"I'm engaged!" A loud thunk sounded on the other end of the line.

"Mother? Mother?"

Well, that went well.

Chapter 8

NICK HAD BEEN IN GRUELING MEETINGS ALL DAY WITH the owner, Marty Hackman; the general manager; and several team attorneys. They had argued over personnel and players' contracts, and at the end of the day, nothing had been settled. Before Nick could head home for a cold beer and dive headfirst into bed, Marty stopped him and gave him another earful about walking the straight line of respectability. Nick reassured him—for the umpteenth time—he was indeed still engaged.

The loss of respect and confidence Marty had displayed toward Nick began to eat at him. Even more than that, Nick started to feel angry. Instead of making smart decisions about the draft, Marty had become hyperfocused on Nick's personal life, making it his life's mission to reform him. As head coach, Nick wanted Marty's respect, not his advice on dating.

Nick admitted his track record with women was iffy at best. And Jenna's topless stunt hadn't won him any trophies. But damn, he didn't want all his hard work and grueling hours playing and coaching to be forgotten in favor of the stupid, f'ed-up choices he'd made. Or for being in the wrong place at the wrong time.

Nick wasn't proud of much in his personal life. The women who made up his world took full advantage of elegant meals, expensive gifts, first-class trips, and great sex. The arguing always came later, when he got bored and the novelty wore off. And the novelty always wore off, because he never wanted to take the relationship to the next level. For good reason.

Memories of Lola and their ugly break-up scene back in Miami after two years of dating came crashing back. All because Nick had made the huge mistake of lingering too long. Lola had wanted one thing: a star quarterback with lots of money. It didn't get any deeper than that.

Since then, Nick had always made it perfectly clear just where he stood in a relationship—halfway out the door. Marriage was great, just not for guys like him.

At the moment, his fake engagement with Marabelle was the closest thing to normal he'd experienced since his middle school crush on Anita Ridgeway. A solid, normal relationship had a peaceful ring to it. Nick wanted someone to be with him, not because of his career, celebrity status, or money, but because of *him*. Nick the person, not the football star.

He stood at the kitchen island in his empty house, eating the Cuban-style steak his housekeeper had left, picturing the other night when Marabelle had cooked a great meal and made his house feel like a home. Suddenly he had the strongest urge to see her and smell her sweet scent. He wanted to argue with her and get her all riled up; then he wanted to kiss her until they were both breathless. Nick fished his cell phone out of his pocket and punched in a number.

"I'm not kidding. These kids couldn't find their way if you left a trail of Krispy Kreme donuts."

Marabelle sipped her peach-flavored beer and listened to her best friend chatter about clueless college freshmen. Paula Carver worked at the university admissions office. She and Marabelle had met two years back at All-Nites, a granola, eco-friendly bar in downtown Raleigh, over flavored beers. Tonight they had settled into their favorite scarred booth toward the back for their usual bitch-and-moan session.

Paula's dark eyes twinkled behind her stylish horn-rim glasses as she played with her long, silky, jet-black hair gathered in a ponytail. They both giggled over funny stories and relaxed in each other's company.

"I spoke with Clay and told him to meet—" Marabelle's cell rang, and she held up a finger for Paula to hold her thought. She slid from the booth with a palm pressed against one ear and her phone against the other.

After she'd hung up, Paula said, "You look like you've seen a ghost. What's wrong?"

"I can't seem to catch a break," she said as she slumped back into the brown vinyl booth.

"What? You look as if someone killed your cat."

Marabelle's gaze scanned the bar. "Is Clay coming tonight?"

"Yeah, he's meeting us here. Why?"

"Making sure all is in place," Marabelle said, a grim note in her voice.

"What are you talking about?" Paula blinked, wide-eyed behind her glasses.

"A story you won't believe. I don't believe it, and I'm living it." She started from the beginning and brought Paula up to speed on the situation with school, the fundraiser, and Nick.

"This guy is the football coach for the Cherokees? And he used to be a famous quarterback?" Paula had finished the last of her pear-flavored beer and set her mug on the table. It came as no surprise that Paula hadn't heard of Coach Frasier. She didn't know a football from a tennis ball, and she didn't care.

Feeling flushed, Marabelle flapped the front of her black sweater to create a breeze.

"Yes, and he's on his way here tonight…to see me. Did I mention he's God's gift to women?"

"Yes, you made that quite clear. Again, why is he staging this phony engagement?" Paula flagged down the waitress with the pierced nose, tattooed arms, and green-streaked hair.

Sweat prickled her forehead, and Marabelle blotted it with a cocktail napkin. "Your guess is as good as mine. Maybe he doesn't trust me. I get the sense he's hiding something, and this fake engagement is a big deal."

"But he's pledging lots of money and helping you reach your goal. Who cares why he's doing it? Maybe he's really into you."

Marabelle fiddled with her organic beer coaster. "Not a chance. Girls throw themselves at him. All. The. Time. He's even dated Jennifer Aniston—"

"Hold that thought." Paula craned her head over Marabelle's. "Don't look now, but the best-looking guy in the whole *world* just walked in the door." Marabelle whipped her head around. "I said don't look!" Paula hissed.

Marabelle locked gazes with none other than Nick. Her breath hitched like the first time he'd set foot in her classroom. "That's him," she whispered out of the side of her mouth.

"OMG. If *you* don't want him…I do," Paula said.

Marabelle shot her friend a disapproving look. "I thought you were immune to guys like that."

"I was until I saw *him*."

Coach Studly parted the crowd like Moses parted the Red Sea. People cleared a path for him while openly gawking. His worn jeans fit him like a second skin, contrasting nicely with his burnt-orange cashmere sweater, and polished off by his signature cowboy boots. He looked like a *GQ* model in a room full of Fashion 101 rejects. Marabelle slunk lower in the booth, wishing she had put a little more effort into her own outfit.

"Tinker Bell, what a surprise," Nick teased as he approached their booth.

"I told you not to come." She glared up at him. "Ow!" Paula had kicked her under the table. She fluttered her hand in Paula's direction. "Uh…Nick, Paula Carver. Paula, Nick Frasier."

"Nice to meet you, Paula Carver." Nick brushed the back of Paula's extended hand with a kiss. Paula's face lit with a goofy grin, and she nodded at Nick's oozing charm.

"Another one bites the dust," Marabelle mumbled. "Paula, close your mouth, you're drooling." The waitress brought their flavored beers, and Nick ordered an organic unflavored one. Marabelle watched him hand over his platinum credit card to cover their bill.

"The perks get better and better," she said to a starstruck Paula.

He slid into the booth next to Marabelle, draping his arm around her shoulder, wearing a badass grin. "I think a hello kiss is in order. I *am* your fiancé."

Yeah, right. "We don't need to pretend in front of Paula. She knows the whole sordid story," Marabelle said, trying for cool when she felt anything but. Her belly quivered, and her chest grew flushed, a common occurrence whenever Nick came near.

Paula still gaped at him, and other patrons watched from where they sat. Some recognized him right away; others seemed to be speculating. In the dimly lit bar, he stood out like a beacon in the night, casting a harsh light on the Birkenstock, tie-dye wearing, granola-eating, geeky crowd.

He dipped his head closer. "Good. Then Paula won't mind if we practice." Before she had time to object, his lips captured hers. His kisses were like warm, salty French fries. She couldn't stop with just one.

Nick pulled back, leaving Marabelle dazed, but his right arm remained, tucking her into his side as if she belonged there. He started a conversation with Paula, who was so dazzled she could give only one-word answers.

Nick looked just as comfortable at All-Nites among its artsy crowd as he did on the football field. Marabelle wondered what it felt like to be that confident and comfortable in one's own skin. She'd felt out of place most of her life, always choosing the path least traveled, gaining her mother's disapproval along the way. Nick seemed to have been born with gobs of confidence and a healthy dose of ego on top.

The surrounding smells of stale beer and wheat germ permeated the air, but from Marabelle's advantageous position, Nick's fresh, spicy scent filled her head. A few curious patrons ventured forward to speak to him. In Nick fashion, he charmed as he stood to talk football, taking his unique scent with him. Marabelle had settled in to watch the show, when Paula caught her attention and pointed to the front door. Turning, Marabelle saw Clay Spencer standing in the entrance.

Clay stopped to clean his wire-rim glasses with a handkerchief. Good. He was practically blind. Maybe he hadn't seen them yet. Marabelle scooted out from the booth to cut him off at the pass, while Nick entertained his fan club with stories of the glory days.

"Hey, sorry I'm late." Clay pecked her on the cheek, shoving the handkerchief back in his coat pocket.

Marabelle grabbed Clay's arm and tried to guide him back out the front door. "No problem. You look beat. Let's take a rain check. We can do this another night."

"Nah, I'm here now. Wow, you look awesome." Clay's gaze lit on her baggy boyfriend jeans, black V-neck sweater over white tank top, and Converse tennis shoes. Once again, she'd opted for comfort. Her most feminine accessory was a pair of large silver hoop earrings.

Marabelle chuckled at his lack of style. "Time to get those glasses checked, but thank you anyhow."

His lips curved into a slow smile, and then his gaze darted past Marabelle. "Hey, is that Nick Frasier?"

She resisted smacking her forehead. "Um, where?"

"Talking to Paula. Yeah…that's him. He's heading over."

Oh goody. Marabelle latched onto Clay's arm and pulled hard. He wasn't nearly as big as Nick, but he wasn't budging either. "Clay, listen. Your office called, and they said you left your computer on—"

"I want to meet Coach Frasier." Clay peered over Marabelle's head.

"No, no, you don't. No substance beneath his perfect facade. Just your typical dumb jock," she lied.

Clay gave her a you've-lost-your-marbles look. "What's gotten into you?"

"Just remember one thing…" Marabelle paused for effect. "I'm sorry."

"Sorry for what?"

"You'll see."

―⁓―

Out of the corner of his eye, Nick watched Marabelle fast-talking with a shaggy, nerdy-looking guy near the entrance. It took him a minute before the pieces fell into place… This must be Clay, the Casanova in the sack. A scowl formed as he felt an unfamiliar clenching in his gut. He chalked it up to the organic beer he'd been drinking. It certainly had nothing to do with Marabelle talking to another guy.

Nick excused himself and made his way over. He could see the panic written on Marabelle's face grow wilder as he approached. *Sheesh.* He hated to spoil her fun, but Junior needed to be set straight.

"Hey, Tinker Bell, who's your friend?" He purposely placed his hand on the small of her back to declare ownership. Marabelle pantomimed, resembling a Persian cat ready to expel a fur ball, toward the disheveled nerd. Nick ignored her signals. "Nick Frasier." He extended his hand.

"Nice to meet you, Coach." The nerd pumped his hand. "Clay Spencer. How do you know Marabelle?"

Marabelle's expression went from twisted Persian cat to killer Doberman as she snarled. Nick held back a laugh. Messing with Marabelle had become one of his favorite pastimes.

"You haven't broken the great news, pumpkin?" he asked, plucking her away from Clay and into his embrace. "What Tinker Bell hasn't told you is that I've asked her—"

"To be his personal chef!" she exploded. Clay stared as if she was a few tools short in the toolbox.

"You're giving up teaching?" Clay asked, confused.

"No. Maybe. It's just that…" Marabelle tried to wiggle free, but Nick held her snug against his chest. He gave a short grunt as her elbow connected with his stomach, but he didn't release her.

"Poor little thing. She's still in shock. We're engaged, and she hasn't gotten used to the idea. Isn't that right, precious?" He buried his lips in her silky curls.

"No! Clay, listen. Coach Crackpot here is joking, and I'm caught in the mid—"

Clay's face went from baffled to pure happiness. "Wow! That's great! Congratulations. I never knew you two were dating. I'm so happy for you."

Nick finally released squirming Marabelle, making her stumble forward. Clay caught her before she fell.

"Happy for me? I thought you'd be upset. What about…what about us?" Her voice trailed off.

Clay glanced at Nick and must've recognized the glint in his eyes. Smart man. "We knew we were never going to be together. We tried it once, and it didn't work."

"Twice, but who's counting," she muttered. "But… but what about our friendship?"

"I'll always be your friend. That's never going to change. Okay?" Clay gave Marabelle a gentle hug.

Then Clay pinned his sharp gaze on Nick. "And from now on, we won't be seeing any more inappropriate pictures of you with other women, right?" Clay spoke with conviction, as if he could do something about it otherwise. Nick had to admire the guy's nerve. It took guts to stand up to someone who could clearly take him down without much effort.

"Absolutely," Nick said without flinching.

Marabelle started to choke. "Wh-what?"

Nick pounded her back. "You okay there, honey?" Marabelle continued to sputter. "We could all use a drink. Clay, what would you like? I'm buying." He signaled for the waitress to bring another round as they made their way back to the table. Nick was in no mood to discuss his predicament right now. He could still feel Marty Hackman's hot breath down his neck. He needed Marabelle on board and playing her part, not spilling the truth to anyone with ears. Her penchant for setting the record straight could get his ass fired.

After her fourth disgusting peach-flavored beer, Nick noticed Marabelle couldn't hold her liquor worth a damn, which explained her small hands curled around his arm and her lack of wiseass comments.

"It's getting late." He turned to Paula and Clay. "I need to get Little Miss Lush here home." He pulled Marabelle from the booth. Paula volunteered to drive Marabelle's car, and Clay would follow in his.

"I can dr…drive myself." Marabelle stumbled into him, bumping her head against his chest.

"Tink, you're sloshed. Let me get you home," he said, balancing her with his hands on her shoulders.

Eyes unfocused, she blinked up at him. "I'm all yours, Coach Hottie." Nick suppressed a huge, satisfied grin. Now he was getting somewhere.

Out in the back parking lot, he opened the door to his green Range Rover.

"Hey, this isn't your Porsche."

"No shit, Einstein." He steadied her as she climbed in.

Marabelle made it halfway and then giggled. "I'm stuck."

Her heart-shaped ass was only a foot away, tempting him to cop a feel. Nick swallowed hard as he placed a hand on her bottom and pushed.

"Oh." She settled in, wiggling her cute behind onto the hard leather seat.

Nick never envied a bucket seat more. Okay, this was going to get tricky. He reluctantly reached over to buckle her seat belt. *Shit.* His arm brushed her breasts. As he snapped the buckle in place, she slid her fingers around his neck, threading them through his hair. Hot breath brushed the side of his face, and she whispered, "You always smell great…like lemon and spice."

Then she licked him.

Damn. His cock shot from semierect to nail-pounding hard. It took every ounce of willpower not to respond to her tongue's invitation. "Not now," he ground out. "Time to get you home." He unwound her arms from around his neck, and Marabelle's head flopped back. Rounding the hood of the car, Nick took in huge gulps of air. He could do this. *Think about water ballet, or Uncle Harvey's eleven toes.*

Nick followed Paula driving Marabelle's Honda out

of the lot, glancing at his drunk passenger as her head lolled his way.

"Did I ever tell you that you have great hair?" Marabelle said.

"No. But you did call me Coach Hottie."

Marabelle's peach-flavored beers kept talking. "I wasn't always a hot mess. Growing up, I looked perfect. It was a requirement from my mother."

That explained the total opposite look she embraced now. "Who says you're a hot mess?"

She shrugged. "It's not important. I make up for it with tons of personality. If I were beautiful, it'd be too much. Don't you think?" She had twisted in her seat to face him.

At the moment, his thoughts were X-rated, starring a certain fairy. But Nick had a long-standing, self-imposed rule: he never touched drunk women, no matter how much they begged. "What I think is those disgusting peach beers must pack a wallop. You're gonna have a bitch of a hangover in the morning."

"Oh, I don't get drunk. I barely drink." She blinked her chocolate-brown eyes at him.

He gave a quiet chuckle. "That explains a lot."

Nick followed Paula into Marabelle's driveway. Paula locked the Honda and jogged up to his window. "Do you need help getting her inside?"

"Of course not. I'm perfectly fine," Marabelle said, wrestling with the seat belt that had somehow gotten tangled up with her bulky sweater.

He rolled his eyes. "I'll be okay as soon as I get Houdini here unbuckled."

Paula tossed the keys to him and hopped in Clay's

car idling behind them. Nick gave a quick wave and climbed out to rescue Tinker Bell. He leaned in from the passenger door and brushed her fumbling hands aside.

"See what happens when you wear clothes that don't fit? What if the car caught on fire? You'd be toast." He untangled her sweater and unfastened the seat belt.

"I suppose it would be safer if I were naked."

"Works for me!"

"I'll take my chances." She half snorted, half hiccupped.

"Come on, let's get you inside." He pulled a squealing Marabelle into his arms and carried her toward the house.

"Put me down. I can walk on my own."

"That's debatable." He climbed her front porch and unlocked the front door, pushing it open with his shoulder. A table lamp had been left on inside, and Nick caught his first glimpse into her private world. To his left, he spied a small but cozy living room with shabby white sofa and chairs framed by pale-green walls, and to his right, an even tinier kitchen with white cabinets and butcher block countertops. He caught a whiff of something homemade, like beef stew, and his mouth automatically watered. Warm oak floors flowed throughout except for the kitchen, where red-and-white vinyl tiles created a checkerboard pattern. Everything appeared miniature compared to his large, sprawled-out home, from the little kitchen table with four mismatched chairs to the hand-painted, half-moon table next to the front door.

"You don't happen to live with seven dwarfs, do you?"

"This coming from the Jolly Green Giant," she said with a smirk.

"Hey, Thumbelina, lead me to your cradle," he teased.

She squirmed in his arms. "You can put me down now."

Nick tightened his hold and headed down the only hallway toward Marabelle's bedroom. "Not until I see what leaf you sleep under."

"Look, Prince Charming, the wicked witch is dead, and I'm no longer under a spell. Thanks for liberating me though." Again, she tried wiggling out of his arms.

He flicked on the overhead light in her bedroom. Just as he'd suspected: a white puffy bed with pink and lavender pillows and pale-pink walls that glowed like the inside of a conch shell. Next to the window sat a chair and ottoman covered in a yellow-and-pink fuzzy fabric that reminded him of an old-timey bedspread. A pair of light-blue skimpy panties with matching bra had been tossed over the back of the chair. Tinker Bell may have bad taste in clothes, but she sure made up for it in great underwear.

He released his arms, allowing her to slide slowly down his body.

"Uh, thanks for the lift. I can take it from here." Marabelle sounded breathy but made no move to step out of his arms. Her sweet scent of lavender and vanilla surrounded him. He gazed down at her expectant face, and the low heat he'd been fighting all night fanned into roaring flames. Her lips parted with a small gasp.

"Damn, Tinker Bell," he groaned, just before rocking his mouth over hers.

As kisses went, this one was close to perfect. Just the way he liked it: long and sensual and wild. Her hot mouth tasted of peach and desire and something even sweeter and innately her. Nick pressed for more.

Marabelle moaned deep in her throat and arched against him, her fingers threading through his hair. He grabbed the ass featured in all his fantasies and lifted her up against his raging erection. She answered by pushing her hips into him, flattening her full breasts against his chest, trying to get as close as humanly possible. Fine by him. He wanted nothing more than to be skin to skin. He suddenly remembered his rule of conduct and didn't want their first time to be a drunken night of lust. Stopping this now was imperative, before he lost his last thread of control.

Hellfire. Nick broke the kiss and lifted his head, breathing unevenly as he fought for air, watching a sleepy, satisfied look spread across Marabelle's upturned face.

"We can't—we can't do this now." His voice sounded rough.

Marabelle gasped and jerked away. "Ohmygod!" Her hands flew to her red cheeks. "I'm so sorry. Please—"

"No." He grasped her hands and held them between his palms. "I meant we can't do this now, because I don't take advantage of drunk women, no matter how tempting." Her gaze flew to the obvious bulge in his pants, and her face turned from red to shocking crimson. He groaned. "Marabelle, you have no idea how difficult this is for me. But when I make love to you, I want you to remember it."

"Oh." She blinked, trying not to stare at the package she'd been humping just seconds ago.

Nick gave a ragged sigh and kissed her forehead, gathering her close until the tension slowly ebbed from his body. "Come lock the door behind me."

Chapter 9

"THE WHEELS ON THE BUS GO ROUND AND ROUND, round and round, round and round…"

Marabelle's head went round and round. She tried hiding a grimace as her students sang with the music teacher. She hadn't heaved—yet—and she swore on her nonna's grave that she would never drink peach-flavored beer again, if *only* she survived this day.

The painful hangover had nothing on her case of acute embarrassment. She barely stifled a groan as she cursed her own stupidity. Ms. Simmons, the music teacher, shot her a death glare…again. Maybe Ms. Simmons would be more sympathetic if she knew what a complete fool Marabelle had made of herself the night before, when she jumped the world's hottest bachelor and clung to him like Velcro tabs on running shoes.

She tried hard not to relive the precise moment when she'd kissed him like some sex-starved, repressed nymphomaniac. She could only imagine what he thought of her today. "Desperate and pathetic" probably topped his list.

Her cell chirped, prompting another glare from Ms. Simmons. She bent down to her desk drawer, careful not to jar her throbbing head, and fished for the phone in her handbag. Paula's name lit the screen, and Marabelle cupped her hand over her mouth to speak with her.

"Hey," she whispered.

"You all right? I was worried about you last night, but I figured you were in very capable hands. I was right…right?"

"Oh God, Paula. I'm dying here," she moaned. "Do you remember how much I had to drink?" She moved closer to the windows for more privacy.

"Four or five beers. Who cares? Did you get it on with Coach Frasier? Who, by the way, is so-o-o gorgeous. Tell me you had amazing sex last night so I can live vicariously through you."

"What kind of girl do you think I am?" Marabelle tried for outrage but sounded more like wounded bullfrog.

"A badass slut."

"I know. I am a slut. I couldn't be more embarrassed."

"So you took advantage of that prime piece of eye candy?"

"Worse. I threw myself at him. Thank goodness he put a stop to what could've been the second-most embarrassing moment in my life. The first being when my mother made me enter the Little Miss Peachtree Beauty Pageant."

"Sounds cute. What was wrong with that?"

"I was thirteen but looked four. The other contestants were at least a foot taller. The judges thought I belonged at the toddler pageant down the hall. I was humiliated, but Edna kept pushing for that crown." Paula had heard the horror stories of Edna and knew how Marabelle didn't stack up against her family.

"Okay, your childhood was a nightmare. But it's over, and it's time to stop worrying about what anyone thinks and just go for it. You've been handed a golden opportunity here…" Marabelle rubbed her pounding forehead. Paula continued, "Any normal, red-blooded female would not be waffling about grabbing that slab of beefsteak love. Do not, I repeat, do not let the sisterhood down."

Paula had been Marabelle's personal cheerleader since the day they'd met, and today she just wanted to gag her with a tennis ball.

"You don't understand. Women are like the subway to him. He misses one and another one comes along. I don't want to be one in a long line of trains."

"You're full of crap. You're scared. That guy could not keep his eyes or hands off you last night, and it's not like you were all glammed up. You have landed a hot one. *Don't* screw it up!"

"Gotta go," Marabelle whispered. "The music teacher is singing 'Down by the Banks of the Hanky Panky.' And it's sounding a little too coincidental."

By dismissal, Marabelle had finished her third Diet Coke and had popped the last of her Advil. After releasing the kids to their mothers, she looked around her quiet classroom to see only Brandon Aldridge remained behind. He shoved his grubby hand inside the guinea pig cage at Chester cowering in the corner.

"Brandon, is your nanny coming?"

"Dunno."

"It's three o'clock. Let's head to the office and call." Brandon pulled his hand from the cage and banged the door shut. Chester shuddered.

"I don't have to go to the office. I can call with my phone." He reached into his navy uniform pants pocket and pulled out the latest iPhone.

Good Lord. Could he be any more spoiled? To gain

his attention, she bent down. "That's great, but you're not allowed to have a cell—"

"Hello there."

Marabelle jerked her head up and regretted her action, because not only did her head feel like exploding, but the reason for it was framed in her doorway.

"Uncle Nick!" Brandon raced over and jumped in his arms.

"Sorry I'm late, buddy, did you have a good day?"

"Uncle Nick, Ms. Fairchild says I can't have my cell phone," Brandon whined.

Fairy-girl slowly rose, looking green around the gills. Nick almost chuckled aloud. He knew she'd be suffering from drinking that nasty peach shit last night.

"I did not say he couldn't have it. I was trying to explain he's not *allowed* to bring it to school. It's school policy."

"See!" Brandon wailed.

"His mother gave it to him before she left for Europe, so he could call her."

Brandon scrunched his nose at her, but Nick regained his attention and said, "But you have to follow the rules, bud. Your teacher is right."

Brandon rubbed his cheek with his dirty paw. "What if I want to call my mommy?"

"You can call her when you get home. Do you understand?"

"Yeah…can we get ice cream now?"

"Sure. Give me a minute while I talk to Ms. Fairchild."

Brandon scrambled out of his arms and ran from the room. "I'll be on the playground!" he yelled from the hallway.

Marabelle shuffled papers at her desk, doing a good job of avoiding looking at him.

"How do you feel?"

"Fine. I feel fine. Why shouldn't I feel fine?" she said in her frosty schoolteacher voice.

Great. Attitude. He stepped in front of her desk and leaned forward on both fists, putting a stop to the busy paper rustling. "Oh, I don't know…maybe because you had quite a few beers last night and were all over me like a cheap suit, with your tongue halfway down my throat."

Her eyes squeezed closed. "Ooh. I'm very sorry about that. I didn't mean to put you in an uncomfortable position."

"Honey, I'm not complaining."

Her eyes popped open. "Nevertheless, I was out of line, and I apologize. I don't want you to think I'm taking this fake engagement seriously. I'll never drink peach beers again. Scout's honor." She held up two fingers on her right hand. "And I'm sorry about the…uh… tongue thing."

He hadn't meant to come off like a prick. He found Marabelle refreshing. The women from his past would've been more than pissed that he put a stop to the action last night. "I'm teasing. It wasn't all one-sided; I was a willing participant."

Mesmerized, she leaned toward him with her lips parted in invitation, and Nick didn't need to be asked twice. He met her halfway, lips mere inches apart when Brandon came bursting through the door. Marabelle jumped back, eyes wide.

"Uncle Nick, can we go now? I want some ice cream."

He hesitated, studying her flushed face before he

straightened, wishing they were alone in his house, preferably in his bed. "Sure, buddy. Ms. Fairchild, would you
care to join us at the Dairy Queen for a dipped cone?"

"Uh...ohmygosh, what time is it?" She glanced at the
plastic blue Swatch watch around her wrist. "We have a
tennis match this afternoon. I need to get to the courts.
Thank you anyway." She began to gather papers and
shove them in her knapsack.

"What time does the match start?"

"Um...warm-up is at three thirty... Where are my
keys?" She rooted through her top pencil drawer. Nick
reached across her desk and tugged on the lanyard
around her neck, jingling her keys. His fingers brushed
her plump breast and lingered a second too long, deliv-
ering a magnetic jolt up his arm and down to his dick.
She must've felt it, too, because her breath caught.

He gave his best slow, sexy smile.

"Th...thanks. I'm not myself today." Her voice was
low and husky.

"Come on, Uncle Nick. Let's go!" Brandon tugged
on Nick's other hand.

"Good luck with your match. I'll call you later," he
said as Brandon pulled him from the classroom.

"Uh-huh. Sure. Thanks."

———

Nick didn't show for the tennis match—not that he'd
promised—and Marabelle tamped down her disappointment. So why did he ask about it? And why did he keep
popping up and almost kissing her and then not kissing
her, but smiling like he knew what she looked like in
the buff? Marabelle was so rattled and hungover she

couldn't remember the tennis lineup. After a shaky start, Beau and Ty surprised her by showing up to watch her guys win. At the end of the match, they congratulated all the boys and did the signing routine for both teams.

After everyone had left the courts, Beau and Ty remained behind and escorted Marabelle to her car. Beau draped his arm around her shoulders and said in a casual voice, "Mary-bell, you own anything that, you know…fits?"

"Why?" Her eyes narrowed.

"Ty and I want to take you out to celebrate your win. We want you to look real pretty."

"You guys want to spend Friday night with me? Don't you have hot dates?"

"Yeah, that would be you." Ty laughed.

"You're kidding, right?"

"Come on, Mary-bell…make our day and wear something sexy," Beau wheedled.

She opened her car door and smirked. "Sure, I'll go, but I can't guarantee the sexy thing."

Beau grinned. "Pick you up at eight."

Marabelle stared at her image in the full-length mirror in her final and fourth outfit. The box from her mother had arrived, with an assortment of St. John knit suits and cocktail dresses that would've been perfect if she were seventy-five and going to a funeral. But for a casual night playing pool with some really hot football players…not so much. Marabelle did own attractive clothes that fit, but they remained relegated to the far corners of her closet, rarely seeing the light of day. Anything resembling an ensemble made her think of her mother and how much she didn't want to be her.

Not tonight. Beau and Ty had been great to her team today and very generous in supporting her cause. She wanted to look nice for them. Heck, she may never get this opportunity again: dating not one, but *two* smokin' hot guys. Okay, dating might be a stretch, but her company tonight would be a huge improvement over exchanging recipes with her elderly neighbors. She critiqued her low-rise blue jeans embroidered with blue flowers, and smoothed her turquoise-and-brown long-sleeve knit shirt that buttoned up the front. Both hugged her petite frame. Yeah, so they fit. Her lips curved into a small smile. She slid a thick brown belt with chunky silver buckle through the loops and slipped her feet in a pair of Michael Kors brown leather wedges to add an extra three inches. She finished with a silver heart neck-lace and hoop earrings, then grabbed her small Fendi bag—a gift from her dad—and scurried to answer the knock at her door.

"Hey. You wanna come in?" she asked, a little out of breath.

Beau Quinton stood on her threshold and stared with his mouth agape. He took an exaggerated step back to check the house number.

"Q? You okay?" He looked more than okay in worn jeans, tight blue polo shirt, and dangerous five-o'clock stubble.

"Am I at the right house? I'm looking for Mary-bell Fairchild, she's about yea-high"—he held his hand up to indicate her five feet—"and she's a real *bad* dresser."

She performed a quick twirl. "What do you think?"

"I'm thinking you look good enough to eat." Beau's gaze lit with heat.

"Funny. I was thinking the same thing about you."

He gave her a lascivious grin. "You could get in a whole lot of trouble looking like you do, funny girl."

"We'll never know unless you take me out. Ready to go?"

"Hell, yeah!"

―⁓―

Corbett's Sports Bar, located between Raleigh and Chapel Hill, smelled of stale cigarettes, stale beer, and smoked fish products. And from the way Marabelle's wedges stuck to the beat-up wood floor, she assumed half of what she smelled had probably ended up on the bottom of her fashionable shoes. But this was where the cool people went to grab a beer. Not that she came close to being in the same league as the football groupies and sex trophies, advertising their wares as subtly as used car salesmen at a Labor Day sale. But it did her battered ego good to notice the envious looks when she walked in with the hottest quarterback in the South. Beau and Ty made a great production of introducing her around and lavishing her with outrageous compliments. Marabelle enjoyed her fifteen minutes of fame. If she had walked in wearing nothing but Saran Wrap, she still would've been no competition for the women who circled the bar like carnivores ready to pounce on fresh meat. They gave new meaning to Jimmy Buffet's song "Fins."

Beau, being the biggest draw of the evening, asked Marabelle if she would stash some of the phone numbers written on cocktail napkins, business cards, and *thongs* in her handbag. His pockets were already stuffed. She agreed only if Beau would get some players to sign up for her auction, as she shoved a scrap of red lace the size of a rubber band in her handbag.

Big Bad Barry Rocker, a tackle for the Cherokees, said he'd be honored to participate in the auction. Marabelle gulped as she mentally measured the width of his neck against her waist. His neck came out thicker, and his ham-sized hand engulfed hers. As scary as he looked, he had a great attitude and would be a huge asset to the auction.

Yes! The auction was looking good. As long as she kept her eyes on the real goal and not on a certain some-one's broad shoulders, steel-blue eyes, and tight butt. Beau introduced her to four other potential candidates, and she pocketed three more lacy concoctions that wouldn't fill a thimble. Lordy, she needed to rethink her own underwear.

Later, Marabelle sat drinking a soda, watching as three tenacious groupies attached themselves like suc-tion cups to Beau and Ty. Ty squirmed uncomfortably when a beauty with sprayed-on jeans sat in his lap and nibbled his ear. Beau, the quintessential stud, held court with a platinum blond named Starr and a Latin beauty named Selena. Both simultaneously rubbed against him, trying to engage him in a game of tonsil-hockey. *Eeewww!*

Beau managed to push his broad shoulders between the two ladies and asked, "Mary-bell, how 'bout a little pool?"

"Sure. But I have to warn you, I hate to lose."

"Q, honey, I don't want to play pool," Starr pouted.

And Marabelle didn't want to sit across from these obvious groupies like a third wheel. She feared her inferiority complex would reach an all-time low.

Beau patted her thigh. "I know, baby. That's why I'm playing Mary-bell."

Starr gave Marabelle a less-than-friendly once-over. "Q, who is *she* anyway?"

"Is she your girlfriend?" Selena asked. "You keep talking to her." Selena had whining down to an art.

"No, no. Mary-bell and I are just friends. She's Coach Frasier's girlfriend." Marabelle tried kicking Beau under the table, but her short legs wouldn't reach. She shot Beau her fiercest glare. The less said about her and Coach Frasier the better.

Starr and Selena looked at each other in shock. "You mean the one everyone's been tweeting about? But what about Ginger?" they both chorused.

Good Lord, she was probably a Twitter hashtag… wait, what? "Who's Ginger?" Neither sex-bunny paid Marabelle any mind.

"Ginger's meeting us tonight. Nick will be here too." Starr directed her remarks at Beau.

Huh? Marabelle straightened in her chair on high alert, sloshing soda over the side of her glass. She gave the bar a quick once-over to see if Nick had miraculously appeared.

Beau extricated himself from the clinging groupies and grabbed her hand. "Forget it. Come on, Mary-bell, let's see what you've got."

Ty peeled off the bunny plastered to him. "Wait up… think I'll join ya."

Nick stopped by his office to pick up some papers and return a few calls, after taking Brandon to Dairy Queen and then to the park to throw the football. Instead of sitting still the way he'd asked, Brandon ran up and down the halls, yelling at the top of his lungs. Nick couldn't believe how out of control his nephew had become. Damn, Marabelle must have an abundance of patience and energy to deal with eighteen five-year-olds every day.

Nick raked his fingers through his hair, remembering the searing kiss they'd shared the night before. He hadn't been able to think of much else all day. As kisses went, it was damn near perfect. It had started out slow and worked its way up to steaming. Which explained why he'd almost lost all control and made love to a sensual, inebriated Marabelle. He'd wanted nothing more than to throw her on her white puffy bed and bury himself inside her. Something about her sent his normally ironclad control right out the window. Without trying, she had captivated his interest. Nick enjoyed her quirky sense of humor and, God help him, even her quirky sense of style.

But he needed to be careful. Nick didn't want to hurt Marabelle, and this fake engagement could do just that. Keeping his reputation aboveboard, and not landing on the front of BuzzFeed or TMZ.com in any more compromising positions was paramount to his career right now. Too much was at stake. His team and staff were all depending on him, and he didn't plan to let them down.

Chantal poked her head in the door. "Coach, you had a couple of calls earlier. Ty said he and Beau would be at

Corbett's tonight in case you wanted to join them. And Ginger called and said the same thing. Your cell phone must be off."

He reached into his pocket and pulled out his cell phone. He noticed several missed calls and texts and nodded at Chantal. "Yep, it was off. Thanks, and have a nice weekend." Brandon stood on his head on the leather sofa in Nick's office, banging the backs of his legs against his office wall, rattling the plaques and framed pictures. Nick sighed. "Come on, Brandon, let's get you home."

Fans and players accosted Nick as soon as he pushed through the door at Corbett's. He threaded his way to the bar, pumping hands, adjusting to the fog of cigarette smoke visible through the dim lighting. Toby Keith's "Beer for My Horses" played in the background, and he could smell Corbett's famous smoked fish in the kitchen.

Nick reached the large, marine-lacquered bar, where the bartender handed him a cold one on the house. He held court as he drank his beer and fielded questions about the upcoming football season and draft. Not his favorite pastime, but he realized most guys dreamed of coaching football. He made vague statements like "the GM saw the draft as not 'fixing' any weaknesses, but building long-term strength for the team," and he agreed with that philosophy. He nodded at a few other well-intended coaching suggestions, when he looked up and spied Ginger Jones heading his way.

"Ordinarily, I'd love to talk sports all night," he drawled, "but right now I'm in the mood for some feminine companionship. You boys understand, don't ya?"

He winked. The men surrounding him laughed as they cleared a path.

Coach Prichard had introduced Ginger Jones to him back when he'd recently moved to the area and had needed a Realtor. She'd been very thorough in locating the right kind of house in the right community that offered him the privacy he desired. They dated with a mutual understanding of the score. Nothing permanent or exclusive. Once in a while, he would need a date for some stuffy function, and Ginger fit the bill nicely. It had worked, but Nick hadn't been with her in over three months, due to his busy schedule, but mostly because he didn't have any interest in becoming her latest acquisition. Yeah, and those damning pictures with Jenna Williams had sobered him up real fast.

Ginger, along with Marty Hackman and a few others, had some issues with the whole "he said, she said" story. Even though Jenna made a public apology—after some very convincing coaxing by Nick's attorneys—the seed of doubt had been planted.

Yet, as Ginger snaked her way toward him, he figured what harm could there be in having a few beers and catching up on old times? It beat talking about his team with a bunch of guys who liked playing Monday morning quarterback.

"I didn't think you'd come. Wasn't sure you received my messages." Nick checked Ginger out with detached interest. She wore a black knit dress with a wide black patent leather belt cinching her small waist. The scoop neck revealed the tops of her breasts, and the red stilettos enhanced her long legs. Nick caught the look of steely determination in the tension bracketing her lips. He compared Ginger's overall polished look to Marabelle's disheveled one in his mind. And surprisingly, Marabelle came out on top.

He brushed her cheek with a kiss. "Sorry. I was baby-sitting my nephew. Didn't get the message until late."

"I'm glad you could make it." Ginger sounded casual, but a flicker of displeasure lurked in her gaze.

Purposely avoiding eye contact, he asked, "Can I buy you another drink?"

"Mmm, in a moment." She placed her half-empty glass of vodka tonic on a nearby table. "Looks like your fans are going nuts on social media again"—he guided Ginger with his hand on her elbow to the back room with the pool tables—"something about you having a girlfriend." He stopped, afraid of where this was going. "Some old schoolteacher, real short with curly hair."

"It's a long story." Nick was not in the mood to explain his fake engagement to Ginger or anyone else. The less the word "fake" was mentioned, the better.

"Interesting. How well do you actually know this girl? Because according to Starr, she's been plastered to Beau's side all night." Ginger gestured vaguely with her hand.

Nick's brows slammed together.

"*What?*" As if on cue, he heard Beau's hoot of laughter. Nick's head jerked up in time to see his star quarterback in the poolroom, leaning over a cute, heart-shaped ass in tight jeans. Both stretched across a pool table as Beau helped direct the next shot with the cue stick. The shot must've been executed correctly, because Beau yelled "Oh yeah!" and the tight jeans next to him squealed.

His nostrils flared as Nick stood rooted to the floor, watching the exchange unfold. He would know that heart-shaped ass anywhere. It had been embedded in his brain ever since the first day he'd met Marabelle Fairchild. *What the hell?* What was Marabelle doing with his famous quarterback…*again?*

Cool fingers touched his arm. "Nick, what's wrong? You look like you're having a heat stroke." Nick barely heard Ginger over the loud roaring in his ears. Marabelle and Beau were hugging and giving each other high fives. And then it hit him like the first sack of the season.

Marabelle was wearing stylish clothes that fit. Clothes that clung to every one of her succulent curves. Tight jeans, and a knit top molded to her generous breasts, exposing a sliver of curvy belly, just enough to tease and tantalize.

He shoved his empty beer bottle at a passing waitress. "Everything's fine as soon as I wipe up the floor with Beau Quinton."

—⁓—

Ginger Jones looked from Nick to Beau and then to the girl squeezing Beau around the waist. She refrained from rolling her eyes, because this had to be someone's idea of a really poor joke.

Her gaze zeroed in on long, curly hair and a petite but curvaceous figure. She'd calmed herself by thinking men found that sort of look attractive, but she had nothing to worry about. Until she spied Nick's furious expression. The reaction of a jealous lover. And that would never do. Oh no. Not at all. Ginger didn't care what people spouted on Twitter. She had intimate knowledge of the real Nick Frasier, and this whole thing smelled of a poorly orchestrated publicity stunt.

"Uh, Nicky, why don't you and I slip out of here? Go back to my place and have a drink." Ginger smoothed her hand on his hard chest, trying to redirect his attention her way...where it belonged. Not on the little ball of fluff jumping up and down with Beau.

His fury tensed beneath her hand like a spring ready to uncoil. For a nanosecond, she felt only relief, glad his anger wasn't directed at her, but just as quickly she felt insulted. He had never acted jealous over her when she'd dated someone else. *Men!* He needed reminding that Ginger was standing before him, willing and waiting.

Using her killer body to block his path as he stepped forward, she forced him to grab her by the arms to prevent plowing her over. She seized the opportunity to mold herself to his front.

"Nicky, baby, don't make trouble. They're not worth it," she whispered in his ear. "She's made her choice. Let's get out of here, and I promise to put a smile on your face," she murmured, kissing his neck.

Marabelle looked up from her celebration, and not ten feet away, she spotted a tall guy embracing some leggy strawberry-blond. At first glance, he appeared to be another good-looking jock snagging a sex bunny. But then her gaze traveled from his ostrich-skin cowboy boots and long, jean-clad legs to the signature blond-streaked hair. And her gaze locked with Nick's steely blue, furious eyes.

For a moment, time stood suspended. Everything in the bar faded away. Then the bubble burst when Beau slipped an arm around her, and all hell broke loose.

"Hey!" Marabelle shouted, shoving fists on her hips. The statuesque lingerie model nuzzling Nick's neck stopped and peered at her with one eyebrow elegantly arched. Marabelle brushed off Beau's arm and stomped forward in righteous rage.

"Excuse me, but what do you think you're doing?"

Lingerie model pressed even closer to Nick in an attempt to shield herself from Marabelle.

"Are you talking to me?" she asked in a choked voice.

"Uh, yeah. And I'd appreciate it if you would unwrap your long-legged bony self from my fiancé!"

"Excuse me?"

"You heard me. Unhand my man!"

A crowd started to gather near the pool tables to check out the commotion. Some unevolved bar bum started to chant "Cat fight! Cat fight!" and others joined in.

Bony model spoke to Nick through tight lips. "Why is she ranting at me? Nick, *do* something."

Nick removed her talons from his shirt and pushed her gently to the side, never taking his gaze off Marabelle. He fought either a grimace or a smile; she couldn't tell which and didn't care. Marabelle crossed her arms over her chest, refusing to be intimidated by the chanting, rowdy crowd.

"Tinker Bell—"

Nick broke off what he was about to say when Beau placed his hands on Marabelle's shoulders from behind.

"Mary-bell, you okay?" Beau asked, squeezing the tops of her shoulders.

Nick's hand whipped out, quick as a snake, and yanked Marabelle in front of him. Startled, she yelped.

"She's fine," Nick snarled.

Nick and Beau stared each other down like two outlaws facing off for a high-noon shoot-out.

"With all due respect, Coach, I'd like to hear it from Mary-bell," Beau dared, his laughing brown eyes appearing flat and cold.

The bar crowd picked up on the new tension, closing in to witness the showdown between the coach and the quarterback. Marabelle could hear wagers being tossed around in the background. Nick secured her firmly to his side.

Marabelle barely breathed as she felt the tautness vibrating off his body, but managed to squeak, "Beau, I'm fine, but thanks for asking."

"Q, take Ginger to her car, and be sure she gets home okay. I'll take care of Marabelle." The steel behind Nick's low voice did not go unnoticed, and alarm bells went off. Marabelle shot a quick glance toward Ginger, the apparent girlfriend.

Beau didn't budge. "Coach, Mary-bell came out with me tonight, and I should be the one to see her home safely."

The crowd grew even larger at the potential throw down between Nick and Beau. Marabelle didn't want to be the reason for either man putting their career in jeopardy. "Guys, um—"

Nick cut her off, his fury barely repressed. "Q, I'm not asking you. I'm telling you. Marabelle is with me." What he left unsaid spoke volumes.

Complete silence descended over the crowd. Nick's order hung in the air like a case of dynamite ready to explode at any second. Ty and Rocker stepped up, flanking Beau on either side.

"Like I said, Marabelle is my guest and my responsibility, *Coach*." Ty clamped his hand on Beau's shoulder to keep Beau from saying or doing something he might later regret. Marabelle had never seen this fierce side of Beau. She'd grown up on the tennis court, the sport of ladies and gentlemen, not the gridiron, where men played for blood…literally.

"Quinton, this is not up for discussion." Nick's tone was clipped and clear.

Ty pushed on Beau's shoulder to keep him in place. "Coach, in all fairness, we'd like to hear from Marabelle. We invited her tonight, and we need to make sure she's okay with this," Ty stated firmly.

"Yeah. She's our friend, too," Rocker added.

Marabelle gulped. How did one small, poorly dressed schoolteacher get four huge, good-looking guys all defending her at once? Not in her wildest dreams had she ever imagined this scenario. She slipped out from under Nick's grip, only because he finally loosened his hold, and took a hesitant step.

"Beau…Ty…please, it's all right. Coach here—"

Nick spoke in her ear, soft but deadly, "*Do not* undermine my authority, or you'll live to regret it."

She gave a jerky nod and took a deep breath.

"Listen, guys, the coach and I have a mutual understanding… He protects me…from myself, and I protect him from pesky, obnoxious women." Marabelle shot Ginger the universal back-off look.

Smiling at all three players, she continued, "It's mighty sweet of y'all to stick up for me."

"Everyone satisfied?" Nick demanded.

Ty and Rocker took their time before nodding.

Beau did an immediate about-face and grinned like a sly fox. "Mary-bell, anytime you need me, you holler, ya hear?"

"That won't be necessary. She'll have me." Nick's words were more threatening than reassuring.

Beau shrugged off Ty's hand and actually laughed.

———

Ginger Jones stood stunned, witnessing the entire confrontation with pure disbelief topped with a little fear and a ton of jealousy. She shook off the first two feelings, but the jealousy got the best of her. Ridiculous. *I will not be ignored.* She hadn't clawed her way to the top to be toppled over as if she didn't matter. No one was going to stand in her way when it came to the man she wanted. Especially some loudmouth, nobody schoolteacher.

She brushed past Beau and confronted Nick. "What is going on here?" Her future had flashed before her eyes, and she refused to accept it. She wasn't about to lose the hottest bachelor in town without putting up a fight.

Nick rubbed his hand over his jaw. "Listen, Ginger, please allow Beau to see you home. I'll call you later and explain."

Ginger pinned him with a suspicious glare, but since she had no intention of lowering herself to a public scene, she nodded and leaned in to give Nick a kiss on the lips.

"I don't freakin' believe this!" Marabelle bellowed. "I thought I told you to back off."

Ginger flinched. This tacky schoolteacher resembled

a ferocious bull out to gore her to death, but before Marabelle could paw the ground and charge, Ginger's breath caught in surprise.

Marabelle was instantly off her feet. Thank God. Nick had grabbed her by the waist and hauled her back before she could inflict any harm.

"Put me down! I can take her. I'm stronger than I look." She tried swinging her arms, but Nick held her upside down against his hip as easily as a football.

Fingers of alarm skittered up her spine as Ginger stared horrified. She couldn't believe that…that obnoxious girl wanted to fight her in a bar. Keeping the lunatic in her sights, Ginger backed away.

"Time to leave. We've put on quite a show for one evening," Nick said, looking none too happy at all the cell phone cameras flashing in his face. He marched toward the entrance, head ducked. Some guys applauded his caveman tactics, hooting their encouragement. Loudmouth Marabelle didn't go quietly.

"You can't carry me around like a football." Nick ignored her cries. "Wait! I need my handbag. It's *Fendi!*" Nick slowed just enough for Ty to toss the bag over. He caught it with his other hand, never breaking stride, and exited the bar with Marabelle secured against his side.

Ginger's eyes narrowed to slits as she clutched Beau's arm. This evening had not turned out as planned, and she had that stupid, *stupid* girl to thank for it.

———

Marabelle flopped along Nick's side as he jostled her out the door. He made tracks and got as far from the entrance and prying eyes and cameras as possible. He couldn't believe the shit that had just gone down. Dammit. Being engaged to a local schoolteacher was not supposed to be this volatile or damaging. This was supposed to be a touchdown, slam dunk, spiked ball in the end zone.

He stopped halfway through the parking lot and dumped Marabelle on her feet, and she came up swinging.

"You can't…just…pick me…up and…carry…" she said, swatting at him with girly hits. Nick seized both her hands in his.

"Stop. Before I turn you over my knee and spank your ass," he said in a rough voice.

"You wouldn't dare!" She glared at him, the blood returning to her head, and her cheeks filling with color.

"You have no idea." He turned and towed her behind him, giving her no choice but to skip along to keep up with his long stride. Of course, Marabelle being Marabelle, she wouldn't leave well enough alone and go quietly.

"I was only doing my job. I could've taken her. She's all legs and long hair. She's not built to fight like I am." Nick stopped moving, because he'd reached the passenger side of his Range Rover, but he also stopped swearing under his breath, because just listening to her idiotic logic made him want to laugh. Too busy trying to wiggle free, Marabelle didn't notice the smile tipping one side of his mouth. But then knowing that pictures of his near-run-in with Beau were being posted to Facebook, Twitter, Instagram, and every other social media outlet, all humor fled the vicinity.

"You off your meds again? Who do you think you

are? Muhammad Ali?" She stopped struggling and lifted her head, brows furrowed. Nick shook his head. "Have you looked at yourself lately?" Her earnest expression didn't surprise him. Nothing about Marabelle surprised him anymore. He rolled his eyes heavenward. "You should be sitting on your tuffet with pink bows in your hair. You're *not* a badass; you're a pain in the ass."

Marabelle's shoulders slumped. The fight leaked out of her like a bike tire going flat. "I resent that," she mumbled.

Now he felt crappy about robbing her of her feistiness. Nick could read the dejection in her face as plain as he could read a second-string defense. He got the distinct feeling that she dealt with rejection a lot, and he didn't like it. Marabelle truly believed she could fight like a guy and win. "Mind telling me what the hell you were doing in there?" Marabelle's head snapped up, and big brown eyes flashed with anger. *Atta girl.*

"Exactly what you told me to do. Beating off that bimbo clinging to you like kudzu. The point of this fake engagement, remember?" Her eyes blazed as she spoke. "Correct me if I'm wrong, but I understood our agreement to mean I keep all women from coming on to you, and you allow me to have my live auction with the eligible players out there." She made a derisive noise. "That skinny lingerie model was all over you like honey on a hot biscuit."

Marabelle's outburst did all kinds of fascinating things to her heaving chest, momentarily distracting him. But even though he enjoyed more than a glimpse of the goods peeking over her blue lacy bra, it led him right back to his original source of anger. He knew damn straight that Beau and every other guy had been ogling the goods, too. His tightly controlled emotions snapped like a dry twig, which put him right back where he'd started.

Pissed off.

"I'm talking about you and Beau. What the hell were you doing with him when you're supposed to be engaged to me? Don't tell me you're not attracted to him, because I noticed you changed the way you dress. Just for him!" His eyes flicked to her navel and the smooth skin exposed between the hem of her shirt and the waistband of her low-riding, awesomely tight jeans.

"Of all the asinine…are you kidding me? You've been driving me crazy about the way I dress. Now you're all in a snit because I look nice for a change?" Her hands talked as much as her mouth, exposing even more of her cute belly. Everything she did messed with his head.

Nick wanted to spank her. Kiss her. Strangle her. Then kiss her until neither one of them could think of anything else. He needed to get his head back in the game and start calling some offensive plays.

"I'm pissed because I came out tonight to have a few beers, and I see my fiancée and my quarterback practically doing it on the pool table," he snarled down at her.

"I…you…you take that back!" Marabelle hauled back and hit him right in the gut with her fist. Nick gave a slight grunt.

"Ooowww! Jeez. What do you eat for breakfast, nails?" She shook her hand as if it stung. "That hurt," she whimpered.

"When are you going to learn?" He cradled her small

hand in his, inspecting it. "I'd kiss it to make it all better, but I'm still too angry at you."

As some rowdy partiers spilled out of Corbett's on their way to their next stop, Nick yanked open the car door and pushed her into the passenger seat, tossing her handbag inside. He quickly got behind the wheel and took off before he became the subject of more social media fodder.

―⁓―

Stony silence filled the car. Marabelle massaged her hand and wondered how in hell her life had gone from mundane to insane in only a week. She still hadn't forgiven Coach Neanderthal for carrying her out like a sack of potatoes in front of the whole world.

Clearly this engagement was not working out. But it was match point, and she couldn't afford to double fault. She needed him way more than he needed her. The success of the auction depended on his total cooperation and participation. And her promotion was hanging in the balance.

And speaking of balance, Marabelle always felt off-kilter after a phone conversation with her mother. She'd felt defeated and depressed listening to Edna's litany of horrible activities and all the things wrong with Marabelle's life.

But tonight with Beau and Ty, she'd felt…um, kinda cool and necessary. Like they really appreciated her. And not because she was some voluptuous hot mama, but because she was feisty and sassy. Maybe it made her pathetic, but she really reveled in all the attention. Especially the intense, laser-like attention from Nick…

as if she mattered. Finally Marabelle focused on the road and realized they were driving in the wrong direction.

"Where are we going?" Signs for North Raleigh flashed by on the boulevard. She lived south.

"My place," he said.

She straightened. "I don't want to go to your place. Take me home." She tried to sound calm, but she was freaked-out.

"Sorry. You and I are going to have it out. And then I'm going to give you the beating you deserve," he explained very succinctly, not once glancing in her direction.

Gulp. "You're not serious…about the beating part." She gnawed on her thumbnail. She caught Nick watching her out of the corner of his eye. As looks go, it wasn't good.

"Dead serious. I'd love nothing more than to wrap my hands around your neck right this minute."

She removed her chewed-up thumb from her mouth. "There's nothing between Beau and me." His eyes got that scary, narrowed look, and she hurried with an explanation. "Beau and Ty watched us win our match today, and they wanted to take me out for a celebration. End of story. Besides, you said you were going to call and never did," she accused.

"Un-freakin'-believable. Don't blame your behavior tonight on me."

"Uh-huh. Who was locking lips with Ginger?" She poked him in the right arm with her index finger. "You owe me an explanation. Word on the street is you guys are dating. Now how do I fit in, Coach? Because I have to tell ya, still not interested in a threesome."

"I bet if Q was the third person, you would be," he

grumbled low. Marabelle noticed his white knuckles as he strangled the steering wheel, thankful it wasn't her neck…yet.

"There's nothing between Beau and me. Can you say the same about you and Ginger?"

"We dated. Past tense. It's over. Ginger is not the issue."

"Try telling her that." She slumped back in her seat.

Beau Quinton did not tingle her insides, nor did he make her want to climb in his back pocket and stay there. Only Nick did that. But it would be a cold day in hell before she ever gave him that juicy bit of information.

Chapter 10

MARABELLE STIFFENED WHEN NICK PULLED HIS Range Rover into the middle of three garage bays and turned off the ignition. Even though she'd crashed his house uninvited before, she'd never pictured herself returning, and definitely not under these circumstances. His shiny Porsche sat parked on one side of the Range Rover, a gray BMW 750 on the other. A blind man could see he had expensive taste in cars, homes, watches, and women. *Especially* women.

She reluctantly moved from the garage through the mudroom as if heading to the guillotine. Once inside Nick's amazing kitchen, the tension tying her in knots seeped from her shoulders. Gleaming stainless steel appliances, honed soapstone countertops, and old wood plank floors would do that to a girl. Marabelle suffered a serious bout of kitchen envy, and her frustrated chef's heart fluttered. Nick hadn't spoken since they'd entered the house, but every nerve in her body knew he wanted to blast her...again.

She tried heading him off. "I gotta hand it to you, you have an awesome kitchen." The aroma of fresh rosemary teased her nose from the herbs in the clay pot decorating his island.

"You wanna see the rest of the house?"

What? She had expected him to say a lot of things, from "Don't interfere in my life again" to "Let's get naked." Not offer a home tour.

"Sure."

He gestured with his big hand. "This is the kitchen."

"The appliances are a dead giveaway. Do you cook?" She fingered the rosemary, infusing the air with more of its pungent scent.

"No, but my housekeeper does."

Nick led her through the kitchen into the big dining room, where an antique rug in faded greens and oranges covered the wood floor. The room felt masculine without being obvious. She could easily picture Nick at the head of the old trestle table, in the host's chair. She touched the draperies in burnt orange, framing the French doors.

"Do you collect antiques?" A collection of antique beer mugs with horn handles was displayed on the large walnut buffet.

Nick shook his head. "Not particularly. My interior designer put most of it together for me. My only request was for it to be comfortable and classic. Let's keep going."

He guided her through the various rooms on the first floor. She'd already spent time in his large media/pool room the day she had barged in and surprised him, but she hadn't seen the library, guest bedroom, and comfortable sunroom, which overlooked his wooded lot.

Nor his home office. Marabelle felt as if she'd stepped into the lion's den, where his antique partner's desk sat on a rug in browns and blues. Four TV monitors covered the wall in front of his desk, surrounded by bookshelves stuffed with books, tapes, pictures, and tons of trophies. Marabelle inched toward the credenza behind his desk to admire photographs of Nick playing pro ball. Gently she fingered some of his trophies, stopping in front of a massive, diamond-studded Super Bowl ring displayed under a glass cube. Marabelle sucked in a breath. Greatness oozed from every nook and cranny.

"Any of these awards yours?" she asked to break the awkward silence.

"A few."

"You some kind of football fanatic?" she teased, lightly brushing a silver MVP trophy. Coach Frasier had played his entire NFL career with the Miami Stingrays before retiring three years earlier. Marabelle had Googled his career and read some of his stats. His list of accomplishments was impressive even to a novice like her. He had racked up a few unbroken records in passing touchdowns, been named to the NFL All-Pro team several years in a row, and was named most valuable player in the NFL twice. And, of course, he'd won a Super Bowl.

Nick shrugged his broad shoulders. "It's just a hobby."

"Very impressive." Marabelle nodded in awe.

Returning to the front of the house, she looked up at his two-story foyer with exposed wood beams. A wrought iron fixture that looked as if it had come straight from King Arthur's castle caught her eye.

"Great house. Your interior designer did a beautiful job. I hear a good designer gets to know the client real well in order to personalize the space." She couldn't stop her fishing expedition.

"That's one way of putting it. We lived together for years." Nick straightened the corner of a gold-framed painting with the tip of his finger.

Duh! Of course they did. His designer was probably Ginger. Ugh. Disappointment weighed heavy in her stomach.

She pasted on a fake smile. "Well, there you have it. What better way to get to know someone." Studs like Nick didn't think twice about stashing a different woman in every room. And Nick was far more studly than most.

"Yep, she knew me better than most, since she's…" Nick advanced on her and turned her to face him. She rapidly blinked as he slid his hand along her arm and cupped her face in his palm.

Whatever you do, don't say Ginger!

"…my sister. Natalie's a designer. She decorated my house." His low, velvet voice had a calming effect. "Stop worrying. I don't have a harem of women coming and going, no matter what you've heard."

Marabelle stepped away from his warm touch. "I wasn't worrying," she lied. "You could be living in the Playboy mansion. Doesn't matter to me." Her attempt at sounding cool and unaffected failed miserably.

His eyes softened, and Marabelle sensed desire, but something more. Affection maybe.

"Your face says differently. Oh yeah, it matters." They still stood at the bottom of the stairwell next to an antique mirror hanging over an English chest.

"Whoa!" Suddenly Nick had gripped her around the waist and plopped her atop the old chest. She gasped as he slipped between her legs, enveloping her in his heat. This position allowed her to see the clear blue of his eyes flecked with bits of gray.

"Uh, Nick…what're you doing?"

"Just putting you where I can get at you."

And right on cue, Marabelle's insides melted into gooey marshmallow fluff.

Finally. For the first time all evening, Nick felt in control. He'd had enough of being led around by the balls. Time to take this thing—whatever it was—to the next level, because little Tinker Bell had no clue. Without dwelling on the ramifications of getting involved with a sweet girl with irrational hang-ups and a high school equivalent in experience with relationships, he went for it.

She nibbled her lower lip, and Nick noted her brown eyes showed excitement shadowed by fear. Relieved to know this attraction wasn't one-sided.

"Remember last night?" he rumbled low next to her ear. "You being wasted and jumping my bones?" She stiffened beneath his palms resting on her hips.

"Ugh. I've purged it from my memory permanently."

"Well, darlin', I can't seem to forget it. If I hadn't put a stop to it, we'd still be going at it like a couple of minks." A pink flush infused her chest and cheeks. Nick had no compunction about playing dirty or running a quarterback sneak play on an unsuspecting rookie. And in this case, Marabelle was the rookie. Everything seemed to click into place.

He proceeded in a matter-of-fact-tone. "I've been thinking. Ever since the day you blurted out that you sucked at sex"—her face went from pink to red, but he ignored her discomfort—"which I assure you is not true, I've decided to help you out." His fingers moved underneath her shirt, spanning her lower back, brushing against her silky skin. He lowered his voice. "It's time you had mind-blowing sex"

"*What?*" She gripped his forearms, and Nick waited for her to push him away. When she didn't, he almost smiled. Damn, this was going to be fun.

"Bottom line. You can't dress sexy and accept dates with my players when you're supposed to be *engaged* to me."

"But no one believes we're engaged."

"You're missing the point." He frowned. "It's only natural we have sex with each other."

"Nothing about this is natural." Her eyes narrowed. "What's in it for you?"

Sex! Nick cleared his throat. "You gain all the experience your heart desires with me. I get to have great sex, and everyone will believe we're engaged. It's a win-win situation."

"I think you're embellishing the great sex part." She looked at him like he had too much yardage between the goalposts.

He continued in a low, soothing voice. "You scratch my back, and I scratch yours." Matching action to words, he lightly scratched her back and then nuzzled her sweet-smelling neck.

She gasped. "If we do this—"

"Oh, we're gonna do it," he whispered around her delicate ear.

Marabelle pushed back. "It's not that simple."

He watched her. "Sure it is. No point in letting a perfectly good engagement go to waste."

She crossed her arms over her chest, and the effort didn't go unappreciated, since it showcased her killer cleavage.

"*If* I do it…it's only going to be once. For the experience and all."

"You keep telling yourself that." He chuckled, unlocking her arms. Unable to resist temptation any longer, he slid his hands up to cup her breasts, loving the way they filled his palms, round and full. Nick gave a devilish grin. "We're gonna take this real slow. Pay attention. There's gonna be a quiz later."

"Quiz?" she croaked.

"Oh yeah." He wrapped her arms around his waist. Then he started in on her tiny buttons. "You're driving me crazy with that sexy blue bra," he rasped.

"Don't you want to go somewhere…dark?" she asked, pressing her hands into his back.

No way in hell.

"Relax and enjoy." He smoothed back the cotton fabric. His thumbs brushed her nipples over the blue lacy bra, and they puckered in tight, hard buds. Marabelle's eyes closed, and Nick unhooked the front of her bra, pushing it aside in one motion. He lost his breath as the chandelier's dim light cast a glow on her full breasts. Marabelle dug her fingers into his back.

"Perfection," he said, impatiently dipping his head. He drew her nipple into his mouth, raking it with his tongue, and sucked long and hard. A throaty moan purled from her throat and almost sent him over the edge. Nick wanted to be buried deep and hard inside her before he exploded.

Marabelle squirmed, hooking her legs around his hips, pushing closer. Nick trailed kisses up the column of her neck and caught her lips as she gasped, plunging his tongue inside. A wave of warmth unfurled deep within his gut. He deepened the kiss, intensifying the hot haze of lust.

Marabelle shuddered, rubbing against his straining erection, practically starting a damn bonfire with the friction from their jeans. She ground against the barrier as if the denim irritated her as much as it irritated him. After several scorching minutes, Nick knew it was time to stop, as much as it killed him. Moving too fast would not help his cause.

He nibbled at her lips and said, "You have to pay the piper."

"Mmm?" She nibbled right back.

"For your behavior." He nipped her swollen bottom lip, and she whimpered. "You have a choice…to be spanked"—his hands cupped her bottom, and her eyes fluttered—"or you can make me something to eat." Her head lurched back, shock fully registering.

"What?"

"Pick your poison."

"You mean we're…we're done kissing?" she squeaked.

A rush of emotions blasted him like a torrential downpour of pleasure and tenderness at the disappointment in her voice. At that precise moment, he knew only one thing: this crazy new relationship would be more enjoyable than he'd ever imagined.

He murmured against her forehead, "Just taking it slow. It's called foreplay. So, what's it gonna be?"

Marabelle snuggled up to his chest, and Nick liked it…a lot. With a satisfied smile, she said, "What are my choices again?"

Nick licked her ear, making her giggle. "Either I get to spank your sexy bottom for being a smart-ass, or you can cook for me."

"Hmmm…that's a tough one. Twist my rubber arm, I'll cook. Anything to get back in that kitchen again."

Nick laughed reluctantly, backing away from her tempting curves. Fascinated, he watched as she rehooked her bra, inwardly mourning the covering of those plump, perfect breasts. With shaky hands, she tried buttoning her shirt. Brushing her clumsy fingers aside, he finished the job and then helped her down from the chest...his new favorite spot in the house.

"You shouldn't reveal your secrets, Tinker Bell. Now I can use my kitchen as bait."

Heading in the direction of the kitchen, she tossed over her shoulder, "I don't care. Don't ever ask me to choose between *you* or your kitchen. You may not like the answer."

Nick threw his head back and laughed again.

—⁓—

Beau obeyed Coach's orders and escorted Ginger Jones home, grinning to himself as he replayed the tense scene earlier at Corbett's. Beau's great instincts made him a terrific quarterback, and his instincts about Coach Frasier were right on the money.

Coach had it bad for little Mary-bell. *Damn.* He hadn't seen Coach that mad at him since he'd thrown four interceptions against the Steelers last season.

Anyone with half a brain recognized the difference between Mary-bell and other women who pursued football players. She was a breath of fresh air, with the added spunk of a puppy. Beau would hate to see Coach lose Mary-bell on a bad throw of nearsightedness. He figured a well-intended intervention never hurt anyone, and congratulated himself for plotting a near-flawless play: he'd persuaded Mary-bell to dress up and asked

Ty to give Coach a heads-up about meeting at the bar. Everything else just fell into place.

Until Ginger showed up.

She almost blocked the winning field goal. But Beau knew how to drop back in the pocket and see what opened up, studying the field to see which receiver became free.

He pulled his Cadillac Escalade in the driveway right behind Ginger's Lexus sedan. Her two-story Georgian brick house was nestled between two much-older homes in one of the newer communities inside Pine Boulevard, the older, more established part of Raleigh. Beau noticed three For Sale signs in the area with her name as the listing agent. Ginger had certainly made a reputation for herself in this high-end neighborhood.

"This wasn't necessary," she said, unfurling her sexy, long legs from her sedan.

"Always a pleasure." Beau followed her up the front steps with his hand pressed to the small of her back.

"I couldn't help notice the tension between you and Nick… It was a little thick. What's going on with that Marabelle?" She dug for her house keys. Time to set pretty Miss Ginger straight.

"Aw, Mary-bell's great. They met last week through some charity benefit they're working on. Coach is crazy about her. Never seen him get all-in-your-face possessive before." Beau shoved his fingers in his back pockets. "Not that I blame him. Mary-bell is one of a kind."

Ginger unlocked her door with shaky hands. "You're saying, after one week, he's serious about that *girl*?" she all but screeched.

He leaned his shoulder against the doorframe. "It's

the most distracted I've seen Coach about a woman in a long time."

"But…but he's supposed to be with me! We've been dating for months."

Now Beau knew Ginger's type like he knew his own stats. Pretty, successful, and in this case, a shark in the real estate community. But none of that satisfied her. She still wanted the status of snagging a high-profile, rich man. Who better to fill that requirement than Coach? Beau also knew Coach had never acted jealous around Ginger the way he had around Marabelle.

Weighing his options, he decided to lay it on thick. "Honey, why are you waiting around for Coach? He's a busy man. He doesn't have the time to devote to a real woman like you. Don't misunderstand…he's a great guy, but the only thing he's married to is his job. You're a beautiful woman. You can be with any man you desire." He pushed away from the door and moved inside, uninvited.

Ginger Jones knew opportunity when it came a-knockin', and she didn't hide her intent as she sized him up with a sweeping gaze from his head down to his Prada suede loafers, making a pit stop on the goods along the way. She didn't disguise the desire that flared behind her eyes either. Flicking her long mane back with one hand, she formed a perfect, pouty expression with her mouth.

"Mmm, you could be right. Why don't we discuss the possibilities further?" she crooned.

Beau shut the door behind him. Sometimes you just had to take one for the team.

—⁓—

"Your mother wishes you lived in Atlanta?" Nick leaned back against the cabinets and observed Marabelle whip up something she called a frittata—which appeared to be a savory egg dish with cheese—from the fresh ingredients in his refrigerator.

She poured the whisked eggs over the sautéed vegetables. "My mother wishes I was married, having babies, and playing bridge at the country club. Preferably in that order, and definitely in Atlanta where she can keep tabs on me."

"So, you ran away from home?"

"Not exactly. I mostly grew up in boarding schools. My mom couldn't handle me." Nick's expression clouded. "She loves me, but I was a handful growing up, unlike Phoebe, my older sister."

"And your dad?"

She focused on stirring the eggs. "Dad wasn't around much. My parents have a mutual understanding: if they live apart, they get along fine." She covered the pan with a lid. "Almost done…just needs a little time to bake."

She bent to put the frittata in the oven below the stainless range, and Nick couldn't stop from admiring her perfect bottom. Once she turned, he got busy, opening a bottle of chilled white wine and the subject of her family again.

"Do you visit your family much?"

Marabelle hesitated as if weighing her next words. "Um, my dad travels with his job. He's not around much."

Nick poured the wine into goblets and waited.

"My mom…well, she finds clever ways to lure me home. My family is…er, they're very shallow and hung up on appearances. Wearing the right shoes, attending the right parties, and marrying the right man are very high up on their lists."

This explained a lot. Marabelle embraced a completely opposite lifestyle from her parents. The Fairchilds didn't sound much different from the groupies hanging around professional athletes, hoping to gain money, notoriety, and maybe a reality TV show.

"I'm gathering your parents aren't too happy with your choices."

Marabelle shrugged, not meeting Nick's gaze. "I guess. My mom, anyway. She's a bit of a control freak."

Nick heard the bitterness in her voice. He handed Marabelle two dinner plates from his cabinets.

"Being a schoolteacher is great…for someone else. My mother would rather I work at something more prestigious. Really, she'd rather I become arm candy to some sugar daddy."

A prickle of alarm ran up Nick's spine. He'd been down this road before. But he shook it off. Not everyone was after his celebrity status and money. And Marabelle had to be the least likely candidate of all. Nick had never met anyone less affected by his position, except in terms of helping with her auction. For that, she had no qualms in using him.

"So you're not into the sugar daddy thing, huh?"

Marabelle pulled the frittata out of the hot oven with two oven mitts and placed it on the stone countertop. "Give me a break. I have no interest in dressing up every day, getting Botox, and buying shoes at Neiman's. Nor do I want to sit around sipping cocktails and figuring out ways to exploit the latest social cause for the thrill of reading my name in the papers the next day. What a boring life." Marabelle sliced the steamy frittata and put the portions on the plates.

"And you know this…" Nick dragged out the last word.

"I've lived around it my whole life. I'm sure the committee at Trinity Academy has sensed my disgust, which is probably why they're more hostile than usual." She waved her hand to prevent him from speaking. "I know. I'm being ridiculous. Not everyone who raises money for charity has selfish motives. But my mother does."

Nick placed both plates on the kitchen farm table. "If you feel this way, why are you working like a dog on this auction? Why don't you tell them to shove it?"

"Because I can't. Because I believe in this cause. I really do want better tennis courts and playing fields for the kids, and I want to grow this program and give these kids the incentive to go for it. And a promotion will go a long way in helping me support myself."

Nick raised his eyebrow and held a chair out for Marabelle. "What about working for the public school system?"

Marabelle nodded her thanks and dropped into the chair. "They don't pay as well. I want to be where I can teach K through sixth and coach varsity tennis. Public schools don't pay their coaches squat, if at all. Most of them volunteer and don't really have much impact on the tennis program."

What the hell kind of expenses did she have? He'd seen her tiny car and rental house. "How much is your rent? Why don't you get a roommate?" he asked, picking up his wineglass.

Marabelle gave him a scathing look. "It's called a mortgage. I have mortgage payments and yeah, it's probably equivalent to your monthly toilet paper bill, but it's enough for me. And I'm in between roommates at the moment, but Paula's moving in with me as soon as her lease is up in a few months. I'm also still paying off school loans."

Nick's parents had gotten lucky with his education because he'd been given a full ride at the University of Florida. But it sounded as if Marabelle's parents could afford her education. Maybe they'd given their daughters a lump sum of money and called it a day.

"Your parents didn't pay for your college?"

"I know this sounds like a poor-little-rich-girl story, but the truth is my mother was more than willing to pay for everything as long as I attended the school of her choice. But I wanted to play college tennis and was recruited by Clemson. My mother was furious and basically cut me off."

Her mother sounded like a real jewel. "What about your dad?"

A sad smile played around her lips. "I wouldn't let him pay. She would've given him holy hell if he had." Marabelle scooted her chair forward, meeting Nick's gaze. "Have you ever wanted to live life on your own terms? Without someone else calling the shots?"

Yeah. Nick thought of Marty Hackman. Even though Nick had enough money to last a lifetime and Marty couldn't bankrupt him, he did have the power to destroy Nick's professional reputation. And at the end of the day, reputation was all that mattered. "Sure," he said slowly.

"For as long as I could remember, I wanted my independence, and once I got to college, I finally felt free. No longer living to please my mother, because she no longer held the purse strings." Marabelle shrugged. "I've been living on my own ever since."

Nick's heart seized as if gripped by iron forceps. He hated knowing she'd been cut off like that.

"Of course, when my dad would send money, I took it. I wasn't a complete idiot." Marabelle smiled, and her eyes lit with mischief.

"Good for you. Did you receive a tennis scholarship?"

"Sure, but it wasn't enough. We all know the bulk of that money goes to the football players, not the ladies' tennis team." Marabelle shot him a pointed look.

Nick stared right back over the rim of his glass. "You don't expect me to apologize, do you? It's a known fact that college football generates millions in revenue. From broadcasting rights, ticket sales, and merchandising, not to mention bowl games."

"I get it. My point being, other sports don't have great scholarship programs, if at all."

"They don't bring in the fans either." Nick forked some steaming frittata into his mouth.

"Sad, but true." Marabelle watched and waited for when the flavor of egg mixed with cheese, peppers, and fresh herbs exploded in his mouth.

"Whoa. Delicious. If this teaching thing doesn't work out, I'll pay you to cook for me." He winked at her pleased face.

"I might hold you to that," she said, closing her lips around her fork.

They both ate in silence, enjoying the food and each other's company. And didn't that sound strange? They barely knew each other, but something felt right with Marabelle in his kitchen. His home.

Marabelle leaned back in her chair. "What about your family? Any other siblings besides your sister?"

"No. My parents still live in Jacksonville. My sister, Natalie, is off in Europe trying to find herself," he said between bites. "She went through a bitter divorce about a year ago. And Brandon is the one suffering." He grimaced, picking up his wineglass.

With eyes cast down, she said, "Even though our parents never divorced, Phoebe and I felt the hardship just the same. Why did Natalie divorce?" she asked softly.

"Not sure. Dan, her ex, is a great guy. At least I thought he was. Natalie can be high-strung and dramatic. And Dan travels a lot for work."

She nodded. "That can wear on a marriage."

"Yeah, with the exception of my parents, I haven't witnessed too many normal marriages."

"Is that why you've never married? Uh, sorry. None of my business." Marabelle dropped her hands in her lap, strangling her napkin.

He chuckled. "Perfectly okay. We *are* engaged."

"Only in public. I really do respect your right to privacy," she said.

"No worries. I'll let you know if you're invading… my privacy." He'd finished his frittata and reached his fork across to snag a bite from her plate. "I've seen a lot of marriages tank in a hurry. For professional athletes, relationships get based on income, physical attributes…you know…star power." The food suddenly tasted bad in his mouth as he pictured Lola and how she had lied and tried to get him to the altar. And the extremes Jenna went to. All for what? Not for love, that was for damn sure.

"Yeah, life's a bitch," Marabelle muttered, gulping her wine.

Nick raised a brow. "I'm not complaining. I've had a great life. More work than fun sometimes, but it paid well." He pushed his empty plate away. "All I'm saying is if a relationship starts out superficial, then the marriage is heading straight for the toilet." He scowled, leaning back in his chair. "Take my sister. She married for love and it wasn't enough. They divorce and look who suffers—Brandon. I'm not ready to make the same mistake."

—∿∿—

Marabelle watched Nick's features cloud over as he talked about *not* getting married. She'd be smart to remember this was all a game.

Nick fiddled with the stem of his glass. "As head coach with the Cherokees, I'm juggling eighteen balls, and two of them are mine, so my hands are pretty tied up. I wouldn't make a good husband for anyone."

No need to spell it out. Heard you loud and clear.

She humphed. "Clearly, you have commitment issues." She picked up the empty plates and headed for the sink.

Nick followed. "Huh? How is not wanting to be a bad husband a commitment issue?"

"That line of reasoning is so old. It's code for 'afraid of commitment.' Don't get too close." She gave the plates a vicious scrub with a kitchen brush, when Nick snatched them from her hands, shoved them in the dishwasher, and slammed the door closed.

"Are you shittin' me? This coming from 'I'm not

getting married just to piss my mother off.' You're the one with the commitment issues."

"Me?" She dried her hands on a dishtowel and threw it on the counter.

"Yeah. You can't even accept a fake engagement."

"Key word there...*fake*." Marabelle pushed his chest with both hands, but he didn't budge. His blue-gray eyes flickered from irritation to amusement.

Nick snatched up the dishtowel and swatted her on the bottom. "Know what your problem is?"

"Don't you dare do that again," she half shrieked, half laughed, backing up and scanning the countertops for something to hit over his hard head.

Nick tossed the towel over his shoulder. "Don't even think about it," he said, reading her mind. "My palm's still itching to spank your ass, and don't think I won't do it."

"Not if you can't catch me."

Nick's face lit up. Uh-oh. Note to self: never challenge a professional athlete.

"No-o-o!" She squealed and attempted to run in her wedge shoes. Marabelle darted into the dining room and through the foyer, away from Nick's diabolical laughter. She raced up the stairs to parts unknown, since the second floor had not been on the home tour. Without hesitation, she dashed through the first door on her left.

Enough moonlight filtered through the windows to indicate a sitting room. She hurried through a pair of double doors to her right, searching for a place to hide, when she stopped cold. Looming at her from under the window was a king-size bed, glowing like the star attraction.

Yowza! She'd managed to land in the master bed-room. The double doors closed behind her with a definite click.

Marabelle whipped around. Nick pushed away from the doors and stalked her like a tiger eyeing his prey. "Uh…Nick, can't we talk about this?"

"Talking is way overrated." He began to unbutton his shirt.

The backs of her knees hit something solid, and she felt the give of the mocking bed behind her. "What are you doing?" she croaked, with her hands outstretched to ward him off.

"Undressing." He pulled his shirt off, balled it up, and threw in the corner.

Marabelle gulped. She licked her suddenly dry lips. The soft moonlight bathed Nick's chest, giving it the appearance of sculpted marble. A study in contoured muscles all the way down to his ripped abs. For a fleeting moment, she agreed with the folks who plastered his rock-hard body all across the Internet. Something this magnificent should not be hidden. Ever.

Nick walked right into her outstretched hands and gathered her in his arms. Her fingers delighted in brushing through the dusting of hair on his chest before she rested them on his strong shoulders. "This is probably not a good idea," she said with a sigh.

"It's the best idea I've had all month." He cupped one breast through the cotton of her shirt. "Which part of you am I going to taste first?" His words whispered across her cheek like silk, making her shiver. "Let's start here."

His mouth dipped to meet hers. His firm lips teased,

demanded, and seduced. Marabelle moaned and locked her hands around his neck.

"You have way too many clothes on." His fingers brushed against her breasts, and he started to unbutton her shirt for the second time that night, when his cell buzzed, vibrating against her middle. Marabelle froze as if hit with a blast of icy water, and Nick's head jerked up. "Shit. Ignore it." He sought the sensitive spot just below her ear with his lips while peeling off her shirt. The jarring sound of the phone pierced the lust-filled air in the room three more times before it stopped.

Marabelle tensed, not able to relax. "Uh…don't you think—"

"Sh-h-h." Nick captured her mouth and unfastened the front of her bra with a flick of his capable hand. Then his cell buzzed again, killing the mood as she pushed back.

"Jesus. Who the hell is calling at midnight?" he growled, digging his phone out of his pocket.

Marabelle covered her chest with her arms.

"Shit." Nick put the phone to his ear. "Hello? Yeah, what's up, buddy? You okay?" His free hand rested heavily on her shoulder as he rubbed her neck with his thumb, sending all kinds of celebratory messages to her unused female parts. "Slow down, Brandon. What's the problem?"

Alarm bells went off, and Marabelle scrambled to get her bra back on.

"Okay…calm down, buddy…everything's gonna be all right… Yes, I'll come over. I'll be there in about thirty minutes. Okay…okay. Let me speak to Paola. Yeah, yeah. I'm coming."

Nick talked with the nanny in Spanglish as he grabbed a sweater from a tall French chest of drawers. Marabelle stifled a cry of frustration as he disconnected and covered his glorious chest. When he disappeared into his huge walk-in closet, Marabelle told herself she was relieved. She'd dodged a potentially embarrassing bullet. But her body was in mourning. Nick emerged with a Cherokees parka in his hand and tossed it to her.

"It's gotten chilly out."

"Everything okay? What's wrong with Brandon?" she asked, slipping her arms through his oversized jacket.

Cupping her elbow, he led her from the bedroom. "He's fine. Just scared. Apparently, he's been trying to reach his mom all day, and she hasn't answered. Says he can't sleep because he's worried."

"Anything I can do?" she asked, hurrying down the staircase.

"Yeah. Restrain me from killing Natalie when I finally get my hands on her," he answered grimly.

Chapter 11

EARLY THE NEXT MORNING, MARABELLE STOOD WAITING for her coffee to brew. Her head felt as fuzzy as the pink slippers on her feet. While the coffeemaker spat and sputtered, she gazed out the window, blinking at the morning light streaming through the pine trees. She spied Lilah Dawkins, her neighbor, sweeping her walk in a bright-blue muumuu with a yellow cardigan thrown on top. Marabelle poured coffee in her favorite mug—decorated with yellow tennis balls—and savored several sips, allowing the coffee to work its magic. She threw on Nick's Cherokees parka over the large Durham Bulls T-shirt she'd worn to bed and stepped out on the side stoop to wave hello to Lilah.

"Looks like you're hitting it early, Miz Dawkins," she said with a smile. "Coffee? Freshly brewed!" She raised her mug.

"Oh, honey, I've already had my coffee, but I thank you." Lilah leaned against her broom. Marabelle picked up some blue glints in her hair from the morning light.

"Why so early?"

"Fresh, homemade apple pies at the farmers' market, and I want to make sure I get there early to get me some."

"Mmm, sounds delicious."

"They are, but you've got to be quick. Last time, Mable Garner beat me to it and bought every last one. I just about died. Can I pick you up one? I bet those fine boys stopping by your house would love a little apple pie."

"Boys?" she asked, sipping her coffee.

"I saw two right good-looking ones last Sunday. And just last night, you left with one foxy fella and came back with another one *even* better."

Marabelle choked, sputtering on her last sip. *Lordy!* She'd had no idea her neighbor had been spying on her.

"Uh, Miz Dawkins, I can explain. Those guys are friends, and I'm—"

"No need to explain, honey child," Lilah interrupted. "Truth be known, I was tellin' Betty Koonce two doors up it's not right for you to live like a nun when you're so young. These should be the best times of your life. Go for it!"

Great. "Gee, thanks, Miz Dawkins…I think."

Lilah waved her hand. "Don't mention it. I'll bring you one of those pies. Nothing like a home-baked pie to lure a good man." Lilah Dawkins strode back in her house to prepare for a busy day of bargain hunting.

Marabelle remained on her side stoop, wondering how many of her other neighbors watched her house like a soap opera. Even her older neighbors had more exciting lives than she did.

With the exception of a few nights out with Paula, her social life sucked. Until last night. Last night had been fun and exciting, not to mention eye-opening. But Marabelle knew it was temporary. She reprimanded herself for falling for Nick's sexy aura and almost sleeping with him. Sex with Nick would be absolutely, totally over-the-top wonderful. Which was all the more reason she couldn't go through with it. Her life would be changed forever, and he'd forget her and move on before the postcoital bliss had worn off. Not that Marabelle would know anything about postcoital bliss, but she could imagine. She had goals to reach and a control-freak mother to prove wrong.

And with that thought, Marabelle felt a surge of panic at the added pressure of coming up with a story about why her fiancé would not be attending her mother's benefit in Atlanta next weekend. Because no way on God's green earth would she be dragging Nick through the quagmire that made up her family.

Marabelle had no clue if her mother had recovered from the whopper she'd told her. She'd been avoiding her calls for days. But she did know one thing.

Edna would not rest until Marabelle produced a fiancé.

On her way to the store, Marabelle's cell rang, and the reason for her lack of sleep and the three Krispy Kreme donuts weighing heavily in her stomach poured through the line.

Nick.

Her heart skipped a beat. "How's Brandon?" she asked, trying to sound casual.

"He settled down when I got there. Sorry about the interruption. Certainly wasn't how I pictured the end to our date."

"Date? You didn't ask me on a date."

"Touché. But since I had you half-naked a couple of times, I consider it a date."

Heat flamed Marabelle's cheeks. "I'm not usually so easy, but I couldn't stand all that whining. You're worse than my kindergartners."

Marabelle turned her car toward the grocery store.

"Funny, I don't remember any whining. Lots of moaning…but no whining." Had she really moaned? "Wish I could make it up to you tonight, but I'm heading to Charlotte right now," he said.

She pulled into the grocery store's parking lot. "What's in Charlotte?"

"My ex-brother-in-law. I need to talk some sense into him."

"Talk or knock? I vote for knocking."

"Spoken like a true fighter. I'm gonna do whatever it takes to get some answers."

Marabelle's heart squeezed at his effort to help his nephew. "That would be great. Remember, Brandon's lucky he has you."

"Will you have dinner with me tomorrow night?"

And then her heart sputtered. She parked in front of the store and killed the engine. "Sunday night? Um…I can't. Beau and some of the guys are coming for dinner after their tennis lesson."

"*What?* Dammit, Marabelle. I don't want you entertaining Q and the guys. They can amuse themselves some other way."

"I've already promised. Besides, I love entertaining."

"I just bet you do." His voice dripped with sarcasm.

"What's that supposed to mean?" Marabelle drummed her fingers on the steering wheel. Any soft feelings she'd harbored quickly dissipated.

"We went over this last night. I don't want you involved with Beau Quinton or any other player."

She scoffed. "Get real. They're no more interested in me than you are. And stop bullying Beau. He's welcome in my home anytime."

"Don't be naive. Beau Quinton has more moves than Allied Van Lines, and you're crazy if you think he's not putting them on you."

"That's ridiculous. I know when someone is putting the moves on me. And for the record, that person has been you!" She grabbed her handbag and slammed the car door.

"*Marabelle*," Nick growled. "I'm warning you. If he touches one hair on your head, I will rip him apart with my bare hands."

Marching toward the store, she used her I'm-talking-to-a-crazy-person voice. "He won't. He's not interested in me in that way. Now drive carefully and stop worrying about Q. Oh, and come by. There'll be plenty of food."

"Damn straight. I'll be there."

Marabelle stood in aisle five next to the salad dressings and oils, checking her list of ingredients. She had decided on a large pot of her famous spicy chili, a fresh salad, and some yummy baked goods for Sunday night's dinner. She wanted her boys to be fat and happy. With their support, she would raise enough money for the school and for her promotion. So, one chili dinner for a few guys was the least she could do.

She grabbed a bottle of olive oil and whirled her cart down the next aisle, when her cell rang. She groaned, recognizing her sister's number. Okay, time to face the music.

"Hey, Phoebe. What's up?"

"You tell me. You haven't called or emailed.

Mother's driving me crazy. Who is this guy you're engaged to?" she railed.

"I'm doing great. Thanks for asking." She shifted the phone to her other ear.

"Marabelle, spill it."

"It's complicated."

"How complicated?" Phoebe's voice sounded tense.

"Very." She tossed six cans of red beans in her basket and then maneuvered her cart to the pasta and rice aisle.

"Start over. What is his name?" Phoebe said in her calm voice.

"Nick."

"Mother said he worked at Coach. Is he a salesperson? Does he manage one of the stores?"

Marabelle choked back a laugh, trying to picture Nick working in a store selling designer Coach leather.

"No. He *is* a coach. A football coach. We met through an auction I'm in charge of," she hedged, tossing a large bag of rice on top of the cans of beans.

"He coaches football for a living?"

"Yeah."

"Oh, Marabelle." Phoebe let out a groan that bordered on frustration. "You'd be better off dating a salesperson at Coach. At least there's potential to move up the corporate ladder. Mother is going to freak out. You know how she is about sports. And he can't possibly make enough money on a coaching salary. Does he have any other talents?"

Sure, he was an amazing kisser, and he might've played a little professional football. And probably has more money than Facebook's Mark Zuckerberg, which would certainly satisfy Edna's criteria. Once

Phoebe laid eyes on Nick, she'd start purring like a cat in heat.

"Let's not make a big deal about this. With my luck it probably won't last." Better to plant the seed now. She pushed her cart toward the produce section.

"Are you kidding? Mother is already making lists on top of lists." Phoebe's point came through loud and clear. *Crikey.* Marabelle had backed herself into a corner.

She loaded up on fresh vegetables. "Phoebe, tell Mother to stop making lists. Nick and I are taking things slow. Like, so slow you might even say we're moving in reverse." She popped a green grape in her mouth.

"You and Nick better be here next weekend so you can explain this reverse thing to Mother." Marabelle remained silent, chewing, but she heard the warning in Phoebe's voice. "Marabelle, you *are* bringing Nick next weekend, aren't you?"

She swallowed and started making static noises into the phone. "Uh…you're breaking up…can't hear you."

"*Marabelle.*"

"Gotta go, there's a special on aisle ten…stuffed jalapeno peppers." She quickly disconnected and dropped the phone back in her handbag.

Nick nodded his thanks to the waitress as she handed him his second drink. In the dark booth at the Regency Hotel bar, he studied his brother-in-law. Dan Aldridge wore the signs of a man on the edge: disheveled hair, dark circles under his eyes, and an ink stain on his shirt breast pocket. Not the look of a successful money manager. However, Nick didn't drive two hours south to feel sorry for his brother-in-law or hold anything back.

He told him in no uncertain terms that he needed to make things right with his family, because his son was suffering from neglect.

Dan's hands shook as he nursed his ginger ale. He opened up and spilled his guts about the breakup. Too much traveling, too many business meetings, and too much time spent with his female assistant.

Christ. What female assistant? First time he was hearing anything about another woman. *Idiot.* He tamped down his fury, then he asked, "Does this woman still work for you?"

Dan nodded. "Yes. She's a valued employee."

Nick barely tasted the aged scotch he'd ordered as he mentally knocked his brother-in-law upside the head. "I'm gonna take a wild stab here, but your assistant…is she…oh, I don't know…hot?" Dan averted his gaze. Nick wanted to give him a swift kick to the balls. "Good-looking enough to make other women jealous?" he pressed.

"Uh, I guess she's attractive."

Great. She could probably model for Victoria's Secret. "Did you have an affair?" *You're a dead man.*

Dan straightened in his seat and looked him directly in the eye. "No. Never! I would never do something like that." The physical hurt etched around Dan's strained mouth and tired eyes led Nick to believe he must be telling the truth.

Nick leaned forward. "Dan, I've known Natalie all my life, and I'll be the first to admit she's a drama queen, but I'd think if she was *this* insecure about your female assistant, then you should've done everything in your power to not make her feel that way."

"What are you saying?"

"You should've gotten rid of your assistant...*not your marriage*." Nick pushed his fingers through his hair. "I guess what's done is done. But both you and Natalie are not taking care of the one person who is truly innocent, and that's your son."

Dan crumbled like a saltine cracker. "Natalie was awarded custody, and she didn't want me living in Raleigh," he tried to explain.

"This is your son we're talking about. And right now, Natalie is off in Europe somewhere, and you're here or on the road. Where does that leave Brandon?"

Dan rubbed his forehead as if easing a pounding headache. "I don't know what to do. I miss him like crazy. But I can't work *and* take care of him."

His misery hung like a soggy blanket over their heads, and Nick almost felt sorry for him. *Almost.* He needed to grow a pair and take charge of his life. "I know you and Nat are hurting. I'm gonna do you a favor and tell you what to do."

Nick held up his fingers, ticking off his points. "First, you come to Raleigh and spend time with your son." Dan nodded. "Second, get rid of your assistant and hire a man."

Dan's face fell. "But, she's loyal and—"

"You want loyal? Get a dog," Nick said, irritated. "The way I see it, you have royally screwed up! Give the lady a great recommendation or promote her, but get her out of your office."

Dan straightened in his seat, alert. "You're right. I'll do whatever it takes to get my family back."

"Good. Because the third thing is the hardest."
Nick paused. "You have to go to Europe and bring
Natalie home."

———∼∼∼———

Nick returned to Raleigh Sunday afternoon and drove
straight to his office to catch up on some paperwork.
After an hour, he pushed the papers aside and leaned
back in his chair, closing his tired eyes. How could two
people who loved each other as much as Natalie and
Dan get so messed up?

Marriage was like being a part of a team: everyone
had to work together to win. Each player had a vital role.
No matter how great the team's quarterback, if he didn't
have good coverage or good receivers, he'd never win
a ball game.

Nick's own dysfunctional relationships jumped to the
forefront. When Nick was the star quarterback for the
Miami Stingrays, Lola had fantasized about becoming
Mrs. Nick Frasier and didn't appreciate her dreams being
flushed down the toilet when he broke it off. One fake
pregnancy, accusations of a "miscarriage" due to mental
stress, threats of lawsuits…the whole ugly enchilada hit
the press and social media. When Nick's attorneys nailed
Lola for both libel and slander, she switched tactics and
found another way to hurt him. In the second-string quarterback's arms, to be exact. Her dream finally came true.
Once Nick retired and her lover became the starting quarterback, she dragged him to the altar. After one year of
marital bliss, she dragged him to divorce court. Classic.
The whole debacle had left Nick cold. He'd vowed to
dodge that poisoned arrow as long as he could.

But when he pictured Marabelle, the shooting pain behind his eyes magically disappeared, which scared him even more. Why was it different with her? She barreled through life as if she had something to prove. And maybe she did. And maybe he admired that trait. A lot.

He smiled, thinking how Tinker Bell almost started a bar fight. Luckily, his Twitter account didn't shut down, and most of the tweets referred to Beau and the starting lineup for next season. Even more luckily, Marty Hackman didn't blow a gasket. But Marabelle's dinner party for a bunch of oversexed football players was a different matter. His smile became a grimace, and the pounding behind his eyes returned. No way was she entertaining those guys without a proper chaperone. Him.

Chapter 12

MARABELLE STOOD PLASTERED AGAINST HER KITCHEN cabinets. Three huge guys she'd never seen before helped themselves to more chili. Besides Beau, Ty, and Rocker, she counted at least four more guys in the house alone, and that didn't include the ones in her backyard. Not to mention the groupies. What had she expected with a house full of football players? Music blared from several Bluetooth speakers as this cozy get together mushroomed into what resembled an unchaperoned high school party.

Not one to lose sight of an opportunity, Marabelle talked two more players into participating in the auction.

Ricky DiMarco gave a great Jack Sparrow pirate impression, with his dark hair and eyes. He only needed a black patch and hook, and he'd be a dead ringer. He cornered Marabelle in the hallway and surprised her by asking if he could take tennis lessons, because there was this young debutante he wanted to impress.

"Ricky, if you really want to snare a Raleigh debutante, you'd better cut your hair and ix-nay the two-carat-diamond stud earring."

"Aw, man. You don't understand. My job is to strike fear in the defense on the field, and this look scares a lot of people."

Marabelle patted his arm. "Including young debutantes." He'd certainly be her go-to guy if she ever found herself in a street fight.

At the eruption of a loud squeal, they turned toward the front room, where Rocker twirled Lilah Dawkins above his head.

Marabelle pushed Ricky. "Go. *Go!* Instill fear and get her down from there."

Lilah and Betty Koonce had crashed the party to whoop it up with the professional football players. Both laughed and kicked up their orthopedic heels as Rocker took turns bench-pressing them.

Marabelle fed, cleaned, advised, and rejected three different spicy propositions before she grabbed a metal spatula and pushed her way through the front room, searching for Beau so she could beat him senseless.

"Great chili, Marabelle."

"Love those cookies."

"Hon, do you have any dollar bills?" Lilah asked.

"Huh?"

"Singles, so we can tip the guys who are gonna strip for us."

"Strippers!"

"Like the Chippendales, 'cept better," Betty said, barely able to contain her excitement.

Marabelle squeezed her eyes closed and groaned. "Ladies, *please* do not entice these men to remove their clothes. Lord knows, they don't need any further encouragement." Lilah's crinkled face held a look of pity. Marabelle switched tactics. "What will our neighbors think?"

"Who cares? They're HOT!" Both women left for the backyard with a spring in their steps.

"Beau Quinton is a dead man," Marabelle muttered under her breath. "With my luck, I'll get arrested for hosting an orgy."

Above the music, she heard banging from the front door. "Whatever happened to a calm game of Pictionary or Scrabble?" she cried, yanking the door open.

Nick stood on the other side with his hand half-raised.

"Oh, thank God." She grabbed the front of his sweater and hauled him inside. "You've got to do something."

—∿∿∿—

Nick stared down at Marabelle's hands, one fisted in his sweater and the other holding a metal spatula.

"What exactly did you have in mind, darlin'?"

"Tell them no stripping and no bench-pressing humans." She leaned into him to gain his full attention. Hooting and clapping filtered in from the backyard. "Hear that?" Her brown eyes grew wild. "Make them stop," she pleaded.

He gave a cursory glance at his surroundings. "What am I supposed to do?"

She babbled as she waved the spatula. "*Wh*—Take charge. Kick ass. Do something!"

"Hey, Marabelle? Lilah and Betty ran out of singles and wanna know if they can use these as tips," Ty said, holding a platter of homemade chocolate chip cookies.

"See?"

Nick plucked her hand from his sweater and shook his head at Ty. "No."

"Yes!" Marabelle pumped her fist.

"Not until I get a couple first." Nick grabbed two cookies from the tray. Ty smiled and returned to the backyard.

"Wait." Marabelle gestured wildly with the spatula. "What's the matter with you? You love to boss people around. You've done nothing but boss me around since we met."

Nick watched her come unglued as he savored one of her cookies.

"What happened to 'I don't want you entertaining the guys'? And your warning about—" Her head snapped up, and the lightbulb went on. He chewed, giving her the I-told-you-so smirk.

Her eyes narrowed. "Fine. I'll take care of it myself."

Tinker Bell squared her shoulders and stormed through the tiny kitchen toward the backyard, wielding nothing but the spatula. This he had to see. Nick pushed through the backdoor to the outside. Everything appeared relatively tame compared to wild parties he remembered during his playing days. He caught sight of Tinker Bell shutting off the blaring music.

"Party's over. Everyone go home and go to bed. Preferably your own."

The partiers started to moan and boo. Guys dancing with half their clothes off slowly stopped.

"We were just gettin' to the good part," some old lady said as she stood on top of a picnic bench and waved a cookie.

"Everyone. Out. *Now*." Marabelle punctuated each word with a wave of the spatula.

The guys picked up their discarded clothing and helped the two women down from the bench, who mumbled something about Marabelle being a party pooper. Beer cans were tossed in the garbage, and her yard returned to some semblance of order.

"Thanks, Marabelle."

"You rock."

"Call you about tennis."

The two old ladies slinked across the yard when Marabelle called out, "Miz Dawkins, Miz Koonce, what do you have in your hands?"

They stopped, hesitated, and then held up men's boxers. "We won these fair and square. No way we're giving them up."

Nick laughed and Marabelle shot him another stink eye.

After the last of the revelers had disappeared into their cars, Nick guided Marabelle back into her kitchen.

Looking over her shoulder into the empty backyard, she said, "I can't figure out what happened to Beau."

The disappointment in her voice irritated him. He'd be damned before he'd watch her moon over Beau Quinton. Nick plucked the spatula from her hand, tossing it on the counter. Pulling a surprised Marabelle hard into his body, he threaded his fingers through her curls.

"Screw Beau," he growled, lowering his head for a rough kiss. He loved the way her body felt pressed against his. Lush and curvy in all the right places. Even through her bulky sweatshirt and jeans. He tried to remember that she had a sassy mouth and a badass attitude, and he didn't trust her worth a damn, but his body wasn't listening. The soft mewling sound she made shot through him like a bolt of lightning. He forgot all about what he didn't like. He forgot about everything except her hot mouth and the crushing kiss.

Nick wanted more. Sliding his hand to the curve of her butt, he deepened the thrust of his tongue, grinding his hips more intimately into her heat. And it still wasn't enough.

"Marab—*oh my*."

Nick and Marabelle jerked apart as if someone had turned the garden hose on them. Marabelle gasped. Her face flamed with desire…then embarrassment.

"Sorry to interrupt. Saw the light on." One of the old ladies who had been dancing on the bench peered through the screen door to the kitchen.

Wobbly on her feet, Marabelle grabbed the countertop. "Uh—Miz Dawkins, is there something you need?"

"I wanted to thank you for a wonderful evening." Mrs. Dawkins extended a clear plastic container with an apple pie underneath.

When Marabelle made no move to take it from her, Nick intervened, opening the door, introducing himself, and thanking her for the delicious-looking pie. Lilah Dawkins batted her gooped-up eyelashes at him and told him the pie came from the farmers' market. Nick kept up the small talk, giving Marabelle time to pull it together.

"Y'all go back to what you were doing now. Forget I was ever here." Lilah sent Marabelle a conspiratorial wink. He helped her out the door, making sure she crossed the yard safely.

Marabelle got busy gathering up dishes and filling the sink with warm water.

Shit. Perfect timing. Nick sighed heavily and moved from the kitchen into the front of the house, picking up empty beer cans along the way. He knew Marabelle needed space. He was willing to give it to her, but not for long. Dammit, she got under his skin like no other woman. And the solution to the problem was mind-numbing sex over and over until he got her out of his system. Or until he was ready to admit…he was in way over his head. *Shit.*

Nick returned to the kitchen with a handful of dirty plates and bowls, and placed them on the countertop. "Everything's put away in your living room."

"Thanks. I'll finish the rest," Marabelle said, not meeting his gaze as she continued to rinse dishes under the running water.

"You okay?"

"Sure."

He squeezed her shoulder. "Okay. New subject. Why are you afraid of sex?"

Her head popped up. "I'm not afraid of sex."

"Uh-huh." He cupped her stubborn chin and gave her a level stare. "Afraid you won't be able to resist me?"

She gave a nervous laugh, jerking her head away. "I'm stronger than you think."

"You know it's okay to be turned on. Even with a jock. It wouldn't be the first time." He chuckled low.

"Yeah? Could be a big letdown. For me. Maybe you're lacking…in some way." She shot him a cheeky grin.

Nick snorted. "I'm not. And you're not lacking in anything except practice." A flicker of surprise mingled with hope chased across her face. Marabelle appeared beautiful and fragile, and he couldn't remember wanting a woman more. If he didn't leave now, her old kitchen table might get a workout, and her neighbors an eyeful. "When we finally make it to the bed, we're gonna set each other on fire. Get used to the idea. Now, I'm beat and need to head home."

"Oh. Your trip. How'd it go?" She wiped her hands on a clean dishtowel.

Nick couldn't resist looping an errant curl behind her ear. "We're going to see some improvement with Brandon...hopefully soon."

She beamed. "That's great news." Hard not to like someone as genuine as Marabelle when it came to her kids.

He nodded. "Yeah, it is great news." Leaning down, he brushed her lips. "Sweet dreams, Thumbelina."

———

Monday, Marabelle had spent part of recess on the phone trying to derail her mother from all things wedding. Edna focused a good portion of the conversation on bridesmaid dresses. That's when Marabelle knew she was up a creek without a paddle.

After work, Marabelle caught Beau Quinton loading empty coolers from the party into the back of his black Escalade when she pulled into her driveway. She had less than three days to come up with an iron-clad reason her fiancé was not coming with her. Something her mother would believe without hesitation.

"Q, we need to talk."

"Mary-bell, sweetie, I can explain about last night." Beau wore a clean Cherokees T-shirt, sweatpants, and a false expression of remorse. Marabelle eyed his slightly damp hair and wondered if he'd finished showering after a workout.

She shook her head. "Never mind. I've got a problem and need to run something by you."

"You in trouble, Mary-bell?" Beau released the cooler in his hands, ready to do battle on her behalf.

Marabelle's heart warmed. "Not the kind of trouble

you're thinking." She glanced around to see which of her nosy neighbors had tuned in. No one appeared out in the open, but she could've sworn Lilah Dawkins's lace curtains fluttered in her front room. "Have you had dinner?" Beau's eyes lit up. "Go inside, and I'll whip something up while we talk."

Rubbing his hands together, he said, "I'll do anything for some of your home cooking."

"Hold that thought."

Marabelle pulled together ingredients for chicken piccata while Beau popped a cold beer left over from the party. Dredging the chicken breasts in seasoned flour, she explained to Beau that her mother was expecting her to attend her benefit with a fiancé in tow.

"And you want me to ask Coach Frasier for you?"

"No. I'm too embarrassed to even mention this to him. Once again my big mouth ran away from me, when like an idiot, I mentioned the word 'fiancé' to my mother. She's not going to let this go until Nick is either kidnapped by aliens or lost at sea or something." She dropped the chicken breasts in the pan of hot olive oil.

"I don't see the problem. He's your fiancé and the perfect solution. Just ask him."

"Yeah, nah. I'm not ready for a real engagement, and he will never be ready for the social dysfunction that makes up my family. We make the Kardashians look downright boring." Beau chuckled. "Please don't mention this to him," Marabelle pleaded, not wanting this kink to create any more confusion in an already complicated situation. This fake engagement was turning into anything but easy. "Isn't there something big and important going on in the NFL this weekend that you can't miss? Something my mother will believe or confirm if she decides to Google the information?"

He crossed his arms over his chest, leaning against her cabinets. "Not really. We're starting off-season workout programs. Draft's not until the end of the month."

"The draft…good one. I know Nick's concerned about it, and he'll need to be here for critical meetings. Perfect. Thanks, Q. Good enough to sound really important, but nothing she can snoop about or track online." She flipped the breasts in the pan, pleased with this great excuse.

"Mary-bell, you're making this way more complicated than it needs to be. Just ask him to go with you."

Marabelle wished it was that easy. Paralyzed, she couldn't take that step. It felt too real…and even permanent. And believing in the fairy tale only got you burned in the end. She removed the chicken breasts, dousing the pan with chicken stock, fresh lemon juice, and capers. "It's better my way. Nobody gets confused or starts believing in things that aren't real."

Usually so affable and easy to read, Beau's blank expression was making Marabelle nervous. "What are you thinking inside that beautiful head of yours?"

―⁓―

Something she didn't want to hear. Beau couldn't stop thinking that Coach Frasier would be seriously insulted, not to mention hurt, if Mary-bell didn't take him to her mother's benefit. Marabelle seriously underestimated Coach's attraction to her. Beau shook his head. How could she be so lost, confused, and lacking in self-confidence? A plan had begun to form, and Beau hoped like hell he'd still play football for the Cherokees when it was all over.

"I'm thinking you're making a big mistake," he said, rubbing his scruffy chin.

She served him a heaping plate of al dente pasta and chicken seasoned with lemon juice and capers. "Okay. But you have to agree that it's my mistake to make. Swear to me you won't mention this conversation."

He stalled, sniffing his food. "This smells great."

Marabelle's plate hit the table with a clatter. "No food until you promise," she said in her schoolteacher voice.

"Yes, ma'am. I promise..." To not tell Marabelle what he had planned. He pulled out Marabelle's chair.

Marabelle craned her neck, peering up at him. "Thanks for understanding, and to show my appreciation"—she pointed to their plates—"this meal is in your honor."

"If it tastes as good as it smells, we're even." Beau slid into his seat. He shoved a huge bite in his mouth and chewed. "Mmm." Swallowing, he nodded. "Delicious. Hell, Mary-bell, I'll marry you tomorrow, problem solved, if you promise to keep cooking," he added between bites.

Marabelle laughed, twirling pasta on her fork. "You don't need a ball and chain just to get some home cooked meals. If you provide the ingredients, I'll make meals for you and the guys anytime."

"You got yourself a deal." He winked and then attacked his food.

Chapter 13

EARLY THE NEXT MORNING, BEAU FLASHED CHANTAL his sexiest smile and charmed his way into Coach Frasier's office. He wanted to catch Coach before he left for a round of golf in Pinehurst.

Coach looked up from his paperwork as Beau knocked and pushed the door open at the same time.

"Q, what can I do for you? I don't have much time."

He and Beau had not really spoken since the night they'd fought over Marabelle at Corbett's. Beau figured Coach was still nursing some animosity toward him. He hoped to change that with this meeting.

"Morning, Coach. This will only take a minute. I need to speak to you about something important."

Nick nodded and indicated for Beau to take a seat. "What's on your mind?"

Beau dropped down in the chair and leaned forward on his elbows.

"It's about Marabelle." At the mention of her name, Beau felt like he'd waved a red flag. Coach's eyes narrowed, and the angry tic in his right jaw sprang to life. Beau almost laughed with relief. Almost. His suspicions were confirmed. "Over dinner last night, she asked me—"

"Excuse me?" Coach interrupted in a tight voice. "You two had dinner? Again?"

"Yeah, I stopped by to pick up the leftover coolers from the party, and it led to dinner."

"And?"

"And what?" Beau cocked his head to one side.

"And *what else* did it lead to?" Coach gripped his pen as if he wanted to snap it.

Beau leaned back and stretched out his legs. Coach showed the classic signs of a man obsessed with a woman. "Nothing. But there's something you need to know."

Coach pinned him with his don't-screw-with-me stare. "I'm all ears."

Game over. Beau sang like a canary. Ten minutes later, he left Coach Frasier's office with all his body parts still intact, and felt marginally better than when he had arrived. Beau believed in playing cleanly and laying all his cards out on the table. Coach deserved the truth, even if it got Marabelle in trouble. She'd thank him in the end. He'd bet his multimillion-dollar endorsements on it.

Marabelle strolled into a Starbucks after school. She spied the blond ding-a-ling at a table in the corner, sipping an iced coffee with a mountain of whipped cream. Yup. Starr had surprised her earlier by calling and requesting they meet to talk. It took Marabelle a minute to recall who she was. She had no idea what they needed to talk about, but Marabelle figured it had something to do with Beau. Starr hadn't been happy at Corbett's the other night when Marabelle showed up wearing tight jeans and Beau on her arm. Marabelle didn't want rumors flying around about her and Beau; she could barely handle the ones about her and Nick. And she didn't want her friendship to cramp Beau's style. So she figured she had some explaining to do.

With her skinny latte in hand, Marabelle sat in the chair across from Starr, who wore some bust-enhancing white top with crisscross gold braiding. Marabelle wore tennis sweats along with cupcake batter in her hair, compliments of her students. Starr openly gave her the once-over without disguising her distaste.

"What's on your mind?" Marabelle asked, cutting to the chase.

"Nothing really."

Big surprise there.

Starr sipped her whipped concoction. "But my friend has a few questions."

"What friend?" Marabelle spotted the answer heading their way from over her cup of coffee.

Ginger Jones.

Marabelle fought to tamp down her insecurities as a confident Ginger glided toward them, wearing expensive navy sailor trousers and a silk coral blouse. Ginger gripped her Louis Vuitton handbag's strap with one hand and her coffee in the other. Marabelle pushed her pathetic JanSport knapsack, along with her insecurities, under the table. Who cared? It didn't matter what she wore or what handbag she carried. She had what Ginger really wanted...Nick. Okay, technically, she didn't *have* him. But hey, Ginger didn't know that, and Marabelle planned to keep it that way.

"Let the games begin," Marabelle murmured into her cup of coffee.

Ginger came to a halt next to the table, fluttering her impeccable French-manicured fingers, for Starr to move over. With her bouncing boobs, Starr settled into the next chair and didn't appear pleased. Ginger took the seat directly in front of Marabelle.

"It's Mary, right?"

"Marabelle actually. Except Nick calls me Tinker Bell, an endearing pet name, don't you think?" Marabelle sent her a simpering smile.

Ginger's cornflower-blue eyes hardened to ice chips. "Aren't you wondering why you're here?"

"Not particularly. I can pretty much guess what this is all about. You wanna go another round?" Marabelle said with her game face firmly in place.

Ginger bristled. Starr's whipped coffee sat forgotten as her gaze darted back and forth.

"You should rein in your violent nature. It's not becoming to a woman. I'm not here to fight you." Ginger appeared calm as she brought her espresso to her lips. "I'm here on Nick's behalf."

"Really? Funny, Nick never told me anything about it. And he tells me *everything*," Marabelle lied. She hadn't spoken to Nick since yesterday, when he called and surprised her by asking her on a date. But she would've bet her last dime he hadn't called this meeting.

A flicker of doubt flashed across Ginger's face. "Listen, Miss Big Mouth, your so-called engagement is not fooling anyone. A man like Nick needs more in a woman than what you have to offer," she said, flicking her mane of hair behind her shoulder.

"As everyone keeps reminding me, and yet…he's still with me." Marabelle smirked.

Ginger laughed. "Not for long. Look in a mirror. There's no comparison," Ginger said, not bothering to conceal her contempt. "Whatever you're holding over his head isn't going to work. He will throw you away like…like a smelly pair of sneakers!"

"Look, men don't use me. *I use them*," Marabelle the badass said, jabbing her right thumb toward her chest.

Ginger's mouth curved into a humorless smile. "You're a real man-killer, huh? I'm warning you…he's going to break your heart."

"Spoken by someone who knows?"

Ginger flinched, and Starr stared at Marabelle with her mouth hanging open. Marabelle swallowed her sigh, suddenly tired of the whole ugly business.

"Listen, I'm sorry. My eyes are wide open. I'm not as dumb as I look, despite the cupcake batter in my hair. I appreciate the warning, but I'm just going to see where all this leads." Marabelle rose from her seat and tossed her empty cup in the receptacle.

"But one more thing. As long as I'm his fiancée, I will fight to keep what is mine." She looked Ginger directly in the eye to emphasize her point. "And right now, he's *mine*."

Ginger jerked back as if she'd been poked with a cattle prod, while Starr leaned forward, mesmerized by the exchange.

Squaring her shoulders, Ginger said, "You're living in a fairy tale if you think Nick is Prince Charming. He will never rescue you from your pathetic life. If you don't believe me, try Googling some of his past girl-friends. You might be surprised by what you see."

Marabelle couldn't say she hadn't been tempted to pry a few times via Internet, but it wasn't like she lived under a rock. She remembered his name linked with a couple of scandalous situations, but once she and Nick became…well, frenemies, she hadn't felt right snooping. It felt like breaking a trust or something. But she didn't like what Ginger implied, and she certainly didn't want her spreading rumors.

Marabelle sucked in a breath and chose the high road. "You've got one thing right…he isn't Prince Charming. You ladies have a nice night."

———

"Whoa, start from the beginning."

Later that night at her house, Marabelle was filling Paula in on the whole saga over pizza and beer. Marabelle recapped the night at Corbett's, the scene of her first altercation with Ginger, and how Nick removed her bodily from the bar.

Paula nodded. "Ginger is Coach Frasier's girlfriend? But he defended you at the bar and pushed her aside?"

Marabelle jumped up from the sofa and retrieved the shipping box that had been outside the front door when she returned home.

"Not exactly. He held me back so I wouldn't whale on her bony ass."

"Let me get this straight." Paula ticked points off on her fingers. "Coach Dreamboat removes you from the bar, takes you to his fabulous house, where you do some serious making out, shows up again at your wild party, uh, more making out, and tomorrow night he's taking you out on your first official date. Right?"

"Yep, you've covered the highlights."

"And there's been no wild gorilla sex?"

Marabelle glanced up from opening the box and blushed. *Not for lack of wanting.* "Um…we're kinda taking it slow." She had glossed over the parts where Nick practically had her naked and begging.

Marabelle rolled her eyes at Paula's chicken sounds. "I'm with Ginger on this one…he ain't gonna hang around long."

"I thought you were on my side."

"Marabelle, all you have to do is look at the guy. How have you resisted him this long?" Paula rose from her seat and moved next to Marabelle and the shipping box.

Marabelle shrugged, not meeting Paula's gaze. "You know how I am about sex."

"No. I really don't," Paula said.

Marabelle crossed her arms, giving herself a hug at Paula's earnest expression. "With Clay…I was horrible. If I don't give in to Nick, maybe I'll get to keep him a little longer. Before he discovers what a dud I am. Does that make sense?" Warped logic, but she couldn't seem to get past it.

Paula shoved her glasses back up on her nose. "Yeah. I guess. In Marabelle's World. What you need is the right person. Someone who's had gobs and gobs of experience. Someone who practically invented it. Someone like Nick." She pointed a finger at Marabelle. "You know I speak the truth."

Boy, did she ever. And yet, she knew deep inside her bones that being with Nick would mean something… probably everything, and how she'd recover from that she had no clue.

"What's in the box?" Paula asked, twirling her long, silky ponytail around her finger.

Marabelle drifted back to the box as if seeing it for the first time. "Clothes my dad sent from Paris for this weekend." Under mounds of tissue paper that smelled faintly of expensive French perfume, she pulled out a beautiful, bronze metallic jersey dress with a criss-crossed gathered bodice and a pair of Manolo Blahnik gold sandals with four-inch heels.

"Wow. That dress is beautiful."

"I know. You should see what my mother sent." Marabelle made a face. "Dad clothes are party appropriate. Mother clothes are Junior League president appropriate."

"What's this weekend?" Paula asked, popping open another beer she'd pulled from the refrigerator.

"Big Edna has summoned me to Atlanta." Marabelle held up her beer in mock salute. "Cheers."

An hour later in Marabelle's bedroom, Paula said, "I agree with Beau on this one… You're making a big mistake not taking Coach Yumballs to Atlanta." Marabelle was changing into some of her new clothes. Paula had kicked off her shoes and was sitting crisscross-applesauce in the middle of the double bed.

Marabelle slipped into one of her mother's gray knit skirts, and pulled on an old jean jacket over a turquoise silk blouse, trying not to appear so dowdy.

"Does this go with this?" she asked, turning in front of the full-length mirror, straining to see all the way around.

"Does *no* go with *way*? You cannot wear that jean jacket with that…that old lady skirt. You look ridiculous. Just don't wear that skirt at all."

"You're right. I hate these clothes my mother sent. What should I do? She's expecting me to wear them." Marabelle peeled them off her body.

"You're avoiding my question."

"What question?" Marabelle said, her voice muffled as she pulled the blouse over her head.

"Why are you going to Atlanta without Nick?"

"Because." She tossed the blouse aside to land on top of the offending knit skirt. "My family is bad enough for me to deal with. Particularly at one of my mother's soul-sucking, mind-stealing benefits. And…and I just don't want to put Nick through that." She wiggled into a hot-pink Chanel bouclé skirt with a tulip hem.

"Aha! You do care about Nick. Don't you? You like him…a lot."

Exactly why she couldn't involve him. Nick was a triple threat—dangerous to her life, her heart, and her future. Marabelle kept her eyes on her hands as she buttoned up a black silk blouse and slipped on a pair of black patent Prada sling-backs. "Of course I like him. What's *not* to like? He's hunky, irresistible, and loaded. I'd be lying if I said I didn't. But I'm not in his league," she said, wrapping several strands of white and gold pearls around her neck.

Paula exploded, "That's the stupidest thing I've ever heard!"

Marabelle jabbed her index finger at Paula. "One look at us together, and it's as clear as the nose on your face that we come from different worlds."

Paula hopped off the bed and slowly turned Marabelle toward the mirror. "Take a look at you now. I'd say those two worlds just merged."

For a quiet moment, they studied Marabelle's reflection in the mirror. "You look fabulous. This is a keeper," Paula insisted.

"Does it make my butt look big?" Marabelle twisted.

"What butt? This looks great on you. You look sexy yet sophisticated. Atlanta will never be the same. Too bad Nick's not going to see it."

Chapter 14

NICK GAVE HIS WATCH AN IRRITATED GLANCE, WONdering who was ringing his doorbell at ten thirty at night. He'd been aggravated and confused most the day over this latest development. Marabelle had confided in Beau about her trip to Atlanta, when Nick was her damn fiancé. She should be talking to him and trusting him. Nick shook his head in frustration. Marabelle kept trying to play quarterback, and she sucked at it.

Earlier that day, he'd managed to play a horrible round of golf, losing a ton of money to Coach Prichard. All because of Marabelle and Beau and their scheming, or closeness, or something… He didn't know what to call it. *Whatever.* If Marabelle didn't want his help, then he wouldn't force himself on her. But how could she not come to him? *Screw it.* Nick was done trying to solve the riddle.

He peered through the sidelights of his front door, and his day just went from bad to worse.

Ginger Jones stood on the doorstep, washed in light from the exterior sconces. She clutched her expensive handbag as if she feared a mugger would jump out at any second. She wore designer labels from head to toe and a grim expression on her face.

Great. Nick pulled the door open.

"Hello, Nick."

"Ginger." He swung the door wider. "What brings you out this late?"

"It's been a while since we've talked, and I happened to be in the neighborhood." She moved past him straight into the great room.

Right. Ginger lived south of him, inside the boundaries of Pine Boulevard, where the homes were older and prices inflated because of their convenient location. She had no reason to be in his newer development at this time of night. Nick reluctantly trailed behind her.

He hoped Ginger would get to the point and leave… soon. Ignoring the seat next to her on the sofa, he dropped into his leather lounge chair opposite the coffee table.

"What's on your mind?" he asked as he leaned back, crossing his legs at the ankles.

"Your girlfriend for starters," she snapped.

His brows lifted. "What about her?" In his defense, he'd meant to call Ginger after the night at Corbett's, but he'd forgotten all about her. Not something she or any woman would be thrilled to hear.

"You can't be serious about that…that *girl*. She's not your type at all."

Funny, a few weeks ago he would've agreed with her, but now he wasn't so sure.

"Just tonight, she threatened to fight me again!"

Tonight? He sat forward. "What're you talking about? When did you talk with Tinker Bell?"

Ginger didn't bother to disguise her eye roll. "We had coffee at Starbucks."

Nick waited for her to continue.

"I was trying to be friendly…"

Friendly, my ass.

"…when she started in on me like the other night at the bar. She's so brash and full of herself." Ginger slipped a silky wave of hair behind her ear.

He smiled to himself, picturing Marabelle threatening Ginger. "How'd you two hook up?"

Ginger tried to appear guileless, clasping her hands in her lap. Except she'd forgotten Nick had never fallen for her act in the past. Tonight would be no different.

"I wanted to have a friendly drink and get to know her better. After the way you subdued her at Corbett's for trying to attack me, I didn't want there to be any hard feelings."

Sure. How dumb did she think he was? "Is that all?" he asked, his tone bored.

"No. I tried to set her straight about us and our relationship."

He frowned, and his next words held an edge. "What exactly did you say?"

"That's just it. I didn't get the chance to tell her you and I are in a serious relationship, before she started threatening me. Really, Nicky, she's taking this phony engagement too far." She retied a silk scarf around her handbag, avoiding his gaze.

Nick grabbed another beer at the bar. The spastic tic in his jaw jumped to life, and tension pinched his neck and shoulders.

"Who told you the engagement was phony?" he asked, twisting the top off the bottle with unnecessary force.

Ginger uncurled her legs and stood. "Beau. The other night. He explained the whole situation. I know Marty Hackman is behind this whole thing." Nick's eyes narrowed. "Don't worry. You've managed to fool your adoring fans, and there hasn't been any more mention of Jenna or any of your other past transgressions. What I don't understand is why you didn't think to come to me first. I'd have been happy to pose as your fiancée."

Nick watched with hooded eyes as Ginger glided toward him with swaying hips, stopping just close enough to trail her fingers down the front of his shirt. Her perfumed scent lingered in the air. He used to find the scent pleasant enough, but tonight he found it too cloying for his taste. He preferred a much fresher, cleaner scent, like lavender with a touch of vanilla.

"Nicky, you didn't have to saddle yourself with a lunatic for the sake of a fake engagement"—Ginger missed his scowl as she fiddled with his shirt buttons— "when you had the real thing right in front of you," she purred in a low, husky whisper.

"Funny, that's not how I see it." He plucked her hand from his shirt and held it between his palms. He knew he needed to be careful in this situation. A scorned woman was nothing to trifle with. He turned on his unfailing charm.

"Ginger, we dated for a few months, and it was great. But we were keeping it light and on the down low, just the way you like it." And then he added for good measure, "I'm not the man for you."

She made a small gasp.

"You were kind to find me a house and help me get settled. I didn't expect you to tie yourself to me." He patted the top of her hand in his palm like she was an old friend. "You can do much better," he said with a self-deprecating smile.

Ginger jerked her hand loose from his grasp and her blue eyes filled with venom. Suddenly she came at him with an open palm, but he stopped her with a viselike grip before she could slap him across the face.

"Careful," he said from between clenched teeth.

She wrenched her arm free. "You stupid jerk! I put my heart and soul in our relationship, and you enjoyed the benefits! I suffered through your boring football season. Waited around for you after all your late nights, working and partying." Her expression contorted into a look of contempt. "You always found a reason to come by, and I was always there. I think *that* deserves some sort of commitment," she sneered.

She stomped to the sofa and retrieved her handbag. "You're right about one thing. You aren't *man* enough for me. You think I'm losing sleep over you? *Ha!*" She snapped her fingers. "I've already replaced you. There's something to be said for a younger man. You don't hold a candle to him…especially in bed," she added in a nasty tone.

"You'd better leave before this gets any uglier." Nick pointed her toward the door. His repressed anger was overridden by his relief.

"Truth hurts, doesn't it? Now you know how it feels to be dumped." With her hand on the doorknob, she glanced back. Trying for sultry, she slicked her collagen-injected lips with her tongue. "Not only is he better in bed, big guy…but he's a better quarterback than you ever were."

If Ginger was trying to shock or hurt him, she'd missed her mark. Nothing surprised him anymore.

Nick's face remained impassive. "He should be. He has a better coach."

Marabelle crawled into bed after Paula left. They'd replaced all the clothes in her closet, separating the dowdy ones so they wouldn't breed. Between her mother's party and Nick's engagement, Marabelle was going to need some serious coping techniques if she planned to survive the next month. Her cell buzzed with a text. She grabbed it, hoping to give her battered head a break.

> You asleep?
> *Not yet.*
> Mind if I call?
> *Nope.*

Two seconds later, her cell rang. "Tinker Bell, I hear you've been busy defending our love."

"Where did you hear that?"

"The horse's mouth. Tell me what happened," he said.

She released a sigh. "Nothing to tell. Ginger warned me to stay away from you."

Nick's soft laugh warmed her down to her toes. "You set her straight?"

"Absolutely. When this whole farce is over, I forbid you to get back with her. She's a real bitch."

"What else did she say?"

Marabelle punched her pillow for a better position. "The usual. I'm not pretty enough for you. You're going to break my heart. Blah, blah, blah."

For a moment, neither of them spoke. Then Nick asked, sounding hesitant, "You believed her?"

"Not exactly. You're not going to break my heart, because we're not serious." Nick didn't say anything to the contrary. Marabelle was glad they were both on the same page—at least that's what she told herself.

"So you tackled her to the ground and beat her up?" he asked.

"I restrained myself. Told her to stay away from me…and you. Honestly, you can do better."

"Well, it worked. Ginger officially broke it off with me tonight," he said.

Hmm, funny. She'd thought they'd been over. "Uh… are you upset?"

"Hell no. We hadn't been in a relationship for months." Marabelle swallowed her pleased sigh.

"Don't forget our date tomorrow night. I'll be by around seven."

"I'll be ready. What should I wear?"

"Something casual—uh, scratch that. Wear something that fits and doesn't look like you borrowed it from a homeless guy."

"See? Now that's something my mother would say. Just makes me want to go all thrift shop, bargain box crazy."

"Great. It'll give me a good reason to strip you."

She coughed. "I promise to be dressed appropriately."

"Too bad." Then in a serious tone, he said, "We still have a lot more to discuss."

After saying good-bye, Marabelle fell asleep, wondering what else needed discussing.

Chapter 15

THAT EVENING, MARABELLE STOOD IN HER CLOSET, assessing her wardrobe again. Lumpy, frumpy, schlumpy. She reached for schlumpy when she remembered the auction committee's latest plan. Marabelle was going to need to do some serious convincing, and it didn't hurt to be dressed well. She could only hope she felt empowered as she yanked an outfit off its hanger.

Marabelle held the front door open.

Nick shook his head. "You disappoint me. I was looking forward to stripping you." His gaze said it all as it traveled over her blue wrap sweater, focusing on the hint of cleavage, and then moving down her skinny jeans to her brown suede booties.

He smiled slow and sexy. "Nice. I even like the jean jacket," he said, referring to his jacket she held in her hand.

"Thanks. Some hunk gave it to me." True to form, Coach Gorgeous filled her small entrance. He towered over her in a black Italian button-down shirt and jeans, with his signature cowboy boots in black lizard. A small pink gift bag dangled from his fingers.

"Would you like a drink?" she asked, trying not to stare at the lime-green tissue paper peeking from the top of the bag.

"Sure." He followed her into her quaint kitchen and tossed the bag on the table.

Marabelle shrugged and figured she'd sneak a peek when he turned his back. She grabbed two beers from the refrigerator and extended a bottle. He leaned against her white cabinets and took a long pull.

Marabelle had a few sips and asked, "Where're we going?" Before he could respond, she held her hand up. "No, let me guess." She tapped her chin with her finger. "Hmmm. Box seats at the symphony? No. Wait. Front-row seats to the Maroon 5 concert? I heard they've been sold out for months." Nick grinned behind his beer. "I've got it! We're hopping on your private jet to some country-western bar in, uh… Austin, Texas!"

"No, smart-ass."

He purposely placed his beer on the counter and stalked over to her. Marabelle laughed as she side-stepped him and her butt bumped the kitchen table. Nick plucked the beer from her hand and trapped her in his arms. She glimpsed his lopsided smile before he rested his forehead against hers.

"You know you make me nuts, right?" he said, his voice rumbling. His warm breath caressed her skin like a soothing balm. Then his head lifted, and he laughed in her face.

Great. Marabelle felt her self-esteem slip. She'd become a hilarious punch line. The one where sexy guy realized he shouldn't be with plain ole frumpy girl. *Idiot.* Her ego didn't need another crushing blow.

"Didn't your mother teach you it's rude to laugh in someone's face?" she said a little too harshly.

He continued to chuckle. "Damn. Ever since the day I laid eyes on you and your hot-pink panties. Just don't understand it." He shook his head. "I'll fly you to Austin or Paris. Wherever you want to go as long as I get you."

"What?" Marabelle couldn't keep the surprise from her voice.

"Whatever you want, Tinker Bell. Name it and it's yours, as long as you're mine."

All signs of laughter had vanished, replaced by a look of stark hunger—not the yummy brownie-pie version, but the I-wanna-get-naked-with-you version.

Marabelle squirmed out of his loose embrace.

"You've been thinking about me?" She pressed her palms over her heart and felt its rapid beat.

"All damn day." Nick reached for her, but she held her hand up for the second time.

"Wait." She shook her head. "What hot-pink panties?"

Nick's sexy grin turned cocky. "First time I was in your classroom, your cute little butt was poking up in the air while you fished for that damn gerbil. Flashing hot-pink panties for the world's viewing pleasure."

Let it be known a person could turn fire-engine red from mortification. "Oh my *God*! Why didn't you tell me? What if someone had seen me?"

Somehow Nick had his arms around her again and backed up against the cabinets. He nuzzled her neck.

"Someone did. Me." He kissed the sensitive spot right below her ear. "Tell me what you want, Tinker Bell," he whispered against her heated skin.

You. Knees, don't fail me now. She managed to wriggle away after luxuriating in his touch for a second, or maybe twenty.

"What's in the bag?" She smiled.

Marabelle's full-wattage smile always stopped rational thought. Her eyes flicked to the pink bag he had tossed on the table moments before. Nick had forgotten all about his gift. Snatching the bag up, he dangled it in front of her.

"Something I picked up in Charlotte."

She grabbed it from him like a child on Christmas day and dug in, pulling out a pink Life Is Good cap with a yellow tennis ball embroidered on the front.

"I love it. Thank you." She impulsively threw her arms around his neck and smacked him right on the lips. Quickly, she pulled away, settled the hat on her head, and fed her ponytail through the hole in the back. "What do you think?"

"Perfect. You should wear pink more often, fairy girl." Nick grabbed her hand. "Let's go. I'm starved." He steered her out of the kitchen and out of the house.

Lilah Dawkins waved from her porch when he and Marabelle reached his car.

"Yoo-hoo! Where you two off to?"

"Good evening, Miz Dawkins," he drawled, opening the car door for Marabelle. "Out for a bite to eat."

"Y'all have fun. Don't do anything I wouldn't do," she said with a cackle.

"That leaves the door wide open then." He winked and waved good-bye.

After dinner at one of his favorite barbecue shacks, they strolled through a quaint village shopping area in Raleigh. Nick found himself in front of Ben and Jerry's, watching Marabelle lick her lips, wishing he were licking them instead.

"What's your pleasure, Tinker Bell?"

"Cherry Garcia. Is there any other?"

He pushed the door open. "Cherry Garcia it is." He ordered two waffle cones, and they sat outside at a small bistro table to eat them. X-rated thoughts invaded Nick's head, as he pictured licking something other than Cherry Garcia, and all involved parts of Marabelle's anatomy.

"Give me some news about the committee. Who'd they try to shanghai today?" he said. Nothing killed his sex drive more than discussing that committee.

Marabelle continued to flick her tongue over her ice cream, oblivious to the discomfort growing behind his zipper.

"Well, they've been busy, that's for sure. They've come up with a great new idea."

He finished his cone and reached for her half-eaten one.

"Wait—"

"You're making a mess." Not to mention he was about to embarrass himself. Nick tossed the remainder in the trash receptacle and handed over some napkins. "Okay, what does the committee want now?"

Marabelle appeared to be busy cleaning her hands. "The usual…more auction items, more eligible bachelors, all the guys posing for a promotional poster in nothing but towels…yadda, yadda, yadda."

Silence.

Marabelle averted her gaze. Never a good sign.

"Wait. What'd you say?"

She fidgeted, wadding the paper napkins into a tight ball. "More auction items?"

"*And?*" His jaw went into lockdown.

"Nothing I can't handle."

"*Marabelle.*"

She huffed. "You're just going to go all crazy on me, and it's not my fault. Look, I can't help it if they keep drinking the Kool-Aid."

Nick continued to frown, not amused. "Start from the beginning."

Marabelle spilled it and told Nick about how the committee had insisted on a promotional poster with all the local athletes posing in nothing but low-slung, white towels. The more he scowled, the more nervous she became, and the faster she talked.

"I tried telling them no, but they ganged up on me."

"No poster."

"Look, don't shoot the messenger. I happen to agree. But what am I supposed to do? Miz Cartwright suggested it. You remember, the ninety-year-old who wants to jump your bones? Every time she opens her mouth, something outlandish comes out, and they all stick to it like a tongue on a frozen pole." She paused. "On the other hand, it would really kick-start the whole event. If I can pull this off, some real money will come pouring in and—"

Before she could finish, Nick shot up from his chair, dragging her with him. "Come along, Tinker Bell. Looks like I'm gonna have to beat some sense into you after all."

Marabelle tripped behind him, trying to keep up with his long stride. "How does this make me the bad guy?

I'm just doing my job—hummph." She ran smack into his hard back as he came to an abrupt stop. His hand swung around to steady her.

"Hey, John, Elizabeth. How are you?"

"Nick, what a nice surprise."

Marabelle peered around his back like a kid playing peekaboo. Elizabeth stood on tiptoe and kissed him on the cheek. Nick pulled Marabelle out of hiding.

"Marabelle, you remember Coach Prichard. This is his better half, Elizabeth." She shook hands and nodded.

"I've heard so many wonderful things about you, Marabelle. You're darling. Just as John described. I hope you two aren't running off. John and I were going for after-dinner drinks at Fire 'N' Ice. They have a nice quiet bar where we can get better acquainted."

Marabelle pegged Elizabeth Prichard as the consummate Southern hostess. She pictured Twelve Oaks with Elizabeth as Melanie Wilkes in a hoop skirt and wide-brim straw hat. John smiled down at his wife, clearly still crazy about her after so many years of marriage.

"We can't—" Nick started to say.

"We'd love to," Marabelle interrupted. Anything to avoid his blistering lecture.

"Wonderful." Elizabeth linked arms with her as they strolled. Marabelle admired her wavy brown hair and peaches-and-cream complexion. The guys fell into step behind them, and she could feel Nick's gaze boring into her back. She knew he still wanted an explanation about the ridiculous poster. Not that she had one. Later she'd have to deal with his wrath. For now, she'd play it safe and hide behind Elizabeth's skirts.

They chose a dark booth in the corner near the bar

for some privacy. Elizabeth made small talk about the weather and her kids while they waited for their drinks.

Marabelle politely inquired about her daughter, Hailey. "Did you read any of those books I recommended to Coach Prichard?"

"Yes, they were wonderful. Hailey particularly loves it when Nick stops by the house and reads to her." *Really?* Her heart melted. "I'm afraid Hailey's quite shameless when it comes to Nick. She's always vying for his attention whenever he's around."

"Even the young ones don't make him work for it," Marabelle said with a smirk. Both Elizabeth and John laughed in agreement.

The conversation eventually turned to the gala, and Nick made it perfectly clear he wasn't participating in the bachelor auction.

"A lot of women are going to be disappointed." Elizabeth gestured toward Nick. "You'd make the auction tons of money, with your handsome looks and high-profile position."

"That's what I said." Marabelle leaned over the table, happy to have found an ally. "And we're doing a promotional poster, with all the guys wearing only towels, and they want Nick in it, too."

John choked on his beer, Elizabeth coughed, and Nick's brows slammed together.

"A poster with the guys in nothing but towels. Well now. Sounds promising. What do you think, Nick?" Elizabeth asked, grinning behind her drink.

"No way in hell."

"Aw, think of Marabelle," Elizabeth coaxed, placing her half-empty drink on a coaster.

"Yeah." Marabelle liked Elizabeth Prichard more and more. "Think of me." She put on her best puppy-dog eyes as she looked from Elizabeth to John. "He doesn't understand what I'm up against. It's like herding cats. Feel my pain. I have a committee to please, auction items to acquire, and a bunch of prima donna athletes to appease. And on top of that, I have the extra bonus of informing Coach Hottie, and he starts to lose it and wants to beat me senseless. I can't win for losing." All three stared at her as if her head were a Chia Pet.

John snickered, and Elizabeth tried to look sympathetic but gave up the fight and started laughing. Nick, the traitor, joined right in. Marabelle slumped further down in the booth with her arms crossed.

"Laugh all you want. I'm getting that poster," she mumbled. She might complain, but when push came to shove, Marabelle was all about the challenge.

John finally composed himself. "Marabelle, how 'bout we compromise? We could convince the guys to pose, but maybe fully clothed. I bet *Coach Hottie* will even agree to that." John grinned at Nick.

Elizabeth elbowed John in the side, telling him to hush. "Hey now, I know Beau Quinton would pose in nothing but a jock strap, but I'm not sure about the rest of them. What if you put them in tuxes? That would make a marvelous poster," Elizabeth offered, appearing genuinely interested. "Have them all autograph their picture, and then you can auction it off. That should bring in a lot of money." Elizabeth's excitement grew as she warmed to the idea.

Marabelle should've felt elated but suddenly felt inadequate for the task. Maybe she wasn't the best person for the job. Elizabeth was right. She needed another idea in order for these guys to agree. "Elizabeth, I wish you could take my place. You'd get a lot further with the fruitcake committee than I ever will."

———

Elizabeth shot Nick a make-this-right-or-else look, and Nick remembered what he'd promised Tinker Bell. He would give her whatever she asked for, if he could.

He pushed his empty glass toward the center of the table. "Come here, baby girl." He gathered her in his arms. She snuggled against him, tilting her warm brown eyes up at him, and his mind went blank. He felt something when Marabelle was around. Something he never had before, and he wanted more of it. More than a temporary engagement. Just more.

"We'll call a meeting with all the guys and come up with a great promotional poster. I promise." He kissed the tip of her nose. "How does that sound?"

"G-good." She nodded.

He glanced over at Elizabeth. "Hey, what if Elizabeth helped with some of the coordinating? She's a true master. She volunteers for more causes than anyone I know." He gave Elizabeth a wink.

"I'd be happy to help."

Marabelle winced. "I'd hate to impose on you. We're not a very well-organized group, and some of the ideas suggested…trust me, you'd rather stick a screwdriver in your ear."

Elizabeth laughed it off. "It's not an imposition. I'd love to help. I know most of the players and their wives. With a little brainstorming, we'll get everyone rallying behind this event. You'll come out smelling like a rose!" she said, clapping her hands together.

Nick gave Marabelle a reassuring squeeze. "Come on, honey, she's offering you a lifeline. I'd take it if I were you."

"I'd love your help. But surely you have more important things to do."

"John and I have known Nick for years, and if he loves you, then so do we. We'd be thrilled to help."

Nick stopped breathing, and Marabelle stiffened at Elizabeth's comment. Yeah, maybe *love* was too strong a term right now, but Nick was sure feeling something, and the sooner he figured it out, the better.

Elizabeth declared the whole issue settled, and plugged Marabelle's phone number in her cell. Nick exhaled and inwardly cheered, knowing Marabelle had found a new friend and ally. Teamwork at its best.

On the drive home, the DJ's voice drifted through the radio. Marabelle closed her eyes and remembered Nick's words earlier. A hot guy had said he wanted *her*. *Amazing*. And when Elizabeth had suggested he loved her…well, she wasn't dumb enough to fall for that. But for a moment…it felt wonderful. And Marabelle had felt cherished. Something she would treasure and hold close to her heart.

Nick lowered the volume on the radio and glanced her way. "What did you think of John and Elizabeth?"

"They're awesome. You're lucky to have such good friends. Elizabeth and John obviously care a lot about you."

"Yeah. They're great. I'm glad you and Elizabeth hit it off. Funny, she's never liked anyone I've dated before."

What a surprise. Marabelle smiled. "I have that effect on people. They don't know what to make of me, so they just decide it's easier to like me." Marabelle reached for the radio and turned it back up.

He snorted loud enough to be heard over the country music. "Your MO is to throw everyone off balance and then go in for the kill."

"Ha. That's absurd. I do no such thing."

He grinned. "Yeah, you do. You have this uncanny ability to turn a situation around to your advantage, especially in my presence."

"It's called survival. I've learned it the hard way. Not everyone is born with superior looks and God-given talent. You have no clue what it's like to work for your small corner of the world."

"Are you freakin' kidding me? You don't think I worked hard to get where I am today?" His grin vanished into a scowl.

She leaned forward, pressed against her seat belt. "You've misunderstood. I know you've worked hard. But you've been blessed with uncommon good looks. Which makes things a whole lot easier. Being beautiful and sexy in this world sells, and you've got that down in spades."

"You know what I think?"

Not really. "Tell me."

"You're full of shit. You've spent your adult life making an effort not to look beautiful and sexy because you're afraid. Afraid of doors that might open for you. You make it harder because of your choices."

She squirmed in her seat, not liking his accurate assessment one bit. "I don't feel comfortable with people fawning all over me. Can you imagine if I fixed myself up all the time? I'd probably steal your lime-light, and then what would you do? I already threaten you with my wit and smarts. I'd hate to outshine you with my beauty."

"Oh yeah. You threaten." He chuckled. "I can read you like my playbook." She snapped her gaze to him. She had no desire to be an open book.

He gave a heavy sigh. "Tink, you're trash-talkin' with a pro. Professional football players don't get where they are without a lot of hard work, sweat, and a huge amount of trash talking. Hell, we practically invented it." A suspicious gleam lit his steel-blue eyes. "Let's try this one more time. How 'bout we go out this Friday to the symphony and dinner afterward. You get all dressed up and see if I can handle it?"

Yikes. If Marabelle didn't know better, she'd think Nick was trying to trip her up, like he knew what she was hiding. "This weekend?" she asked, clearing her throat.

"You do like classical music, don't you? I don't know if I can be engaged to someone who doesn't appreci-ate the classics," he said, sounding sincere. Then she glimpsed his game face. "I *dare* you."

Marabelle hated backing down from a dare. She hadn't played competitive tennis for years by wimp-ing out on dares. But this time she had her mother to thank for going against her natural instinct. She picked at the seam of her skinny jeans. "Well…this weekend isn't good."

"Chicken."

Her head popped up. "Not at all. I have to be in Atlanta this weekend. My mother is in charge of a benefit and insisting I be there." With her fiancé, but the less she revealed the better. Besides, there was no way he could know about that part…she prayed.

"Alone? Or with some hot date?" Nick asked with an edge to his voice.

"No date. I just have to be there. Big Edna has commanded my presence, and there's no way out."

Nick pried her left hand from her tight clasp and interlocked his fingers with hers. "I'd be happy to go with you, Tinker Bell. We *are* engaged. Maybe it's time your mother met me." He brushed her knuckles with his thumb.

"Thanks. But bad idea. Trust me. No sane person wants to meet my mother. Besides, I'm not telling my parents about a fake engagement. I will never hear the end of it." Marabelle hated lying to Nick, since she'd already let the cat out of the bag to her mother.

He pulled into her driveway and cut the engine. Quiet filled the interior. He spoke low, penetrating the stillness. "Who said it's fake?"

The glow from the porch light illuminated the intensity of his expression. She *wanted* to believe him, believe he could actually want her. Believe their engagement could be real. But Marabelle was a realist living in a fairy tale on borrowed time.

He slipped off the hat he had given her. "I like your hair down." He eased the ponytail holder out, tunneling his fingers through her hair. She gasped as his magical fingers massaged her scalp.

"Remember this when you're away this weekend."

Then he bit her lower lip gently and kissed the pain away.

Clutching his shirt, she pressed into his hot mouth, tasting scotch and something else…desire, heat, and possession.

"You're mine. Remember that this weekend," he murmured, nibbling his way past her jaw and down her neck.

She eased away from his delectable lips. "That goes both ways. Don't make me come back and kick any more bony ass."

"Not a problem." He caught her mouth again in a hot, wet, crushing kiss, and all thoughts of bad weekends, mean girlfriends, and difficult job requirements fled her mind. He made her feel wanted, desired. Marabelle soaked in the pure thrill of being in his arms.

Nick broke the kiss suddenly, staring out the passenger window.

"What?" she whispered.

"Lilah." His lips curved into a half smile.

She gasped and jerked back into the seat.

"Front porch. Waving."

"This can't be happening," she groaned. "My nosy neighbors need to get a life."

"Think we gave her something to work with?"

Marabelle started to shake with laughter. "I have a feeling she could teach *even you* a few things."

Chapter 16

MARABELLE BOLTED FROM HER CLASSROOM THE NEXT day, the minute the last student left, and headed for Belk to buy designer makeup. She needed full battle gear to deal with Big Edna. No drugstore brands would cut it. On her way out, she spied a beautiful, lacy pink bra-and-panties set. She plucked her size from the rack and gave it to the sales clerk.

Later that night after packing for her trip, Marabelle was about to whip up a second batch of brownies for some of the guys who'd showed up uninvited, bearing beer and ice cream, when she heard more knocking at her door.

Somehow her tiny two-bedroom, one-bath bungalow had become the guys' new hangout. Go figure. They talked sports, girlfriends, music, whatever, and Marabelle posed as a cooking armchair psychologist, dispensing advice.

"If you make it, they will come…" she mumbled to herself, brushing flour off her hands. The guys were sprawled out, surfing the channels and picking at brownie crumbs in her small living room when she pulled the door open.

"What the hell is going on?" Nick stood on her threshold, scowling down at her like a mean junkyard dog chained to a pole.

Her insides jumped in glee. Even snarling, Nick was

still gorgeous. He'd clearly been plowing his fingers through his tousled hair. She took a moment to enjoy the view.

"You tell me. Apparently, I'm the little sister they never had." Nick's gaze scanned the living room. The guys acknowledged him, and then returned to the basketball game on TV. She reached for his hand and led him to the kitchen where they could talk in private.

"Are they camping out or something?" His expression was still irritated. "Did you have another party and not invite me…again?"

"Nope. Minding my own business, and suddenly I've got football players crawling out of the woodwork. Don't get me wrong. They're sweet in a huge, kinda scary way. I'm just glad we play for the same team. I wouldn't want to get on their bad side."

Nick shoved both hands in the front pockets of his jeans and lounged against the counter. "Do they want anything? Or just the pleasure of your company?" he asked, sounding bewildered.

"I'm going to try not to take that as an insult." She picked up a pink rubber spatula. "It's the pleasure of my cooking with a side of my company." She went back to stirring brownie batter. "They talk about their girlfriends and ask for advice, and because…maybe… I don't threaten them in any way."

"Have you looked at yourself lately?" He cocked his head to one side.

"Funny. You know what I mean. I don't come on to them or want anything from them. I'm like…a safe house." She dipped her finger in the bowl and pulled out a thick curl of brownie batter, shoving it in her mouth.

"Where you can go and get away from your problems," she said around the gooey chocolate.

He leaned forward, snagging her arm, pulling her into his embrace. "You look good enough to eat." He smiled at her upturned face. Marabelle started to lick a little blob of chocolate at the corner of her mouth, but he beat her to it, licking the chocolate with a flick of his tongue before kissing her lips. She gave a throaty laugh and arched into him, sliding her arms around his waist.

Yum. She didn't know what tasted better, Nick or the chocolate. Both were delicious, but Nick was less fattening. Settling in to enjoy another hot kiss, she heard heavy footsteps. Ricky DiMarco stood in the doorway and cleared his throat.

"Yo, we're heading out now." Ricky nodded at her. "Thanks for everything." Nick allowed her to turn, but kept her anchored against his front.

"Thanks for the brownies and letting us crash here," Rocker called from the front door.

Ty shook Nick's hand, pressing something into it, and winked at Marabelle. "We'll see ourselves out."

"You're welcome, guys. Stop by anytime," she called out.

As soon as the front door closed, Nick started nibbling on the side of her neck. "What did Ty put in your hand? That tickles!" She scrunched up her shoulder and attempted to pry open his fingers at the same time.

"Damn, woman. Stop wiggling."

"Show me what you're hiding," she said. He eased up on his hold, and she whirled around, grabbing his closed fist again. "Open up." Nick uncoiled his long fingers to a bunch of crushed bills. "I don't understand." She glanced from the money to his face. "Why did Ty give you cash?"

He shrugged. "To repay you for all the food and stuff."

Marabelle counted the bills. "Four hundred dollars? They don't owe me four hundred dollars. They don't owe me anything." Marabelle had never asked for money, and she hoped she hadn't put off that vibe. She hated being perceived as a charity case. Only Nick knew about her financial struggles. She pushed the money back into his hand. "Give it back. I'm not taking it."

He tossed the bills on the table. "I'm not giving it back. They want you to have it. You deserve it, and they can afford it—"

"Did you tell them I needed money?" Her voice sounded accusatory.

"Hell no. I don't discuss our personal affairs with the guys. Stop worrying over four hundred dollars. That's like handing you a twenty to those guys."

Marabelle was still stuck on "our personal affairs." Personal and affair sounded official. Like they were a real couple.

"End of discussion," Nick said. "New topic. How are you getting to Atlanta tomorrow?"

Marabelle glanced at the cash lying on her table. Even though it would help with her expenses, she didn't want money she hadn't earned from hard work. If she wanted handouts, she could pick up the phone and call home. Except the conditions attached were unbearable.

"Hey, you. Transportation? How?" Nick waved a hand in her face.

She blinked. "Driving, why?"

"I'd feel a lot better if you'd take my Range Rover."

Her brow creased. Was this a conspiracy?

"No way." She shook her head. "Absolutely not. I'm not taking your car."

"Marabelle, be reasonable. You'll be a lot safer in my SUV. You shouldn't be driving that toy you call a car on the highway."

"Nope." She stomped out of the kitchen and swung the front door open. "My car is fine." First the guys gave her money, and now Nick wanted to give her a car. This struck a nerve like no other. She'd already cut ties with her manipulative mother.

"Okay. Let's try this again." Nick stood militant in front of her, arms crossed. "I'll go with you"—she shook her head so hard her curls bounced across her face—"and I'll drive to keep you company." She glared at him. She didn't need a babysitter.

"You choose to go to some benefit alone when you could have a date? And not just any date, but your fiancé!" His voice rose in irritation as he splayed his hands on his hips.

"If you knew my mother, you'd understand. And for the record, you're *not* my fiancé!" She scowled. "Certainly not in Atlanta. I don't want to keep up pretenses in front of them. Being home is stressful enough."

Nick's expression grew darker than a stormy night. Looks didn't get much scarier. But Marabelle stood her ground.

"Have it your way. Dammit, I'm not begging you," he growled, and the tic in his right jaw jumped to life. "You're the most stubborn, foolhearted woman I've ever met. You wouldn't know a good thing if it hit you in the head."

Anger curled her hands into fists by her side. "Yeah? Who said you're such a good thing? My life was a lot less complicated, and less crowded, before I met you." Marabelle instantly regretted the childish things she'd just blurted out.

Nick slammed the front door shut and snarled in her face, "And boring as hell. If that's what you want, then don't let me stand in your way. Keep building your walls, Marabelle. Pretty soon no one will be able to touch you."

She flinched. His words hit her like a packed snowball. "I didn't ask for any of this. I'm trying to do my job and…and—"

"Life happened. It really bothers you to have people around who care. Who want to help. You're afraid of getting close. Afraid you might become dependent." He pushed his fingers through his hair, closing his eyes briefly. "How many relationships have you had? Not counting Clay. How many others?" His piercing gaze ripped through her.

Her chin tightened. "None of your business. I suppose all the one-night stands you've had with a bimbo in every town count as relationships? At least I have standards."

Nick sneered. "If we all lived like you, nobody would get any."

His words were a blow, but Marabelle came up swinging. "Know what your problem is?"

"No. Why don't you enlighten me?"

"You're spoiled, egotistical, and *jaded*. Along comes a plain kindergarten teacher, and you think you'll entertain yourself for a while—"

Nick hauled her against his hard body, slamming his mouth down on hers. This kiss was hard and punishing, and just as mind-destroying as all his kisses. Anger still boiled inside her, but she clung to him as if she were hanging from the side of a four-story building. When she made a soft noise, he broke the kiss. Marabelle grabbed onto the console table to keep from sliding to the floor. She gulped for air.

Nick smeared his thumb across her bottom lip, palming her cheek as her body trembled from aftershock. "Right now, I'm frustrated and hard." His voice was low and raw.

Tears prickled the backs of her eyes. "You should go…now," she whispered.

He stood rooted to the floor. Finally, he nodded and opened the door. "Be careful on the road." He hesitated before walking out.

Marabelle watched from the doorway as Nick drove away, before she broke down and sobbed.

Chapter 17

NICK BLASTED A STRING OF CREATIVE EXPLETIVES AND banged his fist against the steering wheel. That conversation had not gone as planned. Hell, nothing ever went as planned with Marabelle. She was stubborn, hardheaded, and unreasonable. He'd never encountered a woman who flat-out refused much-needed help. As if her carefully built life would tumble like a house of cards if she showed any sign of need.

He almost turned around twice to try to talk some sense into her, but he knew when to cut his losses. She'd dug her heels in so deep she'd left grooves in her hardwood floors. It took all his willpower to leave her there with tears brimming in her eyes.

Those tears had almost brought him to his knees. If he'd stayed, he would've been a goner. If she'd asked him to dress in a Cherokees cheerleading uniform and dance a routine on the fifty-yard line, he would've done it to keep her from crying. When it came to Tinker Bell, he would do just about anything. Too bad she didn't know that.

He'd practically begged her to take him to Atlanta. He never begged women...*ever*. He didn't need this shit. Marabelle disrupted his life and made him do things he swore he'd never do. He needed to call a time-out, bring the first string back in, and get this game back on track.

"Oh, hell."

He picked up his cell as he started to formulate a plan.

———⁓⁓⁓———

Marabelle drove to Atlanta in her perfectly capable Honda Civic. She drummed her fingers on the steering wheel and sang along with the radio, trying to forget. But last night's fight with Nick kept coming back to haunt her. How had it gotten so out of hand? She couldn't even remember her point and why it was so important. But she knew she needed to maintain control. And what was his problem? How could not accepting his offer of the car be such a deal breaker? Marabelle always fought her own battles. It made her tough and taught her how to survive. How come Nick couldn't understand that?

Three hours into her trip, she wished she were driving Nick's awesome, tricked-out Range Rover. She'd be sitting up higher in more comfortable seats and listening to his killer state-of-the-art sound system. What an idiot!

Four hours later, she turned into the country club parking lot where her parents were members and where she'd hit her first tennis ball. She pulled out a small overnight bag she'd strategically packed the night before with a Big-Edna-appropriate outfit. Marabelle knew better than to show up on her mother's doorstep wearing baggy jeans and an oversized tennis team sweatshirt. Entering the club through the nineteenth hole, she went directly to the ladies' locker room to change clothes.

Forty minutes later, Marabelle walked out of the club a different person. She had tamed her curls and applied so much makeup she'd jumped from fright at her reflection in the mirror. She smoothed her hands down the St.

John knit navy skirt and grimaced at the navy Ferragamo pumps on her feet. Big Edna would be thrilled.

Marabelle sat in the driveway of what used to be her home. The digital numbers on the car's dashboard flashed five o'clock. She unpeeled her fingers from the steering wheel, flexing them to ease the numbness. The aged, white-painted brick appeared ancient in the low afternoon sun. Black shutters framed tall, elegant windows and French doors. Trimmed shrubbery lined the length of the driveway. Edna kept a meticulous lawn with gorgeous azalea bushes. When in bloom, they were a spectacular sight. The Southern-style home appeared tranquil from the outside, but Marabelle knew better. Peace did not reign on the inside.

Time to face the music. She scooped up her matching navy Ferragamo handbag, courtesy of her mother, shoved her cell inside, and hopped out of the car. Her step hesitant on the old Chicago brick pavers, she straightened her shoulders and held her head high. Let the match begin.

"Marabelle! Welcome home!" Ed Fairchild flung the front door open before she'd hit the first step.

"Daddy!" She hurried forward and threw herself in her father's arms. Ed hugged her so tight Marabelle feared her ribs might crack. He smelled of expensive linen and of safe haven.

"I've missed my little girl. Let me get a good look at you." Ed held her at arm's length and gave an approving smile. "You look beautiful."

"I've missed you too, Daddy."

In one slow, sweeping motion, Marabelle took in the grand foyer. Some things never changed, like her mother's Baccarat chandelier glittering like a million diamonds, the sunny yellow walls with glossy white trim, the black-and-white checkered marble floors, or the smell of freshly baked bread drifting from the kitchen.

"Where is everybody?" she ventured.

"In the great room having cocktails."

Marabelle strained to recognize the voices. Ed guided her with his arm around her waist across the foyer. Twisting her hands, she said, "Dad, is Phoebe here?"

"Yes, we're all here. But I'm very disappointed in you, young lady."

Marabelle could hear the scowl in his voice, and her step faltered. *Great.* He's calling bullshit on her engagement. Edna must've given him an earful. "Um, I can explain—"

"I'm upset you didn't let me in on your good news."

She swallowed and faced her dad. "Sorry, Daddy. It happened so fast. And there were lots of…things, and I didn't want anything to go wrong so—"

"I'm teasing you. Nick's a fine man. Besides, what could go wrong?" Ed's eyes twinkled.

Marabelle turned and stopped dead in her tracks.

That!

"Hello, Tinker Bell."

She stared at none other than Nick Frasier.

A sudden wave of dizziness came over her. Ed chuckled. "Honey, what's wrong? You look like you've seen a ghost."

"You!" she finally said, untangling her tongue.

Nick strode through the double doors of the great room as if he owned the place and grabbed her hands, giving them a warning squeeze.

"That's what I love about her, always acts so surprised." In his low, velvet voice, he added, "Where's my kiss hello, darlin'?"

Marabelle opened her mouth to blast him, but nothing came out. Nick showed no mercy, taking full advantage, kissing her until her toes tingled. She heard Ed's chuckle and the closing of the double doors. Nick continued to tangle his tongue with hers while he played with her left hand. Finally, he lifted his head, and Marabelle felt disoriented. What the hell had just happened? She leaned back with her hands still on his chest and gasped.

On her finger sat a blinding, emerald-cut diamond ring flanked by two canary diamonds. "Wh…what is this?" she hissed. "And what are you doing here?" She couldn't take her eyes off the bling on her finger.

"*That* is an engagement ring. And I'm here because I'm your fiancé." Nick growled low. "Now it's my turn…what in the holy hell are you wearing? What happened to your hair?"

"Marabelle! Nick!" Big Edna barreled through the double doors. Marabelle managed to drag her gaze from the sparkling diamonds on her hand. Edna brushed a kiss on her cheek and gave her a brief hug. "Oh, Marabelle, you look lovely. That suit fits you perfectly. And your hair is fabulous." Edna had on a black suit almost identical to the one Marabelle wore.

"And, Marabelle, your Nick is a doll. We have very much enjoyed getting to know him."

Getting to know him! How long had he been here?

Edna linked her arms with Marabelle and Nick and strolled back to the great room. "I thought you'd never arrive."

Marabelle fiddled with the ring on her finger and tried to breathe.

"We have so much to discuss at dinner tonight. And, Marabelle, remember, not too much butter, dear."

*Annnnd…*she was home. Marabelle ground her teeth. Some things never changed.

The great room was the only one in the house that deviated from Edna's sherbet color palette. The two sofas upholstered in chocolate-brown chenille faced each other. An antique wood door made up the large coffee table. And the mahogany bar probably got more use than the big screen TV mounted over the limestone fireplace.

"Marabelle!" Phoebe jumped up from one of the matching sofas. "You look lovely. That suit is perfect on you, and your hair…your hair is fabulous."

"Yeah. I know." She hugged her sister, a clone of their mother. Over her shoulder, she gave Nick a see-what-I-mean look. Phoebe wore another version of the same suit in charcoal gray.

"Marabelle, what can I get you to drink? Nick, may I refresh your gin and tonic?" Ed was in perfect host mode.

"Since when do you drink gin and tonics?" Marabelle hissed under her breath to Nick and then called out, "I'll just have a beer, Dad."

"Oh, Marabelle. How gauche. Ed, fix her a gin and tonic with a splash of lime," Edna ordered. Nick gave her a nudge with his elbow. Yeah, even he had trouble saying no to Big Edna.

"Come, both of you, and sit next to me so we can all have a nice chat." Edna patted the seat next to her on the sofa. "Nick was telling us about how you two met. It's such a charming story."

Marabelle yanked Nick into the seat next to her. If she went down, he was coming with her.

Nick removed one of the silk throw pillows from behind his back and draped his left arm over her shoulder, pulling Marabelle tight to his side. Ed handed them their drinks and joined Phoebe on the opposite sofa.

Marabelle squirmed while Coach Charming rubbed her arm in a soothing way. How did he manage to project a comfort she never felt around her own family?

Nick looked at Marabelle with a glint in his eye. "I was getting to the part where I met you for the first time in your classroom. You remember? When you were on your hands and knees with your bu—"

Marabelle took great pleasure grinding her elbow in his ribs and watching him wince.

"Uh, Phoebe, where's Tom?" Marabelle asked, steering the conversation to a less volatile subject.

"Upstairs, changing his clothes for dinner—"

"Marabelle, we don't have much time." Edna never knew how to play along, always interrupting. "Nick tells us he doesn't care where we have the wedding as long as we don't take a year to plan it. He doesn't want a long engagement. Isn't that charming?"

What? Marabelle choked on her gin and tonic and started coughing. Nick placed their drinks on the coffee table before pounding her on the back.

"You okay, darlin?"

"Fine," she wheezed, her eyes watering. *You're a dead man.* "Uh, Mother, maybe we should table the conversation about the wedding for another time." Like never.

"Nonsense. We have so much planning to do. There's no better time than the present." Marabelle blotted her flushed face with a monogrammed cocktail napkin. Suddenly Edna shrieked, and Marabelle jumped a foot in the air.

"Let me see that!" Edna grabbed Marabelle's left hand, dragging her across the sofa. "Nick, this ring is gorgeous. Did you pick it out?" Phoebe jumped up to join the inspection of the huge rock that probably cost more than Marabelle's house.

"Yes. I wanted to surprise Tinker Bell, and I can honestly say I did." Marabelle heard a sneaky quality to his chuckle.

"Take it off. I want to try it on," Phoebe said.

"My, my. Mavis Stone is going to be pea-green with envy."

"I think it's stuck," Marabelle mumbled.

"Edna, let the girl breathe. She hasn't been home for five minutes."

"Oh, Ed. Be quiet. Marabelle doesn't mind that we admire her ring. Do you, dear?"

Marabelle squeezed Nick's thigh with her right hand. He cocked an eyebrow and gave her a lecherous grin. She tried pinching him, but his thigh was as giving as a cement block.

"Ed, bring in Marabelle's bags and put them in her bedroom. She needs to freshen up before dinner," Edna ordered, still admiring the shiny bauble on Marabelle's finger.

Typical. Marabelle had fluffed, buffed, and coiffed herself for a full hour, doing unspeakable things to her face and hair, and her mother still thought she needed freshening up.

Nick jumped at the opportunity for escape, following

Ed from the room. "I'll help with those bags." The big jerk.

Two seconds later, Tom Porter, Phoebe's pompous husband, entered. "Good evening, Marabelle," Tom said in his irritatingly nasal voice. He bent down and formally kissed Marabelle on the cheek. "It's so nice to have you back in Atlanta for a visit. It is only a visit, is it not?" the sanctimonious turd said.

Marabelle bared a grin that bordered on scary. "No amount of money could make me stay longer." No one paid her any mind.

"Nice ring, Marabelle," Tom said, giving her hand a cursory look. Phoebe gave Marabelle's hand a squeeze and followed Tom to the other sofa.

Nick strolled back in the room, settling next to Marabelle, and the insane portion of the conversation started up again.

"Marabelle, Nick said when he retires from coaching the Seminoles—"

"*Cherokees*, Mother. The Carolina Cherokees," she enunciated, rubbing her ring finger.

Edna fluttered her hand. "Seminoles, Cherokees… what difference does it make? They're both Indians." Nick started to cough to cover his laugh. "Anyway, he said he would live wherever you wanted. It didn't matter to him."

"He did what?" Obviously Coach Crazy had been running off at the mouth. She had a sudden wish to pound him in the head with a ball-peen hammer. Marabelle glared at a relaxed Nick from under her lashes.

"I think you should definitely consider living in Atlanta." Words continued to spew from Edna's mouth, all of them ridiculous. Marabelle gripped Nick's thigh for a second time. "Wouldn't it be wonderful? Nick could get a job with the Atlanta Braves, and you could liv—"

"The Atlanta Braves? Mother, the Braves are a base-ball team. Nick coaches football."

"It's no use, Marabelle. They're all the same to her," Ed said.

Edna found a new target. "You wouldn't know what I distinguish between. You're never around long enough to find out," she said.

It hadn't taken long for the bickering to begin. Marabelle rubbed her forehead, hoping to ward off a headache.

"And why is that? Have you ever asked yourself that question?" Ed shot back.

"Oh, I know what keeps you away, or should I say who…"

─────

Nick eased back against the sofa cushions, observing the heated exchange between the family members. Man, no wonder Tinker Bell had issues. Her family had "night-mare" written in bold, neon print. Marabelle deserved a Super Bowl ring for turning out so sweet and driven. From the looks of things, she stood alone in her corner, the exception being when her dad chose to be in town. Words didn't begin to describe the mother. Phoebe was milquetoast and Tom was a pompous prick. Interesting cast of characters.

Nick smiled to himself. Marabelle couldn't possibly shut him out. She needed him…badly. He was the only sane one around for miles. Ole Marabelle had herself a team whether she wanted one or not.

After Ed and Edna's argument wound itself down, Phoebe asked, "Marabelle, have you thought about what kind of wedding you'd like?"

"Wedding? What wedding?" Marabelle said.

The room grew eerily quiet as all eyes fixed on her.

Nick heard Marabelle gasp as she realized her blunder. "Ummm."

He covered her nervous hands with his. "What Tinker Bell means is she hasn't decided on a fancy wedding or if she'd rather elope."

Another pregnant pause, this one the size of a herd of African elephants.

Big Edna's eyes bugged out. "Marabelle Taylor Fairchild, you will do *no* such thing."

Then all hell broke loose.

"What will the neighbors say?"

"Give the girl a chance to speak—"

"If you say Las Vegas, I will faint right here on the spot."

"Ed! Do something."

Shit. He had really stepped in it. He cut his gaze to Marabelle, and his gut clenched at the stricken look on her face. This needed fixing fast.

Nick spoke over the frantic voices. "Uh, folks, eloping is not our preference." Slowly, the fury quieted down, and everyone stared back at him. He shifted in his seat, wishing he were anywhere but here. "Marabelle didn't want to put you to a lot of trouble. She knows how busy and important your lives are. She didn't want there to be a lot of pressure." Talking to families in living rooms used to be his specialty. Not today. He hadn't been this nervous since his last game against Dallas, when they were down by seven with only twenty-five seconds left on the clock. He would take those odds over this explosive situation any day.

"But you can't possibly consider eloping." Edna's voice actually shook.

At that moment, Nick vowed he'd get married underwater if it made Marabelle happy.

"Whatever makes Tinker Bell happy. That's what's most important, right?" He leveled his fiercest gaze at her family, the one his players dreaded, daring them to disagree with him.

"Absolutely. Honey, give it some thought and then tell us what you want," Ed offered.

Tension slowly began to seep from the room like sand through a sieve.

"Tinker Bell? Why does he keep referring to her as that?" Edna asked no one in particular, then started to babble about the benefit and all the people who'd be attending.

Finally Edna ran out of material and announced they had only thirty minutes to dress for dinner. She herded Nick and Marabelle up the stairs as she talked a bunch of shit about the Stones and their good-looking son, George III. Sounded like a real dweeb. The more she talked, the more he was glad he came for Marabelle. Nick wanted to salvage as much of this weekend as possible for her sake.

"Here we go," Edna singsonged. "Marabelle will stay in her room, and Nick, darling, you can have the guest bedroom next door, but I'm not a prude. I understand what engaged couples do these days." Edna gave him a knowing look.

A loud groan came from Marabelle's direction.

"Thank you, Mother. We can handle it from here."
She marched past him and into her bedroom.

"Remember, you only have thirty minutes. We
wouldn't want to be late for the Stones."

Nick closed the bedroom door to Edna's voice trail-
ing back down the stairs.

He turned and stopped. The strangest sensation of
stepping back in time to the late 1980s came over him.
Nick moved his gaze around Marabelle's bedroom. The
fabrics were all yellows and greens, and the furniture
girly white. Her desktop was cleared of any past school
work, but the bulletin board above it was full of old photographs, souvenirs, and winning ribbons from tennis
matches. A faded poster of Kevin Costner hung on her
closet door, and a classic poster of Bjorn Borg playing
tennis was still tacked on the back of the bathroom door.

His lips curved into a slow smile when he spied photographs of a young Marabelle, holding tennis trophies
twice her size. On top of her prissy white dresser, he
reached for a silver-framed photo of Marabelle in a
graduation robe hugging her dad.

—∿∿—

Marabelle watched Nick gather bits and pieces of her
childhood. Her bedroom had always been her one
haven, but his massive presence disturbed the usual
peace and calm.

"Excuse me," she said, breaking the deafening
silence, "we don't have all day. The Stones will be waiting." She planted her fist on her cocked hip.

"Nice picture of you and your dad." Nick reached for
the next frame as if they had all the time in the world.

The man made her insane. How could he appear so calm? And what was he doing here, screwing up all her well-laid plans? Marabelle knew how to survive her family, but she hated to have witnesses. She hated for Nick to see her reduced to acquiescing to keep the peace, like she had no mind of her own. She hated for him to see how little she mattered.

"And this picture—"

"What are you doing here?"

He replaced the photo on the dresser in one long, slow movement that had her gritting her teeth. "Looking at your pictures." He flashed his crooked grin and turned his attention back to the photos. He lifted another silver frame of her holding a large tennis trophy.

Marabelle snatched the photo from his hand and slammed it facedown on her dresser, rattling the other frames. "You know what I mean."

Finally, he faced her, his steely gaze locking with hers. "Your friend Beau, being a clever quarterback, informed me of how you needed a fiancé this weekend, and well, I don't know, I thought I'd lend a hand. Since *I am* your fiancé." He bit the last words off as if each one were a rusty nail.

Beau. He was a dead man. Marabelle couldn't believe he betrayed her like that. He was going to pay. Seeing his buzzard-picked-over-carcass on the side of the road held great appeal.

"Read my lips. We are not engaged," she snapped at Nick's stubborn face.

"That ring on your finger says otherwise, so let's play ball, Tinker Bell." His voice heavy with sarcasm, he grabbed her suitcase and tossed it on her bed.

The man was determined to insert himself into her life whether she wanted him there or not. Marabelle didn't need an audience for her humiliation this weekend. She yanked on the ring in question, but it wouldn't budge past her knuckle. "Where'd you get this, anyway? I think it's stuck. It won't come off."

Nick paid her no attention as he made quick work of plowing through her folded, neat stacks of clothes, turning her carefully thought-out packing into a whirlpool of fabrics and colors.

"Stop. What are you doing?" She forgot the ring, rushing over to gather up the clothes as quickly as he threw them out.

"I'm finding you something better to wear. Here. Wear this." He held out the pink Chanel skirt with the black silk top. "Jesus. Take that awful outfit off. I thought I was watching the Stepford wives downstairs." Nick reached for a black knit cardigan with pearl buttons and shoved it on top. "And take your hair down. I almost didn't recognize you." He gave her carefully arranged helmet head a look of disdain. "And what happened to your freckles? I can't even see them under that thick mask of gunk. Wash your face and put on about half the makeup you have on now."

"Are…are…you crazy! It took me forever to transform into this getup. Did you not see how thrilled my mother was?" She pointed up and down at herself with her index finger. "This is who she wants me to be."

He let the clothes fall on the disheveled mound he had created. "But it's not you. Why come here and pretend to be something you're not?"

"Because when you live in the palace, you serve only

the evil queen." Marabelle watched Nick struggle to keep his scowl in place, but he lost the battle, and a huge smile cracked open on his face.

Marabelle tried biting back her own smile and then she wailed, "This is so not funny. You almost gave me a heart attack down there."

"I could say the same." He looked pointedly at her knit suit. "I never thought I'd say this, but frumpy Marabelle is better than creepy Marabelle."

She whirled away and started pacing. "And don't even get me started on the whole elopement debacle." He at least had the decency to wince. "Nice cover, though. Thank God you think on your toes." She stopped wearing a hole in her carpet. "How long have you been here?"

"I flew in, rented a car, and got here around four."

"Not long enough to do too much damage," she murmured half to herself.

"Yeah, maybe because I'm not lying."

She blinked several times and then groaned. "How can you say that? I had my whole story worked out. And now this—"

"Jesus, Marabelle. Why didn't you just ask me? So far, since I've known you, I've managed to say no to you...oh, I don't know...how about...never." A wave of shock sliced through her. But Nick showed no mercy. "You still don't get it. I'm on your team. And that means I'll back you up and even take a sack for you."

Marabelle lowered her head and fiddled with the beautiful ring on her finger. Nick was right; he'd been nothing but helpful to her. "You don't understand...my family. They're careless—"

"So we deal with it together. You're gonna become a team player if it kills me."

Team player? She snapped her head up. She'd played on a team. In her day, she'd been one of the top-ranked doubles partners in the South. "Okay. But I get to call the plays."

Nick gave a harsh laugh. "Hell no. You suck at it. Now listen up." He glanced at his watch. "You have exactly twenty minutes to get changed. No fiancée of mine is going to be seen in public wearing *that*."

She glanced at the awful suit. "I can't do it. My mother will kill me."

He invaded her space, glaring down at her. "Not your call to make. Either you change yourself or I will gladly do it for you."

She leaned forward, tipping her nose in the air. Nick's don't-screw-with-me stare intensified, and Marabelle could tell he meant business.

Dropping her chin, she huffed, "And I thought my mother was bossy." She snatched up the change of clothes and stomped toward the bathroom door, muttering about arrogant fiancés under her breath.

He chuckled. "Oh, and Tinker Bell…" She stopped and frowned over her shoulder. "Put these on, too," he said, hitting her in the face with her new pink lacy bra and panties. "They're hot."

Exactly twenty minutes later, Marabelle emerged from the bathroom to find Nick stretched out in her overstuffed, green floral chair. He had changed into a charcoal-gray designer suit with a pale-blue dress shirt and silk tie in steel blue that matched his eyes. Clothing designers probably salivated all over him. He could make a plastic Hefty bag look good.

She sighed. "You look amazing."

Her stomach tumbled at his wide grin and sparkling eyes. "Thank you." He rose effortlessly from the chair. "So do you."

Marabelle had changed into the stylish pink Chanel skirt and black silk blouse and combed all the product from her hair, leaving it down and curly. A few strands were gathered and pulled up and away from her lightly made-up face.

"Welcome back, Tinker Bell." He reached for her hand and pulled. "Come here," Not one to resist his husky voice, she walked straight into his arms and sighed. Nick tilted her chin up with his thumb.

"Ahhh, I can see your freckles. Thank God." He kissed her nose.

She closed her eyes, breathing in his masculine scent. For the first time since getting up this morning, she felt relaxed.

"We'd better head down before they send out a search party," he said against her hair.

She shifted away from the comfortable home in his arms and picked up her small black evening clutch. He threaded his fingers through hers and opened the bedroom door.

"Uh, Nick? I can't get this ring off. I think my finger's swollen."

Nick simply smiled.

Chapter 18

NICK WAS PISSED. MAVIS AND GEORGE STONE GAVE Edna a run for her money with their snide remarks and useless gossip. And George III, who preferred to be called Trey, must've grown up with Tom, the pretentious snob, because he talked down his nose to everyone. Except Marabelle.

Trey maneuvered so he sat on Marabelle's right side at the round table, engaging in a private conversation for her ears only. Marabelle nodded a lot, grimaced a lot, and drank a lot. Nick understood her pain.

For once he was thankful for his fans who interrupted the table to speak to him or ask for an autograph. Nick had never been happier to oblige. Anything to break up the tedious evening.

After the fifth interruption, Edna couldn't help herself.

"Have people no shame? It's so rude to interrupt someone's dinner to ask for an autograph. If I were you, Nick, I wouldn't be so gracious, and maybe they'd get the message."

"Mother. *Please.* Nick is used to it and handles it with amazing grace and charm." Despite Marabelle's surprising defense, she sat as tense as a tuning fork.

"Society has so lowered its standards when it comes to celebrities. Why, look at that tramp Miley Cyrus…"

"What about Paris Hilton? That dumb hotel heiress."

"Today it's all about the Kar*trash*ians…"

Marabelle gave his thigh a reassuring pat under the table before slugging down another glass of wine. Nick buttered a piece of hot French bread and handed it to her, hoping it would sop up the alcohol pickling her insides.

Edna's butter radar must've gone off. "Oh, Marabelle, no butter. You'll get fat, dear. Remember the wedding gown." Marabelle dropped the bread on her plate like it was covered in maggots.

Nick picked it back up and handed it to her. "Eat," he ordered, "you are not fat." Slipping his arm around her shoulder, he announced to the entire table, "I happen to like a woman with a few curves on her, and I think Marabelle is perfect."

All conversation stopped. Edna's mouth gaped open, and Phoebe blinked like an owl.

Ed broke the strained silence. "I agree. Marabelle is perfect. And so is Phoebe. Both my girls are beautiful."

"Peyton Carter left Margie the minute she gained weight, after thirty-six years of marriage, and now he lives with a twenty-one-year-old."

"Peyton didn't leave because Margie gained weight."

"No, he left her because she insisted on separate bedrooms and wouldn't let him play golf with his buddies."

"He deserved it."

"You would think that."

Throughout the incessant sniping and gossiping, Marabelle barely touched her food. She was teetering on the verge of getting shit-faced, and Nick couldn't quite blame her.

———∾∾∾———

Marabelle entered the ladies lounge, locked herself in a stall, sat down with her head in her hands, and burst into tears. Poor Nick. How could he possibly stand another minute? He needed to leave before it was too late. Her family gave new meaning to the word "dysfunctional."

But Nick and stubborn were synonymous.

Maybe after tonight's horror show, she could convince him to go. Why did that make her feel worse? Her eyes teared up, and then she hiccupped. Marabelle liked having Nick on her team. To fight her fights and beat everybody up, while she stood on the sidelines, cheering. She wanted to eat bread with butter and wear her hair down. She wanted to curl into his broad chest and never leave.

What a wimp.

She hiccupped again.

Exiting the stall, Marabelle faced the vanity mirror and stifled a shriek at her reflection. With blotchy skin and swollen eyes, she looked as wretched as she felt. She pressed cold, wet paper towels to her face and repaired her makeup as best she could. Reaching for the door, she swayed a little.

"Not good." She gave her head a shake to clear the alcoholic haze. "There's not enough wine in the world to make this night any better. I'm ordering another bottle." She hiccupped, swung the bathroom door open, and stumbled out into the hallway right into Nick's arms.

"Whoa… You okay there, honey?"

"Nick." She gripped his arms to keep from falling. "You have to get out of here while you still can."

"What are you talking about? You're not gonna get sick on me, are you?"

"I don't think so." She paused for a minute to think. She didn't feel sick…yet.

Blinking, she refocused on Nick's gorgeous, kind face, gazing at her with complete affection. "You can't stay. It's not safe. Go…go home to Raleigh. You don't want to get caught when they finally drop the net."

Suddenly Nick picked her up and hauled her inside a dark utility closet next to the restrooms.

"What…where…?" she croaked as Nick locked the door. Complete darkness surrounded them, and the closet smelled of starched linens and industrial cleaning products.

"Shhh. Don't talk, just listen." Nick had her back against the door, and Marabelle felt his hot breath on her cheek. Surrounded by his spicy scent and warm body, she didn't know whether to panic or relax.

"I'm not going anywhere without you." His whispered words sent tingles down to her knees. "And we're not running. There's still another half to play, and I don't plan on losing." He planted a hot, wet kiss on her neck. She was thankful for his weight pressed against her; Nick kept her upright. "We're in this together, okay?"

She felt delicious nibbles on her ear.

"But…my family." She could barely speak past the sensations bombarding her ear, neck, toes, and all her lassie parts in between. He kissed his way down to her collarbone and cupped her breasts over her silk blouse, teasing her nipples into hard buds with a brush of his fingers.

Marabelle's breath caught.

He slanted his mouth over hers in a searing kiss that had her pulse soaring. A mewling sound escaped her lips as she tried to climb him with her legs. Nick hauled her up against him, allowing her the access she craved, wrapping her legs around him for even closer contact, wanting his touch…everywhere. His heat and hardness seared her. It took all she had not to scream.

Nick pulled back, his breathing rough and ragged. The rapid pounding of his heart matched hers beat for beat.

"We have to get out of here," he rasped.

She shook her head. Feeling bizarrely vulnerable, she wanted to stay in the dark closet forever. She wanted to forget her family, the pressures from school, her boring life, and eat, drink, and breathe Nick Frasier.

"No," she choked on a sob.

"Listen. I'm taking you home," he said, rocking her gently. "I'll tell your family you're not feeling well. Stay here and pull yourself together." Marabelle reluctantly slid her legs down. Nick moved back, and her body almost cried over the loss of heat.

"You okay, Tinker Bell?"

She nodded but realized he couldn't see her in the dark. "Yea…yeah."

"Good girl." He cupped her face in his hands and kissed her hard. Then he was gone.

Marabelle sat quietly on the ride home. Nick had hustled her out of the restaurant, but not before pulling their waiter aside, ordering an expensive bottle of champagne for the table, and picking up the tab for the dinner. He wanted to make sure the family from *One Flew Over the Cuckoo's Nest* stayed occupied for at least another hour.

Nick had the top down to the rented convertible, the cool air being the next best thing to a cold shower.

The Atlanta skyline passed by in a festival of lights. Marabelle dropped her head back and exhaled.

"Why the sigh, Tinker Bell?"

"Thanking my lucky stars you saved me from a fate worse than death. Otherwise, I'd still be sitting there, listening to Trey Stone bore me to death with stories about his igneous rock collection." As Nick pictured dickhead Trey in a white lab coat, giving a scintillating lecture on rocks, he burst out laughing.

She joined in and then hiccupped, covering her mouth with her hand.

Oh boy. "You gonna be sick? It's a rental, so I don't care, but I'd prefer if you didn't."

"Nope. Just hiccups. Only thing that got rid of them was kissing you."

"Yeah, I get that a lot," he said dryly.

Another hiccup.

Nick snorted. "Darlin', you're drunk. Why do you think you can drink like a three-hundred-pound lineman, when you weigh next to nothing?"

Marabelle half scoffed, half hiccupped. "I'm not drunk. And according to Big Edna, you can never be too thin."

He arched a brow at her. "Trust me. You're drunk. And thin enough. Do me a favor and don't buy into all that crap about being so thin your bones protrude. I can't think of anything that turns me off more."

Hiccup. "But my mother—"

"Talks a lot of shit. No offense, but your mother and her priorities are way out of whack."

"Ya think?" Her sharp glare said it all. "Now you can see why I didn't want you to come."

Nick pulled into the Fairchilds' driveway and turned off the ignition. He faced Marabelle and her big, Hershey's Kisses eyes. "But aren't you glad I'm here?" He rubbed his thumb across her bottom lip. "To kiss away your hiccups?" he whispered as he pressed his lips against her delicious mouth.

Whoa. Her head swayed back.

"You okay?" He laid a hand on her forehead. Clammy.

"Fine. I'm not drunk." She turned, hiccupped, and fumbled with the door handle.

Nick shook his head. "Here we go again."

Marabelle tumbled out when he opened the passenger door. Nick steadied her on her feet.

"Come on. Off to bed you go. I swear, woman, I think you drink on purpose so I can't take advantage of you."

She swayed into him, grabbing his lapels. "That's ridiculous." Hiccup. "I drink because I get nervous." She sniffed his clothes. "Mmm, you smell divine."

Then she moved unsteadily toward the house. "Hey!" She whirled back, slamming into his chest. Nick swore as he propped her up. "Why can't you take advantage of me? Trey Stone wants to drink rum toddies with me"—hiccup—"in Aspen"—hiccup—"in a hot tub."

"Give me a freakin' break. When I do take advantage of you, we won't be doing it over dumb rum toddies." Nick figured at this slow pace, the Fairchilds would be home before Marabelle reached the front steps. He bent down and pressed his shoulder into her stomach, lifting her up and over in a fireman's hold.

"What the hell?" she said against his back.

"You needed rescuing."

Nick carried Marabelle into the house and up the stairs to her bedroom, depositing her unceremoniously on her bed. He watched Marabelle scramble to a sitting position and try to push her skirt down.

"You're lucky I didn't get sick from all that jostling." She frowned.

He bent and slipped off her heels.

"What are you doing?" she demanded.

"Undressing you for bed."

"You wish." She scooted off the bed. "I'm perfectly capable of undressing myself."

"Mind if I watch?"

"Out!" She pointed to the door.

Nick shrugged. "Suit yourself."

Nick shucked off his suit coat and tossed it on the painted French armchair in the guest bedroom he'd been assigned. He slid his tie off and unbuttoned his dress shirt with a few angry jerks.

Abstinence was taking its toll. Since Nick had met Marabelle, his annoyance had risen to an all-time high. So far he'd only managed a few heavy petting sessions, topped with a lot of arguing and a shitload of frustration on the side. He'd never been one of those guys who took advantage of drunk women. But right now, that lofty commandment didn't seem to be making its noble appearance.

Nick raked a palm over his face. Who was he kidding? It wasn't just the lack of sex that had him on edge. He really, *really* liked Marabelle. They got each other. They laughed and talked…about everything. He respected her more than any woman he'd ever dated. The way she fought her way through life, trying to appear as tough as shoe leather, but treated her kids as if they were her own. And the way she held her tongue and didn't tell her mother to shove it when Edna blatantly insulted her.

Nick peeled off the rest of his clothing. Time for another cold shower. Grabbing a clean pair of boxers, he was about to head into the bathroom when he heard voices in the driveway below. Frustrated, he closed his eyes.

Nick moved to the window and pulled back the silk drape. He watched Phoebe and Tom's car clear the driveway, and then the fireworks began.

Big Edna and Ed started to have words, and it didn't take a genius to figure out over what. Ed wanted to take off for the night, and Edna wanted to kill him. As the fight escalated, Nick's first concern was Marabelle. She carried around more than enough emotional baggage when it came to her family. She didn't need another truckload. He didn't think twice.

Standing in the hallway, Nick tapped and pushed Marabelle's bedroom door open at the same time. Silvery light bathed the room, enough for him to see her clothes tangled on the floor, as though she'd fought to get them off. His gaze tracked the scattered trail and landed on a lump on top of the bedcovers.

Marabelle was crashed out on the bed in nothing but lacy pink panties and bra, her heart-shaped ass exposed for him to admire in all its feminine glory. He appreciated the hell out of the view. Relief washed over him that she was sleeping and had missed the war raging between her parents. Doors slammed below, but she didn't budge.

Nick eased the coverlet from under her sleeping form and covered her, mourning the loss of all that feminine fluff.

Tossing his robe aside, he crawled under the sheets and gathered her close. Marabelle murmured something unintelligible and curled into his chest as if she always slept like that. Nick kissed the top of her soft curls and breathed in her refreshing scent. Closing his eyes, he finally relaxed. A feeling of contentment poured over him for the first time since meeting her. He couldn't explain the sensation, but knew deep down it was right. He drifted off to sleep with Marabelle cradled in his arms.

———⁓———

Marabelle was having the most delicious dream. Nick was kissing her neck at that very sensitive spot he'd discovered, and rubbing her breast, causing other body parts to hum the *William Tell* Overture.

A car door slammed.

What? She cracked one eye open to a mere slit. Soft light filtered through the sheers at her window. She closed her eye. Back to her dream. Cymbals crashed. Trumpets blared.

Wait.

Where was she?

A door closed below.

Her eyes sprang open. A husky voice near her ear swore.

This was no dream.

It all came flooding back. She was trapped in her mother's house, spooning with Nick while he copped a feel. No! That couldn't be right. Suddenly, Marabelle was wide-awake.

She turned her head, only to regret the movement.

"Morning, Tinker Bell. How do you feel?" Nick rumbled as she stared at his sleepy, heavy-lidded eyes. She hadn't realized she'd dreamed about how he might look first thing in the morning. Her dreams were *way* below par. He was disgustingly sexy, and even better-looking disheveled with morning stubble.

She could only imagine how bad she looked, if her pounding head was any indication. She blinked, hoping to clear the heavy haze smothering her brain.

"I'm afraid to ask this…did you sleep here last night?"

Nick pulled her closer and started nibbling on her neck again. "Uhmm…mmm."

She tried to concentrate, but her body got swept up in awareness.

"Yoo-hoo, Marabelle, time to get up."

Until her worst nightmare knocked and opened her bedroom door. Marabelle gasped and not in a good way.

"Good morning, Nick." Edna's perfectly coiffed head peered through the opening. "We have a million things to do today. Breakfast in thirty minutes."

Marabelle shoved Nick's hand off her breast and scrambled for the covers.

"What time is it?" Nick asked casually, as if he always spoke to Marabelle's mother while in bed, groping her daughter.

"Seven forty-five."

"That late, huh?" he added dryly.

"Nick, how do you take your coffee? I'll bring it up."

"No. Mother, *please*. We'll be down shortly." This had to be hell on earth.

Edna nodded, unfazed, and closed the door with a click. Marabelle groaned. Bizarre didn't begin to describe her life. How did she end up half-naked in bed with Nick in her mother's house? Half-naked!

She turned to face Nick, causing the covers to slide down. She reached for them, but his hand got in the way.

"Where are my clothes?" She tried slapping at his hand fondling her breast.

"All over the floor where you dropped them."

"Why would I do that?" she asked, wrestling him and the covers.

"Beats me. But you did leave your bra and panties on." He smiled, taking full control of the covers and her last barrier.

"Huh?" Marabelle glanced down at her naked breasts. "Where's my bra?"

"Well, now that is the damnedest thing," he drawled.

Her gaze flew to his face. He filled his large, warm hand with her breast, and her toes curled.

"Sometime last night, you bolted straight up, squirming your way out of your bra like you were on fire, then flopped back down, dead asleep."

He appeared guileless, but looks could be deceiving. "Why would I have done that?"

"Darlin', people do the strangest things when they're drunk."

"Drunk?" Marabelle tried racking her hungover brain. She remembered driving home with Nick, then her memory got murky.

"Now, where was I?" Her muddled mind gave up at the sound of his velvet voice. Nick covered her with his yummy naked chest and went back to neck-nibbling.

Marabelle lost track of time, reveling in the sensuous sensations of being Nick's next meal, when she remembered what waited for them downstairs. "Nick. That was my mother, by the way." She could feel him smile just below her ear. His hand brushed over her breast, lingering long enough to ignite a spark before moving lower.

And lower.

Heat spread low and fast like wildfire through dry brush. Marabelle bit her lip to keep from moaning. He kissed his way down the column of her neck to her shoulder, to just above her breast. She rocked under him, and he captured a nipple in his hot mouth, creating a shock that made Marabelle jolt halfway off the bed.

"Easy," he whispered. His hand slid to the top of her thigh, easing the elastic of her panties down, his fingers played with her inner thighs, and her legs opened with no further invitation. She needed…him…to… His magical fingers found the spot.

She clutched at his shoulders when he slid one big finger inside her, and her eyes flew open.

Nick raised his head. "Tell me if it feels good."

"Good would be an understatement."

"It's going to get even better."

Marabelle swallowed hard. This felt pretty spectacular. Nick's lips trailed down her body, sucking, licking, and lapping as he went. When he reached her stomach, he played for a while, tonguing her belly button.

Marabelle panted. "Tickles…"

"I'll make it stop." He shoved her panties away and

then bent his head and licked into her heat. Marabelle's eyes rolled back inside her head. She stiffened for one brief second, and then molten lava consumed her. Marabelle clutched the sheets as her lungs seized. "Yes...there." The flick of his tongue caused a pulsing vibration that shook her body. Tension started deep in her belly and grew tighter and tighter. Marabelle's back arched, and her pleasure escalated until she shattered, crying out.

Collapsing back into the bed, she was unable to do anything but feel.

Nick pulled her panties back up, kissing his way up her belly before stretching out beside her. She turned her head, blinking at him in wonder.

"I think I had an orgasm," she said in awe.

He flashed his killer smile. "I know you did."

She touched his cheek and saw Nick's face, tender and intent. "That was amazing. Thank you."

"My pleasure," he murmured, and his gaze locked with hers, glowing with heat and something else...

Worried, she whispered, "What about you?" He swooped down for another kiss, slipping his tongue inside, but quickly breaking the connection.

"*Cold* shower. Mother waiting," he managed in a rough voice, looking as whacked as she felt.

Reality slapped Marabelle in the face. "Oh God."

Nick planted a kiss on her nose and slipped from the bed, wearing black boxer briefs that did nothing to hide his erection. She peeled her eyes from that impressive sight in time to ogle the rest of his glorious physique. His fluid motions made hard muscles ripple just under the surface as he moved. Nick closed the bedroom door behind him, and Marabelle shook her head, which she instantly regretted. Her head still throbbed…and not in a good way.

Even after she'd showered and dressed, Marabelle still tingled from her first fantastic orgasm. Details from the night before eluded her, but she didn't care. A very hot, totally ripped, fascinating guy waited for her downstairs, and for once, she wasn't going to over-analyze it. There'd be plenty of time for hand-wringing, forehead-slapping, head-banging regret. But right now, in Atlanta, she'd pull a Scarlett O'Hara and worry about that tomorrow.

In the large country kitchen, a freshly showered Nick was already seated at the breakfast table. Marabelle stopped at the entrance and admired him in all his stubbled, hunky glory.

Ed peered over the morning paper. "Good morning, Marabelle. Did you sleep well?"

She had no idea.

"Uh…fine." A sharp pain attacked the backs of her eyes, and she winced.

"Headache, dear?" Edna handed her a bottle of Advil with a glass of water.

Edna served scrambled eggs with a side of bacon, buttered toast, and freshly squeezed orange juice to Nick. For Marabelle, a small scoop of cottage cheese and four fresh strawberries on the side.

No eggs. No bacon. No butter. No flavor.

"Nick, how about a round of golf today? Marabelle can join us if you two don't want to be separated," Ed suggested.

"Not today, Ed. I'm taking Marabelle shopping at

Neiman's. We have a lot of ground to cover for the wedding." Edna continued to map out a day from hell that didn't help Marabelle's aching head, until her mother and Ed started bickering. Then she thought her head would explode.

Embarrassed that Nick was a witness to her family's twisted dynamics, Marabelle only played with her food. Cottage cheese tended to make her gag. Not the best breakfast to feed a hangover. To her surprise, Nick switched plates with her.

"What are you doing?" she asked under her breath.

"I like cottage cheese. Eat your breakfast so you can survive this day," he said low, spearing a strawberry.

Edna stopped nagging Ed long enough to monitor Marabelle's food intake. "Why are you eating Nick's breakfast? There's butter in those eggs, dear."

"I insisted. Don't want my fiancée weak from hunger. From the sounds of things, she's going to need to be in top shape," Nick said.

"About that golf—"

Edna glared at Ed. "Absolutely not. I've scheduled an appointment for Marabelle to get her hair cut and styled so it won't look so…so wild." Marabelle grabbed Nick's thigh under the table with her fork paralyzed halfway to her mouth.

"Eat, babe," he encouraged softly. Then Nick blasted Big Edna with his cocky grin. "The first thing I noticed about Tinker Bell was her beautiful curls. It's one of the things I love about her. A man's real particular about the way his woman wears her hair." The more he spoke, the thicker his drawl.

"Here's what I think we should do today." He pinned

Edna with his take-charge stare. "Let's hit the stores until lunch time. After that, Marabelle, Ed, and I would like to play a few holes of golf before the benefit tonight. How does that sound to everyone?"

Ed gave a knowing wink. Marabelle hid the triumph in her eyes by concentrating on her food. And Big Edna gave an excellent impression of a deer caught in the headlights.

Upstairs after breakfast, Marabelle cornered Nick in the hallway before she headed back down to face her mother's wrath. "If I have to be tortured today, then so do you," she said, poking a hole in his chest with her finger. "You're not going off with my dad and leaving me with *Mommy Dearest*." Ed had offered to take Nick to the club for the morning, leaving Marabelle to her mother's evil devices.

"Afraid of her, huh?" He chuckled.

"Terrified."

"Marabelle, you ready?" Edna called up. "I want to show you these adorable hats. They say *Bride* and *Groom* on the front in sequins."

Nick's eyes widened in alarm. Snagging her hand, he yanked her toward the stairs. "Shit. Let's go!"

Chapter 19

"YOU SUCK," MARABELLE SAID TO HERSELF AS SHE showered, preparing for the dreaded benefit. Somewhere between cottage cheese and turkey sandwiches—with no mayo—she'd fallen in love. With the unattainable, notorious Nick Frasier. Even after all the self-lectures on avoiding that slippery slope of unrequited love, she hadn't heeded her own warning. But as Nick didn't feel the same, it would be a huge mistake to tell him.

Nope, her lips were sealed. For now, she had this great guy with an amazing ability to make others feel good, even cherished. No way would she ruin that by blurting "I love you." Somehow Nick had crept under her radar and entrenched himself in her life and in her heart. Since she'd met him, he had supported, defended, rescued, fed, and cared for her more than anyone else she'd ever known. In only a few short weeks, he'd become a constant in her life. Lord knew he handled her mother better than she ever had. Edna couldn't be more gaga over him. How could she ignore something that huge?

She smiled as she slathered lavender lotion on her legs, remembering their round of golf that afternoon. As much as Nick demonstrated his gentlemanly qualities, he was a fierce competitor first and foremost. He and her dad had traded long drives all afternoon, but Marabelle ruled the greens. Marabelle could putt the dimples off the golf ball, and her putter hadn't let her down today. At first, Nick seemed surprised by her talent, but by the end of the round, he was her biggest fan.

Now, if only she could survive this evening.

Marabelle made a face at the matronly black cocktail dress her mother had insisted she wear. How could she get her head in the game wearing that boring dress? She wanted to look glamorous for Nick. Her gaze was drawn to the bronzy, sexy designer dress from her dad.

Gnawing her bottom lip, she glanced up as Nick knocked and entered her room.

Nick's gorgeous frame filled out a custom-made tux. Light bounced off his onyx and gold studs, and his tan complexion made a stark contrast to his white tuxedo shirt. Marabelle mentally pouted. The perfect prince to her imperfect Cinderella.

"Please tell me that is not your idea of formal wear." He indicated the oversized Clemson T-shirt she wore.

"No. But it doesn't make any difference, because no matter what I wear, I'm never going to look like I belong with you. You belong in Hollywood!"

Nick chuckled. "Tinker Bell, you're talking nonsense. Show me what you're going to wear, and don't let it be that ugly black dress, because between that and the T-shirt…I vote the T-shirt."

"Okay. Ugly black dress is option one, or bronze dress is option two." She motioned toward both dresses lying on her bed. "Guess which one my mother votes for."

"Forget it. Wear the bronze thing. Show me the shoes." She pulled out the gold Manolos from her dad. "Very nice." Checking his Rolex, he said, "You have exactly thirty minutes to pull it together."

"Yes, sir!" she said with a mock salute.

Nick deliberately checked his watch again. "Twenty-nine and a half. Don't make me come back up here."

"Out!" Marabelle hurled her shoe at him, only to hit the back of the door. He was already on the other side, laughing.

———∿∿∿———

Nick waited behind the bar in the great room, savoring a tumbler of Johnnie Walker Black on the rocks. The weekend had turned out better than he'd anticipated. No doubt the family, particularly the mother, was certifiable, which explained Marabelle's neuroses. But despite a few hurdles, he'd actually started to enjoy himself. He and Marabelle had worked as a team to keep everybody in line, because this weekend had had the makings of a train wreck.

This morning might go down as one of his best ever. He never knew giving pleasure could be so sweet. He loved exploring her body and planned to keep on doing it until this obsession faded, or Marty Hackman called off the dogs, and Nick could get unengaged and back to his normal life.

Then his mouth pressed into a grim line as he pictured his life before Marabelle. Grueling hours of meetings, media interviews, game films, and practices during the day. Shallow women, promotional parties, and meaningless sex at night. Nick had always been passionate about his life in the NFL, as a player and now as a coach. But his life outside of football could use overhauling. As much as it rubbed him raw, Marty was right. He needed to settle down and to step away from everything and remember what was important. And it wasn't just a piece of ass. Nick cringed at all the bad press he'd garnered over failed relationships and dumped divas. He was not proud of those relationships or his own behavior. But with Marabelle, things were different. He was different. Yeah, they argued and fought and got in each other's face, but in the end, they had each other's back. His time with Marabelle had become his sanctuary. With her, he was able to unwind and forget about everything else.

She was important.

He stopped, his drink halfway to his mouth. Marabelle stood in the doorway, smiling at him. In that moment, his heart actually expanded, staggering him with the breadth of his feelings for her. If he didn't know himself better, he would've thought this was love. He tamped down the flutter in his heart and ignored the tingly feeling spreading through his gut. Because this was temporary. Right? Oh hell.

His gaze slid from her sexy sandals, up around the bronzy fabric molded to her curves, to her breasts where the crisscross dress revealed way more than it covered. *Damn.* He swallowed hard. Curls fell around her shoulders, with several strands gathered on top. His gaze landed on her full, glossy lips as her smile slightly dimmed at his scrutiny.

He returned his drink to the bar with a thud. Satisfaction spread through him better than any aged scotch. She was drop-dead gorgeous, and she was all his.

"Just in time." He tapped the face of his watch. "Let's go."

Marabelle's mouth gaped open. Nick kept moving as he herded her through the foyer toward the front door.

She came to an abrupt halt, removing her elbow from his grasp.

"Is that it?" Brown eyes snapping.

"What?"

"Aren't you going to say something?"

"I did. *Let's go.*"

She rounded on him and exploded. "I'm going to give my mother a fatal heart attack at the biggest event of her life, wearing this dress with these shoes and my hair down, and all you can say is *let's go?*"

Her chest heaved. He feared—more like hoped—her breasts would spill from the front of the dress. *Please.* He watched, fascinated. She stomped her foot.

Christ. Almost.

"Well?"

Nick peeled his gaze away from her world-class cleavage. What were they arguing about? Oh yeah. "I could say you look beautiful and sexy."

She relaxed her stance.

He fingered one of her soft curls. "But you don't want to hear that. I remember you telling me you didn't want to draw attention to yourself. You magnanimously wanted all the attention to fall on me"—he ran his index finger along the slim column of her neck—"where it belongs," he said with a crafty laugh.

Her eyes narrowed.

He bent and brushed her lips with a soft kiss. "You look amazing. If I see one guy look at you the way I am, I will break both his legs," he murmured.

Marabelle's full-wattage smile beamed back. "Good. My work is done here."

"Are you wearing a bra?" He'd sure like to explore

for himself but didn't want to risk showing up late and ending up on Edna's hit list.

"Can you see anything?" Marabelle peered down at the top of her dress.

"Are you?"

She checked her reflection in the mirror in the foyer. "You can't see anything." She stood on tiptoe and kissed him on the jaw.

Damn. He was going to have to watch her like a hawk.

~~~

"Not so fast." Marabelle snagged a second glass of champagne from a waiter passing through the crowd milling around outside the ballroom. She observed Nick, holding court with a group of men dying to rub elbows with a famous football player/coach and a few women dying to rub something else.

"Your Nick is very special," her sister said. Phoebe wore a black strapless tulle cocktail dress and metallic silver heels, appearing cool and collected with her blond hair slicked back in a French twist. Phoebe epitomized tidy and elegant, something Marabelle hadn't quite mastered.

"You could say that again." Marabelle caught some older woman batting her big green eyes at Nick.

"Where's Mother?" The last time she'd seen her, Ed had had to fan her face with the auction program to keep Edna from fainting over Marabelle's dress.

"After Dad had her breathe into a paper bag, she went to check on the band. By the way, you look fabulous in that dress. And since Nick can't keep his eyes off you, I think he agrees." Marabelle glanced toward the stud in question and caught him smiling at something the older woman purred in his ear. He looked up at that precise moment and winked at her.

"You're very brave. I don't know if I could handle someone as handsome and famous as he is."

"What do you mean?" Marabelle asked, surprised at her sister's admission.

Phoebe shrugged her elegant shoulders. "All the men want to associate with him because of who he is, and all the women want a piece of him because of how he looks." Phoebe leaned closer and whispered feverishly, "That's Mimsy Peterson. She's currently on her third husband and has slept with half the men in Atlanta. I wouldn't trust her with my dog."

Oh really? Just then, Mimsy made a big show of pressing her hand into Nick's bicep. That did it. Marabelle lurched forward.

"Marabelle, don't!" Phoebe reached for her but caught only thin air.

Nick looked up in time to see Marabelle push her way through the crowd with that bulldog look on her face. Not good. He quickly excused himself to head her off at the pass before she went postal and her mother never forgave her. Or him.

"What took you so long?" He smoothly veered her away from enemy territory.

"You attract them like flies. I can't leave you alone for one second," she huffed.

"Exactly. Now let's make your mother ecstatic and drive up the bids on all the auction items." Nick steered her away from trouble toward the silent auction tables and entered bids on most of the items being offered. He noticed Marabelle over by the jewelry display, admiring a David Yurman silver-and-gold cable bracelet with diamonds. When she moved on to the next table, he bumped the bid on the bracelet high enough to discourage other bidders.

"Yoo-hoo! There you are. I've got wonderful news." Edna glided toward them, wearing an emerald-green ball gown and a triumphant smile. "The ladies on the committee have decided to hold a live auction for the dancing later. Like *Gone With the Wind*."

Nick squeezed Marabelle's hand as she and her sister exchanged looks.

"The men have to bid on the lady of their choice to dance with her." Edna clapped her hands. "And all the money will go to Magnolia House." Edna patted Marabelle's arm. "Mimsy Peterson wants to add 'ladies' choice' so—"

And then it happened.

Marabelle blurted, "Mother, Mimsy Peterson is a slut. She's not getting within a ten-mile radius of Nick."

A few feet away, conversations stopped, and someone started snickering. Big Edna looked as though she had swallowed a sweaty athletic sock. Phoebe stared wide-eyed, and Marabelle slapped her own hand over her mouth. Nick almost choked stifling his laugh.

Ed approached just in time. He looked from Marabelle's shocked expression to Edna's pale face.

"What's going on?"

"I'll tell you." Edna fumed. She motioned for Ed to lower his head and whispered in his ear. Poor Tinker

Bell. She'd gone and done it now. Nick wrapped his arm around her waist and hugged her stiff form to his side.

Ed showed no surprise. "On this, Marabelle happens to be right. Mimsy Peterson is a slut. Nick, you'd be wise to stay away," he said low enough for their ears only.

"Ed, you're as bad as Marabelle. Do not encourage her outrageous behavior. And, Nick, if you don't get her under control, I will hold you personally responsible." Edna glared at him with a perfected evil eye. Nick appreciated its effectiveness. Edna grabbed Ed's arm and marched toward the ballroom.

Nick dropped a kiss on Marabelle's head. "Damn, honey. Now you've got your mother threatening me. What do you have to say for yourself?" She squared her shoulders in what he recognized as her stance of defiance.

"Just doing my job, Coach."

He grinned. "Atta girl."

Inside the ballroom, Marabelle and Nick wove their way through the decorated tables draped in cloths of varying shades of green moiré, with clusters of magnolias as centerpieces. The evening had barely begun, and Marabelle wanted nothing more than to go home, throw on her comfy sweats, and eat a dozen Krispy Kreme doughnuts. And when she said home, she meant Raleigh.

Marabelle knew this night would be a nightmare. And once again, she'd managed to embarrass herself. She didn't care what her mother thought. But she didn't want Nick laughing at her and looking at her as if she were some joke. Rounding the backs of gold ballroom chairs swagged with ribbon and more magnolias, they reached their assigned seats the same time as Phoebe and Tom.

"Mother has really outdone herself. Oh." Phoebe hesitated, reading the place cards. "Mimsy Peterson is seated next to Nick and—"

Sweeping up the place cards, Marabelle said, "Over my dead body—"

"Excuse us, please." Nick replaced the cards she'd grabbed up and hustled her toward the French doors leading out to the terrace.

"What are you doing?" She tried wrenching her arm free.

He closed the door and pulled her toward the railing away from the party. "Preventing you from making another scene and having the wrath of Edna come down on you. Again."

So this was the thanks she got. "I suppose you'd rather have that black widow spider next to you, groping you under the table," she snapped. "I was trying to protect you."

"I appreciate your concern, but I think I can handle it."

"But that's my job." And then it hit her like a gong to the head—Nick didn't need her. Maybe he had enjoyed or even encouraged Mimsy's come-on.

Marabelle silently counted to ten. "You're right. I'll stay out of your way." Rigid with fury, she turned to leave, but Nick spun her around to face him.

"Listen, you need to exercise some self-control. Your actions affect other people. What do you think will happen if you change the seating arrangement and pick a fight with Muffy?"

"*Mimsy.*"

"Whatever. You go in there half-cocked, and your mother will never forgive you, not to mention half of Atlanta."

The party's muffled noises filtering through the French doors brought her back to reality.

More than embarrassed and wishing she'd never agreed to this charade, Marabelle lowered her head. "You're right. Mother would kill me. I won't make a scene." She lifted her head and locked gazes with the man she loved but would never have. "But you're on your own." Quietly, she turned and went back inside the ballroom. This time Nick let her go.

The cool night breeze brushed past Nick, but he was too tied up in knots to appreciate it. He'd do anything not to return to the stuffy party. He leaned his arms on the stone railing overlooking the golf course. The smell of fresh-cut grass lingered in the air.

He knew Marabelle's outbursts stemmed from jealousy and not from the game they were playing. He was flattered. What guy wouldn't be? Marabelle didn't do anything half-assed. No, she forged full steam ahead, bulldozing anything in her path. And he would give anything to have her unbridled passion directed at him in bed.

But when the fireworks died down, what then? He winced as he pictured her chocolate-brown eyes all hot and bitter. What next when the romance fizzled? His chest tightened at the thought. No way Marabelle would blast her hurt on Twitter or make false accusations. She made scenes, but only because she believed she was righting a wrong. Not because she was vindictive or out to get revenge.

Marabelle was protecting her heart. Suddenly Nick felt all of his thirty-eight years. A part of him couldn't exactly blame her.

"It's getting chilly out here." Lost in his mental tirade, he hadn't heard Phoebe approach. She stood, poised by his side, wrapped in a silver cover-up. "She gets to you, doesn't she?" He lifted a brow, not giving anything away. Nick didn't know whose side Phoebe was on: Marabelle's or Edna's. "Marabelle has always marched to the beat of a different drummer."

"You can say that again."

"Even when we were kids, Marabelle did things her way, no matter the consequences. I've always admired that about her." Phoebe's gaze drifted over the dark golf course. "Mother never understood her, and Marabelle refused to bend." Her voice was solemn. "I used to wish I was more like her. Still do. She's always so brave.

"When we were younger, this neighborhood kid used to bully me all the time." She laughed. "He wanted my attention because he liked me, but at the time, I was terrified. One day he backed me up against the fence, because I wouldn't let him walk me home, and threatened to steal my books and papers and rip them to shreds. Even back then, the thought of anything of mine *not* being perfect was horrifying," she said deprecatingly. "Suddenly Marabelle bounded around the corner and knocked him to the ground."

"Somehow that doesn't surprise me," Nick replied wryly.

"That boy was much bigger than she was, but

Marabelle got in a few good licks before I had to pull her off."

"Now I understand her insatiable desire to fight."

Phoebe fiddled with her wrap. "Marabelle fights for the people she loves. You know, she even warned Tom when we were engaged that if he did anything to hurt me, he'd have to answer to her."

That didn't surprise Nick either, but he kept quiet.

"At the time, I was furious with her. But she did it because she loves me." Phoebe's eyes darted around the terrace as if she had revealed too much. "What I'm trying to say is, that's why she's protecting you. Marabelle thinks with her heart, not her head."

Nick understood, but where did that leave him and Marabelle? Did they have what it took to survive the long haul?

Phoebe sighed. "We should go inside before we're missed." Looping her arm through his, they moved toward the doors. "Oh, before I forget"—Phoebe pierced him with her sharp blue eyes—"if you do anything to hurt her…you'll have to answer to me."

As threats go, it worked.

—∞—

The live auction had begun, and Marabelle had become painfully aware that Nick had made no move to bid on her. She straightened in her seat, facing the dance floor, her back to the table, hoping she didn't look like a loser. Would this evening ever end?

"Marabelle Fairchild! Come on down! You'll be dancing the first set with one of Atlanta's finest…Trey Stone," the auctioneer boomed into the microphone.

And her night went straight to hell. What had she expected? She'd shamelessly flirted with him all through dinner to get back at Nick. She'd made her bed, and now she had to lie in it.

Marabelle and Trey found their place on the dance floor, when the auctioneer called out again. "And the highest bid for the evening goes to none other than the belle of the ball, *Edna Fairchild*. Ed, you've been outbid, my friend. By a much younger man." The chattering ballroom grew quiet as the guests looked on with interest. "Edna, our famous guest from North Carolina has just bid twenty-five hundred dollars to dance the first set with you this evening." Everyone oohed and aahed.

Marabelle whipped around in time to see her mother smiling and waving as Nick led her to the floor. *Good Lord.* Images of Scarlett O'Hara and Rhett Butler flashed through her head. Edna actually curtsied just like Scarlett when she got to the center of the dance floor. *Unbelievable.* Just when Marabelle thought the night couldn't get any suckier.

After the first set, the guests switched partners, and Marabelle danced with her dad, Peyton Carter, and even Tom, her brother-in-law. But not once with Nick.

On aching, crippled feet, she headed back to her seat for a rest. Manolo Blahniks were made to look great, not boogie the night away.

Phoebe plopped down next to her, moaning, "I can't feel my toes. Why do we have to dance just as hard as the men, but in three-inch heels? Life is so unfair."

"Try four-inch heels." They both burst out laughing. Neither dared to remove their offending footwear, knowing Big Edna would admonish them for their inappropriate behavior. Phoebe snagged two champagne flutes from a passing waiter and handed one to Marabelle.

"A toast. To you and your adorable Nick." Phoebe raised her glass, but Marabelle didn't respond. "What's the matter?"

Did she dare confide the truth to her sister?

"Nick is a wonderful guy, and you're lucky to have found him," Phoebe said in earnest.

"I guess. Right now, he's a real jerkwad."

Phoebe's eyes flew open. "Why would you say that? He's charming and absolutely dotes on you. Don't ever take that for granted."

"Yeah, well, so much for doting. He hasn't once asked me to dance tonight," she said as she sulked.

"Oh, Marabelle. He's been graciously dancing with all the women, because everyone is so enamored with him. Give him a break. He even danced twice with Margie Carter." Phoebe said "Margie Carter" all gravelly, mimicking Margie's smoker's voice. Marabelle couldn't help but chuckle. "And he paid twenty-five hundred dollars to dance with Mother. We should've paid him!" The sisters snickered together.

"Now you're making me feel sorry for him. Stop singing his praises. He loves having women swoon all over him." Marabelle snorted in disgust.

"You have nothing to be jealous over. Nick adores you," Phoebe said.

Marabelle straightened in her seat. "Who said I'm jealous? I don't care who—"As the crowd parted, she zeroed in on a drunk Mimsy Peterson plastered to the front of Nick, swaying to the band's rendition of "Sexual Healing" by Marvin Gaye.

"That bitch."

Phoebe looked up, alarmed. "Marabelle, it's not what you think," she said, her tone doubtful.

"If she gets any closer, we'll have to pry her off with the Jaws of Life." Marabelle scooted to the edge of her seat, ready to pounce like a cat on an unsuspecting mouse.

Phoebe pressed her hand on her shoulder. "Stay. I'll handle this."

Marabelle's gaze never wavered from her prey.

"Here. Drink this." Phoebe handed her the remainder of her champagne. Gliding to where Nick and Mimsy were grinding it out on the dance floor, Phoebe tapped Mimsy on the shoulder. Marabelle couldn't hear a thing over the music, but whatever Phoebe said must've been pretty powerful. Mimsy unglued herself from Nick's front and scurried off like a rat. To his credit, Nick looked relieved. Phoebe finished the dance with him with the proper distance of six inches between them.

At least Phoebe won't hit on him. But why hadn't Nick asked her to dance? Marabelle watched in misery as Trey Stone weaved in her direction. Years of good manners drilled into her head would not allow her to say no, even if he seemed a little tipsy. And since she'd had nothing but sucky luck all night, the next song was a slow ballad. She furtively looked around and saw some woman old enough to be her grandmother hanging all over Nick.

Ugh. At least Trey was near her age. Trey pulled her in tight, and she almost moaned…in misery. Trey's hands rested precariously close to the top of her bottom. Oh brother.

—∿∿—

"Scotch on the rocks, please." Nick had finally disengaged himself from some woman who reminded him of his old Aunt Hildy. She gave him the willies when she tried to cop a feel. Usually he could schmooze his way through an affair like this on autopilot, but tonight he was off his game, and it was all Marabelle's fault. His eyes narrowed as she danced by with Trey Stone holding her close *again*. *Oh, hell no.*

Blood boiling, Nick was tired of watching that arrogant dickhead making the moves on Marabelle.

Knocking back his drink, he slammed the glass down on the bar and wove his way back through the crowd to retrieve what was his...Marabelle. Normally, he'd get stopped a half dozen times to talk football or sign something, but he had his game face on, and everyone cleared a wide path.

"Excuse me. You have something that belongs to me...my *fiancée*," Nick said in his don't-screw-with-me voice.

Both stared at him in shock. Dickhead recovered first.

"Look, Frasier, Marabelle and I are old friends," Trey said in his snotty, entitled voice.

"Right. Now beat it," he growled, plucking her from Trey's clutches and dragging her off the dance floor, away from the crowd.

"N...Nick. What are you doing?" Marabelle said from between clenched teeth.

"Doing you a favor. Or do you prefer douchebags groping you all night?"

"Excuse me?"

"I told you what I'd do if some guy tried to make a move on you. That dickhead can't keep his eyes off your breasts or his hands off your ass. Nothing would give me greater pleasure than beating the living shit out of him."

"Are you kidding me? What about your fan club? Did they all go home for the night to soak their teeth? The young ones aren't enough? Now you're hitting on grannies?"

"You think I enjoyed them rubbing against me?"

Hurt and doubt passed over Marabelle's face. "I didn't see you saying no. You seemed to enjoy all that bumping and grinding with Mimsy. Everyone noticed," she hissed.

Nick plowed his fingers through his hair, wanting to yank it all out. "Un-freakin'-believable. You've been in a royal snit all night, not even looking my way at dinner."

"Me?" Marabelle snorted. "That's ridiculous."

"Yeah, you. While you were pouting, I had to endure everyone, down to a woman I could've sworn was a clone of my eighty-year-old Aunt Hildy." He jabbed his finger at her face. "And you flirted with that dickhead and countless others."

"Flirting? Now that's rich. Coming from the infamous skirt chaser," she mumbled.

He released a heavy sigh, rolling his shoulders. Why was he fighting with her? Sometimes it was smarter to drop back and punt, and this was one of those times.

"Tinker—"

"Don't. Don't call me Tinker Bell." She crossed her arms. "You didn't even bid on me to dance during the auction." She gulped, her eyes swimming with tears.

Nick felt two inches tall. He'd never meant to hurt

her. He'd rather eat Astroturf than make Marabelle cry. "Aw, honey." He gathered her unyielding form close. "Don't be mad about that. I wanted to flatter your mother and make her evening successful." He tilted her sad face up with his finger. "Don't cry, babe." He caught a tear with the pad of his thumb as it slid down her cheek. "I only wanted to be with you tonight."

With his arm anchored around her waist, he gently propelled her toward the dance floor. "What're you doing?" Remaining stiff against his side, Marabelle sniffed, slanting him a suspicious look.

"Dancing with the prettiest woman here for the rest of the night." Tucking her tight against his body, he wrapped his palm around her hand. The music was soft and low, and Nick swayed until the tension eased from her body and Marabelle snuggled against him, resting her cheek against his chest. Much better.

"Hey. We're all meeting at the Stones' for a late-night breakfast. You want to join us?" Phoebe asked, interrupting their slow dance.

"No. Thank you. I need to get some rest before hitting the road tomorrow." Marabelle moved from the circle of his arms.

"We'll miss you. I'll be by in the morning to say good-bye." Phoebe hugged her sister and whirled to leave, when Marabelle stopped her.

"Wait, what did you say to get rid of Mimsy earlier?"

A mischievous smile lit Phoebe's face. "The truth. That I saw her husband heading into the ladies' restroom after some young blond."

"You *didn't*!" Marabelle's eyes rounded.

"She deserved a taste of her own medicine."

Nick grinned at Phoebe, the perfect debutante gone rogue.

"Thanks. I don't think I would've been that subtle," Marabelle said.

"No shit," Nick added.

Phoebe laughed. "Oh, in case you're wondering, Mother raised more money this year than ever for Magnolia House. Thanks to Nick." Phoebe gave him a wink. "Don't forget to pick up your auction items on the way out."

Nick didn't need any further encouragement. He hustled Marabelle toward the entrance. "Meet me at the front while I settle up." He couldn't believe his stroke of luck: a few hours alone with Marabelle, *and* she was sober.

"Coach Frasier, we have all your wonderful purchases right here," the eager volunteer said from behind the checkout table. "You got the—"

"Thanks. I'm just gonna write a check and include the twenty-five-hundred-dollar pledge for the dance." He dug for his checkbook in his coat pocket. "Will that cover it?" He ripped the check from the register and pushed it across the table.

"Goodness! Yes, that will more than cover it. Thank you so much for your generosity."

"Don't mention it." He started for the lobby.

"Uh, Coach Frasier!" He turned, his impatience clear. "Don't forget your items." The volunteer waved a green Magnolia House tote bag in the air.

"Christ." He snatched the bag. "Thanks."

"Wow. Do you have any idea what you have in this bag?" Marabelle rummaged through the tote as he pulled away from the clubhouse. Nick accelerated past the speed limit through the empty streets.

"No clue."

She held up a certificate. "It says you're the proud owner of an *original commissioned portrait*."

"Just what I need."

"Four days and two rounds of golf at Sea Island, Georgia. It's beautiful there."

"Good. You can plan the trip. Anything else?"

"Yeah, you have a full day of salon services at Miss Pitty Pat's Salon."

He snorted. "Yours."

"*And*…you're a proud member of the Fruit of the Month club!" Marabelle burst into hysterical laughter.

"Huh? I didn't bid on that."

"I kn…know. I did," she said in between hoots.

He chuckled. "Gimme that." He snatched the certificate and tossed it over his shoulder. "What else is in there? And you'd better not say implants or Botox treatments."

"Hmmm, let's see." Marabelle held up a black velvet jewelry pouch. "What's this?"

"Open it and find out." She reached inside the pouch and pulled out a bracelet.

"Wow. The Yurman bracelet," she breathed.

Nick parked in the Fairchilds' driveway and turned off the car. He unlatched his seat belt. "Yeah?" The bracelet's diamonds sparkled in the outdoor lights. Marabelle slipped it on her small wrist. "You like it?" he asked.

She nodded. "Sure. What's not to like?"

"Good. Then my sister should love it, too."

Her head snapped up. "Sister? But I thought—"

Marabelle clamped her mouth shut, and pink infused her cheeks.

"Gotcha. That's for the Fruit of the Month Club." He laughed. "If you could see your face." Pink turned to red, and she scowled. He cupped her chin. "You're so transparent. It's yours, Tinker Bell," he said against her lips. *I'm yours.*

Chapter 20

"INSIDE...*NOW*!"

Somehow Marabelle had found her way across the convertible's console, sprawled on top of Nick, when he tore his mouth away from hers, gasping for air. He had her dress pushed up around her waist, and his big, warm hands cupped her bare ass.

"What?" She blinked at him.

Nick smoothed her dress down, patting her bottom. "We're going inside, straight to my bed. Now."

Nick's hands never left her body as he practically pushed her up the stairway toward the bedroom.

"Tinker Bell, get a move on. I've waited long enough. We're going to do it until this crazed obsession runs its course."

Marabelle bit her lip. "So, this feeling is new to you, too?" Marabelle had no doubt the earth would shatter for her, but she wanted to be more than a notch on a bedpost for him.

"Yeah, and it scares the crap out of me, but I'm going for it anyhow. Now, hurry up before your mother gets home."

She spun around at the top of the landing. "Do not mention my family. I'm hoping you're good enough to make me forget."

In one smooth motion, Nick scooped her up, almost sprinting up the hallway with his long strides. "You can count on it."

Marabelle had wanted this since the first moment she'd clapped eyes on Nick Frasier in her classroom. And now that the moment had arrived, she couldn't help being both thrilled and scared to death. Hopefully, he didn't have high expectations, because she wasn't too sure she could deliver.

Nick closed the bedroom door with a resounding snick. A sliver of light trickled in through the sheers at the windows. Marabelle's face, only inches from his, could make out the glitter in his steely blue eyes. She gulped at the intent she saw there.

"Uh…Nick? Not to put you off your game, but you do remember I'm no good at this."

He dropped his arm from behind her knees, keeping her close as she slid the rest of the way down his body. "Darlin', you're going to do just fine. Neither one of us is going to last very long…the first time," he murmured.

Nick brought both her hands to his mouth. He covered the backs with hot kisses, slipping his tongue between her pinky and ring finger. The suggestion didn't go unnoticed.

"Mmmm." She shivered at his touch. If he could make her fingers fall in love, God help the rest of her body.

"Shhh." He curled her into his broad chest, claiming her lips in a melting kiss, and her doubt faded like mist in the early morning sun. He took his time, kissing her slowly and thoroughly. Her body responded instantly, and she gripped his arms.

His warm breath came out in a rush as he slipped the straps of her dress down her arms. His gaze sought her breasts and heated. "I knew you weren't wearing a bra. And to think that dickhead Trey wanted some of this."

He flicked a nipple with his hot tongue and then closed his mouth over it and sucked.

Marabelle helplessly whimpered. Nick paid homage to her other breast, licking and sucking. Sensations swarmed over her like a whirlwind. His big hand slipped under the hem of her dress and skated from the outside to the inside of her thigh. He wickedly palmed her over her already-wet panties. Too hot and greedy to be embarrassed, Marabelle rubbed against his hand, pushing his jacket off his broad shoulders. Yanking the end of his bow tie with one hand, Nick brushed her hands away and jerked his shirt off. Studs scattered across the room, bouncing off the carpeted floor. Marabelle's hungry hands roamed over his sculpted bare chest.

"You have an amazing body," she breathed, loving the way he felt, like hard, warm clay beneath her fingers.

"So do you, darlin'." He unzipped her dress and pushed it down until it pooled at her feet. She stood only in her strappy sandals and lacy black thong. "I do like your choice of panties." His voice was husky as he scorched her with his gaze. He lifted her effortlessly and placed her in the middle of the bed.

Oh yeah, this was good, she thought lazily as he covered her with his powerful body. She rotated, bringing herself more in contact with his erection. Desire flowed higher and hotter. He kissed her neck, going for the sensitive spot until her entire body pulsed. She moved restlessly, wanting his lips on hers. He drew back just enough for her to catch the passion and heat swirling in his eyes. She needed more.

Nick stood, slipped off her sandals, and shed the rest of his clothing in one fell swoop.

Nick Frasier in a tux was hot, but Nick Frasier in the buff was phenomenal. Like a powerful warrior, his body was built for battle and had some rather interesting scars to show for it. She couldn't help but catalog the imperfections of her own body as she faced his finely tuned chest, arms, and abs. When she lowered her gaze to his impressive erection, she swallowed.

"Like what you see?" he asked, his voice thick with desire.

She nodded and reached for the coverlet to shield herself. Nick was on top of her before she had a chance. He grabbed both her wrists in one hand and pinned them above her head.

"No way," he rasped. "You're not covering anything up." He rubbed against her. She felt his desire and had to bite her lip to keep from moaning.

"I don't even know what you like," she whispered.

"I like you. I want you." His mouth crushed onto hers. "You're mine," he muttered as he hungrily kissed her.

That's when it hit Nick like a three-hundred-pound tackle and took his breath away. Deep down he knew he'd always feel this way about this crazy, sassy, disarming fairy, and he hadn't even gotten inside her yet. Marabelle belonged to him. No way in hell was he letting go. Nick's hand cupped her breast. "Damn. You're sexy." This felt right. It felt *perfect*.

Marabelle squirmed, arching her back. "Nick…I need…to touch you," she panted.

He showed no mercy, keeping her hands pinned as he feasted his way down her slim neck and chest until he hovered above her breasts. "Later. I need to do this my way. I've waited too long." He latched his mouth on a raspberry nipple, and she thrashed beneath him.

Nick stroked, touched, kissed, and tasted his way around her body, making her even wilder for him. Finally he released her wrists as he slid the rest of the way down, stripping off her black thong and pitching it over his shoulder.

Marabelle had nothing to grip but the coverlet at her sides. "Nick, we need—I'm not taking—" Words escaped her.

"Easy. I came prepared." He stroked her flushed skin, lingering on the smooth curve of her belly, and then lower to the silky feel of her thighs. She opened for him without even realizing it. His fingers slicked between her legs against her wet heat. A low moan escaped her throat, and he could feel her need pulsing against his hand.

It would be so easy to push into her heated softness and thrust home, but he wasn't about to let this moment slip by without making it mean something. Barely able to control his reaction to her, he continued to worship every inch of her body…again and again. She gasped and grasped at his shoulders, writhing beneath him, her nails digging into his skin.

"Oh…my…"

"Soon," he murmured against her belly.

Fire consumed his body, and his cock throbbed. He moved to the juncture of her thighs. Her body shook, and her hips bucked at the slightest touch, making him ache for her. Her eyes were closed and her teeth dug into her swollen lower lip as he spread her thighs. He bent and pressed a gentle kiss to her center. A deep shudder ripped through her. And that's all it took. His tongue teased and tormented, daring her to come for him.

She clutched the coverlet, fighting for control, but Nick wanted her out of control. He grabbed her hips, raising her up to meet his tongue.

Her body tightened into a coil; tension coursed through her veins until she exploded with release. Crying out, she shuddered against his mouth, and then she lay there limp, unable to move.

Nick slid forward, dragging his hot, slick body against hers, making her gasp again with need.

"Did that feel good?" He lay next to her on a bent elbow.

"Oh, yeah," she whispered at his devastating grin.

"I'm glad." He reached over, smashing her down with his body as he opened the drawer to the nightstand, withdrawing a condom. She watched with fascination while Nick rolled it into place.

"Tell me that's your condom and not something my mother keeps on hand for all her guests."

He settled himself next to her, tucking her close. "Yeah. Told you I was prepared." His lips were on her as he pinned her all the way beneath him. Marabelle wrapped her arms around his neck, her body ready for him. He lifted his head. "Open for me, honey," he whispered.

Marabelle locked her legs around his hips and dug her fingers into his broad shoulders. He began to ease inside her, but she surged forward to take all of him at once.

"Slow down, babe," he bit off through clenched teeth. Instead, she lifted her hips higher. He groaned. "*Please*…easy…you're so tight."

"I need…it's…oh…"

"I know," he muttered, his voice strained.

She wanted more. Her nails sank into his arms, and she rocked forward.

"Easy." His body rigid with desire, he couldn't hold back any longer. He drew a ragged breath and thrust deeply, her warm wetness pulling him closer and closer. Deep, heavy thrusts. Stretching her.

But Nick wanted her with him. "You have to come for me."

Her eyes fluttered open, and he built up speed to match the rocking of her hips. She whimpered, and with a cry, arched against him as her second climax hit.

That was all it took. Nick unleashed his tenuous hold. He pumped once, twice, three times, and let himself go. Collapsing on his forearms, he buried his face in her neck. The aftershocks seemed to last forever. For a long moment, neither of them moved. Nick could feel Marabelle taking in huge gulps of air. With a deep sigh, he rolled onto his side, gathering her close.

"You okay?" he asked in a hoarse voice.

Still trembling, she snuggled around his body. "Perfect." A look of concern etched her face when she asked, "Was I okay?"

He closed his eyes and threw his head back, half groaning, half laughing. "Any more *okay*, and we would've both gone up in smoke."

She propped herself up on one elbow. "Really?" she asked, eyes bright.

He peered at her excited face through slitted eyes. "Tinker Bell, I know you don't have much experience in this department, but take it from me, it doesn't get any better than this."

"Phew! Good to know." She flopped back down. "You wouldn't mind…you know…doing it again, would you?"

A deep warmth worked its way into his bones. What

man didn't want to hear that? "I need a little recovery time. Not as young as I used to be."

"Like how much time? Because this time, I want to be on top."

Nick's laugh shook the bed.

———

Marabelle gave a leisurely stretch as a big yawn escaped her mouth. She reached her hand out and felt around the sheets. Nothing. She lifted her head, peering through her mass of tangled curls at the empty guest bedroom. Sunlight streamed through the pale-blue sheers over the windows. Nick was nowhere in sight.

She flopped back onto the pillow, pushing hair from her eyes.

Sheesh. She'd gone and done it now.

She'd fallen…hard. Just one more thing to add to her ever-growing list of really dumb things. Especially when they'd be breaking up in just a few weeks.

Her head pounded from lack of sleep and too much sex. Wait. Could that be right? Too much sex? Her body flushed from the memory. When did she become an insatiable nymphomaniac? Good Lord, she didn't even like sex.

Marabelle heard footsteps down the hall and wondered about the time. She needed to hit the road. A light tap sounded at the door, and Marabelle started to sit up. She swallowed a whimper for the second morning in a row, when her mother's blond head peered into the room from the cracked door.

"I was wondering where you ended up. I should've known to check here first," Edna said without a hint of censure. "I was about to fix some breakfast. What would you and Nick like? Where is Nick?" She scanned the bedroom the same way Marabelle had moments before.

"Uh...I'm not exactly..." The man of the hour entered from the connecting bathroom with a fluffy white towel slung low around his hips and another one draped around his shoulders. Small drops of water slid their way down his muscled arms. Marabelle physically gulped, and Edna's jaw hit the floor.

"Oh my." Edna's tone was reverent, mirroring Marabelle's thoughts exactly.

"Good morning, ladies," Coach Glorious drawled. "Edna, I hope I didn't wake you when I left for an early morning run."

"Oh no. I didn't hear a thing. I was just taking breakfast orders. What would you like? Waffles, pancakes, omelets?"

"Omelet sounds great. Let me throw on some clothes, and I'll be down to help," he offered.

Edna twittered. "Well, don't go to any trouble on my behalf." Marabelle gaped at the mischievous expression on her mother's face.

"Marabelle, will you be joining us?" Edna asked.

"Yeah," she croaked, her throat dry.

"See you in a few." With a wink, Edna closed the door.

Marabelle slumped down and pulled the covers over her head. This couldn't be happening. Her mother was ogling Nick.

"Hey, sleepyhead." The bed dipped with his weight. He slowly drew the cover away from her face.

She slapped her hands over her exposed face and moaned. "Go away."

"Is that any way to greet your fiancé? I don't know why you're hiding. I've seen everything…up close and personal."

"What's so amazing is that you're still here," she said, her voice muffled behind her hands.

Nick pried her hands away from her face. "I'm not going anywhere." He leaned down and kissed her. "Get a move on. I'm starving."

Marabelle struggled to sit up, clutching the covers against her chest. "You wouldn't happen to have a shirt I can borrow? It's one thing to be naked with you in the dark. It's another altogether in broad daylight. I'm not quite that cavalier."

Marabelle painted a sexy picture with her tousled hair and sleepy eyes, making Nick want to crawl back in bed and make love again, and show her how important she was to him, but there wasn't enough time.

"What time do you want to leave today?" He tossed a Cherokees T-shirt at her head.

She grappled to pull it on without relinquishing the covers. Her head popped through the top of the shirt. "After breakfast. What time is your flight?"

He zipped a pair of jeans up over his black boxer briefs. "Thought I'd drive back with you. I need to turn my rental in, and then we can head out after that." She scrambled from the bed. His T-shirt fell close to her knees, covering everything important, unfortunately.

"Huh? You want to ride back in my car? You hate my car."

He buttoned a green-and-white striped designer shirt

with blue paisley cuffs. "Would you consider driving it in a ditch so we could take the convertible instead?" Her gaze roamed his body before she glanced up and blushed. Nick grinned.

"Uh, no. But I also don't expect you to ride back to Raleigh with me. You've served your sentence. You've more than earned your parole."

His hand shot out, grabbing a fistful of the T-shirt and dragging a startled Marabelle into his arms.

"I don't want you driving back to Raleigh alone. Unless you want me to call downstairs and tell Edna we won't be down in time for breakfast, I suggest you get a move on." He gave her bottom a quick swat.

"Ow. That hurt." His hand lingered and rubbed the spot he'd just abused. Several inappropriate thoughts flashed through his mind. They really needed to get out of here before he acted on them.

Marabelle went up on her toes and kissed his jaw. "Let me grab a quick shower, and I'll meet you downstairs."

―――

"Damn, Marabelle. How do you drive this thing?" Nick slid behind the wheel of her little blue Honda, pushing the driver's seat as far back as it would go, trying to get comfortable.

"It drives fine, spoiled rich boy."

"Why couldn't you have listened just once and driven my Range Rover? Bumping down the highway in this lawn mower for seven hours is going to make my ass sore. Not to mention my back," he groused.

"Poor baby. Maybe if you're sweet, I'll massage them for you."

"Oh, you can count on it. After this weekend, I deserve a full body massage along with complete servitude on your part. You might as well get used to the role of sex slave," he said, leering at her.

Marabelle studied Nick as he drove. As usual, he exuded confidence and sex appeal without any effort. Just looking at all that perfection depressed her. Not to mention, he'd charmed her mother again over omelets and orange juice. The entire weekend, Edna never brought up Marabelle's job or love life or moving back home or joining the Junior League. It had been progress. And Marabelle had Nick to thank for it. But instead of feeling grateful, she felt sad.

Nick fit into her family in one short weekend better than she ever had in her whole life. He'd won over both her parents and half of Atlanta. Even Phoebe had fallen under his spell. And he was great in bed!

Marabelle had a big problem. Make that two problems.

Nick and phenomenal sex.

She'd probably never experience anything that great again. She'd had sex with the hottest bachelor in the South, who made her feel like a goddess. And she'd experienced an earth-shattering orgasm…four times.

But nothing good lasted forever. Marabelle's short-lived fairy tale was coming to an end. She was in love with a fairy-tale prince, and knowing he'd never feel the same way made her heart hurt. A sound of distress slipped past her lips.

Nick glanced over, arching a brow. "You devising another wacky plan?"

Marabelle straightened in her seat, along with the

mess inside her head. "Since the weekend is over, we don't have to pretend anymore, and you don't ever have to see my family again." There. She felt better locking all her defenses back in place.

"What are you talking about? I promised your mother we'd be back after the school gala."

She twisted to face him. "We are not coming back. She thinks we're getting married, and we don't even have a…a…real…" She gestured frantically with her hands, searching for the right words.

Nick's eyes narrowed. "Relationship. Is that the word you're looking for? What the hell do you think we've been doing all this time? Or do you always have incredible sex with guys you don't have relationships with?"

"Of course not. I told you I don't have sex at all." Marabelle crossed her arms and lifted her chin. "And that's the way it needs to stay."

Nick wanted to pull this piece-of-shit car off the highway and shake Marabelle until her teeth rattled.

Jesus H. Christ. The kind of sex they'd shared the night before was phenomenal. Beyond amazing. They'd burned the sheets up and still weren't satisfied. That was not something to take lightly. They were great in bed and great as a couple. A rare combination that shouldn't be thrown away on a knee-jerk whim, or because of some insecurities.

Okay, he'd admit he wasn't making sense, and Marabelle was doing exactly as they'd agreed, keeping everything casual. And sure, he might not be ready for marriage this very second, but hell, he wasn't saying *never* anymore, and that had to count for something. This little charade of theirs had bloomed into a relationship, and it was going to stay that way until it ran its course or they decided to take it farther. It had taken a lot of unsatisfying flings for him to realize what he shared with Marabelle was special and should be nurtured and allowed to grow.

Marabelle had taken up permanent residence in his head, making him forget all his past toxic relationships, including Lola and even Ginger. Nick drew some deep, calm breaths. If anyone understood Marabelle's resistance, he did. Time to calmly talk her off the ledge.

"You still have a gala to pull off, and everyone in Raleigh thinks we're engaged. Do you really want to break it off before you've fulfilled your commitment?"

Marabelle remained quiet for so long Nick thought she hadn't heard him.

Finally she cleared her throat. "No. But just because I'm willing to continue our fake engagement for appearances doesn't mean I'm going to continue to sleep with you."

"Bullshit!" Nick exploded. "I'm going to chalk this whole ridiculous conversation up to your complete lack of experience. I don't know why you're hell-bent on destroying what we have, but I'm not playing."

"What's that supposed to mean? Look, I'm not one of your players. You can't tell me what to do or how to think."

"*Marabelle*. Shut up." He gripped the steering wheel so hard he thought he might pull it from the steering column. He gritted his teeth and kept his eyes glued to the road.

Nick counted out-of-state license plates, devised new plays for his offense, and ran drills in his head. Anything not to dwell on Marabelle and her hang-ups. After an hour of driving in silence, he glanced over, expecting to see her asleep. Instead, what he saw sucker punched him in the gut. Tears streamed down her face.

"Aw, honey." He covered her thigh with his hand. "Please don't cry." Marabelle gulped, and a sob spilled forth. Nick felt lower than pond scum. He spied the next exit and eased into the right lane. Two minutes later, he pulled into a McDonald's and parked the car.

"Come here." He gently gathered Marabelle in his lap and rocked her in his arms.

"I'm sorry. I never meant to upset you," he murmured, hating that he'd caused her any pain.

She buried her face in his shirt, wetting it with her tears. "I'm the one who's s-sorry," she said between sobs. "I don't know what got into me. I do appreciate all you did for me this weekend. Really, I do." She hiccupped. Nick kissed the top of her head, then leaned forward and opened the glove compartment, pulling out some paper napkins. He blotted her tears, and she wiped her eyes and blew her nose, balling the napkins up in her fist.

"What can I do to make it all better?" He stroked her back with his hands.

Between sniffles and hiccups, she said, "Nothing. I'm being s-stupid and petty." She gazed at him through watery eyes. "My family likes you better than they *ever* liked me. It's humiliating."

Nick's heart took a dive. He didn't want Marabelle believing that for one second. "Sweetie, that's not true. Your family loves you very much. And they're very protective of you, as they should be. I only wanted to make this weekend easier for you by being there."

She sniffed. "And I acted like an ingrate. You were wonderful and perfect, and everybody loved you." She wiped her eyes again. "Just give me a minute, and I'll be back to normal."

Marabelle was game-tough, and Nick loved that she could shake herself off and face her challenges. With spiky dark lashes and red nose, she never looked more beautiful.

"You're perfect just the way you are." He cupped her wet cheeks and brushed her lips with the barest of kisses. "You want a soda or something to eat?"

She gave a sniffle and a nod.

As he pulled back on the highway, all signs of crying and hiccupping had vanished after he'd fortified her with hot fries and cold soda, and Marabelle had her plotting-something-outrageous look on her face. Nick was beginning to loathe that look.

Licking her fingers, she said, "I've been thinking."

"Okay," he said slowly. "What's the plan this time?"

"We continue our fake engagement until we get through the tournaments and gala. I definitely get a lot farther attached to you. Besides, I can't seem to get this rock off my finger." She gave the diamond ring another tug. "As for the 'relationship'…" Nick could feel a sharp pain building behind his eyes. "I think we should call it what it is."

"And what would that be?" he asked, already knowing he would hate the answer.

"Affair. Fling. Hookup. Whatever. I've never had one before, so this is all new to me."

Oh boy. "Hmmm, you're willing to have an affair, but you don't want to be in a relationship? That about sum it up?"

"Yeah, I think so," she said slowly.

This should be good. "I'd say an affair implies sex. Lots of sex. Wherever-and-whenever sex. Would you agree?"

Marabelle swallowed hard. "Um…I guess so."

"Just so we're perfectly clear, I'm talking about head-banging sex. On the hood of the car sex, up against the wall sex, shower sex, swinging from the chandelier sex. The type of sex that leaves bedsheets torn, things broken, neighbors complaining—"

"I get it! Stop saying 'sex'!"

Nick leered at her flushed face. "Glad we're on the same page."

"You also know all that sex has to be consensual."

"Absolutely." But Nick had personal knowledge of what turned sweet Marabelle on, and he had every intention of playing dirty.

"Okay then. It's settled." She poked her pert nose in the air. "Because it's no secret I get bored easily. All that sex with you will be no exception." She feigned a yawn.

Nick burst out laughing. Marabelle shot him a dirty glare and cranked up the radio to drown him out.

Chapter 21

AFTER THE EMBARRASSING HANGING FROM THE CHANdelier sex discussion, Marabelle and Nick settled into a comfortable conversation about music, food, travel, sports, and more sports.

Curious, Marabelle asked him questions about his football and coaching career. "Do you think you'll ever retire from coaching?"

"Sure. It's grueling and demanding, and if you don't win a few championships, then you're shit out of luck and shit out of a job."

From her playing days in college, Marabelle understood the inordinate amount of pressure all professional athletes felt, and that pressure tripled as a coach in the pros. "You'll win a championship. The Cherokees are tough and getting stronger, especially with you as their leader."

He gave her a half smile. "And you know this how?"

Because she'd done some snooping on the Internet and read what the sports analysts were predicting. Racy photos involving another coach's wife and Nick on some island also popped up. But for all his celebrity status and fame, he really was a decent guy. Marabelle's heart tripped over how he'd treated her family and how supportive he'd been all weekend.

"I just do. You have that leadership thing going. Men, especially young men, will want to follow you. That's not something that can be taught. You come by it naturally. But you don't lord it over people. You use it in a good way."

Nick reached for her hand and brushed the back with the softest kiss. Marabelle's hand tingled from his warm lips.

"Thanks. That's the nicest thing you've ever said to me."

She gave his fingers a reassuring squeeze. "I speak the truth. I wish I had half your confidence and natural talent."

"Baby girl, you do just fine. I'd pick you for my team any day." Marabelle's heart smiled. Coming from Nick, that was one of the best compliments ever.

They arrived back at Nick's house around six that evening. After the seven-hour drive, they decided to get some exercise before grabbing dinner. Marabelle jogged on a regular basis, but her short legs were no competition for Nick's long, effortless strides. She huffed, disgusted that she couldn't keep up. After jogging a three-mile loop, they finished at the end of Nick's street.

"Remind me never to exercise with you again," Marabelle panted on her cooldown. "You don't even sweat. That's not normal."

"Sure I do. You forget I already put in a five-mile run this morning while you were still dreaming about me in bed," he replied with cheerful arrogance.

"Don't your shoulders get tired, carrying around that huge ego all the time?"

"Nah. What do you want for dinner? I know a great Thai place that delivers."

"Sounds good. Do I have time for a quick shower?"

Nick opened the kitchen door from the garage. "Sure." He handed her a water bottle from his beverage refrigerator. "Hey, I'll race ya. Last one showered and dressed pays for dinner."

Marabelle studied him over the top of the bottle. A strange ripple started in her chest, causing all sorts of hot images of Nick to flash through her mind. She deliberately ran the tip of her tongue over the top of the bottle, catching his undivided attention.

"As much as I love a challenge, I have an even better idea," she said in a sultry voice she never knew she possessed.

"What do you have in mind?" he asked, his voice husky.

"How about that shower sex you were boasting about earlier?" She shrugged. "For the sake of the affair."

Marabelle's heart raced at his wicked grin. "That's pretty advanced stuff. Think you can handle it?"

"I'll be with a professional, won't I?"

"Absolutely."

The minute Marabelle arrived home from work on Monday afternoon, she kicked off her shoes and dove straight for bed, exhausted. She had no idea how long she'd been out, when pounding on her front door woke her.

"Hold your horses, I'm coming," she called out in a groggy voice as she stumbled down the hallway.

"Open up. It's me, Paula."

Marabelle pulled the door open. "Hey, what're you doing here?"

"Checking on you. I tried texting, but you didn't ans—YOU'VE HAD SEX!" Paula said loud enough to wake the dead.

"What? Am I wearing a sign or something?" Marabelle shuffled back to her bedroom to look in the mirror.

Paula followed on her heels. "I can just tell. YOU'VE HAD A LOT OF SEX!"

"Yes, and now the entire neighborhood knows. Please stop proclaiming it for all the world to hear." Marabelle ran a brush through her messy hair.

"Holy shitski. I can't believe you finally broke down."

Marabelle dropped the brush with a thud. "I'm only human, you know."

"Good for you. This calls for alcohol." Paula held up a six-pack of Coronas and a bag of limes. "You better start from the beginning," Paula said, marching to the kitchen. Marabelle quickly changed into jeans and a T-shirt and joined her.

Paula supplied the beer, and Marabelle offered the chips and salsa and her accounting of the weekend.

"You mean to tell me Coach Gorgeous gave you that incredible ring you can't get off your finger, and he says this is only an affair? Am I missing something?"

Marabelle hedged. "Not exactly. We came to a mutual agreement after I told him we should call it off. He pointed out that I still needed him for the auction." She gave a dismissive gesture with her hand.

"I swear, girl, sometimes you're thicker than a concrete block."

"Thanks. What makes me so thick?" Marabelle dipped her chip in the spicy salsa.

"A man like him does not buy a diamond you can see from space, fly to Atlanta to be with his fake fiancée's weirdo family, charm your doodle of a mother, give gobs of money to her charity, have smokin' sex with you, *and* drive seven hours back in your wind-up car because he's *only* having an affair."

"Why not?" Marabelle said around a mouthful of salsa. "Men do all kinds of things for the sake of an affair. Cheat on their wives, dye their hair, lose thirty pounds—"

"Uh-huh. Are you blind? Are you forgetting who he is and how he looks? Nick doesn't have to do any of those things to have an affair. Women probably pay him." And didn't that reality smack Marabelle in the face. Why exactly was he with her?

Paula pointed a salty chip at her. "Stop your belittling thoughts."

Marabelle cut her gaze to Paula's knowing face. Paula understood all about her dysfunctional relationship with her mother.

"Face it, he's not going to all this trouble to get in your pants. He could've had you up against your whiteboard the first time you clapped eyes on him."

Sad but true. "Okay, why is he doing it?" Maybe Paula could shed some light on a very confusing situation that had Marabelle's heart soaring and stomach doing cartwheels.

Paula slapped herself in the forehead. "Wooing you, of course. Don't you see?"

Paula voiced what Marabelle had been too afraid to whisper inside her head, let alone her heart. She didn't dare. Years of competition taught Marabelle how to lock down distracting thoughts and stay focused on her goal. *Keep my eye on the ball—my promotion—and anticipate my opponent's—the committee's—next shot.*

Marabelle chugged her beer. "No. Don't start spinning this. I'm using him to rock that auction. That's it."

Paula chewed, giving Marabelle her I-can't-believe-we're-friends look. "Okay. Then what's in it for him?"

"That's easy. Um, well. He wants me to scare off those gold-digging women who only want to be Mrs. Nick Frasier."

Paula smirked, "And how's that working out?"

Every woman who had blatantly flirted with Nick this past weekend popped into Marabelle's head. And then there was perfect Ginger with her designer clothes and bony ass. And yet, Nick had been with Marabelle.

Paula rolled her eyes. "Fine. Have it your way."

"Can we change the subject?" Marabelle needed time to process this information on her own.

"Yeah. Just one more question." Paula tipped the beer to her lips.

Marabelle hesitated at the calculated expression on her friend's face. "What?"

"Can I be a bridesmaid?" Paula fell back hooting with laughter.

Marabelle threw a chip at Paula's head. "You're sick. You and Big Edna should get together."

Paula grabbed Marabelle's hand to examine the engagement ring more closely, whistling low. "I'd love to see what he'd buy if this was a real engagement."

Yeah, so would Marabelle. But this ring was growing on her. It was real to her, and she wanted to savor it as long as she could. Her heart cartwheeled smack into a brick wall just as she heard a knock at her door. Good thing. Marabelle's thoughts would lead to nothing but trouble. Beau Quinton stood on her front porch, not looking particularly contrite.

"Hey, Mary-bell. You still speaking to me?"

"Well, well, well, look who's here. Brutus. Here to stab me in the back or dig for more secrets?" Marabelle turned, shutting the door on Beau's cocky grin, except, being a sneak, he'd stuck his foot out to prevent it from closing.

"I brought a peace offering." He held a bouquet of fresh spring flowers and a bucket of fried chicken. Pushing his way inside, Beau followed her to the kitchen.

Marabelle snorted. "Paula Carver, meet the infamous Beau Quinton. Quarterback for the Carolina Cherokees and professional snitch. He brought you flowers."

"Hello there, beautiful." Beau laid on the charm thick as Crisco. "Aren't you a sight for sore eyes?" For someone who wouldn't shut up only moments ago, Paula appeared dumbstruck.

Beau's good looks tied a lot of tongues, and Marabelle would've laughed except she was still hurt—no, furious—with his underhandedness.

"Don't let her dumb-ass expression fool you. When she snaps to, she'll be the most intelligent person you converse with for the next month."

"I deserve all this shit you're throwing at me, huh?" He smiled, unflustered as usual.

"Where do you find these guys?" Paula asked after several hard gulps.

Marabelle put water in a bright-yellow Fiestaware vase for the flowers. "This one crawled out from under a rock. But they're around. All you have to do is cook something, and they'll swarm you like flies at a picnic," she said, arranging the spring flowers. "Be careful what you say, Paula. Q here is a known narc." She placed the flowers on her windowsill next to the sink. "Thanks for the flowers and the food. You can leave now." Marabelle glared at Beau.

Beau casually opened a Corona and straddled a kitchen chair, dangling the beer from his long fingers. Paula sat across from him for an unobstructed view and openly gawked.

"Look, I'm sorry I let Coach in on your half-baked plan. And before you go all schoolteacher on me and rap my knuckles with a ruler, Coach seemed pretty pleased with himself this morning. You could say I did you a favor. I didn't get all the details, but it sounds as if the weekend wasn't a disaster." Beau shrugged his broad shoulders.

"How would you know? Were you there?" Marabelle slapped silverware and plates on the table. "Crossing a minefield is less stressful. Between Nick bossing me around and my mother, well, being herself, I came this close to losing it." She pinched her thumb and forefinger an inch apart.

"And yet, it worked out." Beau tipped the beer to his lips.

Did it? Marabelle wasn't sure of anything. "How do you think I felt when he showed up with a diamond ring?"

"Happy. Ecstatic. Elated." Beau didn't disguise the interest lighting his dark eyes.

"More like shocked, stunned, and speechless." Marabelle dumped the chicken on a platter, and Paula and Beau pounced on the food like hungry puppies.

"You're right. Diamond rings piss off most women," Beau said between bites.

"Talk about a suck-up," Marabelle muttered under her breath, suddenly not feeling the love. And she wasn't only referring to Beau winking at Paula. Nick sucked up better than her Dyson vacuum cleaner. "You know what he did at the live auction?" Marabelle pointed a drumstick at Beau.

"No, but I'm sure—"

"He bid twenty-five hundred dollars to dance with my mother."

Beau paused, wiping his hands on a napkin, and then whistled low. "Damn. He's got it bad."

Marabelle sniffed. "Then he spent tons of money on the silent auction, endearing him to my mother for life."

"That bastard," Paula said in mock outrage.

"Oh, you don't understand." Marabelle pushed her plate away, no longer hungry. The more she recapped the weekend, the sicker she felt. Because she'd fallen hopelessly in love with the unattainable man. How could she explain that to Paula and Beau?

"Mary-bell, what are you really trying to say? None of this sounds like a nightmare to me," Beau said patiently.

Marabelle plopped her elbows on the table. "Don't you see? Because of his convincing performance, everyone thinks he's wonderful and I couldn't do better for myself."

"So?" Beau and Paula said in unison.

"*So?* Hello, people. There's not going to be a wedding. Fake engagement, remember? Which means I'm left to clean up the mess when he finally dumps me." God, she sounded whiny and pathetic.

Wordlessly, Beau and Paula stared at her.

After a few beats, Beau hopped up and carried his plate to the sink. "Let me explain something to you about guys. No guy goes to all the trouble pretending to be engaged, buying expensive jewelry, and sucking up to his girlfriend's family if he isn't in a serious, committed relationship."

"That's what I said," Paula added.

Beau worked his strong fingers into Marabelle's tense shoulders. "I don't see much of a downside. From where I'm standing, this fake engagement looks pretty real."

Holy Serena Williams. Marabelle twisted in her chair and glared at Beau. "You're still in the doghouse. Because of you, I'm in a freakin' hot mess."

Beau raised his hands in surrender. "I had nothing to do with your fake engagement. That was between you and Coach."

Paula jabbed her finger at Marabelle. "Yeah, don't be blaming Beau."

Marabelle rolled her eyes. "Sure. Take the hot guy's side."

"Hey, I like you, Paula Carver. How 'bout hanging out with me tonight?"

Beau could tempt cloistered nuns with his sexy smile, the wily fox.

"I'd love to." Paula reached for Beau's outstretched hand, and they both bolted for the door. Marabelle followed. "Go. Have fun. Leave me here to wallow—" She froze. Another car sat parked in front of her house.

"*Nick.*" She pushed past Paula and Beau and raced down the steps. Nick closed the door to his Porsche just in time as she flung herself into his arms, wrapping her legs around his hips, and hugging him around the neck.

"Hey there, baby girl." He smiled, giving her a tight squeeze.

"I missed you," she breathed, pressing her lips against his for a long, deep kiss.

"You'd think they hadn't seen each other in months," Paula said with a sigh.

Beau smirked. "Yeah, it's obvious she can't stand the guy."

Marabelle clung to Nick and kissed him in front of her house for all her nosy neighbors to see, and she didn't care. She was in his strong, supportive arms, and that was all that mattered.

Still holding her in place, Nick said in his dark-velvet voice, "Invite me in."

"So, no hood-of-the-car sex?" Marabelle sounded breathy, and she never did breathy.

Nick gave a wicked smile. "Sure. We can ask Lilah Dawkins to score our performance."

Carrying Marabelle inside her small foyer, he released her legs slowly. Marabelle buried her nose in his chest, inhaling his signature scent.

"You hungry? T-there's food in the kitchen."

Nick walked her backward down the hallway; his hands never left her body. "No. I'm more interested in your bedroom, Tinker Bell. More specifically, your bed."

They made quick work of removing all their clothing. Nick tossed Marabelle on her bed and followed her down, covering her with his body.

He kissed and stroked until she was mindless with need. Marabelle delighted in his warm, muscular body beneath her palms. She loved how he made her feel and how he made her forget. Forget this wasn't real. And he wasn't hers. And she wasn't worthy.

"We should slow down. I'm going too fast." He

rained kisses over her face and chest. But Marabelle didn't want slow. She wanted fast and hard, and she wanted Nick more than she'd ever wanted anything in her life. And for this moment, he was hers, and that would have to be enough.

She rubbed against him, reveling in his moan of pleasure. "I need you now," she breathed. Emotions she couldn't name unfurled inside her chest, but she treasured their intensity. Impatient, she pulled him down and stole another kiss, opening her legs to cradle him. Nick prodded the entrance to her body and gently rocked.

Marabelle wanted all of him…now. She clasped her legs around his thighs and lifted her hips, sheathing him completely inside her body. Pleasure spread like a liquid inferno. Nick stroked slow and deep.

"More. Faster. Harder." She locked gazes with him.

Suddenly her urgency became his. Nick thrust, and Marabelle clung to him, digging her nails into his back. Small cries broke from her throat, and her hips rose convulsively against him.

Mindless with need, Nick's breathing grew more labored. Until—

"Fuck!" Suddenly he stopped.

"W-what?" Marabelle's eyes flew open.

His arms shook from holding all his weight. "No condom," he rasped.

Marabelle gasped.

"Say the word, babe, but hurry," he growled in frustration with sweat beading his brow.

The ramifications of what they were doing didn't go unnoticed. Marabelle watched the tension in his neck and corded muscles. But she never felt panic. She felt right. She felt loved.

"Don't stop," she breathed.

That's all it took.

Nick slammed into her. She felt him all the way to the core of her heart, climaxing on the third deep thrust. She bucked against him, his name exploding from her lips.

Nick barely held on, making a guttural sound and shuddering his release only moments later.

Chapter 22

"No." Marabelle sat in her kitchen, wearing Nick's button-down shirt and a scowl. "I'm not marrying you. I want an affair. I don't want marriage. You promised an affair and all kinds of sex, and…and…now you're reneging."

Nick calmly devoured several pieces of chicken, washing them down with beer.

"For the umpteenth time, we just had unprotected sex, and I will not have my child growing up a bastard. We're getting married."

Marabelle recoiled in horror. "But I'm not pregnant!"

"You know that for a fact?" He watched her over the top of his beer bottle.

Her hand flew to her stomach. "No. But chances are remote. It was only one time."

Nick arched a brow. "Darlin', I wonder how many thousands of women said that very statement while staring at a positive pregnancy test. When's your next period?"

Marabelle blushed. Somehow her life felt like a roller coaster, rounding a curve too fast and lifting off the tracks. *Holy John McEnroe.* She hated roller coasters.

If she ended up pregnant, Nick would be with her every step of the way and do the upstanding thing. He'd be an awesome dad. And somewhere in the far recesses of her heart, that made Marabelle smile. But…

Marriage? Not under those circumstances.

She could've said no. He would've stopped. She hadn't wanted him to. She was too consumed with wanting him...*all of him*. She might be reckless, but she wasn't stupid. Marriage was hard enough when two people loved each other.

"The thing is, I'm not very regular," she mumbled. "I'm not sure when...you know." Her hand fluttered in the air between them.

The intensity with which Nick watched her had Marabelle's heart thumping erratically. Like he had X-ray vision and could actually see her ovulating. She squirmed in her seat.

"I expect to be the first to know whether you get your period." Lifting her onto his lap, he wrapped in her in his arms. "And if you're pregnant...we're getting married." His tone dared her to disagree. "Deal?"

Distracted by Nick's hand sliding up her thigh and under her shirt, stroking her belly, Marabelle focused on not moaning aloud.

"I want to hear you say it, Tinker Bell," he pressed, giving her a gentle shake.

"Deal," she whispered.

⁓

Nick hurried home from his meeting at Cherokee head-quarters to get changed. Tonight, he was picking up Marabelle and heading out to Harmony, a small town twenty minutes from Raleigh where John and Elizabeth lived, for the ridiculous photo shoot. And he'd prom-ised not to be late. Beau, Ty, Ricky, and Rocker had all agreed to be photographed for the promotional poster.

As long as it didn't border on raunchy, Nick figured he'd participate too.

One puppy-dog look from Marabelle, and he was a goner. Saying no to her was not an option. But after the bullshit publicity shoot, he could finally relax, because Marabelle was his for an entire weekend. No interruptions.

The negotiations regarding the draft had been demanding the past few weeks. Tempers had flared as they'd narrowed down the scout's choices. The ultimate decision was up to the GM and Marty Hackman, but Nick fervently hoped they'd take the talent evaluator's advice on potential players. The future of his team's performance, and his job, hung in the balance. He couldn't build a winning ball program if he didn't have strong players, and if he didn't have a winning season, his building days would be over, because he'd be out of a job. Nick had argued his case. Now all he could do was wait.

But none of that mattered to him right now. Because what he wanted even more than a winning football season was Marabelle. And that shook him down to his very core.

Marty Hackman had pulled Nick aside after the meeting to say he thought it was time to hold a press conference with Marabelle, officially announcing Nick's engagement, and have them pose for publicity shots. All would go a long way in cleaning up Nick's bad boy reputation—and wouldn't hurt the Cherokees' standing in the community either.

That would certainly make everything official in everyone's eyes…except Marabelle's. She was sticking to her affair like tar to the bottom of a car. No amount of coaxing on his part had persuaded her otherwise. A small part of him actually hoped she was pregnant so she'd have to marry him.

Nick hadn't planned this particular line of attack... unprotected sex was *never* in his playbook. But what the hell, he'd work with what he had. Nick wanted her with a fierceness that terrified him. He needed her like he needed food and water.

Now the tricky part...to convince her she felt the same way.

Nick knew Marabelle was scared of her feelings for him and was using the "affair" as a protective shield. He'd go along...to a point, but if she dragged her feet much longer, then he wasn't above using every weapon in his arsenal to get what he wanted. He'd pull out all the stops and use whatever and whoever at his disposal to change her mind.

***

Ginger Jones checked her reflection in her rearview mirror one last time as she pulled in the driveway of the two-story English Tudor home. She'd been salivating for years to get a crack at one of the properties that sat on the most prestigious street inside Pine Boulevard. When the call came in from Carol Evans about listing her house for sale, Ginger had practically kicked up her Gucci heels. Because Carol would tell all her friends, and soon Ginger would be the Realtor *en vogue* to the rich and snobby. Exactly what she wanted to be.

That...*and* Mrs. Nick Frasier.

Nick was the only thing that eluded her in her well-mapped-out, meticulously constructed, perfect world.

The last piece of the puzzle. And Ginger was determined to make him fit somehow…someway.

Ginger's world hadn't always been perfect. She'd left the trailer park she'd grown up in and never looked back. She'd put herself through school by waitressing and handing out socks and jocks at the university's gym locker room. She had even jumped out of her fair share of bachelor party cakes. She hadn't worked this hard all her life to lose now. This was a simple setback and nothing more. She knew how to go after what she wanted.

And she wanted Nick.

According to Beau, Nick was head over heels in love with that stupid, brassy bitch, Marabelle. Ginger snorted to herself. A temporary lapse in good judgment. It would run its course and fizzle out. Ginger never doubted her abilities to keep a man satisfied. She knew he would be hers…soon, very soon.

Ginger sipped on a glass of Chardonnay while Carol Evans gave her a guided tour of her home. Ginger made mental notes of the home's nice finishes and painted cove ceilings as Carol kept up a running monologue, detailing her extracurricular activities and charity work. Ginger got the distinct impression she should be duly impressed with Carol's status in the community. She made all the appropriate comments of praise.

"My latest project at the moment is spearheading Trinity Academy's gala and auction. *Quelle* nightmare," Carol groaned, descending the grand staircase back to the large foyer.

"Nightmare?" Ginger's ears perked up at the mention of Trinity Academy.

Carol reached the bottom step and turned. "You have

no idea. I'm working with a bunch of imbeciles, and the gal in charge of the live auction is a disaster. Don't misunderstand, Marabelle Fairchild has lined up some great bachelors except"—Carol held her index finger up for emphasis—"the biggest draw of all. How she gets engaged to the guy is beyond me." Carol heaved a huge sigh.

Ginger almost spewed wine onto Carol's oriental runner at the mention of Marabelle's name. Obviously, Little Miss Big Mouth had more enemies than she realized.

This was good. Real good.

Ginger recognized a gift when she saw one. She would get back at that brat, and have Nick all to herself, if it was the last thing she did. She savored another sip of wine, mulling the options over in her head. Carol proceeded to spill juicy details about the gala, Marabelle, and the live auction, until the tour ended on her craft room and fifth and final bathroom.

"Fascinating. You're saying Nick Frasier is not participating in the live auction because he's engaged to Marabelle?" Ginger asked with a touch of innocence as Carol led her back to the formal living room.

Carol nodded. "Yes. It's such a shame and a waste. Our profits would more than double if we added his name to the list. I'm not lying when I tell you this girl has nothing. I hear she's a wonderful teacher and deserves a promotion, but her wardrobe is atrocious and her manners are appalling and she's certainly not much to look at with all that curly hair…"

"She certainly isn't," Ginger mumbled under her breath.

"…but somehow she's got something on Coach Frasier…"

"She certainly does," Ginger murmured into her glass of wine.

"...I wish I knew what it was, so we could work around it. Coach Frasier was the whole reason behind this year's gala. I mean, I'm happily married, but lemme tell ya, that man is wicked hot." Carol's New Jersey accent started to leak out. "Marabelle doesn't seem to be going anywhere. Whatcha gonna do?" Carol shrugged her Chanel-clad shoulders. "And Coach Frasier seems to really like her. Oh well."

Ginger always made it a point to get to know her clients, warts and all. She'd sized up Carol Evans and realized she could be a formidable enemy or friend. Ginger wanted to make sure it was the latter. Carol sat next to her on a Queen Anne sofa, nibbling a sugar cookie from a silver platter the housekeeper had produced.

Ginger settled her half-empty wineglass on a linen cocktail napkin. "Carol, today just happens to be your lucky day. Not only can I sell your house and make you a lot of money, but I think I can help you with your Marabelle problem."

Carol's brows arched. "Really? I'm listening. What exactly did you have in mind?"

Ginger slid a contract across the mahogany coffee table toward Carol. "First, read this and sign on the bottom. Then you and I can have a productive chat about Marabelle Fairchild."

Indecision flickered across Carol's face as she glanced at the contract.

"I assure you, it will be worth your while," Ginger encouraged. "According to Twitter and the rest of social media, this engagement is a publicity ploy. Something

Marty Hackman has cooked up to increase ratings and goodwill for the Cherokees."

"Well, of course, we've seen the tweets too, but I'm not so sure. Now Facebook's holding a contest on guessing the wedding date."

Ginger gave the contract a nudge. "Trust me. I have personal knowledge of Nick, and I can safely say there will be no wedding." To Marabelle at least.

Nick waited in Marabelle's living room while she zipped up her overnight bag for the weekend. The hum of small wheels rolling down the hallway signaled she was finally packed and ready to go.

"I'm so glad you finally agreed to come tonight." Marabelle parked her bag by the front door. "Thank goodness Elizabeth agreed to host this photo shoot. One more thing ticked off my to-do list," she said with a big sigh.

Nick adjusted his white linen pants. "Yeah, the sooner it's over, the sooner we can get out of there," he rumbled.

Marabelle ran her hand along his long-sleeved, light-blue linen shirt…the stupid "outfit" everyone had agreed on for the publicity poster. Hell, it beat standing there in nothing but boxer briefs.

"We can't be rude. Elizabeth has gone to a lot of trouble. She's even holding a meeting for the committee from hell to finalize the event." She wrapped her small hand around his wrist.

Nick tucked a curl behind Marabelle's ear, allowing his finger to trail down her neck. "She's great that way." He loved the silky softness of Marabelle's skin.

"Absolutely. So, please don't be difficult tonight," she pleaded.

Nick slowly backed Marabelle up against her front door. "Don't push it, Tinker Bell, I haven't even decided if I'm going to participate." He had to give the pretense of still being in charge, when nothing could be further from the truth.

"Wait. You already promised. Are you backing out?"

He curled his hands behind her head and pulled her in for a long, slow, burning kiss that frustrated more than quenched.

Nick sighed against her plump lips. "If the photographer wants us to stand on our heads with our asses in the air, I'll go along, if it will make you happy."

She leaned back, lips wet, casting him a doubtful look. "No questions asked?"

"Only one…did you get your period yet?" He slid his hand under her short jean skirt and up her bare thigh.

Marabelle gasped, clamping her hand down on his arm. "No!"

He let a wolfish grin unfurl. "Good, I'm glad." His fingers inched up, unimpeded, brushing her panties, slipping beneath the elastic.

"S-stop. And stop asking… I… Don't…start something…"

"You're wet," Nick rasped as his fingers rubbed between the juncture of her thighs, "and hot and… soft…" Her grip slackened, and her breathing turned choppy. His dick shot to full attention. He wanted to strip her naked and sink into her *now*, claiming what was rightfully his.

"Christ. We can't do this now." He let out a ragged

breath and reluctantly reined in his lust. He pressed a hard kiss on her mouth, removed his hand from her wet heat, and squeezed her hip until control returned to his body.

"Let's get this over with." He yanked on the handle of her overnight bag. "I want you in my home and in my bed...*soon*," he growled.

—◦—

On the drive over, Marabelle admired the small town of Harmony and its picturesque Main Street. Nick pointed out the funky diner called The Dog, short for Dogwood Diner and Grill, where he and John met for dinner sometimes. It had become a local draw with its colorful interiors and karaoke/roller derby nights.

"Maybe we'll go one night. How are your pipes, Tinker Bell?"

"I probably sing about as well as you play tennis. But I can skate. What about you, Coach?" Marabelle asked.

"I'm more of a spectator. But the owners, Cal and Bertie Anderson, are always looking for new talent. I bet you'd look sexy in those short derby outfits. Tight, short, hot pants and low-cut top, showing lots of cleavage." He chuckled.

Marabelle shot him a wry look and snorted. "Yeah, sure. I'll wear that outfit as soon as *you* wear it."

Inside Elizabeth's cleared living room, Nick and the players gathered around in varying shades of pastels and linen, looking like a bunch of Easter eggs. Elizabeth said the outfits contrasted nicely with their masculinity and set off their toughness to perfection. Whatever that meant.

The photographer continued to fuss over their positions, shooting frame after frame, adjusting the lighting, and positioning the guys until he seemed satisfied with Nick standing front and center, holding a football, and the guys angled off on each side of him.

The photographer motioned for Marabelle to check the photo on the digital camera.

"Wow. This is gonna make an awesome poster." She graced the photographer with her smile. "Just for kicks, why don't we take one without shirts—"

"That's a wrap. Come on, guys, let's move the furniture back in place," Nick said over hoots and whistles and Elizabeth's musical laughter.

After adjusting the sofa according to Elizabeth's instructions, he hustled Marabelle to the door to make a quick escape. He'd given John and Beau enough ammunition to use against him because it was obvious to a blind man he couldn't keep his hands off her, and he didn't want to embarrass either one of them any further. With other women, it had all been an act. He knew the difference now. With Marabelle, there was no acting involved…he was whipped.

Elizabeth escorted them to the door. "Marabelle, the gala committee will be meeting here Wednesday afternoon. Will you be joining us?"

Marabelle nodded. "You still okay with hosting the meeting? It's a lot of work, and the Blondie Twins can be like two ticks with no dog between them."

"She's right on this one. Those two give new meaning to the word *bitch*," Nick said.

"And Miz Cartwright is sweet but comes up with the zaniest ideas," Marabelle added.

"Don't worry about me. I can handle it. This event is going to be spectacular. I'll make sure everyone is on their best behavior," Elizabeth said, her game face in place.

"Better you than me." Nick heard the relief in Marabelle's voice.

———

"That went rather well, don't you think?" Marabelle asked for the third time, standing inside his kitchen. Nick could hear the nerves talking. She had chattered and rambled the whole way home. This would be the first time she'd stay with him the entire weekend. Like a real couple. Like a real engaged couple. He knew it scared the hell out of her, because it scared the hell out of him.

Nick dropped her overnight bag by the door and waited in silence.

"You want me to make something? I do a really great gooey calzone. It'll beat any pizza you order." Marabelle ran her hands over the soapstone countertops.

Nick could think of a thousand things he'd rather she slid her hands over, starting with his chest and ending in his pants, but he kept quiet. She needed to adjust to being in his home with him for two full days.

"Gooey calzone sounds perfect. We'll eat in front of the TV," he offered. The tension in her shoulders eased. "Let me change out of this fruity outfit, and I'll be down to help." He picked up her bag and headed toward the stairs, wanting to bottle the memory of her standing in his kitchen.

Nick finished his calzone and half of Marabelle's

as they sat in front of the flat-screen TV and surfed the channels.

"Wait. Don't change that. I wanted to hear the secret ingredient," Marabelle said. Nick had changed the station away from the Food Network and landed on a rerun of *What Not to Wear*.

"You need this more. Pay attention. You might pick up some valuable pointers," he teased, tossing the remote in her lap and then gathering up dirty dishes. "Cherry Garcia? You interested?" Marabelle nodded, cringing at clothes being tossed in a large garbage can.

After ice cream, Nick switched to the Travel Channel where they were doing a piece on island destinations. Marabelle sighed at the aerial views of various exotic locations with first-class resorts.

"I'd love to get away to some faraway island and do nothing but sunbathe, swim, and drink piña coladas."

He grinned, brushing a kiss against her sweet-smelling temple. "I had no idea you were an exhibitionist. You know they sunbathe nude on those islands."

"Not *all* of the islands." She twisted to stare up at him.

"Pretty much."

"What about Bermuda? I want to go there and see the pink sand. And I want my own private villa with my own private infinity pool overlooking the water. Then maybe I'll sunbathe nude." She settled back against his chest.

The idea of Marabelle sunbathing nude captured his imagination. "Remind me to call my travel agent first thing in the morning."

She answered by turning slowly in his arms, rubbing her breasts against his chest. "I can think of something better I'd rather do," she whispered, sealing her lips over his.

Nick turned the tables and flipped Marabelle onto her back as he followed her down.

"Is this what you had in mind?" He kissed the column of her neck.

"I was hoping you could do better," she said through gasps, her arched back asking for more. Nick chuckled, brushing his stubble into her soft, creamy skin just above her barely-there lacy bra.

"Pay attention, Tinker Bell," he said for the second time, "you're about to get your first lesson in sofa sex."

Chapter 23

"YOU WANT BUTTER AND SYRUP WITH YOUR HOT-cakes?" Marabelle called over her shoulder as the back door to the kitchen opened. She stood over Nick's stove on Sunday morning, wearing another one of his yummy-smelling, button-down shirts and a satisfied smile.

Nick had gone for a run while she'd lounged in bed, reliving all the incredible sex from the weekend. She'd had no idea sleepovers could be so much fun… or so aerobic.

As she'd stretched her arms over her head in the middle of the bed, she'd tried to decide which was better: sofa sex, up-against-the-wall sex, Jacuzzi sex, or dreamy-barely-awake morning sex. Hmmm, such a close call. Guess she'd have to do each one again to make her final verdict.

Nick was a most generous lover, always making her feel cherished and loved. He'd taught her the art of give and take. Frankly, Marabelle thought he gave way more than he took, but he didn't seem to mind.

Whenever they were together, he devoted 100 per-cent of his attention to her. That had to mean something. No one in Marabelle's family ever acted as if she had anything interesting to contribute. But the way Nick actively listened when she spoke and encouraged her, made her believe she had more to offer.

On Saturday night, Nick had taken her out to the symphony and a romantic dinner afterward, never leaving her side the entire evening and always introducing her as his fiancée. He had Marabelle believing in the impossible…*a real relationship*.

And then Marabelle's good friend, Doubt, with its wart-like head, showed up, yapping and telling her how foolish she was to believe in fairy tales. Why would Nick keep her around for the long haul when he could have his pick? How long before the novelty of dating a simple schoolteacher would wear off? Before someone way more glamorous caught his eye? How long before she saw her pictures posted all over social media with the headlines: Scandal! Plain schoolteacher jilted over SI's bathing suit cover model.

The kitchen door closed with a loud bang. "Excuse me?" an unfamiliar feminine voice asked.

Uh-oh. That wasn't Nick.

Marabelle whipped around, still holding a metal spatula in her hand.

A tall, glamorous woman dressed in designer jeans and pale-blue silk blouse stood in the kitchen. *Holy Roger Federer.* Her depressing thoughts had become reality. *Dammit.* Marabelle didn't want her fantasy ending today. She wanted more time. She needed more time. She couldn't give Nick up yet. Where the hell was Nick, and who was this beautiful woman?

Marabelle's face grew heated. "May I ask what you're doing?" Glamour Girl's eyes narrowed; clearly she was not pleased.

"Making hotcakes?" Marabelle squeaked.

With a sweeping gaze, Glamour Girl assessed the domesticated mess in the kitchen. "Where is Nick? And *who* are you?" Her exasperation was rising.

"I…uh…Nick is out running." Marabelle frantically scanned the kitchen for a place to hide. Maybe if she stepped inside the pantry and never came out. "Would you like a hotcake? They're homemade." She tried to keep the panic from clawing at her throat as she slid pancakes onto a platter.

"No, thank you." She placed her designer handbag on a kitchen chair and stared pointedly at Marabelle. "I'm Natalie, Nick's sister. And you are?"

What? *Nick's sister!* Suddenly the resemblance was crystal clear. Same blue eyes. Same streaked blond hair. *Damn.* This was bad. She'd rather be dealing with one of Nick's disgruntled ex-girlfriends. She had experience with that. But his sister? A member of the family? How should she put this? *Hi, I'm Nick's current sex partner, who just happens to be your son's teacher.* That should put Natalie's mind at ease. Marabelle could feel a hysterical laugh coming on. She tamped it down and cursed Nick at the same time.

"Nice to meet you. I'm…um…Marabelle Fairchild. Orange juice? Freshly squeezed?" She held up a glass, staying behind the island, not wanting to expose any more of her half-naked self to Nick's disapproving sister. Could this get any worse?

Natalie shook her head. "Fairchild? How do I know that name?" She studied Marabelle with the same piercing gaze as her brother.

Oh, I am so busted.

Bile churned in her stomach, and Marabelle swallowed the urge to vomit. "Uh, I'm Brandon's teacher at Trinity Academy," she mumbled, praying Natalie was hearing impaired.

Natalie recoiled. Horror registered on her face, and she covered her mouth with a shaky hand. "You teach Brandon?" she whispered. "And you're standing in Nick's kitchen in nothing but a…a shirt?" She sank down onto a kitchen chair as if she'd lost the strength to stand.

Crap. Natalie had perfect hearing.

"It's not exactly what you're thinking." Yeah, right. She taught her kid by day and had sex with her brother by night. "I know this looks bad, but there's a perfectly logical explanation… I just can't think of what it is at the moment." Marabelle wiped her hands clean with a dishcloth. "How 'bout I just grab my things and be on my way?"

Natalie continued to sit as if paralyzed, blinking up at her.

"Do you need to breathe into a paper bag or something?"

"What smells great, Tinker Bell?" Nick strolled into the kitchen, wiping his sweaty face with his T-shirt, when he stopped short. "What the fu… Natalie?" He looked from his sister's stricken expression to Marabelle's embarrassed one, and knew he'd just stepped into a steaming pile of buffalo shit.

"Hey, Nat, when did you get back?" He leaned down and gave his sister a peck on the cheek, careful not to drip sweat on her silk blouse. No one spoke through the thick, tension-filled pause. In his peripheral vision, Nick caught Marabelle sidling away from the kitchen island. *Great.* Panic mode. Then Natalie cranked up snobby mode, glaring at Marabelle as she spoke.

"I got home last night. I wanted to talk with you,

so I headed over this morning." Natalie glanced at her watch. "It's almost afternoon," she said absently. Nick grabbed a water bottle and picked at a hot pancake sitting on a platter. Marabelle continued to do the side step toward the exit.

"I would've called, but I wanted to surprise you."

Great surprise.

"I'm home for good," Natalie said as Nick watched Marabelle slip from the room. Another pause, more painful than the last. Nick rubbed the back of his neck in frustration. He should've stopped Marabelle from disappearing, but he needed to deal with his sister and all the jumping to conclusions running through her mind. "What happened here?" He pinned Natalie with his fiercest scowl.

She glowered right back. "You tell me. I'm not welcome in my own brother's home? What are you doing screwing Brandon's teacher?" she hissed.

Nick's eyebrows arched. "Is that what she told you?"

"She told me who she was. I managed to fill in the blanks on my own."

"It's not what you're thinking. So just stop it."

"Why don't you explain it to me? I think I have the right to know, since she's Brandon's teacher."

Nick rolled his eyes and snorted at the same time. "That's lame, even for you. The truth is that Marabelle has taken really good care of Brandon while you've been off 'trying to find yourself.'" He made air quotes with his fingers. "Which is more than I can say for you."

Natalie winced at his accusation. "I guess I deserve that."

"You're damn right you do!" he almost yelled. "You should be thanking her instead of maligning her." He pointed an accusing finger at Natalie. "And before you continue to put her down, you should know we're engaged, and I'm going to marry her."

Natalie's eyes bugged out. *"What?* You're…*getting married*? When did all this happen? Does Mom know?" she sputtered.

He picked up a fork and dug into the pancakes, wishing he were sharing them with Marabelle instead of arguing with his sister. "I haven't told Mom and Dad yet. It's complicated. And after today, I'm going to have a lot of ground to make up," he said with a sneer.

Natalie approached him with her arms outstretched. "Nick, I had no idea. She didn't mention any engagement. I'm sorry. It's just…what do you mean it's complicated? What ground do you have to make up?" she asked.

He tossed his fork into the sink, having lost his appetite, and crossed his arms, propping his hip against the countertop. "Marabelle's kinda in denial. She doesn't believe we're getting married."

Natalie stepped around the island. "I don't understand."

"It's a long story. In the beginning, we were trying to help each other out, and now it's the real thing. I'm not clear on how it all happened." Nick shrugged. "I'm not clear on anything. But all I have to do is convince Marabelle. Piece of cake, right?" he added derisively.

"Absolutely." Natalie eyes flashed. "How could she not want to marry you? You're wonderful. Do you want me to talk to her?"

Nick gave a humorless chuckle at Natalie's immediate change of heart. Still, it was nice to know she supported him, no matter what. "Nah. Let's drop it for now." He pushed away from the counter. "I'm glad you're home. How's Brandon?"

Natalie's face lit with pleasure. "Wonderful, and I'm so happy to be back. I just came by to thank you for all you did. Dan and I are going to try to work it out... thanks to you." A pretty blush colored Natalie's cheeks.

"I have no idea what you're talking about," Nick lied.

"Mmm, whatever." She leaned forward and kissed him on the cheek. "I'm going. Don't worry about Dan and me. It's going to take some work, but we're meeting with a therapist, starting this week. I think we have a real chance this time." She squeezed his arm and then scooped up her handbag, stopping when she reached the door.

"Nick, if Marabelle is the one you want, don't let anyone or anything stand in your way. Go get her."

Nick smiled for the first time since entering the kitchen. "Nat, next time...send a text."

———※———

"Idiot. Moron. Stupid. Idiot!" Marabelle shoved her clothes in her overnight bag. How embarrassing.

Marabelle had rushed upstairs after literally escaping the heat in the kitchen, and took the world's fastest shower before she started packing up her clothes. She needed to get out of here. She needed to be alone. She needed shock therapy.

What had she been thinking? Cinderella was way past her curfew. Time to pack up her glass slippers and go home. She did not belong in the castle with the gorgeous prince and his evil sister.

"Come on." She tugged a pink bra out from under

the bed, threw it in her bag, and zipped it shut. Then she turned and froze. Her heart leapt into her throat.

"Don't go."

Nick stood in the doorway with a look of pure anguish on his face, as if his best friend, best dog, and best friend's dog had died. Marabelle had never witnessed visible pain on him like that. Ever. She wanted to wrap him in her arms and cover him with kisses, to assure him everything would be okay.

"Hey," she whispered, afraid to say more.

His gaze locked on the packed bag in her hand. He plowed his fingers through his hair and sighed. "Don't go...like this."

Her heart pounded so hard against her chest wall, she was certain he could hear it from across the room. "Nick, I'm sorry. I had no idea she was your sister. I didn't threaten to beat her up or anything. I swear." The bag slipped from her stiff fingers, hitting the carpet with a thud. "But God knows what she thinks of me. I'll never forget her look of utter disgust when she realized who I was. I'll probably have nightmares and need years of therapy. I just think—"

"Don't think," he said hoarsely. Marabelle blinked, and suddenly he stood within inches of her. He cupped his large hands on her shoulders. "Stay with me."

Marabelle searched his face for clues. The strain around his eyes and the tension bracketing his mouth nearly unglued her. This was so unlike her fearless, cocky, tough-as-beef-jerky Nick. Marabelle's stomach tightened in a knot, and her heart flipped like one of her hotcakes on the griddle.

"It's good. *We're good*," Nick murmured, lips

hovering above hers as he pulled her into his body. His damp shirt soaked the front of her cotton blouse, and the combined scent of sweat and outdoors filled her nose. Steamy heat sent shivers from her breasts down to her knees as she relaxed against him.

They still had issues. Insurmountable issues. But when Marabelle examined the tanned face and steel-blue eyes she loved, none of those problems mattered.

Nick brushed her lips with the gentlest of kisses. "Please," he whispered.

And that one word melted Marabelle's heart and sent her rude friend, Doubt, packing. Throwing her arms around his neck, she kissed him with everything she had. Nick was hers for another day.

Nick hoisted her up, wrapping her legs around his waist. His mouth moved over hers with a hard rest-lessness, as if the idea of losing her had rocked him to the core.

"Where're we going?" she gasped as they started to move.

"Shower," he growled.

She drew back. "I've already showered."

His grin turned mischievous. "Then you can just stand there and watch."

"It's gonna cost you," she said in a sly voice.

"How so?" he asked, reaching inside the massive shower and turning the lever.

"Oh, I think a little striptease is in order," she suggested in a teasing tone.

His brows arched. "I'll get naked, but I'm not stripping."

Marabelle laughed at the indignant look on his face. "I'm not asking for a pole dance. I just want to watch.

I love your body," she murmured as she nipped his bottom lip.

She could feel his hard erection jump, and a smile curved her lips. He quickly released her and stepped back. First he toed his shoes off and kicked them aside. Next went his socks and then his sweaty T-shirt.

Her mouth dried up as she watched the fantastic display of rippling muscles. She wanted to grab him right then and rub up against him like a big, fat, happy mama cat.

He was hot.

Very hot and hard.

His fingers slipped inside the waistband of his jogging shorts, causing them to ride low…way low. He pushed his shorts past his hips and kicked them on top of his sneakers. *Thank you, Lord.* Marabelle had found religion.

"Now what?" he asked, holding his arms wide.

"I pay you right back," she said, slowly unbuttoning her blouse.

———⁂———

Marabelle felt restless as she wiped down the clean kitchen countertops for the second time that night. The gala was just around the corner, and her volunteer job would soon be over. She had worked harder than anyone for the school, putting together an incredible group of athletes and celebrities for the live auction and tournaments. If it all went as planned, the school would rake in more money this year than ever before. And yet she didn't feel any more secure about her promotion than she had before it had started.

She poured herself a glass of iced tea and stared out

her kitchen window. Recently, Mrs. Crow had become very evasive every time Marabelle mentioned the teaching position. And the committee members, all busy with last-minute details, barely acknowledged her or what she'd accomplished. The Blondie Twins had given her a wide berth, still resenting her engagement to Nick. Like they had a chance with him. No one had a chance with him. Not even Marabelle.

Nothing had been resolved. Especially her situation with Nick. Marabelle was in love with a great guy, and it was making her sick. Yep. She'd fallen head over heels for Nick Frasier, and it was making her sick to her stomach.

Talk about stupid. She grimaced into her glass of tea.

And for the life of her, she couldn't come up with a single plausible way to get out of it without looking like a fool. She was setting herself up for the biggest, most humiliating breakup since Blake Shelton and Miranda Lambert.

She was going down. Knocked out cold.

She tossed her iced tea down the drain. "Face it, you're too weak to walk away first," she mumbled.

She started scrubbing her clean kitchen sink. For the record, she knew Nick had feelings for her. He desired her and made love with a ferocity that stunned her, but…he never talked about anything long-term except when he nagged her about being pregnant. But that was responsibility talking. Marabelle didn't want Nick to feel responsible. She wanted him to need her above anything else.

She wanted him to *love* her.

She poured herself another glass of iced tea and then

absently put it back in the refrigerator. If he loved her, shouldn't he be pushing for a wedding date? At the very least, shouldn't he be begging her to move in with him? But the topic never came up. Unless there was an audience—then he made a big production of introducing her as his fiancée. If that wasn't fake, then she didn't know what was.

The ringing of her cell interrupted her mental tough-love lecture. Maybe it was Nick. She scrambled for her phone inside her handbag. Could she be any more pitiful?

After Nick had dropped her at home early Monday morning before work, he'd left town to visit his parents in Jacksonville and wasn't returning until Thursday. He'd still managed to call as he'd sat at the gate waiting for his flight. To declare his love? Nah. But he did say he missed her, which she lapped up like chocolate syrup.

Stunned, Marabelle disconnected the call. Somehow her prayers had been answered. Fate or karma or good ole faith had come through. She'd been given the most perfect solution to her problem. A solution that was flawless and pure genius in its simplicity. Trinity Academy's sister school in Birmingham had invited her to fly out for an interview as soon as possible. They had an opening that would be just right for her. A full-time—with benefits—teaching position. And coaching tennis was on the table too.

What an opportunity. This could solve all her problems. Right?

She'd interview for a new teaching job with a really great school. She'd get the job and *presto*! She'd leave her current shaky situation and her fake fiancé with her head held high.

Marabelle paced back and forth in her small living room. This setup had potential. She would neither be the dumpee nor the dumper. Everyone understood how careers got in the way of relationships. It happened all the time. This could save her from being a pathetic loser. She was driven by her career. She'd be a fool to pass this opportunity up.

Yes! She stopped pacing.

And she'd be doing Nick a huge favor, too. This way he could save face and not look like a schmuck when he dumped her. Social media would have a hard time slanting this any other way. This would allow Marabelle to slink away, lick her wounds, and glue her broken heart back together without an audience. It might take a lifetime to get over Nick, but by physically removing herself from the situation, at least she had a fighting chance.

The plan wasn't foolproof. At close examination, it was probably shot full of holes. But she couldn't worry about it anymore. Besides, she had a more urgent problem needing her attention at the moment. Marabelle scooped up her car keys and headed out the door. She needed to make a stop at the all-night pharmacy.

She needed to buy a pregnancy test kit.

"You're what? You can't be. I don't believe it," Paula said, glaring at Marabelle from behind her horn-rimmed glasses.

Marabelle ladled homemade spaghetti into bowls, trying to remain calm, as if she hadn't just dropped a bomb.

"I'm sorry, but I think you have truly cracked," Paula said.

Beau Quinton leaned against the counter, staring at Marabelle as if she'd sprouted fangs. "I'm with Paula on this one. You can't be serious."

Marabelle placed the bowls of spaghetti and tossed salad on the table. "What's the big deal? People do it all the time," she responded with a conviction she didn't feel.

"Um, just taking a wild stab here, but I'm assuming you haven't told Coach." Beau pulled out Marabelle and Paula's chairs.

"No. I don't tell him everything. He doesn't own me, you know," Marabelle snapped, resenting Beau's implication.

Beau groaned and rubbed his stomach as if it ached. Paula shook her head in disgust.

"And you better keep your big trap shut on this one. I still haven't forgiven you for tattling last time. You're worse than my five-year-olds." Marabelle frowned in Beau's direction.

"Beau has already apologized, and besides he only did what you should've done yourself." Paula pointed her fork at Marabelle. "Tell Nick! He's your fiancé and has the right to know," Paula insisted.

Dammit. Their shocked reactions were unnerving her more than she cared to admit. Marabelle pretended to concentrate on the plate of spaghetti in front of her. "It's no big deal. Look, I may not get the job. Why borrow trouble?" she said, twirling pasta into a perfect coil on her fork. "Besides, he's not my real fiancé."

"Try telling him that," Beau mumbled around a mouthful of spaghetti.

Marabelle noticed Paula hadn't touched her food. "Let me get this straight. You're going to move to Birmingham to teach at another school, leave this great house you struggled to buy, great friends, and wonderful fiancé, who happens to be the hottest guy in the state of North Carolina—"

"Present company excluded, of course," Beau added with a smirk.

"Because *this* is the most logical thing you came up with to protect your fragile heart?" Paula asked, reading the guilt written all over Marabelle's face.

Marabelle lowered her head and fiddled with the napkin in her lap. "No. That's stupid. I don't know what you're talking about."

No one spoke for several strained moments until Paula couldn't keep quiet any longer. "The rational side of you has to know that you and Nick are not your parents. You can have a successful relationship and marriage. You love and respect each other…that's a huge foundation to build on." Paula covered Marabelle's hand with her own. "You need to stop running."

The seriousness in her friend's voice scared her. Marabelle didn't know what to think. Was there any truth in what Paula had said? Could she and Nick really make it? Could they live happily ever after?

Doubt tapped her on the shoulder and shook its nasty head, reminding Marabelle that fairy tales were nothing more than pretty lies. Big lies. In the real world, love sucked. Fabulous guys like Nick didn't end up with ordinary girls like her.

Paula smacked her palm flat on the table, making Marabelle jump and Beau stop eating. "You know what you need? You need an exorcism to get rid of all your childhood angst. But mostly you need to tell Nick you love him."

Marabelle squirmed in her seat. Her gaze shifted from Paula to Beau and back to Paula.

"I can't," she whispered, dropping her head.

Paula pushed back from the table, standing. "Well, I'm tired of your wishy-washy self. Go to Birmingham and ruin the best thing that's ever happened to you. I don't want any part of it." She took her plate of uneaten spaghetti to the sink. "I'm leaving. Q, you coming?"

"I'm gonna finish up here first."

"Suit yourself." Paula turned to go.

"Paula—"

"I'll let myself out. See you around." Paula left without a backward glance. Acid churned inside Marabelle's stomach, and she felt like the worst friend ever.

The mood was heavy in her tiny kitchen. With Beau's help, Marabelle put away the leftover dinner. They hadn't spoken much since Paula's sudden departure. Why was this so hard?

Finally, Beau broke the silence. "When do you leave for Birmingham? I mean for the interview?"

She swiped a dishcloth over the clean kitchen table for the third time. "This Thursday through Saturday. The gala's next weekend, and I have to be here."

He moved between the table and the door. "Coach returns on Thursday. You going to be talking to him?"

"Probably. He calls or texts every day." She tossed the dishcloth in the sink and rounded on him. "Promise me you won't tell him. Why bring it up when it could be nothing?" Marabelle reached out, squeezing her hand around his forearm, her voice deepening. "Don't you see that I have to do this?"

---·····---

What Beau saw was a girl afraid of love. And afraid of taking that leap of faith. He shook his head. "You're in serious denial, sweetheart. I think you should tell Coach how you feel. You may be surprised at the outcome." She pressed her lips together, jaw tightening.

He shrugged and tapped her nose. "It's your decision. But I think you're wrong. He's going to be royally pissed off, and he's going to take it out on us. If you don't do it for yourself, then think of the guys…Ty, Ricky, Rocker, me." He rubbed his forehead. "Jesus. Training is gonna be a friggin' nightmare."

Marabelle wrapped her arms around her waist. "Not true. Nick would never take it out on you guys."

Beau snorted. "That goes to show what you know. I need to use the john, and then I'm out of here."

Marabelle might as well strap dynamite to Coach's Porsche and light a match…that was how bad this was gonna blow. When the shit hit the turbo fan, Beau didn't want to be within striking distance of Coach Frasier's foul mood.

He washed up and started to dry his hands on a linen towel, when he spied a home pregnancy kit, sitting next to some bottles of lotion on the countertop. Beau had no qualms about picking it up. Only one test remained.

He whistled softly. "What is Mary-bell up to now?" He replaced the kit back where he'd found it.

"Another shit storm. Here we go again."

Chapter 24

NICK WAS HALF ASLEEP AND PRETTY SURE HE'D HEARD Marabelle wrong. He'd left his parents' place at six in the morning to catch a flight back to Raleigh, and he hadn't had his morning coffee yet, when his cell indicated a voice message from her. Something about leaving for Birmingham for a meeting. What meeting would she have in Birmingham?

He pressed the phone to his ear again. *Damn.* She wouldn't be home until Saturday night. If he knew Marabelle, she was probably chasing another celebrity, like Bradley Cooper or Rafael Nadal, to con them into participating in her school auction. Nick had texted her back, but she hadn't responded.

A wave of disappointment rushed over him. He'd looked forward to getting back to her. He had missed her and wanted to get their relationship back on track. They had made huge progress in the last few weeks, and he didn't want any setbacks. And Nick knew only too well that the slightest thing could set him back. Just flying down to see his parents had been a risk, especially after the kitchen episode with his sister.

Marabelle had been mortified at meeting his sister, wearing only his shirt. He couldn't have cared less, but she had some warped image of the way people perceived her, and she was always in great fear of screwing up. Thanks to Edna.

Nick knew Natalie would come around in time and love Marabelle as much as he did. And there was never any doubt about his parents. They were already over the moon from the stories he'd shared with them. His mother couldn't stop beaming and hinting about babies. He agreed it all had a nice ring to it. He wanted that family his mother gushed over. He wanted it with Marabelle. And deep down he knew it wouldn't hurt his career either.

Now he needed to convince Marabelle. He leaned his head back on the cushioned headrest in first class and stretched out his legs, closing his eyes in an attempt to relax. But try as he might, he couldn't get Marabelle's message about Birmingham out of his head. Marabelle's impulsivity always made him nervous.

Very nervous.

———— ∼∞∼ ————

Once again, Beau found himself between a rock and a hard place. On one hand, he had Marabelle acting like a frightened kitten, ducking for cover, and on the other hand, he had Coach, who controlled his career. He'd be real smart to remember that one.

This time he was not getting involved. Little Mary-bell could fend for herself. He didn't want to be within striking distance when the bullets started to fly.

Right. Who was he kidding? Mary-bell really sucked at this deception stuff. She sucked at falling in love, and she sucked at knowing when something was right and when it was wrong. What she had with Coach was right.

What she planned to do was wrong.

"Damn," Beau muttered as he hopped in his Escalade

and headed for Cherokee headquarters. He didn't know how much Coach knew, but he had a strong hunch Marabelle hadn't told him about the interview. And he'd bet his right testicle she hadn't told him about those pregnancy tests.

Beau hesitated before rapping his knuckles on Coach's office door. "Here goes nothing," he mumbled.

Fifteen minutes later, he left Coach Frasier's office with a cramp in his side and a full-blown headache. Had he done the right thing? After the look on Coach's face when he ratted out Marabelle, he wasn't so sure. This sucked. He felt terrible. Marabelle had begged him not to breathe a word. And there'd be hell to pay if she ever found out. She was his friend, and he didn't want her to get hurt, but he couldn't see any good coming out of her running away and leaving all her friends and Coach behind.

Coach had sat frozen like an iceberg, with eyes to match. The only movement Beau had detected was a tic in his right jaw that looked downright painful. As he stumbled through the explanation, he could see Coach becoming more and more remote.

He hurried on to explain that Marabelle was running scared, and he and Paula had tried to talk her off the ledge. It hadn't made a difference.

In a word…Coach was *furious*.

Beau had broken out in a cold sweat as he'd watched Coach's eyes go from chips of ice to bloody daggers. For once, he was glad he'd never had to play against him, because he was one scary mother when he was really angry.

He'd done his best to plead Marabelle's case. He'd

ended by saying, "For what it's worth, she loves you but is too paralyzed to admit it. She's got some serious self-esteem issues. She doesn't think she's worthy of love. Something about her parents' relationship"—Coach had never even blinked—"for what it's worth."

Nick sat for what felt like hours in his office, replaying Beau's conversation in his head. Furious didn't begin to describe his feelings.

He wanted to roar, pound his chest, drag her off to his cave, and never let her go.

Had he been flying solo throughout this whole relationship? Was he the only one who felt something every time they were together?

Not just when they were together. All the time. Every damn day.

What a freakin' moron.

To think he'd gotten excited about making their engagement official and actually setting a date. He'd even told his parents. Hell, he was even considering Marty Hackman's press conference. Nick wanted to announce it to the world. He winced, thinking of what Marty would say now, not to mention what he might do to Nick's career.

All these years, he'd managed to avoid marriage, dodging all kinds of women who wanted a piece of him. Beautiful women, placed on this earth to do nothing but look good and cater to his every whim. But he hadn't wanted to be put in a vulnerable position…until now. What a stupid schmuck.

Now the one person he'd decided to take the plunge

with wanted to run away. All this time, she'd been off plotting some covert operation on how to get away from him. She'd planned to pack up and move to another city. Another state.

While possibly carrying his baby.

Over his dead body.

He'd handcuff her to his side before he'd ever let that happen.

He couldn't believe he'd thought they loved each other and had a committed relationship. Had he seen only what he'd wanted to see? Okay, so she'd insisted she only wanted an affair, but that had to be nerves or fear talking. He'd never believed it. He'd thought he really knew her. He'd thought Marabelle loved him. How could he have been so wrong?

A buzzer sounded, and he became aware of Chantal's voice over the intercom. She'd interrupted his mental tirade to announce he had a call from Elizabeth Prichard.

Nick took a deep, slow breath and picked up the phone. After a few strained pleasantries, he tried not to howl out loud as he gnashed his teeth.

"Anyway, I just thought you might want to know what I overheard at the meeting on Wednesday night regarding Marabelle," Elizabeth said.

His ears perked right up. "Tell me."

"Those two women, Carol Evans and the other one, her name escapes me for the moment"—Nick knew she meant the Blondie Twins—"they were talking about some job in Birmingham at Trinity Academy's sister school. Apparently they have some contact there, and they've arranged for the school to offer Marabelle a job."

"*What?*" He sounded choked to his own ears. Marabelle was set up? That still didn't excuse the fact that she went for it and never discussed it with him. As if he didn't matter.

"Yeah. They seemed delighted about how easily Marabelle went for it," Elizabeth said, sounding disgusted. "Do you know anything about it? I'm really worried about her."

"No," he growled, "but I will."

"Here's to a very successful open house," Ginger Jones said, lifting a flute of chilled champagne in Carol Evans's large breakfast room.

Carol clinked glasses with hers. "That's wonderful news. Serious buyers or just snoopers?"

"Several couples were very serious. I'll follow up with phone calls. But I have even more good news." Ginger's lips curled into a sly smile.

"Do tell."

"It seems Operation Get Rid of Marabelle is working like a charm."

Carol's eyebrows shot straight up. "What have you heard?"

Ginger savored the bubbly champagne on her tongue before answering. "I called my cousin, the dean of students, in Birmingham, and he said Marabelle's interview went very well. The school has already made her an offer, and they want her to start right away."

"Has she accepted?"

"He wasn't sure, but she only has a couple of days to make up her mind. They need to know ASAP."

Carol drummed her French-manicured nails on the glass kitchen table. "Do you think we can sweeten the pot…you know, encourage her to go somehow?"

"Already thought of that, and taken care of it."

"Really?" Carol sounded surprised. "What do you mean?"

Ginger's gaze darted around the room to make sure they were alone; her voice lowered. "Let's just say somehow the school here knows all about her interview. And they're not too happy about it. She might not have a choice after all."

Carol's eyes widened as her mouth fell open. Her look of shock gave Ginger a moment of discomfort. But she'd only taken care of a problem Carol and the other women had talked about but didn't know how to solve.

"They wouldn't fire her, would they?" Carol sounded uneasy. "I'm the first to admit I find Miss Fairchild annoying, but I don't want to be a party to interfering with her right to make a living."

Her tone unnerved Ginger just a twinge. She didn't want this to come back and trip her up. She had spread a little useful gossip to the right people to better the cause for everyone's sake. Carol should be thankful.

It wouldn't be wise to upset her newest client. Ginger said, "I seriously doubt they'll fire her. I'm sure they'll let her know in no uncertain terms they are onto her. Marabelle will have to make a decision one way or another without too much delay. Everything will work out. Don't worry."

"If you say so," Carol said in a doubtful tone.

Ginger touched her hand. "And with any luck, maybe

we can convince Nick to get up on that auction block."
And back in my bed.

Marabelle had reached a final decision on her taxi ride
home from the airport Saturday evening. She really liked
the school in Birmingham. They had made her a generous offer, but as she sat staring out the dark window of
the car, she knew she could never pull the trigger. No
way could she leave her house she'd worked so hard to
buy, or her cute neighborhood, or friends who meant so
much to her, old and new. No way. She loved all of it
too much.

A calmness came over her. No way could she leave
Nick.

She loved him most of all.

If this weekend revealed anything, it proved she didn't
have the strength or the heart to leave him. She needed
to give their relationship a chance. If she left town now,
she'd never know if he really loved her or not.

She stiffened her backbone. From this moment forward, Doubt would no longer tell her what to do. She'd
be kicking it to the curb. No more running and hiding.
Marabelle would face her fears and conquer them. Just
because Edna and Ed were screwed-up didn't mean she
was doomed. She could *and* did have a normal relationship with Nick. And just because Edna thought she
never made the right decisions or choices didn't mean
Marabelle should keep listening to that inner monologue. Marabelle already knew Edna approved of Nick.

And if it didn't work out…well, she would survive.
Maybe a little more banged and beaten-up from the

process, but she'd survive nonetheless. She leaned her head back. She wouldn't think about that right now. She'd think about that tomorrow. She was getting really good at this Scarlett O'Hara thing.

As she fished for her wallet, her fingers brushed her busted up cell phone, and Marabelle cursed under her breath. She had dropped it on Thursday, running for her gate, and it had shattered on the tile floor. Tomorrow she'd head to the store to buy a new phone and retrieve any calls or messages she might've missed. After she paid the driver, she faced her front door and noticed a light from her living room peeking through the wood blinds. She didn't remember leaving one on when she'd left, but she'd been in a huge hurry, so maybe she had. She bumped up the front steps with her carry-on, unlocked the door, pushed it open with her hip, and stopped dead in her tracks.

Nick sat slouched on her sofa, facing the door with a beer bottle dangling from his fingers. He didn't move to stand. He watched her from under heavy lids, staring as if he'd never seen her before. He looked cold and remote, and Marabelle's heart skipped several beats... in a bad way. A very bad way.

Something was off.

Right away, Marabelle noticed his disheveled appearance. His wrinkled dress shirt looked slept in and hung out over an old pair of jeans. And his stubble had passed the cool stage, bordering on scary. Three more empty beer bottles sat on her glass-and-rattan coffee table.

Either someone had died, or someone was about to die.

Marabelle had a sinking feeling it was the latter.

She eased the door closed behind her. "Nick? You okay?" she whispered, afraid to speak any louder. His distance and demeanor unnerved her.

He stared stonily at her until panic pricked up her spine. When he spoke, she jumped at his raw voice, as if he'd overused it.

"You moving to Birmingham?"

Oh God. What was going on? What did he know?

Her mouth felt as dry as chalk; she swallowed hard. "Uh, no. How did you get in?" Nick didn't have a key to her place. Had he resorted to breaking and entering?

"Lilah." He took a pull on his beer, his hard gaze never leaving her face. She shifted her weight, still standing on the threshold of the room, remembering she gave Lilah Dawkins a key in case of emergencies. This must've been an emergency.

"Nick, I'm not sure what you've heard, but—"

"I heard plenty from your good friend Beau."

Dammit. This can't be happening again. Beau butted in when she specifically warned him not to. Anger and anxiety tightened her chest.

"Are you pregnant?"

"*What?*"

He rose on what seemed to be rusty knees, like he'd been frozen to that spot for hours. He invaded her space, blasting her with the intense heat radiating off his body. Usually she felt safe and comforted by his presence.

Today she felt cold and afraid.

A dangerous spark lit his expression. A strain showed on his face, as if he hadn't slept in days. This close, she could feel the rage rolling off his body like a clap of thunder. The air felt thick, crackling all around them.

"Simple question. Are. You. Pregnant?" he said in a voice devoid of any emotion.

Her head jerked up. "No. What gave you that idea?"

"This." He raised his left hand, shaking the opened pregnancy kit from her bathroom. She hadn't realized he'd been holding it this entire time. She tried snatching it away, but he yanked it out of reach.

"Where did you get that?" she snapped. "Are you adding pilfering to your breaking-and-entering repertoire?"

"Two tests are missing. How do I know you're telling the truth?"

She sputtered, "Because I am. Why would I lie about that?"

He gave a humorless, hollow bark of a laugh. "Because you've lied about everything else. Why should I believe you? Why did you use *two* tests? I want the truth!" he shouted. "And don't tell me I can't handle it!"

"I am telling the truth. I'm not pregnant." Her hand motioned toward the kit between his fingers. "I used two tests because I wasn't sure I did it right. End of story. Why are you so upset? I would've told you if I were."

Something flickered behind his cold eyes…a sadness, but it was gone before she could analyze it.

"Yeah, right," he snorted in derision, "like you told me about Birmingham and taking a job there. When were you gonna let me in on that one? After you'd already moved? Did you plan on sending a postcard?" He mimicked, "'Dear Nick, I've moved. Later, Marabelle. P.S., I'm not pregnant.'" She flinched. "I know damn well you would've never called or texted. Just like you didn't return all the texts and messages I left on your cell."

"I'm sorry. My phone shattered at the airport. I was without service the whole weekend. I didn't get any messages." She kept her voice calm, as if crooning to a wounded wolf about to strike.

He shook his head, disgust on his face. Abruptly he turned and flicked the pregnancy kit on the coffee table. He rubbed the back of his neck as if it ached. Without facing her, he said, "Why'd you do it? Go away without discussing it with me?" He spoke so low, she strained to hear him.

What a colossal mistake this whole exercise had been. All her reasons for leaving before seemed less than noble now. She should've listened to Paula and Beau. She should've banished her stupid fears. How could she explain to him without sounding selfish?

Marabelle worried the engagement ring on her finger. "I…uh…thought it would be a solution to our…my problem." She continued to talk to his rigid back. "I mean, the auction is over next weekend. We won't need to pretend anymore about the fake engagement." Her voice shook. "I thought if I left, it would be easier for both of us…" As she spoke, she felt her words polluting the air, making it difficult to breathe. Nick slowly turned around. The anguish etched on his face was so raw that Marabelle had to avert her gaze. She'd never meant to hurt anyone. Especially Nick.

"I love you," he rasped, "and you love me. Why would you do that?"

Loved her?

Hot tears welled behind her eyes as her gaze flew to his face. She couldn't bear his anger and hurt and accusations. She started to shake, locking her knees for control. "I d-d…didn't know. You never told me. This was all fake…a game…a…a fling. When did it stop being that?" she choked.

His response was as bleak as the expression on his face, and he shrugged. "I don't know. But it did. You know it, and I know it. Did I ever once give you the impression it wasn't real?"

Fire burned her cheeks. He looked away as if he couldn't stand the sight of her. "I did everything in my power to make you feel desired and…and loved. Instead of believing in what we had—*believing in me*—you run off and take a job in another state." His accusation pierced her shattered heart.

She stumbled forward on stiff legs. "Nick, I was scared. I wasn't thinking. How was I supposed to know? You…we never said anything. Please—"

"I should've walked out of your classroom the first day I met you and never looked back. You've been nothing but a shitload of trouble from the moment I laid eyes on you."

His words hit worse than a hard tennis ball to the face. "*What?*"

"Marabelle…" He reached out his hand.

She stumbled back, twisting the ring on her finger. He'd just confirmed her deepest, darkest fear.

I'm not worth it.

Her face burned with shame, then anger welled up inside her and spewed out of her mouth. "If you recall, none of this was my idea. But thanks for being so accommodating." She tugged hard, and the engagement ring finally slid off her finger. Surprised, she looked down.

Definitely a sign.

The ring bit into her palm as she squeezed her hand shut. "You were great. I mean in every sense of the word. Particularly in bed. You taught me a lot. Thanks again." Sarcasm dripped from her voice.

He moved closer; disappointment and regret filled his face. "Marabelle…I'm sor—"

"No. Don't say any more. I think we've both said enough." She gulped back a sob. "Here. Take it." She extended her hand. When he didn't move, she picked up his right palm and placed the ring in it. "You need to leave." Her voice quivered.

Motionless, he stared at the ring, which looked very small in his large palm, and then slowly he closed his fingers over it. "Don't do this." His voice was hoarse.

"Go!" She pointed a shaky finger at the door. "Please." Tears streamed down her face. Marabelle didn't know how much more humiliation she could stand.

Nick hung his head and nodded, moving toward the door. With his hand on the knob, he dropped the ring on the table by the door. "Keep it." She watched it bounce and ping, stopping just short of the edge. When she looked up, he was gone.

Chapter 25

MARABELLE SHOWED UP AT SCHOOL MONDAY MORNING only to find out she shouldn't have bothered.

She was out of a job.

Mrs. Crow had called Marabelle into her office to inform her that Mrs. Harris would be returning from maternity leave, and they no longer needed a teacher's assistant, but she'd appreciate it if Marabelle would finish out the week, concluding with the gala and auction. Then she proceeded to congratulate Marabelle on her new job.

Marabelle didn't even question how she knew about Birmingham. She didn't care enough. She didn't care about anything anymore. She spent all her energy working on last-minute details for the upcoming tournaments. She had an obligation to the people who were coming out to support her and Trinity Academy, and she did have some pride left. Besides, if she worked long and hard enough, she might squash all feelings until she was completely deadened, and then maybe, *just maybe*, she could make it through the day without curling into the fetal position and crying her eyes out.

After Nick had left Saturday night, she'd cried buckets. As for her broken heart, she chose not to deal with it. She stayed busy to keep from thinking. Period.

And yet, news had traveled fast. This time she almost smashed her new cell phone on purpose, because she received frantic calls from her mother, Phoebe, Beau, Paula, Elizabeth Prichard, her mother three more times, and even her dad. So much for no more tears. She had no strength to deal with the accusations and disbelief slung her way from friends and family. Nor did she have the energy to field all their questions. She did the most mature thing she could think of: she turned off her phone.

Shock and numbness had set in.

If she could survive this week, then…she hadn't a clue. But she knew one thing: she was out of here. Not sure where, but she'd come up with something.

Marabelle pulled her car into her driveway that afternoon, and Beau stood on her front porch with his arms crossed, wearing a scowl. Marabelle couldn't believe his nerve. With friends like him, she didn't need enemies. Marabelle shot him the evil stare as she dragged herself out of her car, pulling the cardboard box of supplies from the backseat.

"Why haven't you returned my calls or answered my texts? I've been worried sick," Beau said.

"Do I really need to explain it to you?" she said as she stomped up the steps. He unfolded his arms and plucked the box out of her hands.

"You look like hell. And I don't mean the ugly sweater you have on. Your eyes are all puffy, and you look like you haven't slept in days."

She pushed open her front door. "Thanks for the news flash. If you're done insulting me, you can leave." She dumped her keys on the table by the door and flopped down on the sofa.

"Get changed. I'm taking you out to eat," he said, dropping the box on her coffee table.

"I'm not in the mood for food or you. Why are you here? If you're snooping for more dirt to screw me with, I'm all tapped out."

His voice lowered. "Come on, Mary-bell, we need to talk. I'm really sorry, okay? I thought I was helping. I never meant to hurt you. If it makes you feel any better, everyone is having a crappy week." He eased down next to her on the sofa.

"Did everyone lose a job this week?" she asked with heavy sarcasm, picking at the loose threads on her ugly sweater.

"What?"

"Nothing. Just forget it. No one knows yet, and I want to keep it that way." She gave him a stern look. "That means keeping your loose lips zipped, got it?"

Beau nodded, wearing a grim expression. "Aw, Mary-bell. I don't know what to say." He pointed to the box. "Cleaned out your desk?"

She jumped up from her seat and grabbed the remote, pointing it at the TV and punching buttons, trying to drown him out. Beau plucked the remote from her hand and pushed the Off button. He gathered her in his arms.

"Come out with me tonight. Let me make it up to you," he said, rubbing her back. "Somewhere quiet so we can talk. Maybe it will help."

Unwanted emotions started to bubble to the surface. She didn't want to cry anymore. And she didn't want to rehash the scene with Nick…ever. But she also didn't want to be alone at her self-loathing party one more night. She sniffed back tears as she leaned against Beau and took what little comfort she could find in his arms.

"Okay. Let me change."

———

Beau created his third fajita while Marabelle picked at the burrito on her plate at Taco Town, a dive that offered authentic Mexican food, really cold beers, and really dark atmosphere, which added to her anonymity. Maybe talking about the breakup would be therapeutic. It couldn't hurt. She didn't think she could feel much worse.

Marabelle pushed the refried beans around on her plate. "What I tried to do was wrong. I knew it before I even returned home. But then Nick and I fought and said some pretty awful things to each other." She moved her plate of uneaten food to the side. "It's for the best. It was never meant to be in the first place."

Beau refreshed their margaritas from the pitcher on the table. "I'm sorry again. I didn't know he'd lose his shit with you. This whole thing sucks, but I think you're doing the right thing by finishing up the gala and auction. Maybe the auction will be so successful, you'll get your job back."

She sniffed. "Yeah, right. I could secure a million-dollar donor, and I wouldn't get my job back. I'm not even sure I want it back." She paused. Did those words just tumble from her tongue? Everything had been about job security and making her own living. She did have bills to pay, and her bank account was anemic. But it had also been about not caving to her mom's dictates and standing on her own. For some reason, all that didn't seem important. A few months ago, that wouldn't have been the case, but things were different now. Marabelle was stronger, more confident, and she would find another coaching or teaching job. One that paid more and where her efforts were appreciated.

Marabelle straightened her shoulders. "I'll finish up with the tournaments, but I'm not going anywhere near the gala."

Beau looked up from the packed fajita he'd just assembled. "I understand how you feel, but it's important you be there—"

"No." She shook her head.

"Let me finish. Ty, Rocker, and Ricky will support you the entire evening. Come as my date, and we'll make sure your auction is a huge success," he pressed.

"I can't. Nick will be there. I'm not that strong...yet." Her voice wavered. *Maybe never.*

"Four NFL players will be holding you up. You'll be great. Come on."

She didn't need another venue for her heart to break again. What if she couldn't hold it together and broke down crying? In front of everyone? In front of Nick? She twisted her napkin in a knot as she re-created various humiliating scenarios in her head.

She'd lost the love of her life.

She'd taken a gamble and blown it. At least she'd played the match. What was one more night? The damage was done.

Beau smiled as if her thoughts flashed on a jumbotron above her head. "I promise you won't regret it."

She heaved a huge sigh. "I already do."

Later, after dropping Marabelle home, Beau thought it would be a good time to pay Ginger Jones a visit. As

Marabelle had spilled her guts at dinner, something about her story struck him as odd. The timing felt forced. Orchestrated. Suddenly a job appeared out of nowhere in Birmingham and ultimately led to getting Marabelle fired. Who else knew she had an interview besides Paula and him? Obviously, little Mary-bell had made herself a few enemies. He'd felt guilty about his role in the whole debacle. Watching Marabelle beat herself up pierced him in the heart. He had to come up with a plan. He had to fix this.

Coach and Mary-bell had to get back together. Because they belonged together, and because he didn't know how much longer anyone could take Coach's nasty-ass mood. This needed resolving before training camp officially started, or the whole team was gonna be effin' miserable.

Ginger opened her door wearing a long, silky peach robe and most likely nothing underneath.

"I was surprised to get your call," she purred. "Haven't heard from you in a while." She opened the door wider, inviting him inside.

"Right. It's been much too long." He pulled her into his embrace, giving her a slow, leisurely kiss, rubbing his hands up and down her back. Yup. Nothing underneath.

"Got any beer?" he asked.

Disappointment flashed across her face. "Sure."

He drank his beer while Ginger sipped some nasty green tea as they sat around the pedestal table in her breakfast room. They chatted about nothing in particular, when he finally broke the ice.

"You planning on attending the tournaments and gala

at Trinity Academy this weekend? A bunch of us are going up on the auction block. Maybe you could put in a bid." He winked.

She swirled the tea in her cup. "I've seen your posters all over town. I just listed a house with one of the head coordinators of the gala. She says the auction is going to be fabulous."

"Yeah, all for a good cause."

She chuckled, leaning forward to fiddle with a bowl of lemons decorating the center of the table. "Good thing everything is set to go, because I understand Marabelle Fairchild has been fired, and she was in charge of the auction."

Bingo. Just as he'd suspected. As her robe slipped, Ginger revealed more than her fake tits. And Beau appreciated the information as well as the view. How had she known Marabelle had gotten fired? This had the makings of a fake play written all over it, and he hated fake plays unless he was the one pulling it off.

Beau stretched his legs and leaned back in his chair. "Well, now, that's awful. She put together the entire event. How'd you hear she got fired?" He gave an easy smile, sliding his gaze up her legs and over her breasts.

She tightened the knot on her belt. "Well, like I said, I know people who are involved."

I'm sure you do. "Yeah, it's too bad for cute little Mary-bell." He crossed his arms over his chest. "Did you hear she and Coach broke up?"

Ginger bolted upright, sloshing tea onto the table. "Uh, no. When did that happen? Nick and I haven't... you know, recently," she added, blotting the spilled tea with a napkin.

"Just happened. He's been biting everyone's head off since Monday. Must've been bad." Beau shook his head. "Damn, poor Marabelle...loses her job and her fiancé in one week. That's gotta suck."

Ginger's chin tightened. "She's young. She'll bounce back. I wouldn't be surprised if she gets another job offer right away. I understand she's an excellent teacher." Placing her teacup in the sink, she said, "And we all know Nick will be fine. He never took their silly engagement seriously."

Obviously, you didn't see the rock on her finger. "Maybe you're right. So, you gonna bid on me?"

She had her back to the countertop, posing with one long leg slightly bent, exposed almost to the top of her hip through the silk of her robe. "Mmm. I don't know. Depends on what you're offering."

He moved in front of her, skimming her body, placing his hands on either side of her face. "Let me see if I can convince you," he murmured against her lips.

"Did you hear that Marabelle was fired?"

Nick groaned, regretting opening the door to his sister. He wished everyone, including Elizabeth, John, and the whole team would get off his back. His mood had gone from bad to down the shitter ever since Saturday night. He'd just as soon forget the whole damn thing. But everywhere he went, someone gave him a rash of shit or ripped him a new one, while singing Marabelle's praises. He could've sworn the lady behind the deli counter at the Harris Teeter had given him a look of disgust. The whole town had painted him as the bad guy, and not one person had asked for his side of the story. Elizabeth Prichard even went so far as to threaten his family jewels if he didn't make up with Marabelle immediately.

As if he had a choice!

She was the one who'd lied, run away, kept important information from him, and then had given his ring back. She had no faith. In him or in their relationship. Marabelle wasn't tough. She was complete and total chickenshit.

And she'd never even told him she loved him.

That hurt most of all.

He'd bared his soul to her and she hadn't reciprocated.

Screw it. He was done begging. There were plenty of fish in the sea. Not that he wanted any of them, but it felt better just to know they were out there swimming.

Natalie pushed her way into his great room. "I found out today at school. I can't believe it. She's wonderful with those kids. Something's going on, and I don't like it." She plopped her large handbag down on the pool table and stared at him.

"You look like death." She studied him.

"Thanks. Why don't you make yourself at home?" he said, making a production of removing her bag before she ruined the felt on his table.

"When was the last time you slept?"

"Drop it." He grabbed her upper arm and propelled her farther into the room. "What exactly do you want from me?" He shoved a pillow onto the floor and pointed at the sofa. "Sit."

Natalie watched him with a concerned expression etched on her face as she gracefully eased down onto the cushions. Nick dropped down beside her and waited.

"I want you to get back together with Marabelle, and I want you to get her job back. I don't care which you do first. Just do something." Her voice grew louder and more anxious as she spoke. He would've been amused at his sister's sudden staunch support of Marabelle if he weren't so damn pissed. Only a week and a half ago, Natalie sat in his kitchen, accusing Marabelle. He shook his head as his shoulders slumped. It felt like ten years.

"Look, Nat, I'm not the issue here. She broke off the engagement. For all I know, she probably beat up a parent or something, and that's what got her fired."

"That's absurd!"

"You don't know Marabelle," he mumbled as he leaned his head back and closed his eyes.

Natalie poked him in the ribs with a pointed, manicured nail. "Don't be ridiculous. She's adorable and she's a wonderful teacher *and* you love her." He opened one eye and peered at her. "Don't get all supercilious with me, Nicholas," she snapped. Another nail poke. "I know you love her."

He raised an eyebrow. "Yeah? How?"

"Because I've never seen you like this after any of the thousand breakups you've had in the past. You certainly weren't this upset after that heinous bitch Lola ran off with the other quarterback. But with Marabelle, you're…a wreck."

Just the kind of stupid crap he didn't want to hear. Why couldn't everyone just leave him alone so he could move on and forget Marabelle? Forget her curly hair and luscious body and eyes the color of Hershey's Kisses. Forget her sassy, sensual mouth, the sound of her laughter. Forget how she slept sprawled on top of him, and the soft sighs she made. And God knows he'd like to forget the way she felt when he was inside her. Every time, it took his breath away.

He didn't want to remember her fierce competitiveness and the way she trash-talked as if she could back it up. He sure didn't want to remember her delicious meals and how she made his house feel like a home.

Nick missed talking to her. He missed arguing with her. He missed being with her.

Nick jumped up from the sofa and moved to stand in front of the French doors overlooking the front yard. If everyone would leave him alone, he could go about shoving the memories away in the far corners of his mind. He raked his fingers through his hair and told the biggest lie ever. "It was just a fling…nothing more. Let's forget the whole thing."

"Ha! That's why you flew home to tell Mom and Dad…about a fling?"

He whipped around and roared, "Goddammit! Just drop it! You're one to talk. Go work on your own failed marriage." Nick cringed at the color leaking from Natalie's face.

"Nat, I'm sorry. I didn't mean it." He dropped his head and stared at the fibers in the carpet. "Seems I'm saying a lot of things I don't mean these days."

She gave a heavy sigh and said, "You're right, but take it from me. Don't throw someone away because of your pride. I should know. If you love her, then she's worth fighting for." Natalie kissed Nick on the cheek, retrieved her handbag, and secured it over her shoulder. "Think about it. But not too long. I'll see you at the gala." She kissed his cheek again and left.

Nick felt particularly pathetic later that evening as he sat on his patio, wallowing in scotch on the rocks... alone. Natalie's visit made him think, but the bruises from Marabelle's betrayal were too fresh for him to make the first move.

Cursing, he thought of his upcoming meeting with Marty Hackman on Monday morning, and how his breakup would impact his career. It wasn't enough he had problems with a young, inexperienced team that needed to win a championship. He should be focusing on football. Not bachelor auctions and engagements to inexperienced schoolteachers and their insecure hangups. He hoped and prayed Marty would understand and let him get back to what he did best...nothing but football. Then maybe the stabbing, debilitating pain in his gut would recede.

Nick's cell rang. Not recognizing the number but fearing it might be a call about the draft, he answered. "Hello?"

"Nicky, honey, it's Ginger. I've been concerned about you. Are you okay?"

He stretched out on his chaise, cradling the phone on his shoulder. "Great. What's up?" he said with no enthusiasm.

"Glad to hear it. Well, I've been talked into attending the gala this weekend, and I need a doubles partner for the tennis tournament. What do you say? For old times' sake?" Ginger wheedled.

What the hell? He had to attend, might as well make the most of it. "Sure. Sign us up as a team."

"Wonderful. I hope all those lessons I've been taking make a difference."

He smiled. Finally a conversation that didn't involve

Marabelle. "You'll make a great doubles partner." And before he thought about it or could stop himself, the next words slipped from his mouth. "Would you like to attend the gala with me?"

"Yes! But I don't want to keep you from your responsibilities as the main sponsor."

He gazed up at the dark, starless sky. "It's not a big deal. As long as I show up, shake hands, and sign autographs." Already he regretted his rash invitation. "It'll probably be a big bore. If you'd rather not—"

"I'd love to!" she said.

He hesitated, then said, "Okay. I guess it's settled. Pick you up Saturday morning around nine so we can warm up."

"I'll be waiting," she purred.

Chapter 26

MARABELLE WORKED ON AUTOPILOT. SHE HAD slammed the door on her emotions gone wild and shut the floodgates on her tears. There'd be plenty of time later to alternate between falling apart and beating herself up.

The Friday afternoon golf tournament had been a big success, and all the celebrities put on a great show. Everyone had a terrific time. *Yippee.* Marabelle skipped the barbecue that evening due to pure exhaustion, but mostly she didn't want to chance running into Nick. She needed to work on the format for the mixed doubles the next morning. She noticed Ginger had signed up with Nick as her partner.

Barf. They deserved each other.

Marabelle tried making the draw as even as possible, knowing some of the professional athletes would end up competing against each other in the end. To make the tournament more exciting, she purposely put Beau and his partner at the opposite end of the bracket from Nick and Ginger.

Early Saturday morning, Marabelle posted the doubles teams on a big easel outside the tennis pro shop. She scanned the courts to see if Nick had arrived. Sure enough, he and Ginger were warming up against another couple.

Since he was hitting three courts over and couldn't see her watching, she took the time to observe him.

Mmm, not bad. He hit with an open stance and had a nice follow-through on his forehand. What had she expected? He was good at everything.

And gorgeous.

But Ginger? What a dork. She had dressed from head to toe in the latest hot-pink Nike ruffled short skirt and halter tennis top that showed more cleavage than it covered.

Marabelle almost laughed. Ginger hit like a wimp, not putting any muscle behind her shots.

"Hey, Mary-bell. I need you." Beau jogged over to where she stood on the veranda.

"For what?"

"My partner can't make it. You need to play with me," Beau said.

She shook her head while keeping a lookout on court three. "No way. Not in a million, gazillion—" Ginger giggled as she missed an easy overhead, and Nick gave her a playful swat on the bottom.

"Give me five minutes to get changed," Marabelle said with steel in her voice.

"Way to go!" Beau smiled as she stomped off to the locker room.

Marabelle was as serious about her tennis as the NFL players were about their football. She took no prisoners and always played to win. This charity tournament was no exception.

Beau and she easily won their first three matches. Beau was just as competitive, but he managed to have fun at the same time, laughing and joking with his opponents during the changeovers.

Not Marabelle. Strictly business. She barely cracked

a smile. And as she suspected, Nick and Ginger were winning their bracket, too. Perfect. It came down to the finals, and Marabelle couldn't wait to kick some bony ass.

As she recorded the scores on the board, the air around her changed. The hairs on the back of her neck stood up as she peered over her shoulder. Nick had leaned against one of the white pillars in front of the clubhouse with his arms crossed, blatantly studying her. She sucked in a breath and stiffened; their gazes locked, and time stood still. Then Ginger sidled up to him and whispered something in his ear and the spell was broken.

You're going down, girlfriend.

Nick surreptitiously watched Marabelle the entire morning. He couldn't believe how much power she put behind each shot. She might look pint-sized, but she packed a real punch. She had game, and he couldn't be prouder. She was a helluva tennis player.

He knew they would probably meet up in the finals. Marabelle had annihilated her opponents, playing not for fun, but to win. And today, she played for revenge. He'd be laughing if he still weren't so pissed off.

He couldn't help notice she looked cute as hell in a short black tennis skirt with a fitted white sports bra top. Every time she served, her top crept up and showed her belly. He missed that curvy belly and how ticklish she was whenever he kissed it.

Screw it. Get your head in the game, man. If he was going down, it wasn't going to be without a fight.

The final match would be the best of three sets. Everyone gathered around the club veranda to watch. Marabelle glanced up as she changed the overgrip on her racket and saw some familiar but worried faces. Elizabeth and John sat together, Elizabeth's attractive face marred with concern. Marabelle knew word had spread about her broken engagement. She figured everyone was waiting for this showdown. Well, so was she. *Bring it.* The tennis courts were her turf. She had the home field advantage.

"Hey, Coach! Rocker and I have some money riding on this," Ricky DiMarco called out in jest from the rocking chairs in front of the pro shop.

Before Nick could respond, Marabelle piped up, "Make sure you place it on me…*to win.*"

Ginger's hiss could be heard even over the guys' whooping and hollering. Beau chuckled, but Nick remained silent.

"Come on, partner, let's do this." Beau patted her on the bottom in full view of Nick.

She grabbed Beau by the arm, gaining his attention. "Listen to me," she whispered. "No fooling around. I want to win. I *have* to win. Remember…keep it low and deep and come in on the short balls."

Beau nodded and winked. "I always keep it low and deep," he said in a sexy voice, loud enough for Nick to hear. Then he pecked her on the lips. "For good luck."

"Whenever you two lovebirds are ready," Nick called out in a dangerous tone from the other side of the court.

Marabelle whacked two balls over the net at him. "Serve it up, Coach."

Ginger disapproved. "Hey, shouldn't we spin first to see who serves?"

"No!" Nick and Marabelle said in unison.

Marabelle never knew revenge could be so sweet. She loved their easy three-one lead in the first set. But even sweeter was the sight of Nick getting more and more irritated as Beau and she high-fived after every good shot.

At first, she hit every ball to Ginger, not because she feared Nick, but because she took great pleasure in watching her pink–bubble gum butt scramble all over the court. Ginger started to sweat, and it wasn't pretty. Her fair skin turned blotchy, and her long ponytail hung lifeless and limp. After Ginger missed a deep forehand in the corner, Nick looped his arm around her shoulder, whispering some sort of strategy in her ear.

Fine. Marabelle wouldn't hit to Ginger anymore. She could win either way.

"Whenever you lovebirds are ready, I'd like to serve," she called out. Ginger glowered at Marabelle as she took her position at the net. Skin prickling, Marabelle felt rather than saw Nick's steely blue gaze. When she glanced at him from under the bill of her hat, the corners of his mouth were turned up.

———

Nick wanted to pump his fist every time Marabelle hit a winner. He loved her competitive streak. She had proved to be a true athlete. She was also furious, and it showed in her intensity, but more important, it showed that she cared. *Really cared.*

He took his first calming breath since last Saturday

night. He could deal with Marabelle's anger any day. What he couldn't bear were her tears and betrayal. That tore him up inside and left him with a big, gaping hole where his heart used to be. Today, she wanted to prove something to him. But he wouldn't make it easy for her. *Nah.* That would only piss her off…more. He planned to give her the fight of her life.

Nick turned up the heat to overcompensate for his weak partner. The battle lines had changed as he and Beau tried to outmuscle each other. The second set was a lot closer than the first. And if Beau patted Marabelle's bottom one more time, Nick would not be responsible for his actions. Nick purposely hit Beau with a ball in between points.

"Sorry." *Asshole.*

Marabelle stayed in her zone. The score was forty-thirty, and she had returned one of Nick's hard forehands crosscourt when bubble-gum Ginger decided to poach. Only she moved too late, and Marabelle hit her with the ball…not quite on the boob, but close enough—her boobs were so huge, they were kinda hard to miss.

"Owww! You hit me!" she screeched as she pressed a hand to her front. "What's the matter with you?" Ginger rubbed her chest, trying to determine if there was a mark.

Marabelle raised her racket for the universal apology in tennis and walked off the court. The score was now five-four in Marabelle's favor. Ginger continued to squawk about getting hit. Nick and Beau made a big production of checking out her "injury." *Idiots.*

"Nicky, did you see that? She did it on purpose," Ginger accused with fake tears.

"Let's get some ice on it, and I think you'll be just fine," he said as he examined her boob a little too closely. Marabelle drank water and reapplied sunscreen. Someone from the crowd brought over a cup of ice.

"When did tennis become a contact sport?" Ginger whined, frowning at her. She jumped as Nick applied ice to her chest.

"Careful, they might explode," Marabelle said under her breath. Someone in Nick's direction coughed or laughed. She couldn't tell which.

Marabelle headed over to the other side, stopping in front of Ginger. "Just a little friendly coaching advice. If you decide to poach the ball, you have to go. Don't hesitate, or you're going to get hit…again."

Ginger's mouth gaped open. Beau had trouble suppressing his grin as he picked up his racket and trotted after Marabelle. And Nick had some coughing, choking, throat-clearing thing going on.

The next game pitted Nick's strength against Marabelle's finesse. Nick seized the opportunity, rushing in on a short ball and angling it wide for a winner. Marabelle dove for the shot, falling near the players' benches off the court. She hit the bench and bounced back on her butt on the clay. The crowd gasped, and Nick and Beau rushed over.

Beau reached her first. "You okay?" He tried to help her up, when Nick bent down and knocked his hand out of the way.

"Do you hurt anywhere, honey?"

She heard the alarm in his voice, laced with concern, as he checked her arms, knees, and legs for injuries.

"Only my butt and my pride. I'm fine. Let's play." She did her best to ignore him and his large, warm hands as he tugged her to her feet.

Sore butt be damned. She refused to whine like Ginger. Beau made a big deal of brushing clay off her bottom, and that triggered a low growl from Nick.

"Keep your hands to yourself, Quinton. *I mean it.*"

Beau patted her on the back and grinned, unfazed. "Come on, partner. Let's put the nail in the coffin."

For the next several points, all four players battled to the death.

Ginger dumped the ball in the net, making the score ad-in. Match point for Marabelle and Beau. Marabelle hit her killer slice backhand that gave Ginger no choice but to pop the ball up.

"Mine!" She reached up, snapped her wrist, and hit a beautiful overhead. The ball came down hard and missed hitting Ginger only by inches.

The crowd roared. Beau jumped up, tossed his racket in the air, and hugged Marabelle, twirling her around before planting a big kiss on her lips. She laughed and squeezed him back. Ginger stormed off the court and threw her racket down. Nick's lips curved into a smile of pleasure until he witnessed the kiss.

Nick strode to the net to shake hands. He squeezed Beau's hand with a murderous gleam in his eyes. Beau toned his brash act down a smidge. Marabelle figured he didn't want to warm the bench for next season's opener.

Nick clasped her hand and drew her toward him. The holey net was the only thing that separated her from falling into his broad chest. Her breath hitched. Was he going to kiss her? *Dear God… no, yes, no!*

"Way to go, Tinker Bell," he said, wearing his sexy, crooked grin. "You're one rockin' tennis player." She could feel his hot breath brush her sweaty face and smell his distinct, spicy scent. "But I want a rematch."

She plastered on a cocky, bored expression. "Name the time and place, Coach. I'll beat you like a drum… again." To her surprise, he threw his head back and howled with laughter.

—•••—

Afterward, before the awards ceremony, Ginger held court with Nick by her side, bellyaching: the match was unfair, Marabelle tried to kill her with the ball, blah, blah, blah. Marabelle didn't stick around to hear more.

She headed home for a much-needed soak in her tub and to plot the rest of her life. Smothered in bubbles in her claw-foot tub, she finally returned her dad's call and many texts. She hated to tell him the truth about Nick and the stupid stunt she'd pulled, but she needed some advice. She didn't have to see her dad's face to know he was hurting for her.

"What're you going to do now?" Ed asked.

She gathered her courage and said, "I've been thinking. What if I come to visit you for a while in France?"

"I would love to have you visit. But don't you think you're running away from your problems?"

"Yes. But if it helps me get over Nick, how can it be wrong?"

"Because you need to face your problems. I know I only met him for a short weekend, but Nick is a good man. You need to swallow your pride and go after him. Running away is not going to solve anything. It could be your biggest mistake ever."

She sniffed. The water had turned cold. Her toes looked like prunes, and her face probably looked even worse from all her crying. "How can you tell he's a good man? How do you know for sure?"

"Anyone who goes out of his way to make you feel special and puts up with your mother and me is an *excellent* man. He won't let you down. He deserves a second chance."

She nodded, trying to keep from blubbering like a baby. "What do I do now, Daddy?"

"Dry your tears, get dressed up real pretty tonight, and then go to that gala. You've worked hard, and you deserve it. And the first chance you get, ask him to dance. I promise the rest will fall in place."

"You think?" she croaked.

"Nick loves you, but his pride has been wounded. I'll bet he hasn't suffered many blows to his ego. You're probably the first woman ever to break up with him. I'm sure he feels he laid it on the line for you. He's waiting for you to make the first move. You can do it. Hold your head up high, be the bigger person, and go after him. He'll appreciate the effort, and I know he'll reciprocate."

"How can you be sure?"

"Because behind every good man is an even better woman. Nick is a good man, and he wants you because you're the best. Now fix yourself up and go have a good time tonight."

Marabelle felt better after his pep talk. "Okay, Dad. I will."

"Good. One more thing...now don't get upset. I'm not trying to control your life, but do you need some extra money? Just until you find another job?"

"Nah. I'm fine for—" She stopped and sat up, splashing water over the side of the tub. The low balances in her checking and savings accounts blinked red in her head. She swallowed her pride. "Uh, yeah. I could use a little money, but I'm paying you back. I promise."

"Sure, honey. I'll transfer some to your account."

She unscrewed her eyes and released a pent-up breath. At least she didn't have to worry about her mortgage for a few months while she figured out the rest of her life.

"Now forget about the money for once... I've got your back. Think about Nick," Ed said.

"Thanks, Dad."

"I love you. Now, go get him!"

"Love you, too, Dad."

"Whoa! You look fantastic." Beau whistled low when Marabelle answered the door that evening.

Just the reaction she'd hoped for. She wore a short, baby-doll dress she'd bought on a whim with Paula one afternoon. She hadn't had the nerve to wear it until tonight. A satin band circled the empire waist and hem. She ran a hand down the magenta-colored layers of silk fabric. Thin spaghetti straps held satin cups covering her breasts. The salesgirl had said it fit her small frame perfectly.

She had styled her hair in a loose French twist with a few stray curls brushing her neck. A gold and pearl necklace sparkled against her skin and dipped into her cleavage. She paired the necklace with large gold hoop earrings and her gold Manolo strappy sandals.

She *wanted* to be noticed, and for once, she didn't care what anyone thought. She just hoped everyone reacted the way Beau had.

Before Beau backed out of the driveway, he reached in the backseat and handed her a large tennis trophy and an envelope.

"What's this?" she said, flipping the envelope.

"You won a thousand dollars."

"We're supposed to split the winnings." She attempted to push the envelope back in his hand.

"Believe me, you earned it. You were totally awesome. You should've stayed for the ceremony afterward. Everyone wanted to congratulate you. Besides, you're gonna need that money when you bid on me at the auction," he replied with all the self-confidence of a stud.

She laughed, shoving the envelope in her gold evening clutch. "That won't even cover the opening bid. You're gonna bring in way more than that... I'm counting on it!"

The ballroom was a huge crush. Everyone who was anyone in the Raleigh area had come out for this much-touted event. Marabelle wished they were there for the sake of the school, but she knew better. People packed the ballroom to rub elbows with all the celebrities. And she had to admit, the lineup was impressive.

Of course, the Cherokees players were a big draw, being the local heroes, but so were members of a local country band and a few basketball and baseball players.

Marabelle scanned the room for Nick the minute she walked in, but he didn't seem to be there…yet. *Thank goodness.* She breathed a little easier. Well-wishers swarmed her about her win, as well as eligible and not-so-eligible men trying to hit on her. All because she wore a short dress and real cleavage. Jeez, men were so easy.

Ricky DiMarco saved her just in time from a lecherous coot old enough to be her grandfather, and swept her onto the dance floor. After Ricky, Ty claimed her for a dance, and even Rocker—if it could be considered dancing, as her feet never touched the ground. Beau cut in and brought her feet back to the floor.

"You don't have to babysit. Won't your adoring crowd miss you?" she teased as they swayed to the music.

Beau nuzzled her ear. "There's plenty of me to go around. I want to dance with the prettiest girl at the party." Marabelle laughed, finally enjoying herself as he swooped her around the dance floor.

Chapter 27

NICK IMPATIENTLY GLANCED AT HIS WATCH FOR THE fifth time as he paced Ginger's foyer. The gala had already started. He remembered a time when he used to appreciate her efforts to gain his attention, but not tonight. Not now.

And not ever, as long as Marabelle remained in the picture. And he wanted to make damn sure she remained in the picture. He didn't know if Marabelle would even show up tonight. She'd run off right after the match, before he'd had a chance to speak with her. But he hoped like hell she'd be there. He needed to apologize and set things right.

He needed *her*.

If he had to crawl on his hands and knees and beg, he would. She belonged to him, and he belonged to her. He just had to convince her of that.

Nick tugged on his collar. Showing up tonight with Ginger on his arm was *not* one of his more brilliant moves. He'd been feeling sorry for himself when he asked her. What a moron.

What the…? Where had she bought that gown? Nick stopped fidgeting as Ginger descended the stairs, wearing a long, strapless, slinky dress in some sort of leopard print. The slit up the side looked like it never ended, and the fuck-me stilettos were fuchsia. He tried not to stare. He had no clue what held up her huge breasts. The dress had no back. He wished like hell she'd put something else on...like a trench coat or an army blanket...but they were already late, and he didn't want to wait a second longer. This sucked. Marabelle was probably wearing that hideous black dress from her mother, along with all her insecurities. She didn't need to see Ginger in this Frederick's of Hollywood getup, hanging all over him like a high-priced hooker.

His head throbbed. He couldn't afford any more social media gossip, speculation, or pictures with a Playboy bunny wannabe, and he didn't want Marabelle believing he'd replaced her...already...with Ginger. He deserved whatever backlash came his way for showing up with Ginger so soon after his breakup. His stomach roiled, and he thought he might be sick.

At the gala, the coordinators accosted Nick the minute he walked through the doors. He shook hands and examined the ballroom at the same time. He didn't see Marabelle anywhere. He spied most of his players dancing and entertaining the ladies.

Beau Quinton hadn't lost any time hitting on some hot chick in a very short purple dress. *Figured.* He bet that before the night was over, Beau would have that dress over her head.

Nick kept checking the perimeter of the party as he made the obligatory rounds to see if Marabelle sat alone or hugged a wall somewhere. *Damn.* Where could she be? He knew better than to call. She wouldn't pick up her phone. Maybe he could sneak away and see if she was holed up at home.

He handed Ginger a vodka tonic from the bar, giving her a wide berth as he continued to scrutinize the rest of the room and avoid as many camera phones as he could.

Over the rim of her glass, Ginger gasped. "Well, well, well… Q sure doesn't waste any time. Looks like he's with Miss Innocent Schoolteacher Gone Wild."

Schoolteacher? His ears perked up.

Ginger indicated with a tilt of her head. "Over there."

Nick had been watching the entrance, hoping to catch Marabelle arriving. He pivoted to face the dance floor. What was Ginger talking about? He picked Beau out easily, still dancing with the babe in the short dress. "Who are you—" He stopped midsentence, unable to keep his eyes from bugging out.

The *babe* twirling around in Beau's arms in a nothing dress and a whole lot of skin was Marabelle!

He wheezed as though he'd been bodychecked in the gut. Tinker Bell had dared to wear that in public? The part of him that craved her every minute of every day appreciated the hell out of it. She looked amazing. But the possessive, jealous part of him wanted to kill anyone looking at her the way he was.

Especially Beau Quinton.

His scowl deepened as Beau twirled her, exposing her great legs. She appeared to be having the time of her life.

That does it. He didn't care if Twitter crashed from too many tweets or Marty Hackman fired him for his public display. Marabelle was his! Nick made a lunge for the dance floor, but before he could take two steps, Carol Evans and her husband blocked his path, and Ginger had an iron grip on his arm.

"Coach Frasier, we can't thank you enough for all the

support you've given the school and for lending your name as our sponsor. So far, it's been a huge success, and I'm sure tonight will not disappoint." Carol beamed at him.

"Uh, you're welcome. Now, if you'll excuse me." He made another attempt to leave.

"We're going to start the live auction in just a bit," Carol said, halting him again. "As soon as everyone is seated for dinner. We can't wait much longer. The natives are getting restless," she trilled.

He barely listened. His gaze was glued on Marabelle as she danced with John Prichard. Better. John was safe. *Maybe.* The way she'd dressed tonight, he wouldn't trust his own father.

"Everyone's hoping you'll change your mind and join the auction." Nick dragged his attention back to Carol's babbling, when suddenly the idea of the auction sounded like a solution to his problem. His mind did some fast calculating. It was a long shot, but he had to take the risk.

He nodded. "Certainly. Anything for this worthy cause."

"That's marvelous! And Ginger won't mind if we borrow her escort, will you? It's so nice seeing you two back together again." Carol leaned into him and said in a conspiratorial whisper, "Ginger explained about the fake engagement with…you know." Carol waggled her drawn-on eyebrows. "We truly appreciated the sacrifice you made for the cause." Nick curled his hands into fists, but Carol didn't notice.

"Ginger, you were absolutely correct…she did get fired as you predicted. Gracious. Who knew what she was really up to?"

Ginger gave Nick a nervous glance and said through a fake smile, "We'd better take our seats. Looks like they're going to start the auction." She looped her arm through his, trying to propel him forward.

"Follow us. We're both seated at table five," Carol said as the emcee took the microphone.

Nick leaned down and growled in Ginger's ear, "How did you know Marabelle was going to be fired?"

Ginger gave him a coy look, as if they were having an intimate conversation. "I didn't know. I only mentioned it was possible with how volatile she is. Oh, Nicky, stop scowling. You're the main sponsor; you're supposed to be having fun."

He managed to smooth the scowl from his face, but these meddling bitches were up to something, and he was going to get to the bottom of it.

Marabelle watched Nick and Ginger cross the ballroom to their table near the stage, heads drawn together, obviously enjoying a cozy chat. She had known the minute Nick had entered the ballroom. The air had become electrified, and the little hairs on the back of her neck had stood straight up for a second time that day.

Ginger clung to him in a drop-dead dress that had every head in the room swiveling for a better look. Why Ginger? Why did he have to go back to her? He could have any woman in this town, and he chose Ginger. How could she compete with that?

Marabelle wanted Nick with every fiber of her being, but only if she could have him all to herself. Totally, completely, forever. Watching him with Ginger made her feel a little ill and a lot inadequate. As she worried over her next move, her table started to fill in. Elizabeth Prichard sat to her right and Beau to her left.

"Why the sad face, Mary-bell?" Beau asked, slipping his arm around her shoulders.

"Take a wild guess." Her gaze shot to Nick and Ginger across the ballroom. "Oh, Beau, why did he have to pick her? I think I could stand almost anyone better than that wretched, whiny, lousy tennis player!"

"Don't pay them any mind," Elizabeth Prichard piped in. "Nick is not interested in that conniving bitch, I can assure you." Marabelle sat up, giving Elizabeth her full attention. "He's hurt. You bruised his ego. He's never had a woman break up with him before. Only you hold that distinction." Elizabeth patted her hand. "His ego needed to be taken down a notch or two. He'll come to his senses soon. I've already threatened him if he doesn't," she added smugly.

"What did you say?"

"You don't want to know," John said on the other side of Elizabeth. "But Nick does *not* want to be singing soprano."

Marabelle sat stupefied, not knowing what to do with that interesting bit of information. Then, to her horror, Nick's sister, Natalie, and her husband, Dan, came rushing to the table.

"Did we miss anything?" Natalie said, out of breath, as Dan held her chair. "The babysitter was late, or we would've been here earlier."

Marabelle's face blanched. What was Nick's sister doing here? She hadn't seen her since that god-awful morning in his kitchen. She noticed how elegant

Natalie looked in an off-white sheath gown. Suddenly, Marabelle's "party-girl" dress didn't feel so appropriate anymore.

Natalie flashed a warm smile. "Marabelle, it's wonderful to see you again."

Was she speaking to her? Marabelle glanced around the table to see if maybe another Marabelle was present.

"I enjoyed watching you play tennis today. I'm thinking about getting Brandon started. Would you have time for some private lessons?"

Nothing but time, now that I'm jobless.

"Sure. Be happy to."

Natalie's smile brightened, as if she and Marabelle were the best of friends. "Great. We'll talk later."

Marabelle gave the table another quick glance, surprised by all the friends surrounding her. Ty, Ricky, Rocker, the Prichards, and even Natalie all seemed to be on her side.

Her team.

How could she let her team down? Marabelle never played to lose. Not now. Not tonight.

The emcee explained the rules of the live auction, cracking a few jokes about how it was only an innocent outing and not an invitation for sex. *Right.* Then he began calling the bachelors up one by one. Rocker and Ty brought in twenty-five hundred each as they hammed it up on stage to keep the ladies bidding. Their packages consisted of first-class accommodations for an entire day spent in the North Carolina Mountains.

Ricky DiMarco turned up the heat as he wowed the women with his dangerous looks and sexy moves. He promised some lucky gal tickets and backstage passes to a Keith Urban concert, including champagne and limo ride.

Marabelle laughed, enjoying the antics as everyone went wild. Ricky's bidding got very interesting. She noticed a young, pretty blond bidding. In the end, the young blond won to the tune of thirty-three hundred dollars. Ricky jumped down from the stage and swung the pretty, squealing girl around in his arms. Everyone cheered.

When Ricky reached the table, he said, "Hey, Marabelle, looks like I'll be going out with my debutante after all."

"What? You mean that's the one you've been talking about?"

Ricky winked and nodded.

"Lordy," she breathed as she sat back. She sure hoped the girl's father didn't own a shotgun.

Several other celebrities took the stage, as well as a local sportscaster, a young attorney, and a heart surgeon. Then finally Beau's name was called.

Beau taunted the guys at his table. "Watch, listen, and learn, boys." He surprised Marabelle by hauling her up for a long, slow kiss. "That's for luck," he said at her dazed expression.

Beau strutted his stuff as he made his way to the stage. Embarrassment flooded her cheeks. Marabelle looked around the table, but no one seemed to notice. Everyone was laughing and cheering for Beau. Elizabeth tossed out the first bid, only to be outbid by Natalie, then both of them were knocked out of the competition as the real bidders took over.

"What if you had won him?" Marabelle asked Elizabeth, shocked at her nerve.

"Oh, honey, it would've served him right. He's too cocky for his own good," Elizabeth scoffed. Marabelle was amazed at the harmless ribbing and overall camaraderie everyone seemed to share. She glanced from Elizabeth to John to Natalie, when she happened to look over at Nick's table.

Her breath lodged in her throat as time stood still.

Nick was watching her with an intensity she'd never seen before. Her heart banged clear through her chest. Her dress left little to the imagination, and she was sure he noticed from across the room. Beau continued to work the crowd, and the women went crazy. The room could've been on fire for all she noticed, because she was so drawn to Nick's mesmerizing gaze. His expression went from intense to calm as the corner of his mouth quirked up, flashing his lopsided grin. He wasn't laughing at her or even mocking her. He looked at her with—Marabelle blinked as a waiter reached in front of her to refill her wineglass. When he removed his arm, Nick was no longer watching her, but the stage where Beau was racking up the bids.

Anticipation tingled her skin. She knew she hadn't imagined it. Nick hadn't been smirking or looking at her with loathing or even hurt in his eyes. For a brief moment, she could've sworn she saw kindness, forgiveness, and…even love.

Especially love. If only for a split second. She *felt* it from across the room. Her pulse quickened, and her palms started to itch.

I need to get to him…now.

"Are you okay?" Elizabeth Prichard asked, touching her arm.

"Uh, yeah." She shook her head to clear it, reaching for her water glass.

Elizabeth laughed. "You looked like you were in a trance. Can you believe Beau?"

"What?" Marabelle tuned in to the excitement on the floor. Beau had sold for forty-four hundred dollars to some Kim Kardashian look-alike dripping in diamonds, and they were taking a day cruise off the North Carolina coast.

"Sheesh. These women have more money than sense," Elizabeth remarked.

Beau sauntered back to the table and high-fived all the guys. "Forty-four hundred, boys. You are looking at the mack daddy!" he bragged.

Marabelle's skin felt prickly, and her heart was doing that weird erratic thumping. She couldn't let any more time go by. She murmured some excuse and started to slide her chair back, when she heard a collective gasp around the entire ballroom.

"Damn. He's gonna do it. I didn't think he would," Elizabeth said.

What? Then Marabelle knew as the emcee began his big announcement.

Nick took the stage.

Marabelle gasped. *Oh, Nick. Don't do this. It's not important. Who cares about the school?*

"Ladies, this is a wonderful surprise. Nick Frasier, head coach of the Carolina Cherokees, is offering some very lucky lady a weekend in Bermuda at a private villa. All expenses paid…"

Marabelle didn't hear any more due to the loud rushing in her ears. *Bermuda?* Nick was taking someone to

Bermuda? But he knew she wanted to go there… She shivered, lifting her gaze and staring into Nick's steely blue eyes.

His smile seemed to be saying, *Bid on me!*

"Wake up! You need to bid on Nick," Elizabeth urged, shaking her arm.

"Come on, Mary-bell. This is your chance," Beau said, dropping into his seat next to her.

Panic threatened to paralyze her. "But I'm not sure if—"

"That's thirty-five hundred from Mrs. Hazel Cartwright. Do I hear thirty-six?"

Her head whipped around. Mrs. Cartwright! Oh no! Nick needed saving—now.

Bids started to fly fast and furious.

"Mary-bell, you need to bid," Beau insisted.

"I know Nick wants you. Please bid on him," Natalie pleaded, leaning across the table.

Marabelle did some fast calculating—with the money from her dad and the thousand-dollar check sitting in her purse, she could maybe go up to five.

"Do I hear thirty-nine hundred?"

"Yes!" She raised her hand.

"Thirty-nine to the pretty little lady at table ten. What's your name, honey?"

"*Marabelle!*" The entire table called out.

Nick laughed, looking ecstatic.

"Do I hear—"

"Four thousand."

"That's four thousand, from Ginger Jones at table five. How about…"

"Forty-two!" Marabelle shouted and shot her meanest glare at Ginger.

Someone else bid forty-four.

"Come on, Mary-bell, keep bidding." Beau nudged her with his elbow.

"I've only got five thousand," she whispered furiously when she heard Ginger bid forty-five. "Dammit. I hate that bitch."

Beau rotated her shoulders to gain her full attention. "Listen to me. Keep bidding. Go as high as you have to," he said, ferocity lacing his voice.

"I can't."

His fingers dug into her flesh. "Do it for the guys, Mary-bell. We're backing you."

Marabelle's mouth fell open at what he had implied. "*What?* I can't take money from you and the guys. I'll never be able to pay it back."

"Come on, Marabelle!"

"Keep bidding!"

"You've got this."

Beau gave her shoulders a shake. "Look at me. You get Coach, and we get peace of mind instead of training camp from the bowels of hell. Do it for the team!"

Ginger had just finished bidding five thousand. Beau turned her toward the emcee.

"I've got five thousand on the table, who wants to bid fifty-one hundred? Anybody? Remember, this is an all-expenses-paid trip to Bermuda with none other than Coach Nick Frasier."

Pressure from the table was tangible. She stole a glance at Nick, and his gaze burned a hole through her as fiercely as before.

"Fifty-five hundred!" someone said before Marabelle realized it had come from her mouth. Her table went wild, celebrating. She gave a shaky smile, praying it was over at the same time.

"Fifty-five hundred going once, going twice—"

"Six thousand," Ginger cried out clear and strong.

Marabelle gasped, gripping the edge of the table. Beau slid a cocktail napkin in front of her and nodded.

"Do it."

She almost choked at the amount she saw written on the napkin. "Are you sure? I can't…" she whispered.

"Now!"

"Going twice—"

"Ten thousand!" she yelled out as her hand clutched her throat.

The entire ballroom erupted in cheers, hooting, and hollering. She could barely hear over the noise. She looked up in time to see Nick fist-pump the air as the master of ceremonies said, "Sold! For ten thousand dollars to the lovely Miss Marabelle!"

Chapter 28

PANDEMONIUM BROKE OUT ALL AROUND MARABELLE. The guys cheered, and Beau wrapped her in his arms for a huge bear hug. He quickly released her and gently shoved her toward Nick, weaving his way through the crowd.

Marabelle lurched forward and threw herself in his arms as he hugged her.

Home at last. This was where she belonged...in Nick's arms.

Finally.

Nick squeezed her as if he couldn't get enough, kissing her hair, cheek, nose until he landed on her mouth.

Everything fit perfectly.

He hoisted her up, and Marabelle wrapped her legs around his waist and looped her arms around his neck. The party raged on around them as guests took to the dance floor, but they were oblivious as they continued to embrace.

Marabelle finally leaned back. "I'm *so sorry*. I never meant to hurt you. Can you ever forgive me?" she said, feasting her eyes on his gorgeous face.

Nick answered with another scorching kiss. "As long as you believe this is for real. We are *not* playing a game."

Her insides went all squishy, but she nodded. She believed him with all her heart and felt the first flicker of hope in his arms. She really wanted him to hold her forever.

"Does this mean you still want me?" Doubt and hope laced her tone.

"Oh yeah," he rumbled against her lips.

Her head began to swim, and it wasn't from the wine. Maybe fairy tales did come true. "I think we're good for each other. You take care of me, and I take care of you."

"I wouldn't have it any other way."

A shiver prickled her spine, and she blurted, "Nick, I lov—"

"*Excuse me*," Ginger sniped.

Hussy harlot! That woman had impeccable timing, interrupting the biggest declaration of Marabelle's life. She wanted to slap her across her overly made-up smug face.

"Nick, the committee chairs would like a word with you. And may I remind you that I'm your date this evening." Ginger blasted a look of pure evil at Marabelle.

Nick groaned, slowly releasing Marabelle until her feet touched the carpet. He gave Ginger only half his attention. "Yeah. Tell them I'll be there in a minute."

"Nick. Now." Ginger yanked on his arm.

He squeezed Marabelle's hand. "Hold that thought." Marabelle knew he had obligations, but she refused to let go. He squeezed her hand again and winked. "I'll be right back."

Marabelle barely refrained from throwing herself at him. She wanted to stomp her feet and scream.

He's mine!

She still had a lot of making up to do. Like telling Nick she loved him. Tears burned the backs of her eyes.

Marabelle never wanted to watch Nick walk away with another woman again as long as she lived.

Especially Ginger!

They strolled away like a couple. A couple that belonged together. She stood there like a ninny, wondering what to do next, when she blurted, "Nick!"

He stopped and turned his head. She rushed forward, practically tackling another couple in her haste, and grabbed his arm. The look she shot Ginger dared her to say one word. Then Marabelle peered at Nick, knowing her face was flushed.

Nick said in a husky voice, "Tell me, Tinker Bell."

"Pick me. Want me. *Love me,*" she pleaded, barely above a whisper.

"Forever," he murmured. He swooped down for another bone-melting kiss. She swayed into him, holding on for dear life until he lifted his head.

"Give me fifteen minutes. Don't go away."

She watched him leave, unaware of her surroundings. She licked her tingling lips, tasting him there.

"You don't know who you're messing with," Ginger said, yanking her back to reality. "This game has just begun." Venom dripped from her voice. Marabelle thought about tripping Ginger as she slithered after Nick, but for the moment, she was too happy to cause a scene.

Fifteen minutes turned into thirty and then forty-five. Marabelle headed to the ladies' lounge as the party continued in the ballroom. She couldn't stand around any longer waiting for Nick. The longer she waited, the more time she had to think.

Not good thoughts.

The most pressing one being she just blew nine thousand dollars she didn't have, and she had no idea how she was going to pay it back. She needed to find a job fast. And she needed to have her head examined…again.

And Nick. Had he meant what he'd said? He wanted her, forever? If yes, then where did that leave good old Ginger, the slutty, shitty tennis player?

Marabelle stared at the mirror in the ladies' room, wincing at the look of horror on her face. She gave her head a vicious shake. Everything would work out. It had to.

She reapplied her lipstick and stepped out of the lounge, almost plowing someone over. "Excuse…oh."

Ginger wore a snooty expression as Marabelle attempted to skirt around her, but Ginger seized her arm in a surprisingly strong grip, halting her.

"Not so fast. You and I need to come to a little understanding."

"I don't think so." Marabelle tried wrenching her arm free.

"Nick is leaving *with me* tonight. And we both know how the evening will end." Her voice oozed with innuendo. "When I'm done with him, he won't have any desire to be anywhere else." She smirked like a woman very confident of her sexual allure. "So, out of the goodness of my heart, I'm offering you a way to save face."

Marabelle yanked, freeing her arm. "This I've got to hear," she sneered.

"It's simple. You go to the committee and tell them you can't afford ten thousand dollars, which I know for a fact you can't, and Nick and the Bermuda trip will go to me…the next-highest bidder."

She jerked back. "Why should I? How do you know I can't afford ten thousand?"

Ginger gave a humorless laugh. "Who do you think got you fired from your job?"

Stunned, Marabelle blinked. "*What?*"

"You're such a dumb-ass. I'm the one who set up the interview in Birmingham, thinking you'd have sense enough to take the job. I had no idea you're too stupid to seize a golden opportunity."

"Are you freakin' kidding me? Because I didn't take the job, you had me *fired*?" Hysteria filled Marabelle's voice as she clenched her fists.

"No, you simpleton." Ginger flashed a look of contempt. "I had you fired so you *would* take the job. Why you didn't is beyond me. I tried to help you."

Marabelle could not see past her blinding rage and Ginger's arrogant expression. "I am going to kick your bony ass!" Marabelle pushed hard until Ginger hit the wall behind her, next to the ladies' lounge door.

Ginger screamed, "*You're crazy!*"

"And don't you forget it!"

"Marabelle! Stop!" Before she could take a swing, she found her feet in the air and Nick's arm around her like a steel band. Marabelle struggled against him, trying to break loose. Ginger froze with her back against the wall, her eyes wide with fright. "Stop, honey. Calm down," Nick said gently.

Ginger took advantage of the moment. "She attacked me! You were a witness. I'm going to press charges."

"I'm not the only witness," Nick said in his scary-calm voice as he held Marabelle close to his chest.

Ginger's gaze darted beyond Nick and landed on

Beau and Carol Evans, standing a few feet away. Beau shook his head in disgust, and Carol looked as if she'd witnessed Ginger in an illegal-drug bust.

Ginger gulped hard, then started backpedaling. "I don't know what you think you heard, but I'm an innocent victim. I was minding my own business when this…this…*stupid bitch* attacked me!" She pointed a shaky finger at Marabelle.

"Ginger, enough. One more word out of you, and I'll kick your ass myself," Nick snarled. Anger vibrated off his body and rattled Marabelle as he still held her close. "You sabotaged Marabelle's job and her reputation. That alone is unforgivable. But if I ever hear you slander or smear my future wife's name again, if you so much as whisper her name, you will have to answer to me. And I can promise, you will not like the consequences." Nick leveled his deadly gaze at Ginger.

Ginger's face drained of all its color. "Nicky, it's not what you thi—"

"Well! I've certainly heard enough. Ms. Jones, my husband, the attorney, will be calling you in the morning." Carol then spoke directly to Marabelle. "Ms. Fairchild, I am sorry to hear about your job. I will personally speak to the school on your behalf. Now, if you will excuse me, I need to find my husband." Carol scurried away from the scene of the crime.

Beau appeared at Ginger's side. "Coach, I'll take her home," he offered, not looking real happy.

"Hey." Nick stopped Beau with a hand on his arm. "Thanks…for everything."

Beau fist-bumped him with a big grin. "She's worth it."

Nick grinned back. "I know."

Marabelle stood dumbfounded after Nick released her, watching Beau escort a belligerent Ginger out. What the heck just happened?

Suddenly, Nick had her up against the wall, caging her in with both arms on either side of her head. "Now, where were we? I think you had something to tell me."

Marabelle blinked and gazed up into the face she knew she would love for the rest of her life. "Did you just call me your future wife?"

"I did indeed. What do you say?" Hope, a smidge of uncertainty, and a whole heap of love passed across his features.

"What I should've said a long time ago. I love you, Nick. I want to be with you forever."

His lips hovered over hers. "I love you, Tinker Bell." He kissed her swiftly at first, then lingeringly. "Now, will you marry me for real?" he said against her mouth.

She plastered herself to him, too distracted by his smell and his touch to think. "For real."

Nick chuckled. "Is that a yes?"

Marabelle leaned back and beamed. "Yep, I love you, and I'll marry you!"

Epilogue

THE SALTY AIR TICKLED HER NOSE AS MARABELLE enjoyed the view of the turquoise-blue ocean just beyond the infinity pool. She relaxed on a cushioned lounge chair built for two.

Nick dropped down next to her, and she peered over her sunglasses. "What's that?"

He handed her a frosty orange drink. "Bermuda Triangle. Tomorrow, we'll try one called Bermuda Bouquet."

She sipped the fruity rum drink and sighed. "Isn't this beautiful?" She looked out from the privacy of their villa, and a warm breeze lifted her curls and brushed them across her face.

"Yeah." But Nick's gaze never left her face.

Marabelle had pinched herself so many times in the last two months that bruises had started to appear, reassuring herself she was no longer dreaming. It would take some time for reality to sink in. But for the next two weeks, she had Nick all to herself. In Bermuda. On her honeymoon!

Marabelle had chosen not to return to Trinity Academy, even though she'd been offered a permanent position with much groveling on Mrs. Crow's part. She'd decided to teach private tennis lessons, play in a competitive 5.0 league, and practice some of her favorite recipes. Nick had encouraged her to start a take-out business, feeding busy professionals and athletes home-cooked meals, all from his fabulous kitchen. Beau, her first customer, signed up for three meals a week. There were enough hungry ball players to keep her business thriving.

As for the wedding plans, she had given Edna full rein to plan and make lists to her little heart's desire. As long as Nick was in the wedding, she'd be happy. But Edna had other ideas. She had bombarded Marabelle with daily calls and hundreds of texts about the dress, music, food, flowers, linens, and guest list until Marabelle thought her head would explode. The only thing Marabelle insisted upon were individual cakes in the shape of footballs and tennis balls.

Thank goodness for her bridesmaids: Phoebe, Paula, Natalie, and Elizabeth. They took their roles seriously and more than once kept Marabelle from killing her mother. Especially when Edna had insisted on practicing the hesitation step down the aisle *not* once, but six times.

"What was your favorite part…about the wedding?" Marabelle asked Nick as the drink slid down her throat and warmed her insides.

"Kissing the bride."

She blushed, recalling how Nick had crushed her in his arms and kissed her until the minister cleared his throat several times.

"Mine was watching my mother race across the dance floor to save Lilah Dawkins from Rocker twirling her over his head." She laughed, remembering the look of horror on Edna's face.

"I loved when the guys presented you with your own personal Cherokees jersey with *Tinker Bell* on the back, and you pulled it over your designer wedding dress."

Nick laughed, and Marabelle giggled. "I thought Edna was going to need mouth-to-mouth, and Beau was going to give it to her," Nick said.

She rested her head back on the lounge cushion with a dreamy smile. "I love that jersey. I'm going to wear it to bed every night."

"Not if I have anything to do with it," Nick said in his low, velvet voice. He crowded her on the lounge chair and rumbled close to her ear, "Now, about that nude sunbathing."

"Bermuda doesn't have nude sunbathing." Marabelle gasped as his lips nibbled below her ear.

"They do now. We haven't tried sex on the beach. Pay attention. It might be our favorite."

Acknowledgments

First and foremost, a tremendous thank-you to all the great readers, bloggers, and reviewers. Your support and love of small-town romances (especially mine!) cannot be measured.

To everyone at Sourcebooks for all your hard work editing, designing, and marketing. Your commitment to quality shows from the cover to the very last page. To Deb Werksman and Nicole Resciniti, thank you for your continued help and encouragement.

To my favorite personal assistant, Jessica Faulkingham, I'm forever grateful that our paths crossed at the perfect moment. You make marketing look so easy!

Thank you to my friends and family for sticking by me all these years.

Lastly, to my husband and wonderful kids for your tolerance, patience, and love. And for being the real tennis players in my life. Your drive and talent never cease to amaze me. You guys rock. And for that, I might actually cook again. Maybe. Don't hold your breath. ;-)

About the Author

Michele Summers writes about small-town life with a Southern flair. She has her own interior design business in Raleigh, North Carolina, and Miami, Florida. Both professions feed her creative appetite and provide a daily dose of humor. When she isn't writing or creating colorful interiors, she is playing tennis, cooking for family and clients, knitting, reading, and most importantly, raising her two great kids. Michele's work has won recognition from the Dixie First Chapter, Golden Palm, Fool For Love, Rebecca, Fabulous Five, and Beacon contests. She is an active member of the Heart of Carolina and Florida Romance Writers chapters of RWA. You can contact Michele at her website, www.michelesummers.com, where you will also locate her other social media buttons.

If you loved *Sweet Southern Trouble*, keep reading
for a sneak peek at The Shaughnessy Brothers series
by *New York Times* and *USA Today* bestselling author
Samantha Chase

A Sky Full of Stars

Chapter 1

THERE WAS A GIRL IN OWEN SHAUGHNESSY'S CLASS.

A. Girl.

Okay, a woman. And she wasn't a scientist and she wasn't awkward. She was…pretty. Beautiful, actually. Though he had no idea if she was awkward or not. She had walked into the lecture hall minutes ago, and there were only five minutes left in his talk, so…why was she here? Maybe she was the girlfriend of one of his students?

Looking around the room, he ruled that out. He seemed to be the only one taking note of her presence. He chanced another glance her way, and she smiled. He felt a nervous flutter in the region of his belly, and as he continued to look at her, her smile grew.

And now Owen felt like he was going to throw up.

He immediately forced his gaze away and looked at the notes in front of him. "Next time we'll be discussing dust trails and dust tails, which represent large and small dust particles, respectively. Please refer to your syllabus for the required reading material." Lifting his head, Owen scanned the large lecture hall and noted the almost universally bored expressions staring back at him.

Except for her. She was still smiling.

He cleared his throat before adding, "Class dismissed."

There was a collective sigh of relief in the room as everyone stood and began collecting their belongings.

As the students began to file past him, Owen did his best to keep his eyes down and not react to the words he was hearing.

Geek. Nerd. Weird. Awkward.

Yeah, Owen not only heard the words being murmured but knew they were being used to describe him. It was even worse considering the students in the room were all interested in the same subject he was—astronomy. So even in a group of his peers, he was still the odd man out. He shrugged. He'd learned not to let the hurtful words land—to fester—but sometimes they stung a little.

Okay, a lot.

Packing up his satchel, he kept his head down as the class of two hundred students made their way out. Or escaped. Maybe that was the better word for it. He didn't make eye contact with any of them—he simply went about his task of collecting his papers and belongings so the next instructor could come in and set up on time. He was nothing if not polite and conscientious.

His phone beeped to indicate a new text, and he couldn't help but smile when he pulled out his phone and saw it was from his twin brother, Riley.

Skype. Tonight. 8 your time.

Refusing to acknowledge how once again he and his brother were in sync with one another—Riley loved to say it was because they were twins—Owen couldn't help but be grateful for the timing. There were just times when he needed to talk to someone—or, more specifically, Riley—and there he was.

And the more he commented on it, the more Riley would go on about twin telepathy.

It was ridiculous.

As a man of science, there was no way Owen could accept the phenomenon as fact. Coincidence? Yes. Fact? No. His phone beeped again with a second text from Riley.

Whatever you're stressing about, we'll discuss.

He read the text and chuckled. "Nope," he murmured. "It was just a coincidence."

The last of the students exited the lecture hall as he slipped the phone back into his satchel, and Owen relished the silence. This was how he preferred things— quiet. Peaceful. He enjoyed his solitude, and if it were at all possible, he'd stick to speaking at strictly a few select conferences and then spend the rest of the day doing research and mapping the night sky.

"Excuse me," a soft, feminine voice said.

His entire body froze, and he felt his mouth go dry. Looking up, Owen saw her. Up close, she was even more beautiful. Long blond hair, cornflower-blue eyes, and a smile that lit up her entire face. And that light was shining directly at him.

She wore a long, gauzy skirt with a white tank top. There was a large portfolio case hanging over her shoulder, along with the sweater she'd obviously chosen to do without in the too-warm classroom, and multiple bangle bracelets on her arm.

Gypsy.

No. That wasn't the right word. Gypsies were more

of the dark-haired variety and wore a lot of makeup. This woman was too soft and delicate and feminine to meet that description.

Nymph.

Yes. That was definitely more fitting, and if he were the kind of man who believed there were such things, that's what he would have categorized her as.

He couldn't form a single word.

Her expression turned slightly curious. "Hi. Um... Dr. Shaughnessy?"

She was looking for him? Seriously? Swallowing hard, Owen tried to speak—he really did—but all he could do was nod.

The easy smile was back. Her hand fluttered up to her chest as she let out a sigh of relief. "I'm so sorry for showing up so close to the end of your class. It was inconsiderate of me. I meant to be here earlier. Well, I was supposed to be here for the entire lecture, but I lost track of time talking to Mr. Kennedy." She looked at him as if expecting him to know who she was talking about. "He's the head of the art department," she clarified.

Again, all he could do was nod. He cleared his throat too, but it didn't help.

"Anyway, I'm supposed to meet my uncle here— Howard Shields. He suggested I come and listen to you speak. He thinks very highly of you and thought I'd enjoy your lecture."

Seriously? Howard Shields thought someone would *enjoy* hearing him talk about meteor showers? That wasn't the normal reaction Owen received from his talks. Informative? Educational? Yes. Enjoyable? Never.

Not sure how he should respond, he offered her a small smile and felt a flush cover him from the tips of his toes to the roots of his hair. She was probably regretting listening to her uncle. As it was, she was looking at him expectantly.

"Anyway," she said, her voice still pleasant and friendly, "Uncle Howard talks about you all the time, and when he told me you were in Chicago guest lecturing, I knew I had to come and meet you. My uncle really respects your work."

Owen finally met her gaze head-on because her words struck him. It was no secret that Owen looked up to Howard—he'd been a mentor to Owen for as long as he could remember—but to hear it wasn't all one-sided? Well, it meant the world to him.

Most people in his field looked at Owen a little oddly. It wasn't because he didn't know what he was talking about or that he wasn't respected; it was because of his social skills. Or lack thereof. It seemed to overshadow all of his fieldwork, research, and teachings. He was more well-known for being painfully shy than anything else. He was filled with a sense of relief—and pride—to know that Howard had said something nice about him.

And now he also knew he was going to have to speak.

"Um…thank you," he said softly, feeling like his mouth was full of marbles. When he saw her smile broaden, it made him want to smile too.

So he did.

But he had a feeling it wasn't nearly as bright or as at ease as hers.

"Ah, there you are!" They both turned and saw Howard walk into the room, his white lab coat flowing slightly behind him. "I was on my way here and was sidetracked talking with Dr. Lauria about the waiting list for the telescope." He shook his head. "Students are up in arms over the lack of availability."

Owen nodded but remained silent.

"I see you've met my niece, Brooke," Howard said before leaning over and kissing her on the cheek.

"We haven't been formally introduced," she said shyly, smiling at Owen.

"Well, let's rectify that," Howard said, grinning. "Owen Shaughnessy, I'd like you to meet my niece, Brooke Matthews. Brooke, this is Dr. Owen Shaughnessy."

Brooke smiled—a genuine smile—as she held out her hand to Owen. "Feel free to make fun," she said.

Owen looked at her oddly. "Fun?"

Her head tilted slightly. "Yeah…you know. Because of my name."

Now he was confused. "I'm sorry," he said nervously, "is there something funny about the name *Brooke*?"

Howard laughed out loud and clapped Owen on the shoulder again as he shook his head. "Don't mind him, Brookie. He doesn't get pop culture references."

Pop culture references? Owen looked back and forth between the two of them for some sort of explanation. Then he realized Brooke's hand was still outstretched, waiting for him to take it. Quickly wiping his palm on his slacks, he took her hand in his and gave it a brief shake. He murmured an apology and averted his gaze before stepping back.

Tucking her hair behind her ear, Brooke continued to smile. "My parents named me after Brooke Matthews, the model." When he still didn't react, she added, "She's also an actress." Still nothing. Looking at her uncle, she shrugged and let out a nervous chuckle. "Well, anyway…um, Uncle Howard, I'm afraid I was late to Dr. Shaughnessy's class."

Howard placed an arm around her and hugged her. "I knew pointing you in the direction of the art department was going to be a problem." He chuckled and turned to Owen. "Brooke is an artist and looking to either intern here at the university or maybe get a lead on a gallery where she can work and perhaps get her paintings looked at." He smiled lovingly at her. "She teaches painting classes during the summer semester at the community college, but she's far too talented to keep doing it."

"Uncle Howard," she said shyly.

"What? It's true!"

Owen still couldn't quite figure out why Brooke was here or why Howard had thought she should come to hear him lecture. He was just about to voice the question when Howard looked at him.

"Brooke's specialty is painting the night sky."

For a moment, Owen wasn't sure how to respond.

Brooke blushed and then looked at Owen to explain. "I know most people would say the night sky is simply dark—or black—with some stars, but I don't see it that way. I see the way the stars reflect off one another and how it causes different hues in the sky." She gave a small shrug. "Most of the time my work is a little more… Well, it's not abstract, but it's more whimsical than a true portrait."

"Don't just tell him about it," Howard suggested. "You have your portfolio with you. Why don't you show him?"

"Oh!" Brooke turned and took the leather case from her shoulder and laid it on the desk in front of her.

Owen watched in fascination as she worked, noting her slender arms and the music that came from her wrists as her bracelets gently clattered together. Her long hair fell over one shoulder, and it was almost impossible to take his eyes off her.

"I hope we're not keeping you, Owen," Howard said, stepping closer. "I probably should have asked you earlier about your schedule before we both sort of bombarded you like this."

He shook his head. "I…I don't have anything else scheduled for this afternoon. I had planned on heading back to the hotel and doing some reading before dinner. I'll talk with Riley later." Howard and Owen had known each other for so long that he didn't need to specify anything regarding his family—Howard knew all about them.

"How's he doing? Is he back in the studio yet?"

"Not yet. He didn't want to do another solo project, but getting the band back together isn't going as smoothly as he'd hoped."

Hands in his pockets, Howard nodded. "That's too bad. Still…I'm sure the time off is enjoyable. How is Savannah doing?"

Owen smiled at the mention of his sister-in-law. "She's doing well. She found an agent, and she's submitting proposals for a book she's been working on."

"Wonderful! Is it based on her work interviewing rock stars?"

Beside them, Brooke straightened and gasped.

"Are you okay, my dear?" Howard asked.

But Brooke was looking directly at Owen. "You're Riley Shaughnessy's brother," she said. It wasn't a question but a simple statement of fact.

A weary sigh was Owen's immediate response. This was how it normally went—not that it happened very often. At least not to him. But he heard from his other brothers what usually occurred when a woman found out they were related to Riley. And it wasn't as if Owen knew Brooke or was involved with her, but he braced himself for the disappointment of knowing that from this point on, she was probably only going to want to talk about his famous brother.

And for the first time in a long time—possibly since high school—he resented his twin.

Might as well get it over with.

Clearing his throat, Owen nodded. "Um…yes. Riley's my brother."

Brooke nodded, her smile just as sweet as it had been since she walked into the lecture hall. "How fascinating! I mean, I think it is, anyway, to see such diversity in a family."

And here it comes, he thought.

"You're both so talented but in such different occupations. Your parents must be incredibly proud of you both!" Then she turned and straightened her pictures.

Wait…that was it? She wasn't going to obsess or go on and on about how talented Riley was or how much she loved his latest song?

"So let me ask you," she began as she turned to face him, and Owen braced himself again. Now she was going to do it. Now she was going to gush. "What colors do you see when you look up at the night sky?

Do you just see black, or do you see different shades of blue?"

He stared at Brooke.

Hard.

And his jaw was quite possibly on the floor.

"Owen?" Howard asked, stepping forward. "Are you all right?"

He shook his head as if to clear it and then focused on Brooke and said the first thing that came to mind. "Why aren't you talking about Riley?"

She looked at him as if he were a little bit crazy and then turned to her uncle before looking at Owen again, shrugging. "I'm sorry. Did you want to talk about him? I thought I was going to show you some examples of my paintings."

He blinked, still unable to believe what he was hearing. Glancing at Howard, he saw the older man smirking as if he knew exactly what was going on in Owen's mind. People always wanted to talk about Riley. He was big news. People liked celebrities, and he was far more interesting than most. Certainly more interesting than Owen.

"Oh…um. Yes. Yes. You were going to show me your paintings," he said nervously, and he stepped forward to take a look.

And was rendered speechless.

Not that it was hard to do—Owen was already a man of few words—but the canvases Brooke had strewn across the desk were nothing like he was expecting.

The colors were bold and bright, and made with large brushstrokes. He thought of Van Gogh's painting *The Starry Night* and admired how she had layered the paint.

He stepped closer to the desk, picked up the closest painting, and studied it. This one was darker—it portrayed gravitational waves—and Brooke had managed to capture all of the light and the colors, and make it feel as if you could reach into the painting and touch the stars. It was brilliant. It was compelling. It was… He put it down and picked up the next one. A shooting star. It was a little more whimsical than the previous one, but the colors were just as vibrant, and looking at it made Owen feel as if he were looking through his telescope and watching the stars fly across the night sky.

"So what do you…?"

He placed the painting down—ignoring Brooke's attempt at a question—and picked up the third painting. This was the one that reminded him of Van Gogh. This had depth, texture. Owen wasn't in the least bit artistic, but he knew what he was looking at was amazing. Gently he ran his hand over the canvas, taking in the feel of the paint, and was mesmerized. How many times had he wished he could reach out and touch the sky, to feel the heat of a star and study its contours? And standing here now, that was exactly what he felt he was doing. Unable to help himself, he looked at Brooke with wonder. "This is…amazing." And then he wanted to curse himself because that description didn't do her work justice.

And yet she looked pleased.

Relieved.

Her hand fluttered up over her chest as she let out a happy sigh. "Thank you. I know they're all different. I'm trying to find the style that calls to me the most and reflects how I'm feeling, but they all do. It sort of depends on the night. Does that make sense?"

Owen had no idea if it did or it didn't—he certainly had never tried this medium, so who was he to judge? But he was still confused. What did her artwork have to do with him? And again, as if reading his mind, Howard spoke.

"Brooke's favorite subject is nature—particularly the night sky and sunsets, that sort of thing. She's been talking about wanting to go out to the desert and paint, and I immediately thought of you and the Nevada project."

It still didn't make sense to him. "The Nevada project?" Owen parroted. "But…that's to watch the meteor shower, and it's for students and undergrads. I…I don't understand."

Beside them, Brooke cleared her throat and began collecting her paintings. "I should probably let the two of you talk," she murmured. "I thought it was already—"

Howard cut her off. "I meant to discuss this with Owen sooner, but our schedules haven't quite matched up. You don't need to leave, Brooke. It's good that you're here and we can go over it together."

Nodding, she continued to put her things away and then stood back silently while her uncle explained his idea.

"I fully support Brooke's work and her desire to experience different places to paint. But her heading off to the desert alone just isn't practical or safe. Her mother has some…issues, and Brooke is willing to respect them for the moment. So she needs to go with a group."

Nodding in agreement, Owen offered a suggestion. "Perhaps she could find painters interested in doing the same thing. Make it an artist's retreat." That was a thing, wasn't it?

"I want you to hear me out, Owen. I have a proposition for you."

Dread sank like a lead weight in his belly.

"You and I both know you're going to need help on your upcoming trip to Red Rock. An assistant. Someone to help you manage your time and keep you on task."

"I don't have a problem with staying on task, Howard," Owen argued lightly. "I have excellent time-management skills—"

"No, what you have is excellent social-avoidance skills. You get too wrapped up in reading and studying, and you forget there are people around you are supposed to be interacting with. This project is going to require you to lead a group of twenty, and that means you have to be accessible to them and able to communicate with them without having a panic attack."

All Owen wanted at the moment was to hide—especially from Brooke. While Owen knew of his own shortcomings, he didn't appreciate them being pointed out to an audience.

Howard placed a reassuring hand on Owen's shoulder and squeezed. "You are an amazing teacher and scientist, Owen. But your people skills could use a little… help. There's nothing wrong with admitting that."

Easy for him to say, Owen thought. The man was one of the most personable professors and scientists he'd ever worked with. "Howard—"

"Brooke is at ease in front of a class and working with people. She's friendly and personable and very sociable. She would be an asset to your team and would free you up to concentrate on the science aspects. And while she's in the desert with you, she could paint. It's a win-win."

"But…" And how did he put this without it coming off as arrogant or a put-down to Brooke? "She's not a scientist, Howard," he said softly, hoping to cushion his words. "I think it's important to have someone working with me who understands the project and what we're doing so if anyone has questions and I'm not available, that person can answer them."

"Owen—"

"No, it's okay, Uncle Howard," Brooke said, her voice soft and not sounding at all offended. "I understand what Dr. Shaughnessy is saying." Then she turned to Owen. "I know I'm not someone you would normally consider having as an assistant, especially here on campus or in the normal scope of your work. What my uncle is proposing is just for the time you're working on this trip to Red Rock. I do have excellent organizational skills, and I'm comfortable working in an office environment and am proficient with all the computer programs you may need to get information ready for this trip. I can make phone calls and set up schedules for you and your group. And once we arrive in Red Rock, I'll be there to help you with the group on a…social level. If that even makes sense."

It did. It seriously did. But Owen wasn't sure he was comfortable with it.

Brooke must have sensed his hesitation because she smiled and then looked at her watch. "I'll tell you what, why don't you think about it and let Uncle Howard know? I have an appointment to get to." She held out her hand to Owen, and this time he didn't hesitate quite so long to shake it. With a quick wave to Owen, she gave her uncle a hug and wished them both a good day.

Owen watched her leave and immediately felt as if the sun had gone behind the clouds. The lecture hall felt dark and quiet and…lonely. He stood and watched the empty doorway for several minutes until Howard cleared his throat.

Damn.

He looked over at his mentor and hoped he didn't look like some sort of lovesick puppy.

"Think about it, Owen. I believe Brooke is the perfect person for you." He paused. "And for this project."

And then he was gone too and Owen was completely alone and left wondering if Howard's words were somehow a double entendre.

Brooke slipped into the first empty lecture hall she could find feeling completely defeated.

Not sure what to do with herself, she walked over to the first row of desks and took a seat. A long, slow sigh came out as she sat there and replayed the last several minutes. It wasn't as if she had been expecting Owen Shaughnessy to jump at the chance to have her work with him, but she still couldn't help but feel…disappointed.

It shouldn't have come as a surprise. She looked down at herself and shook her head. What serious scientist would want someone who looked like her to help him on such a prestigious event? She looked like some sort of bohemian. Why hadn't she thought of that sooner?

Dress for the job you want, not the job you have.

Ugh. How many times had *that* phrase been thrown at her? Too many. And honestly, the job she wanted was to be an artist. Well…to be taken seriously as an artist. But so far, no such luck. Sure, Uncle Howard supported her, but he was the only one. Which was why she had relocated to Chicago from Long Island—because her parents just didn't get it. And they never would.

In their minds, Brooke was wasting her time and energy by pursuing her love of painting. Not that they had high expectations for her in general, but they certainly had been vocal about her need to find a suitable husband from a "good family."

Not interested.

The thought of settling into the type of marriage her parents had was beyond unappealing. The last thing Brooke wanted to do was get married—especially to someone chosen because he looked good on paper and would impress the country club set. It almost made her shudder with revulsion. And her parents were getting even more vocal about their desire to have grandchildren. Right. Like she wanted to inflict the kind of relationship she'd had with her brother on kids of her own.

Again, not interested.

Growing up, she hadn't been particularly nice to her brother—as a matter of fact, she had been out-and-out bitchy. While she had been popular in school and seemed to make friends wherever she went, Neal had been the object of teasing and bullying because he was a computer geek. A nerd. Completely unpopular. While Brooke had been winning beauty pageants, Neal had been tucked away with his nose stuck in a book. It was both comical and sad how their parents had pushed them toward such typical—and outdated—gender roles. The beauty queen and the brainiac.

Just the thought of it made her entire body tense up.

It wasn't until recently that she'd had the epiphany about how unjustly her parents had treated them. It was more than the roles she and Neal had been put in; it was the way they were taught to view one another. She was never allowed to focus on her education, mainly because her mother was busy entering her in pageants. And Neal? Well, he had been encouraged to study hard and make something of himself since he was old enough to read.

Which was at age three.

Her brother was a genius—no one could doubt that—but for the longest time, he had been a major social outcast, and even though he was older, Brooke and her friends had teased him about his social status mercilessly.

Not her finest time in life.

As an adult, things had changed, and Brooke came to realize how being the captain of the cheerleading squad and waving to a crowd while wearing a sash and tiara were only enviable when you were in high school. Out in the real world and dealing with everyday life, her former status didn't benefit her in any way, shape, or form. Yeah. Reality had hit her hard when she went to college and found out there were dozens of girls on campus who had the exact same titles. There was no one to *ooh* and *aah* over her. There was no special treatment from her professors.

And no one was impressed.

As her star was fading, Neal's had started to shine.

He'd finally hit his stride, had stopped looking like he was a young boy and grown into a man. He'd gained confidence, and all the people who had once scorned him were now praising him. And while her brother had been making a name for himself, Brooke had been floundering.

Was still floundering.

When her uncle had offered her the chance to come and stay with him in Chicago to look for work, she had grabbed it like a lifeline. Out of all of her relatives, he had always been the one to see how she was more than just a shallow, spoiled girl with a pretty face. She couldn't remember a time when he'd even talked to her about her pageants. He'd always talked to her about school and things that made her think.

It hadn't been easy to ask him to help her get a meeting with the head of the art department here at the university—she didn't want to take advantage of his generosity. It was one thing to encourage her to find work. It was quite another for him to actually have to get personally involved and risk looking foolish to a colleague if she wasn't any good.

Stop thinking so little of yourself!

But here was the thing—it wasn't as if she were asking him to actually *get* her a job. She just needed a little help making some connections. If Brooke was completely honest with herself, she wasn't even sure why she was seeking his help. Hell, she wasn't even sure what job she was looking for or what she hoped to achieve by coming here. She loved painting and drawing, and had an appreciation for art history, but she wasn't quite sure if teaching was her thing. Or if she was even qualified to teach beyond the community college level. Night school, essentially. She didn't have a degree in teaching. She didn't have a degree in anything.

So why am I here?

Good question.

In her typical pattern of over-researching everything, she'd found that the head of the art department was truly talented and had done very well in multiple showings and galleries. More than anything, Brooke wanted to pick his brain—and maybe see if he could give her some direction on how and where to focus her time and energy to get her own name out there, as well as her work.

Over the last week, Uncle Howard had pretty much been in cheerleader mode, encouraging her choice of trying to make art her career. She wished she shared his optimism. But she wasn't like him. Uncle Howard had known since he was eight that he wanted to be an astrophysicist. He'd been fascinated by the solar system his entire life, and he had turned that love into a respected career, teaching and traveling to different colleges and universities to give lectures. There wasn't a doubt in Brooke's mind that, even if she poured all of her energy into her art, it was unlikely she'd have a career as successful as her uncle's. There were thousands of artists out there, and she was quickly becoming familiar with the phrase *starving artist*. If she didn't find work soon, she'd be able to drop the *artist* part of that statement.

It was tiring to keep searching for creative ways to pay the bills—working part-time jobs at galleries—and doing her best to network with people who could help her and also have time to travel when she found a lead. And though she appreciated her uncle taking her in for the next couple of months, she just hoped it wasn't all for nothing.

When he'd mentioned working with Owen Shaughnessy out in Red Rock three days ago, it seemed almost too good to be true. The chance to paint in the desert and have someone so highly respected take her on as an assistant? It had seemed like the perfect opportunity. And even though Brooke initially felt excited about it, it didn't take long for her own insecurities to come to the surface.

In a lot of ways, Owen reminded her of Neal—quiet, shy, and scary smart. When they were younger, Brooke took great pleasure in making fun of him because he was socially inept. She'd outgrown it, had apologized for it, but she'd never been able to forget it. And she certainly never received his forgiveness. And now…

She stopped the train of thought and sighed. She had a feeling Owen had probably experienced a lot of the same bullying Neal had—and probably at the hands of people just like her. It would serve her right if he didn't want her to work with him. As a former "mean girl," she knew she didn't deserve anyone's forgiveness for her behavior. No mercy. Which was exactly how she used to view those she deemed to be socially beneath her.

Maybe someday she'd be able to forgive herself.

But she doubted it.

Taking a deep breath, she stood and knew she needed to get going. There was no way she could stay here in this empty lecture hall and hide out all day—no matter how much she wanted to. Securing her portfolio strap over her shoulder, Brooke made her way to the door and pulled it open. There were several people in the hallway, but luckily none of them were her uncle or Owen Shaughnessy.

She looked around at the display cases as she made her way toward the exit. The science department wasn't a place where she was comfortable. Even though she loved painting the night sky and the cosmos, she certainly didn't know anything about them. And with no one having to say a word to her, she felt inferior. With every step she took, she could hear voices mocking her, telling her she wasn't smart enough to be there. Wasn't smart enough to assist someone as brilliant as Owen Shaughnessy.

Another sigh escaped before she could help it.

He had seemed nice. Sweet. His shyness had been endearing, and when he looked at her—well, when he had finally looked at her and met her gaze—she felt something she'd never felt before.

A connection.

Maybe she was crazy. Maybe she was imagining things. But as soon as Owen's dark eyes had met hers, she'd felt…well, everything.

He was younger than she had expected—not that her uncle had said too much about him, but for some reason, she had pictured Owen Shaughnessy to be older. After meeting him, she figured him to be in his early thirties, and he was tall but not overly so, with thick, dark-brown hair that probably could have used a haircut but on him looked good. Mussed. A little bit wild.

A giggle came out before she could stop it. She was sure no one would look at Owen and think "wild," but she certainly did. That wasn't to say he didn't have his nerdy vibe going on—because he did—but there was something about him that called to her. And not in a professional "let's work together" kind of way, but as a man.

She swallowed hard and tried to calm her thoughts, which were now starting to wander toward how wise it would be to work with him if she was already feeling like this.

Giddy.

Fluttery.

Totally crushing on a man who'd said maybe five words to her.

Yeah. Maybe this wasn't such a good idea.

Pushing through the heavy exit door, Brooke stepped out into the crisp and cold Chicago air and cursed the fact that she had forgotten to put on her sweater. Shaking her head, she stopped and quickly slipped it on before walking down the steps to the parking lot at a fairly quick pace and making her way to her car. Just as she was opening the door, she saw him off in the distance.

Owen.

He must be through for the day too, she thought, and watched him walk toward what she assumed to be his own car. Why she stood and watched, she couldn't say. She found she enjoyed watching him. He was so different from almost every man she knew, and part of her longed to walk over and talk to him some more.

He seemed lonely.

Her uncle had mentioned how Owen wasn't based out of Chicago but was doing a short-term lecture series here before going to Nevada to prepare for the meteor shower project. And after that, who knew where he was going to go? From what she could tell, Owen

Shaughnessy hadn't settled anywhere. He traveled too much. She almost envied him for it and then immediately took the thought back.

No wonder he was lonely.

Brooke wondered if he had any family other than his brother, Riley. Was it just the two of them? Did Owen have anyone he connected with when he wasn't working? Was he involved with someone? That thought stopped her cold—it bothered her. Here she was just meeting him, yet the thought of feeling the connection she'd felt and then finding out he was involved with—or married to—someone else upset her more than it should have.

Maybe she'd talk to her uncle a little more at dinner tonight.

Maybe she'd have to do a little investigating of her own.

Either way, whether she got to work with Owen Shaughnessy or not, Brooke knew today couldn't be their only interaction.

—⁓—

Relief.

It was Owen's immediate reaction when he had returned to his hotel room and closed the door. The entire drive had been spent thinking about Brooke Matthews.

And that reminded him—he needed to do a Google search and figure out who she was talking about because he had a feeling it was a pop culture reference he should know. Of course, it was too late to undo the awkwardness of not knowing it already, but that couldn't be helped. She seemed to recover from his faux pas, so at least there was that.

Right now, all Owen wanted was some peace and quiet to unwind. Maybe read the copy of *Sky & Telescope* he'd picked up just this morning—that would be a great way to relax and forget about the possibility of having a beautiful woman working as his assistant.

Right. As if he was going to forget *that* anytime soon.

Things like that didn't happen to him. Ever. Not that he didn't date attractive women—he had, but… Wait a minute. He wasn't dating Brooke; he was going to work with Brooke. Maybe. Sighing, he put his satchel and laptop case on the desk and took off his jacket. And whether the assistant was Brooke or somebody else, Howard was right. He needed the help. Badly. As it was, Owen had been warned, repeatedly, that he needed to hone his social skills because his students weren't connecting with him.

If he wasn't on this lecture circuit, Owen knew he wouldn't have to deal with things like this—with the constant stream of people wanting to socialize with him and talk about what he was doing. If he had stayed the course of his original plans, he'd be enjoying quiet time safely ensconced in his research.

Unfortunately, his career had taken a slight detour, and because of his inability to say no, he was stuck doing short-term guest lectures at universities all over the country. If he'd only been able to decline the very first time he'd been asked, Owen had no doubt he'd be happily situated in an office of his choosing right now.

He just wasn't sure where that office would be.

The thought of working close to his family in North Carolina was appealing. More so now that he'd been away for so long. It seemed as if everyone was slowly making their way back to their childhood hometown, and he had to admit he was a little envious, but it wasn't in the cards for him yet. Maybe in another year or so he'd be able to reevaluate his schedule and dictate where he wanted to be, but for now he had commitments he needed to honor, and that meant more time away.

Later that evening, he would have time to Skype with Riley. Just the thought of his brother made Owen smile. They hadn't had a whole lot of time together in person in the past couple of months—mainly because his brother was on tour, promoting his new solo album—but they always tried to make time to talk via Skype. And lately Owen had felt the need for the connection.

Maybe he was feeling homesick, or maybe he was at a crossroads in his life because his brothers were all settling down and starting families and Owen just didn't see that as a possibility for himself. He didn't have much of a social life, and even though he dated occasionally, Owen had never felt a connection with a woman in a way that mattered. He dated other scientists, and even when they were on dates, they talked about…science.

And the more he learned about his brothers and their wives, the more Owen realized that solid relationships— the kind where you fell in love and formed a bond and wanted a future together—weren't always based on common interests.

Like work.

His eldest brother, Aidan, had met and fallen in love with his wife, Zoe, when she had started working for him. But even though they did have their work in common, they were opposite in a lot of ways. Zoe had been all about starting her life over and forging a new path, while Aidan had been so deeply entrenched in living his life in the past. But it hadn't taken long for his control freak of a brother to let his guard down and learn to accept—and enjoy—their differences.

All the women around Owen were exactly like him.

It was no different with his brother Hugh. Hugh had been emotionally cut off and seemed unlikely to ever settle down in a relationship that was based on love. There had been a time when Owen had actually been able to relate to Hugh the easiest because of that outlook. But after working with the carefree Aubrey, Hugh too had taken the plunge. Hell, last Owen heard, they'd been on a trip to Belize and were teaching their young son, Connor, to snorkel and swim with the dolphins. And Owen could only listen with a bit of envy because Hugh had come out of his self-imposed emotional exile and was finally living his life.

At the last big convention Owen had gone to, no one had even wanted to get within ten feet of the hotel pool, let alone swim with a dolphin.

And then there was Quinn, the ultimate middle child. He'd been the love-'em-and-leave-'em type for so long that for the longest time, Owen never thought Quinn would settle down either. And for the most part, everyone accepted how that was just the way Quinn was. But through it all, Anna had been there—playing the part of the best friend even though she was secretly in love with Quinn. Then—and this part still made Owen chuckle—Quinn had seen Anna in a bikini and suddenly realized his best friend was a beautiful woman. The entire Shaughnessy family had been happy to see him wake up and notice what had been right in front of him for years.

Having been too shy to even talk to girls when he was younger, Owen had no female friends, let alone any harboring a crush on him, or vice versa.

Riley. His twin. His other half. They were fraternal twins, and it wasn't only their looks that were completely different. Everything about them was. Things came easily to Riley, especially women. And when he met Savannah and she blatantly told him she didn't like him—and hadn't for some time—it had come as quite a shock. Yeah, that was another story that made Owen laugh, imagining his rock-star brother being told there was a female alive who wasn't in love with him. Of course, Riley had changed Savannah's mind, and now they were happily married, but other than their love of rock and roll, they'd had to work hard to overcome some of their differences.

There wasn't even anyone Owen knew of who he'd be able to try to overcome differences with. And there was no way he was going to seek out any kind of relationship advice from Darcy. She might be his sister, but she was so much younger than him. He chuckled to himself. Although she probably had a hell of a lot more experience than he did. Then he shook his head. No. Darcy still scared the hell out of him just because she was so…different from him.

A sigh came out before he could stop it. He definitely needed this time with Riley tonight. Not so long ago, Owen had helped his twin when he was at a crossroad. Now he was hoping Riley would return the favor. The only problem was that Riley had known—sort of—what his problem was. He'd had writer's block and couldn't complete the album he'd been working on. Not that

Owen wasn't oversimplifying Riley's issue, but at least there had been a definitive problem for them to work on. Owen couldn't define his problem. He had an overall feeling of discontent in his life, and no amount of looking up at the sky and watching the stars was helping.

And it used to always help.

No matter what was going on.

Hell, when his mother had died, Owen had…

The alarm on his phone beeped, reminding him of his upcoming time to Skype with Riley. Not that he was going to forget it. He was looking forward to the call. Needed it. He might even call his brother early.

He opened up his satchel and went about the task of emptying it out and organizing everything neatly on the desk—his laptop, his phone, his chargers, his notes, and his magazine. Looking at the clock, he confirmed the amount of time he had until Riley's call—two hours and thirty-seven minutes—and sighed.

With nothing left to do, he quickly called and ordered room service—a turkey club sandwich and french fries—and then started up his laptop. He was intent on finding out all he could about Brooke Matthews.

The model-slash-actress *and* the beautiful artist he'd met today.